MORE BY THE AUTHOR

SPECIAL AGENT KIM KUPAR

Jade Eyes
They
The Why Files

THE TSCHAAA INFESTATION

Book 1: The Gathering Storm
Book 2: The Tsunami
Book 3: Typhoon of Steel
Free Range Protocol: Tales of the Tschaaa
Beyond the Great Compromise: Tales of the Tschaaa
Survivors: Escaping the Tschaaa

ANTHOLOGIES

Monstrosity (Unnerving Anthology)
Descent (Unnerving Anthology)
Wicked (Unnerving Anthology)
Nightfall (Unnerving Anthology)
The Mighty Pen
Unconditional
Cascadia
Tales of the Slug
Super: Unexpected Heroes Arise

COLLECTED WORKS & MORE

Inhumanity: A Year of Stories
The Island (The Haunting of Orchard House)
Shane (Angels of Anarchy)

THE TSCHAAA INFESTATION
VOLUME 1

The Gathering Storm

MARSHALL MILLER

BLUE FORGE PRESS

The Tschaaa Infestation: The Gathering Storm (Book 1)
Copyright 2017, 2022
by Marshall Miller

First eBook Edition November 2018
Second eBook Edition March 2022
First Print Edition November 2018
Second Print Edition March 2022

ISBN 978-1-59092-968-1

Blue Forge Press is the print division of the volunteer-run, federal 501(c)3 nonprofit company, Blue Forge Press, founded in 1989 and dedicated to bringing light to the shadows and voice to the silence. We strive to empower storytellers across all walks of life with our four divisions: Blue Forge Press, Blue Forge Films, Blue Forge Gaming, and Blue Forge Records. Find out more at www.BlueForgeGroup.org

Blue Forge Press
7419 Ebbert Drive Southeast
Port Orchard, Washington 98367
blueforgepress@gmail.com
360-550-2071 ph.txt

*To my wife, who puts up with my ramblings and ranting,
and serves as the two-legged mother to our four dogs.*

ACKNOWLEDGEMENTS

This is the Second and Revised Edition of *The Tschaaa Infestation*, a three-volume chronicle of what was once referred to as "the War and Peace of alien squid invasion novels." Thanks to the hard work of my publisher, Blue Forge Press, I now can present a new and improved version of a long labor of love and creativity. I have had many people help me in learning my craft of being a 'Wordsmith.' This is a career and an endeavor of beating words and phrases into a finely tempered work which, like a blacksmith does with steel fresh from the forge, cuts with a clean blade, but ideas rather than wood or flesh. At the same time, like a samurai's katana mentioned in the series, it can also bend to new concepts and opinions without breaking due to its flexibility.

Of course my wife, Sheri, has often times been a Writer's Widow as I disappear for hours on end, especially late at night, to hone my craft. Thus, without her understanding and support, this would have been a stillborne offspring.

Author and Esquire Thomas Mengert helped me with the first editing of this work of speculative fiction as well as suggested a companion volume of short stories. Thanks for all the hours spent with me on this futuristic War and Peace.

My good friend Gregory Brashear, an accomplished local teacher, was a sounding board for many of my ideas. Truth be told, a main character of the series is based on his life and adventures. I'll let the readers figure out which character fits this mold.

All the members of Kitsap Literary Artists and Writers helped provide ideas on designs, marketing, and publishing. The Bremerton Kitsap Access Television interview show I do on a monthly basis is an outgrowth of this group. The KLAW show was the reason I met Jennifer and Brianne DiMarco and became affiliated with Blue Forge Press, which is leading to bigger and better things. Sometimes it takes a while for "good things and people" to come into one's life.

I hope all "wannabe" Authors read my artistic endeavors and think "Hey, I can do that!" For writers must write. We all hope that what we write will find a group of readers who will appreciate our ideas, concepts, and the worlds we create as we spin our web of ideas. Especially when those ideas involve humans being cattle for invading alien squids.

In closing, I also must thank all the people I have met and worked with over the years as yes, you all provided models and fodder for my characters and stories. Hopefully, those who knew me will read my books and say "Hey! Cool!"

As a final thought, remember:

Watch the skies! The *Tschaaa Cometh*!

THE TSCHAAA INFESTATION
VOLUME 1

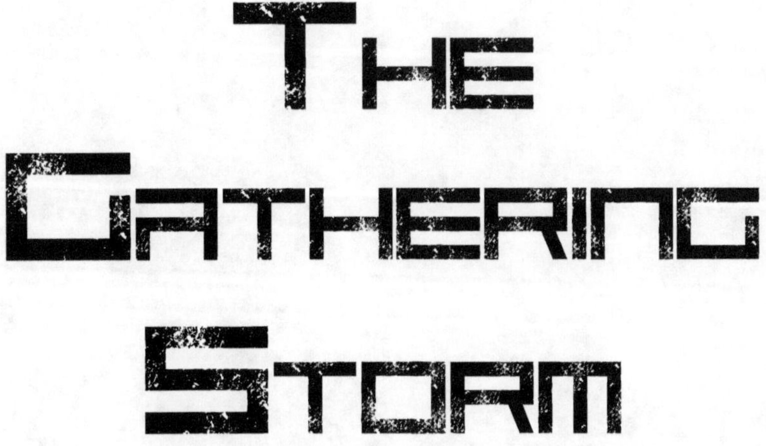 The Gathering Storm

MARSHALL MILLER

CHAPTER 1

Princess Akiko of the Free Japan Royal Family sat at her desk. She was still for a long, silent moment; she was not a woman who rushed anything. Finally, slowly and deliberately, Akiko looked down at her manuscript. She agreed with authors before her that writing a book was like giving birth but with months of labor instead of hours. She'd heard writers even attest to having labor pains.

She picked up what her publisher had called the "proof copy," a bound draft of her finished manuscript. It was not a small work, both the subject matter and the number of pages required to record the events had a distinct heft to them. Actually, when she was first approached by the American publisher, she doubted her ability to complete the project.

Not only had a significant amount of time passed since the events she'd been asked to record, but the memory of those events–despite the passage of time–was still bitter for Akiko and for many others. After all, she was no fairytale caricature but a true Samurai Princess; she had played her own active role in the resolution of that chapter of human history. The origin of the Great Compromise–which had allowed two dominant species to share dominion of Earth–had been so startling in its advent that it had seemed almost unbelievable. That the Tschaaa were willing to accept the human race as more than just a food source had been a game changer of immense proportions. And to encapsulate that story into a single volume of history? Yes, it had seemed an impossible task many times. But it had to be done. The story had to be told while memories were still first-hand but not so raw that no one would be able to endure the recollection.

Akiko nodded to herself. Now that it was complete, she felt confident she had captured the bright spirit and the dark reality of those times. Even though she was Samurai first and foremost, she felt within herself the abiding instinctual drive to produce and preserve life on this planet. She understood well the importance of recording such a pivotal events between two species. What other option had there been, really? Coexistence was predetermined from the moment the Tschaaa discovered the oceans of Earth. The life giving reefs, the warm water of the tropics, the sun lit blue waters, and the diverse deep sea life– specifically the Tschaaa's seeming cousins, the Deep Ocean Giant Squid–created a magnetism for the aliens that imprinted an indelible psychic impression upon them. The Tschaaa weren't going away... and neither were humans.

Her publisher had been emailing, voice calling, video calling, and generally yelling at her to, "Get it done!" But Akiko did not bend to pressure, especially from a pushy American Northwest publisher who hadn't even been there to see the events Akiko committed to paper. She knew she had to get it right, not just get it done. She had to pay homage to all those who had been there. The title, of course, was *The Great Compromise* and the subtitle was longer than most:

The History of the Coming of the Tschaaa of the heroes and villains the Coming produced and of the Great Compromise which allowed two species of apex predators to exist together in relative harmony

It almost read like a poem. And there was a type of beauty to it; the truth always has a layer of beauty... and a layer of darkness.

The publisher's cover was colorful, with eye-catching bright oranges, reds, blacks and whites symbolizing the major participants and events of those seven years, from the first Rock Strike to the Great Compromise itself.

Inside, Akiko had dedicated the book with careful and sincere words:

This work of history is dedicated to those who fought, loved, coped, survived and died during the period of the Tschaaa Invasion, as well as to those who created the Great Compromise and made it work. They did not just strive to preserve a certain way of life. They struggled, sacrificed, bled and sometimes expired so that homo sapiens as a species were preserved and could co-exist with their former sworn enemy, the Tschaaa. These members of humanity are truly our Greatest Generation.

She did not care that the publisher had wanted the book done months ago. This is what she felt in her bones, her heart, and her soul. Even if there had been even one small revision in this history, Princess Akiko would not be sitting here today, the proud mother of twin daughters, both away at military school to follow in her footsteps.

Akiko paused as she felt a moment of frustration. She had hoped they would find a different path. But she had raised them to be just as independent as she was–though her father (and many others) used a different word: Stubborn. Maybe someday they would emerge from her shadow and strike out in a different direction. But no matter, Akiko was fiercely proud of them. As was their father, the newly-elected Prime Minister of Free Japan. Also was their cousin Ichiro Yamamoto, who had also been a major participant in the Great Compromise.

The Princess looked at another stack of papers on the corner of her desk and smiled again. She reached over for the title page of her newest work-in-progress, *Banshee: The Complete History of the 101st Special Attack Unit and the Sisters of Steel, Madam President's Own.*

Banshee was another labor of love from someone who was there from the very beginning. Akiko considered the two projects. They would tell a companion story of all that had occurred, all that had helped to create and cement the relationship between humanity, the Tschaaa… and any other alien species.

She wanted to publish her work as close to the twenty-fifth anniversary of the signing of the   Great Compromise as possible. Everyone, especially   the younger generations, needed to be reminded just how close they'd all come to a War of Extinction. If not for the actions of small bands of people–the prototypes of the current new family paradigm–any homo sapiens who may have survived Harvesting would either be hiding in caves or mines, deep forests and jungles… or they'd be service animals or pets of the Tschaaa Lords.

Banshee, which mostly covered the aftermath of the Great Compromise, would be published in a year.

Akiko leaned back in her high-backed desk chair and closed her eyes. On and about her desk were pictures of humans, of War Dogs, and even a few Tschaaa who had become part of her story and often her family. It was hard to believe she had a photograph of her "holding hands" with the Tschaaa Warrior Pilot, Dorothy. Dorothy had been a fellow Banshee–just over a year after they'd been sworn enemies. Not for the first time, Akiko mused that how learning to love and respect the Tschaaa had evolved them from calamari, tako, and sashimi to comrades. It seemed too simple, almost childish, but it was the truth. Today, she counted Dorothy as one of her dearest friends; they had faced death together.

The photos gazed back at her: Torbin Bender and his wife Aleks Smirnov; Ichiro Yamamoto and his wife Abigail Jorgensen-Yamamoto; Brynhildr Jorgensen; Commissioner Miller; General Reed and, of course, the late Madam President, she of the Spine of Steel. Then those of the other side: the Director and his wives, Kat and Mary, and his best friend the Chief, plus Andrew the cyborg. An image of the Tschaaa Lord Neptune scrolled through Akiko's mind. Memories of times, actions, faces, births and deaths.

A large wet tongue made her eyes snap open. General, her War Dog from the long line that started with Abigail's Sergeant Fuzz, brought her from her reverie.

"What is it, my large and faithful friend?" Akiko asked as she scratched his ears. Akiko knew that with each generation these War Dogs became smarter and even more sentient. Soon… who knew?

Maybe someday they would take over and run things far better than Tschaaa and humans. For now though, General just snuffled her then gazed into her eyes. Theirs was a true love just has as Abigail had had with Sergeant Fuzz. Akiko hugged the great animal then kissed his massive muzzle.

"Did I ever tell you the story, my General, of how this all was started? How this younger daughter in the Japanese Royal Family became the great and grand Samurai Princess Akiko, heroine of many an anime epic?"

Akiko chuckled at her own words and tone and General wagged his tail.

"Well, my good sir, it started far before me, with other heroes and heroines, with perceived and actual villains and monsters. Do you have a while to listen to me? How about if I give you a dog biscuit? A large one."

Akiko leaned back in her chair, remembering, deciding where to start. General laid his mighty head in her lap and absently–comforting him as much as herself–she stroked his head and began.

"How do the Americans say it? Always start by explaining who is trying to do what to whom...."

CHAPTER 2

The radio woke Adam Lloyd with a soft rock hit of the late 1980s or early '90s. Even before the Invasion, he had always preferred music that was just loud and snappy enough to wake him up without overwhelming his senses. Now, per his mandate, the only remaining radio station played soft rock between the hours of 6:00 and 8:00am. And as usual, he was awake in an instant–a survival characteristic that he had developed over the past six years.

Although fully alert and aware of his surroundings, he did not immediately leap up. All that would do was possibly lead to a pulled muscle, not to mention upset the other occupant of his spacious king-sized bed. But so far there had been no complaints from other listeners, as if that mattered.

Adam lay quietly, turning his head just enough to see the time on the clock radio. 6:45am. Mary Lou stirred next to him. He turned in her direction and saw that, once again, she had no bed covers on. Her back, and full, rounded curves were an inviting sight. She stirred, playfully reaching out her hand to caress his inner thigh. He gently pushed her hand back, then reached over and kissed her on her right cheek.

"Later. Don't forget the new arrivals will be at the theater at 9:00am. You young ladies need to be there on time also."

"Don't worry, we'll be there." She rolled over, and eyes still half closed, grinned. "Party pooper."

Jeanie and Jamey, whose identical blond hair and proportions made them appear almost as twins even though they were not related, began to stir in the adjoining room. As usual, they wound up sleeping with their nude bodies pressed up against each other. Adam surmised some time ago that they liked each other's bodies more than his. He smiled. It didn't matter as long as they were there for him in other ways were important, and occasionally–when the mood hit them all–in his bed as well.

All three women had been by his side for the past three years. Under his watch, they were among the few special women who did not have to explain why they weren't trying to get pregnant as their conquerors had demanded.

Adam rose quickly from the bed, reset the alarm for the ladies to 7:30am, and left the bedroom. He passed through the connecting door between his office area and the extended living quarters, locking it behind him to insure privacy. His living room office, built to his personal specifications after he had taken over the Naval Command Headquarters at the former Key West Naval Air Station, was now the equivalent of a huge suite, with a large entry way and reception room on the main floor to receive guests and hold staff meetings. His assistant, who held the moniker Chief–from the days when he was Chief Master Sergeant in the Air Force–had even created a small armory to store his favorite weapons as well as any new acquisitions waiting to be tested.

With speed Adam had developed over years of practice, he showered, shaved, put on some deodorant and then his undergarments. A high end three-piece gray suit with matching tie followed, along with his two ornamental as well as functional pistols. He knew exactly what made him look his best, and an old-fashioned U.S. flag lapel pin was the finishing touch. Some people thought he was rubbing salt in recent wounds with the pin. The old U.S. of A. may not exist as a real entity, but he knew where his roots were.

Adam looked at his image in the mirror. He was proud of his body, his height a shade over 5'10", with broad shoulders and a fairly slim build from hours spent working out in the gym and practicing martial arts. Adam thought he cut a fine picture for someone approaching forty. He still had a full head of brown hair and his blue eyes were still crystal clear.

He paused, recalling the dream he had last night. It was the same dream he usually had once a week, the one he always had before welcoming new arrivals to Key West. It was difficult to accept that in reality it was not just a dream at all, but the memory of when that first large meteor struck in Atlanta, Georgia, as he and the Chief were meeting in a local diner.

One minute, they were bullshitting with each other as usual, the next hitting the diner floor as the the impact levelled the parking garage next door, while the force of the same simultaneously caused the diner's front windows to shatter inward. After that, normal life too was shattered, and nothing was the same. It became all about survival.

A sharp knock on the outer door jarred him from his reverie and let him know that the Chief was here already with his morning coffee. It had become a ritual that the Chief brought him a mug of coffee on such mornings, usually some high quality blend that he had discovered in his many travels.

Chief William Hamilton, of the former U.S. Air Force Security Forces, had done the traveling for both of them during the last six months, as Adam Lloyd had been spending more and more time with the Tschaaa Lord who owned North America. The area from Panama Canal on up to the Arctic regions was now often referred to as the Reconstructed States of America, although people residing outside the Tschaaa-controlled areas often called the area the Occupied States, or the Infested States.

"Come on in, Chief."

A rather short and stocky red-headed man with a handlebar moustache entered the room, steaming cup in his hand. Chief William Hamilton–Willie, or Chief to Adam–seemed laid back but his alert eyes caught everything. He also had a reserved strength, coiled and at the ready, that appeared when necessary. "Here's your coffee, Boss."

Adam sniffed the contents of the mug. Then slowly, he took a sip and eyes narrowing, responded. "This is different. New kind of Columbian?"

"Nope. Bet you can't guess."

"Hm. South of the border?"

"No Sir, guess again."

"Someone's homegrown stash?"

"No again. Give up?"

"Chief, you're just too sharp for me."

"Yep. That's why I stayed a Chief and let you be the Director. You get to have all of the headaches, and I'm the brains behind the throne."

They both chuckled. This private joke had been going on for years. However, both men knew the truth behind the jest. They had survived by watching each other's backs, shooting first at times, and on other occasions, running away to fight again. Now Adam was *Director* Lloyd, of the Reformed States of America. In reality, the Tschaaa owned and controlled all real estate, and the Director's job was simply trying to keep as many humans alive and well as possible.

"Actually, I cheated. It's not real coffee from beans. It's a chicory syrup substitute that was popular in Canada. I recovered a small quantity during my trip to the Puget Sound."

"That's why I like you, Chief. You cheat."

Chief Hamilton gave his best imitation of a shit-eating grin, then smiling even more broadly added, "Oh, by the way, she's here."

Adam abruptly set down his coffee mug. "Kathy Monroe? You got her here in time for the orientation?"

"Of course, Boss. That's what you wanted. I had to do some last minute horse trading, but she's here." After a beat, the Chief continued. "She's a lot feistier and more stubborn than you probably even realized. She refused my promise of a shopping spree within an abandoned mall or two... Something about she can't be *pre-bought* until she hears the offer from you. I'd watch my balls around her."

"Huh. I guess I will."

Adam mused to himself, Who would have thought that a former adult film star would be picky about her standards in this day and age? The film and television worlds were, thanks to his efforts, just starting up again with regular broadcasts in some areas. A few movies were being made for general consumption. But he had not heard of anyone with the wherewithal to start making porn movies again. At most, there were some nudie joints in the old former Navy towns and that was it.

Sex was a form of currency in many of the now growing areas of human habitation, but not an official one. Actually, the Tschaaa hoped humans would screw themselves silly, as long as an increase in pregnancies was the result. They liked plenty of food and possible draft animals around. Conversely, those women who refused to be bred were long ago sent to the larders, thanks mostly to the efforts of some of the nastier human minions of the Tschaaa. If you were female, you'd better be willing to at least *try* to get pregnant. Feminist ideas of birth control were extinct.

Adam looked at his watch. "Let's head out now. I want to be at the auditorium early enough to get a good look at the new arrivals before the orientation begins."

"Your wish is my command, oh Great Potentate."

"You know Chief, you can really be corny sometimes."

"Yes, Boss. Helps to break the monotony."

Downstairs, at the front of the building, a muscular six foot plus tall soldier in urban camo combat fatigues stood at parade rest by a jet black polished Humvee. Upon seeing Adam, he came to attention, saluted, then opened the back door of the vehicle. The Director thanked him and clambered into the Humvee, the Chief going around to the other side. Adam noticed the troop had a complete set of battle rattle on the passenger front seat, with an assault rifle clipped in a rack on the roof interior.

In addition to all of the outward armaments, Adam thought he noticed that the troop had an additional concealment Kevlar vest under his fatigues. The Chief had tried to get Adam to wear some kind of body armor around the base, but he had refused. If the people believed the Director himself was afraid and did not trust them, all of this would quickly fall apart. Trust in him and what he was doing was his primary motivation for selecting personnel in what was now the new capital of North America. It may not be complete blind trust, but Adam needed it to maintain the decorum of law and order that remained.

The Humvee was escorted to the front and rear by Harley motorcycles with old fashioned sidecars, two troops per vehicle. Adam chuckled to himself for the at least the hundredth time. Chief Hamilton had a strong predilection for *retro* back to Double U Double U Two (WWII) whenever he could get away with it and still get the job done. He had even obtained a bunch of BARs–Browning Automatic Rifles–from where, Adam had no idea. They were carried by the Special Response Teams and even used were all still functional.

It was a short five minute drive to the auditorium. The Humvee pulled up to the back entrance, where an attractive blond female military member in former U.S. Air Force Class A uniform was waiting.

Major Jane Grant, an athletic yet feminine thirty-something year old woman, saluted Adam. "Good Morning Director."

"Good Morning, Major. And of course, everything is ready to go, as usual."

She smiled. "Of course, Sir. That's what you pay me for."

"Do I pay you enough?"

"It's not for the pay, Sir. It's for the adventure."

Adam smiled at her, the question and answer a well-worn exchange. He noticed that Jane had finally worn a uniform skirt and dark high heeled pumps, increasing her already substantial sex appeal. But, Adam had learned from his days as a commissioned officer, not to start poking his staff. It always led to trouble. Yes, his three ladies were referred to as staff, but a special staff outside the normal chain of command. Mary Lou acted as his receptionist and gatekeeper, with Jeanie and Jamey acting as social directors, as if the state was a cruise ship. They worked directly for him, and all three knew better than to abuse their relationship. Maybe if he ever could resign, he'd grab the Major, make her an honest woman, and then screw her brains out. But who was he kidding?

Major Grant escorted him through the entrance, down a hallway, and to the Operations and Surveillance room. The Chief hung back a bit, watching the Director's back as usual. The room had a large bank of television monitors that surveyed the entire auditorium and the area adjacent. As needed, it had the capability to hack into other surveillance cameras all over the base. If the primary command post, at the Security Headquarters, was ever compromised, this room would also serve as the emergency backup.

After putting the room personnel at ease, Adam quickly took control of one of the monitor stations. He used the cameras to pan and scan the crowd of new arrivals in the back of the auditorium. Six hundred, no, six hundred and one nervous–no, likely scared–human beings were drinking hot and cold beverages, eating bagels and donuts, and milling around, attempting to socialize. This was the largest group of new arrivals he had processed at one time. It may well be the last one for quite some time as well. He looked for one person in particular.

There she was. Kathy Monroe. She was slim but curvy in all of the right ways and the right places. Sure, her blond hair probably came from a bottle, but who cared? It looked good and she looked even better. Bright blue eyes, brighter smile and perky demeanor completed the package that had won over probably millions of men and a few women fans, before the first rock strike. Adam had admitted it to himself, she was his ideal type. Ever since he had first seen her on some talk show years before, defending adult entertainment, he had been smitten with her. Badly. Without the strike by the Tschaaa six years prior, he never would have met her. Now, she was going to work for him.

Adam also saw his three ladies arrive and spend a few minutes circulating among the new arrivals, then make their way to the front of auditorium. Dressed to the nines, in high heels and stockings, he saw the other women look at the clothes they wore with a *how do I get those* look while the men tried to imagine what was under the clothes. Adam smiled at the thought.

"Almost time, Boss." Chief Hamilton had slipped up behind him. "Including Miss Monroe, guess how many people are assigned here as of today?"

"I'll bite. How many?"

"Six thousand, six hundred and sixty-six."

Adam paused. "I think I see where you are going with this. That makes it six, six, six and six?"

"Yes, Sir."

Adam gave a short laugh. "I guess it's good that I never really held much stake in the story of Revelations."

"Right, Boss."

He turned to Jane. "Major, let's get this show on the road."

"Yes, Sir." Major Grant clicked on the public address system, and launched into her standard presentation. "Good Morning, ladies and gentlemen. If you could please find a seat at the rows of tables toward the front, nearest the stage. The Director will be with you shortly. Thank you."

Ten minutes later, at 9:00am sharp, everyone was seated except for the armed security officer at each corner of the auditorium. Adam had watched Kathy on the monitor take a seat three rows back. Some young stud kept trying to chat her up, maybe because he recognized her. Or maybe he was eager for the opportunity to pop his cherry with an older, more experienced woman. No matter. If he bothered her too much, Adam would see that he was permanently reassigned to Bumfuck, Egypt.

It's showtime, Adam told himself as he drew a deep breath and confidently walked onto the stage to face six hundred and one pairs of penetrating eyes.

"The Director, the Honorable Adam Lloyd." The Chief's voice boomed loudly throughout the room, not needing help from the PA system. Adam saw some people start to rise to their feet, but others who read the instruction sheet handed out the day before reminded them to retake their seats. Adam had no need for the trappings of ceremony. People already knew who was in charge; anything else was a waste of time.

Even the handful of children present fell completely quiet. Then again, six years of on-again, off-again conflict and strife had a way of encouraging all to learn the value of silence.

Adam reached the center of the stage, and turned to take in all of the new faces.

"Good morning. Hopefully, everyone was able to enjoy a little of the beverages and food items provided. I need everyone to be fully awake and energized, so that they can pay attention. It might interest you to know that this feast, other than those unique breakfast tacos and burritos, were made right here in our kitchens. The tacos and burritos came from the Conch Republic, the nature of which will be explained later. Hopefully, this helps to allay any fears that you will not be provided for if you all choose to stay here."

A low murmur could be heard in some parts of the auditorium.

"That's right. After hearing today what we do here, about our history and mission, you may leave voluntarily. If the Chief at times seemed like he was drafting you, well, he has a tendency of being aggressive when he sees something he wants, or something *I* want." A few nervous laughs were heard.

"But before I share any additional details, my assistants, Jeanie and Jamey, will bring the children to a room nearby for entertainment, so they won't be bored by our little talk. Don't worry, I promise, they've done this many times before and haven't lost anyone yet."

Jeanie and Jamey both had a way with children which was natural and genuine. Adam watched as the two experienced women escorted some dozen boys and girls between the ages of five and twelve to the waiting room. A couple of the mothers gave them stern looks which clearly stated, "If anything happens to my child, you're going to wish you weren't born." This was understandable, especially given recent history concerning children.

When the last of the youngest audience members had gone, Adam continued. "Since I do not like to beat around the proverbial bush, let me be clear; you must listen attentively and understand everything I present. Today is your last chance to have second thoughts, to vacillate. Tomorrow morning, you will either leave, or sign on to be part of a larger plan involving all of North America, and possibly more. After that, only *I* can decide if you can leave, when you can leave, how you can leave."

One could almost hear a pin drop.

"Now, to fully understand how Key West became the new capital and what brought you here, a history lesson is in order. Trust me, a lot of this will be new to you."

A PowerPoint presentation, run by Major Grant, began on the large screen in front.

"Almost exactly six years ago today, at 9:13am Eastern Time, the first rock from space struck…"

Approximately two hours later, Director Adam Lloyd plunked down behind his huge desk. It wasn't the first time he had appreciated the comfort of the luxuriously padded chair the Chief had found for this desk. On days like this especially, when the chair eased the pressure of the burden that felt like extra gravity on his weary body. He still could not really understand why these orientation briefings took so much out of him, despite the many times he had done them. Maybe he was just getting old. Maybe it was because even after all of these years, he still put his complete heart and soul into it, because of the importance of helping the assembled humans to understand where they all stood. And, of course, how they fit into the Mission.

Adam opened a lower desk drawer and pulled out a bottle of pre-strike scotch. It was past noon in some part of the world, he told himself. He spun his chair around and opened his personal mini fridge, late from some luxury hotel. He dropped fresh ice cubes from a small bucket into a large highball glass. The scotch soon followed. He turned back around, reclined in his chair and closed his eyes, sipping his drink.

He mentally replayed the PowerPoint briefing Jane Grant had so expertly created years ago. Damn. It had been some four years since he had found the Major and brought her here to be his Executive and Operations Officer. Time sure as hell flies when you are having fun.

Pictures of the various sized rocks the Tschaaa aliens (called Squids by the masses) shot out of the huge mass drivers aboard Asteroid 18666 always got the audience's attention. Especially when the following images showed their effects worldwide. Rocks, usually with high metal content and unique composite heat shields to keep them from burning up, varied from the size of basketballs to semi-truck trailers. Their combined speed and mass produced high levels of kinetic energy, causing large bomb-like destruction. The first forty-eight hours, just under a thousand were released, and another two hundred pinpointed to areas of resistance over the following three weeks.

People who heard the facts of the Invasion for the first time in these briefings were always surprised that all the destruction was done without nukes. In reality, just ten nuclear warheads were used during the Invasion following the rock strikes. And only four of them were of Tschaaa/Squid origin. The remaining six were human-built and detonated. Three of those were Pakistan and India launching at each other, and Iran trying to hit Israel.

Adam shook his head. Stupid goddamned humans. They were their own worst enemy; even as an greater enemy was killing and harvesting them as meat, they were still trying to kill each other. The United States, Russia, and Israel had each used a nuke on a main Tschaaa harvester ark landing area before it was recognized that this strategy would result in a complete scorched earth scenario. Besides, it was soon realized that the Tschaaa with their manufactured greys, front men, and their client lizards had developed a very human-based Fifth Column movement, using a bunch of sleeper cells of racists, skinheads, bikers, sociopaths, anarchists and self-hating human renegades to attack the rear areas, spreading confusion and fear.

One hundred thousand malcontents proved just how destructive Homo sapiens could be against their own species. Some knew they were working for an alien race, others did not. But the fanatic desire to fight against the New World Order, Zionist occupation government, non-believers, and other long-perceived "undesirables" was enough for many to not care that a cephalopodan alien race bent on *eating* fellow humans was behind their efforts at destruction. Hate was a powerful thing.

Adam poured a bit more scotch in his glass. Squids. Good name for the Tschaaa. Ten-limbed creatures that looked like a graphic novel idea of some Lovecraftean concept of the Ancient Ones. Three to four hundred pounds that were weirdly amphibian in nature, they originally had limited mobility on land. In the Earth's oceans, however, they demonstrated their alpha predator status. The nation's navies were soon decimated.

Over time, they evolved means of compensating for being a primarily aquatic species with their inventions, mechanical constructions, and tactics, borrowing heavily from human culture itself. Falcon destroyer aircraft looked suspiciously like a star-cruiser from a popular movie series, delta fighters were overgrown versions of U.S. fighter interceptors, and cyborg warriors nicknamed "robocops" because they resembled a character in a movie series. Harvester robots on six-wheeled ATV chassis chased people down, and took them for slaughter.

Ninety percent of those creations and tactics used in the Invasion were because of the efforts of one Tschaaa Lord, the one Lord to whom Adam reported and paid homage. This Tschaaa Lord had studied human culture through their broadcast media to the point his fellow Tschaaa thought him borderline crazy. "Lord Neptune," Adam chuckled to himself. The Squid had picked that as a human pronounceable name, since Tschaaa speak was a series of whale and dolphin sounds, a series of clicks and rude-sounding snorts and whistles. It was also connected to a bit of an odd sense of alien humor on this Lord's part.

Unbeknownst to him, Adam and the Chief had almost first run into Lord Neptune and his entourage of young Tschaaa warriors–including a harvester robot, and a cyborg named Andrew–some five long years ago on Miami Bay. As he later told the Director, at the time His Lordship had been looking for the two crazy humans who were rumored to run around trying to keep their fellows from killing, raping, and eating each other. Such actions had piqued the alien's curiosity and unusual sense of humor, and he endeavored to locate these humans and try to make use of them.

Upon the recruitment of the Director, Lord Neptune had communicated the Tschaaa's grand plan for the human race. A specific type of protocol had been envisioned. Adam came to know it as the Protocol of Selective Survival. They were to be a client species like the lizards (a reptilian species), the manufactured grey clones, and the cyborg robocop warriors and front men who were created from human genome samples.

Adam opened the physical folder containing the original materials he used for the briefings and looked at the photos inside. The Tschaaa were a spacefaring race who had conquered the bipedal lizards, and in the process found the remains of other alien civilizations, including genetic material from Earth species with the remains of another humanoid race from an unidentified planet. Included were frozen ova, sperm and DNA samples from human ancestors. Lord Neptune told him they were from Gigantopithicus and Homo erectus. Apparently, someone had visited Earth in ancient times. But unfortunately, along with the human samples and other artifacts of alien technology, they had brought back something hidden. Something sinister that would be their undoing.

The Plague. The White Plague which would nearly destroy all of the Tschaaa major source of meat and protein.

Adam scanned some of the additional slides he used for the orientation briefing. The Tschaaa had moved from sea to land at one point in their evolution, becoming amphibian. Their octopus and squid like-structures being modified by Darwinian pressures to incorporate a pliable cartilage rudimentary skeleton. Thus, they could scuttle along for short distances similar to a crab, a cartoon octopus on tippy toes. At the same time, they kept their ability to change the color of their skin to blend in with their surroundings, becoming excellent ambush hunters on land.

Adam looked at photos of their primary prey. The meat creatures were a primate-like species, with chocolate-colored skin and faces like an Earth tarsier. He examined the before and after pictures of what the White Plague did to the primate meat prey. As the Plague progressed, the dark skin became bleached out, nearly white. But even more importantly, the primate meat itself became poisonous, especially to the Tschaaa young. Other mammal species were affected as well, to a lesser though often still disastrous degree.

Culture collapse, pure and simple, began for the Tschaaa. The closest situation on Earth that Adam could imagine would have been if the African Maasai tribesman had been told that, after several hundred years of being a culture of cattle herders, meat and beef blood eaters, were told overnight they had to become vegetarians. No matter the comparison, the Tschaaa civilization began to collapse. The thought of going completely back to their large oceans for life was not an option, even if they had wanted to return. They had outgrown their original environment.

For the first time in Tschaaa history, inter-Crèche conflict began, with one Crèche that had pushed for a recognition of the sentience of the prey primates and a return to the old ways of the oceans being blamed for the Plague. Before the actual origins of the Plague were discovered–and for the very first time in Tschaaa history– a genocide resulted in a bloodline all but being wiped out. Then the human samples were re-discovered, as was their planet of origin, Earth.

This revelation in turn launched two massive projects by a species that had a history of cooperation many times greater than had ever been demonstrated in Earth humans. First, the Tschaaa began to grow human-based meat samples in vats, their biological science being much more advanced than anything than had ever been accomplished in the history of human science.

Millions of Tschaaa had died due to poisoned meat or malnutrition during the first year of the White Plague. A small breeding population of their homegrown primates was kept alive in isolation and a test program of vat grown meat products, both from the native primates and Earth-based species, was expanded as quickly as possible. Actual living specimens were created from the Gigantopithacus and Homo erectus materials. Within twenty years, a viable breeding population for both Earth primate species was created, in addition to the vat grown meat.

The Tschaaa had great difficulty producing viable Tschaaa offspring with their available resources. There was a limit as to what could be done with the available genetic material and breeding population. The population of available sea-based food creatures had significantly diminished over the years. These realities led to the development of the second project–the construction of huge generational starships as *the* solution to the crisis–visit the home of the Homo genus. Earth.

No longer would the Tschaaa base all their hopes on one idea; being married to the idea of cultivating meat creatures on their home world had been their undoing. They would go to Earth, to harvest fresh dark meat and genetic material. The White Plague caused them to think that "white meat was bad, dark meat was good", despite the fact that early produced examples of human flesh showed pigmentation of the meat source did not matter. All the Earth hominid samples seemed immune from the effects of the White Plague.

The Tschaaa next developed warp or hyperdrive technology to cheat the speed of light limitation. However, due to the stupendous energy sources needed to propel craft using these methods, that technology was reserved for smaller scout ships and military raiders. Instead, thirteen huge, slower-moving, multi-generational starships were also produced, each one with the volume and space of an Earth city. Each would carry large numbers of a single breeding Crèche, a bloodline, similar to a huge human extended family. Meat-producing growth vats were placed on the ships, as were areas where populations of Earth primates could be housed as sources of fresh meat.

The final project was the stupendous hollowed-out asteroid, which later became known to the humans as Base One. Several mass drivers were mounted as oversized projectile weapons in and around Base One, also being used as spacecraft propulsion in a pinch.

After some twenty years of construction and preparation, the harvesting fleet was launched toward Earth. Acceleration of the starships was slow, a little over half the speed of light being reached in the first decade. The near Thousand Year Trek began. And, unfortunately for humankind, the voyage successfully ended here on Earth.

In light of this knowledge, Adam had to somehow convince the new arrivals to the project that they would not be cattle, meat for the larders of the Tschaaa. It was especially rough when he had to acknowledge the elephant in the room–that the Squids liked human young, as some humans used to enjoy veal cutlets. It always triggered some gag reflexes for the audience when that informational tidbit sank in. The Protocol would be successful if and only if the people working for the Reformed States of America and really believed the Director when he said they were a protected class. So far, so good.

The loud buzz of his intercom brought Adam back to the present. "Chief is here, Director," Mary Lou announced from the outer office.

"Send him in, Mary Lou." Adam knew the Chief was as much checking up on him as he was coming to discuss any possible fallout from the orientation briefing. It was not uncommon for individuals to ask to leave after Adam had explained the conditions and expectations at Key West. But often that could have been communicated over the telephone.

Chief Hamilton opened the office door and closed it behind him. "Ruminating again, Boss?"

Adam smiled at the oft-repeated question. "You know me too well, Willie."

"Hell, Boss, we've been together as long as some married couples. Of course I know you."

Adam laughed. It was a good release of tension, after the stressful orientation. "Here's the bottle. Fix yourself a drink."

"Never turned that offer down." The Chief took the bottle, strided purposefully to the full wet bar in the corner of the office, and expertly poured himself a scotch on the rocks. He then pulled up a chair and sat near the corner of the desk.

"Kempai, as we used to say to each other on Okinawa."

"That seems like ages ago, Chief."

"Hell, Adam, it was. We are in a completely different age of Homo sapiens development. Thanks to our Squid... masters."

Adam took a sip of his drink, then took the bottle and freshened it. He looked directly at the older man. "Still think about woulda, coulda happened?"

The Chief snorted. "All the time. It would have been a helluva lot simpler if a piece of that rock that broke up over Atlanta during our meeting had hit us. Quick, sure. And I would have gone with my wife and kids."

Adam was lucky, in a way. He had been single when things blew up. He did not have to suffer the pain of a dead spouse or children.

"But," the Chief continued. "We wouldn't be here, saving at least part of the human race. It all worked out for a purpose."

Adam raised his glass. "To the Mission, Willie."

"To the Mission, Adam." They each took a large swig from their drinks.

"Now, to current business. How many are making noises of leaving after my presentation?"

"Surprisingly, Boss, just the one person who I had already pegged as questionable."

Adam frowned. "Who's that?"

"Professor Joseph Fassbinder's wife, Professor Sarah Broadmore-Fassbinder. She had a burr in her saddle, as they say, the minute I showed up at their survival compound. She let me know she thought you and I were devils incarnate."

"Then why did she come here?"

"I think it was a combination of not willing to let hubby go, out of her control–you're seeing him later this afternoon–and the chance to tell you exactly what she thinks of you. Maybe throw a drink in your face."

"Well, she'll have a chance at the icebreaker shindig we have tonight. We'll see if the new attire I provided to her and the other women will soften her at all. Any children?"

"Nope. I suspect the Ice Queen's womb would freeze any invading sperm before it got to the right place." Adam began to laugh. There were times when Chief Hamilton had just the right way of putting things.

When he stopped chuckling, Adam asked, "Suit and tie, right Chief?"

The older man's face showed his displeasure. "Yes, Boss. I'll put a monkey suit on just for you. But only for you. If you ever get bumped off, however, every one of those suits is being buried with you."

Adam grinned. "I'll just have to make sure, with your help, that doesn't happen."

"Which reminds me... are you still wearing your Glock 26 and SP101 like I asked?"

Adam opened his suit coat. "Look for yourself. Gold plated with a bit of pearl in the handle for the Ruger .357. All showy yet will still blow a hole in someone."

"Consider it a trade-off, Boss. You wear the pistols for me, I wear a monkey suit for you."

"Hey, I thought I was the Director–the head mofo in charge."

The Chief's expression registered fake surprise. "Oh, you are. You just do this for me because you love me. After all, we've been together as a couple now for…"

Adam began to laugh again. "Out. Go harass the troops some more. I have more new people to meet this afternoon."

"One being a sexy blond?"

"Out!" The Director picked up a pencil from his desk, and gestured toward the door. "I'll see you tonight, Chief."

"Right, Boss. With bells on." Adam threw the pencil at him as he left, and began to laugh again.

CHAPTER 3

The character of Adam Lloyd remains one of the most disputed aspects of the history of the coming of the Tschaaa, often referred to as the Tschaaa Infestion. Some have concluded that Adam Lloyd had acted the part of a traitor in being so willing to sacrifice some individuals to save others. Why should a man who had left the U.S. Air Force as a mere rank of Captain been given complete discretionary power over the life and death of thousands? And how could only one man determine the criteria that would determine those who would be victims and those who would be survivors? My research indicated that it was the unique personality characteristics of the Captain that had led to the degree of trust reposed in him by the Tschaaa.

What were these points of character in which Adam Lloyd surpassed most of the surviving men of his time? As a Royal Princess, trained in the code of the Samurai, I had been sensitized from a young age to a code of behavior which I found echoed in the particular character of Adam Lloyd. One of the principles of my early training was that 'groundedness' was the first principle of the Samurai. The Samurai must know his Lord. A Samurai cannot be a effective servant without grounding. But, once knowing the direction in once he is to move, he may proceed with confidence. Adam Lloyd recognized the inevitability of his contact with the Tschaaa or its minions. Thus, he shaped those around him into a proto-organization that would fit the Protocols of the Tschaaa.

Others have proposed the idea that Adam was merely an opportunist, possibly with a hint of sociopathy, selfishly driven to feather his own nest and insure his own comfort and survival. After all, Adam Lloyd lived rather well during the period in question. The third theory was that Adam Lloyd was willing to make the best of a bad situation and take responsibilities for his action because no one else was willing to do so. It should never be forgotten in these times of comparative peace what it was like to have every governmental structure lying in ruins. Nor should it be forgotten that complete anarchy reigned supreme in the areas designated as Feral. Compared to this reality, the selective harvesting in the areas presided over by Adam Lloyd seemed comparatively civilized. Of course, those conditions were in direct contradiction to the existence of those in what was eventually called Cattle County.

> —Extract from the *Literary Works of Princess Akiko,* Free Japan Royal Family

ATLANTA, CATTLE COUNTRY

Martin Luther, acting Mayor of Occupied Atlanta, wished again for the thousandth time that his father had not named him after such an important historical figure in history. That seemed to make people expect more from him. He rubbed his hand through his prematurely graying hair. There was a time when someone might have called his proud mane of curly hair by a more derogatory name, which might have started a fight. That time was long gone.

He reached into his top right hand drawer and removed a bottle of pre-strike bourbon, and refreshed his glass. Straight up, no ice, because decent alcohol was at a premium and he wasn't about to water it down. He replaced the bottle, next to the Luger pistol Joe had found for him. Guns and ammunition were at a premium also. At least for some people. Which happened to be the reason of the meeting with the gentleman who just arrived. The room he now occupied was a hotel suite in one of the few high end buildings still left standing in downtown Atlanta. It was referred to as the Mayor's office now, the original first class hotel chain name long forgotten.

A loud knock sounded at the door, and a huge shadow of a man opened it. Joe, his aide and protector, entered the room. "He's here, Boss."

"Thanks, Joe. What name is he using now?"

The former NFL draft pick gave a wry smile. "Malcolm X. Carter."

Martin grunted. Another young black man with delusions of grandeur? God, he hoped not. "Show him in, please."

"Right, Boss."

A muscular young man with cropped hair, dark glasses, and dark suit that complemented the tone of his skin entered the room. Martin quickly noticed he had a Samsonite briefcase handcuffed and chained to his left wrist. He also remarked to himself that his was the darkest black man he had seen in years, even darker than Joe.

Joe had survived through a fluke, Andrew believed. How had "Malcolm X. Carter" survived? The Squids had been drawn to darker-skinned humans as soon as they noticed the color variations in our species; the humans that had the darkest skin in any population were harvested first. The automated harvester robots would sometimes be overwhelmed with the quantity of meat available. Eventually, this led the programmed machines to overload and reject those same individuals, freeing the fortunate ones who had not been culled previously. That apparently had happened to Joe. The same with this young man?

The Mayor did not offer a hand, but nodded in the young man's direction. "Have a seat, please, Mister… Carter is it?"

"My name isn't important. What I have to offer is."

Malcolm set the briefcase firmly on the large desk in front of Martin. He unlocked the handcuff from his wrist and opened the case. As the youth reached in, Joe appeared as if by magic, his huge hand on a large Bowie knife he kept concealed under his suit coat. "Careful, son. Nice and slow."

Malcolm smirked. "Do you think I would have come by myself if I wanted to cap someone, old man?"

Joe visibly clenched his jaw, but a look from Martin stopped him from reacting with a fist. They had worked together for five years, so Joe knew by a look and didn't need a further word to confirm what his boss might be thinking. Joe took a step back, while Martin leaned over the case to take a closer look. Inside were three Sig Sauer .40 caliber automatics, in near pristine condition.

"Hm. Seems you definitely have the goods, Mr. Carter."

"Malcolm. Malcolm X. will do for today. How many you want?"

"At least six. Plus ammunition and spare magazines."

Malcolm calmly answered, "That can be done."

The Mayor was surprised. This young man seemed not to have a care in the world. "So, what do you want in return?"

In response, Malcolm made himself at home in the chair behind him. He pulled out a cigarette case from an inside suit pocket, removed a cigarette, lit it with a gold lighter, and began to slowly smoke. Martin was an itinerant smoker, and could not help but enjoy when others indulged. Malcolm saw this, and offered him a cigarette, which Martin gladly took. As the Mayor lit his cigarette, Malcolm began. "Let me tell you a story, Mister Mayor. A story of a young man whose path started one way, and ended up another.

"His father was a federal agent for Homeland Security when the first rock hit, here in Atlanta. His father had been on the fast track for promotion when all hell broke loose. Because he worked for the government, with a Top Secret security clearance, he knew what was happening after the first twenty-four hours. He knew who was being eaten, where, and why. He figured that out real quick.

"He and his partner went to the field office, each grabbed a duffle bag full of pistols and ammo, and as many shotguns and M-4s they could carry. They then headed to the suburbs where they lived, and barricaded themselves in their respective homes. They each lasted about a week before a harvester landed nearby, and a shitload of those little ATV looking robots started running up and down the street, breaking doors in, looking for humans.

"The father, defending his wife, two sons and daughter, blew several of those little ATV robos away before a robocop showed up. As his two sons and daughter fled out the back, he and his wife took on the robocop and actually managed to take it out. Five minutes later, a second robocop showed up and blew the front of the house off, leaving the parents for dead. And harvesting."

"The one son returned, saw his dead parents, grabbed the duffle bag and some of the long guns, and hot-footed it out. Unfortunately, he lost track of his other brother and sister, never to see them again."

Malcolm stubbed out his cigarette, and pulled out another one.

"A month later, the son was back in Atlanta. How he made it there is hard to say. Sometime later, a large electronic and physical fence was placed around a three state area by the Squids, and here we are.

"So, since it's nearly impossible to get out, and if you did, you don't have the firepower to fight the Squids–especially not without some pistols–why do you need my services?"

Martin finished his cigarette after smoking it down to the nub.

Tobacco was almost impossible to get, so he wasn't about to waste any. "It's complicated."

"No, it sure as hell isn't," Malcolm retorted.

"How's that?"

Malcolm looked at Martin with an unwavering gaze.

"You are the 'house negro' of days past; your help keeps your 'massa' happy, and things in the 'big house' running smoothly. The rest of us are just 'field niggers', expendable pieces of meat.

"Now, wait a minute..." Joe started toward Malcolm.

"Go ahead, big man. Gut me. Do you think killing me ends it, fixes it?" Malcolm slowly stood up. "Everyone in this death camp you call the Cattle Ranch is already dead. The only question is the exact time of death."

He pointed toward the briefcase."Keep those three. But they need firing pins to work. I just came here to see if the Mayor actually existed. You do. And you need guns to help keep the troublemakers in line, so you 'house negroes' can keep 'massa' from eating you and yours." Malcolm sighed in exasperation. "This has happened before. Some Jews became kapos in the death camps, sold out other Jews to the Nazis. Africans sold Africans into slavery. Revolutionaries sold their own kind to the secret police. Hell, people have sold their own children for drugs."

The man called Malcolm stared at Joe. "So, big man, am I free to go?"

Joe tilted his head toward Martin, who nodded. Joe stepped back.

"Thank you. Like I said, keep those. As a gift. I have lots of others. If you want more, I need food and specific medical supplies. You see, I plan on keeping us 'field niggers' alive past your deaths. I'll be in touch."

Malcolm left. The Mayor sat quietly for quite some time. "Joe, any idea where his people are?"

Joe shrugged. "Heard sewer lines, caves, just some place underground. Anyone who claims they have info winds up dead."

"That's just great. A troublemaker who actually has ideas, not delusions of grandeur."

"Please, Joe. Bring me some lunch." Joe left him to his thoughts.

Martin Luther stayed alive because the Squids, through Director Lloyd, wanted him to run things, and to insure breeding, the reproduction of the species. He kept order so as to provide certain levels of fresh meat to the Squids. At first, criminals, dope fiends and the like were enough. Now, they are pretty much gone. You cannot keep providing individuals under the guise of malcontents when that applies to ninety-nine percent of the population now. Like his granddad always said, it's "nut cuttin' time".

Now, who could get some firing pins?

CHAPTER 4

There were those humans who clearly embraced the idea of a superior alien culture represented by the Tschaaa. There were humans who embraced the tasks of controlling other members of humankind designated to be dark meat and prime veal for the Tschaaa tables with a zeal not seen since Nazi death camp commanders, Cambodian followers of Pol Pot and those Russian Communists who supervised the Gulag system in Siberia. They were soon collectively known as the Krakens.

Krakens started from a name and symbol for a motorcycle gang formed by one John Talbot, one of the leaders of Renegade Flying Squads that operated as a Fifth Column in the first days of the Invasion/ Infestation. Then one Reverend Kray appropriated the name and ancient symbol of the giant Kraken cephalopod sea monster for his Church of Kraken. For Reverend Kray, a religious fanatic of the same ilk as Jim Jones and David Koresh in North America and ISIS leaders in the Middle East, believed with all his heart and soul that he was serving a monstrous ocean-dwelling Divine and Ancient God. He soon imbued many of his followers with the same zealotry and fanaticism, often to the point where they ate members of their own species, an act which even the Tschaaa considered as an abomination.

Even without examining all the mental characteristics and inner motivations of the Krakens, it is easy to identify them as the result of that same old evil and depravity that lurks, waiting to burst out, in the souls of our unfortunate species.

The Tschaaa in their own evolutionary history had undergone species characterological deformation. My research from the sources available to me demonstrate that the Tschaaa originated in the seas of their home planet. There original source of protein was of an aquatic nature. The first interface between primate like animals and the Tschaaa on their own planet had been apparently accidental. Over perhaps eons, the original proto-Tschaaa evolved into a more highly evolved organism manifesting higher mental capacities and terrestrial mobility. It was then the Tschaaa, led out onto the land by apparent Prophets, began to codify in both writing and deed the culture and belief systems that we now attribute to all Tschaaa.

>—Extract from the *Literary Works of Princess Akiko,* Free Japan Royal Family.

MYRTLE GROVE, FLORIDA

As Mayor Luther ended his meeting, something was about to happen that would eventually resound up the highways and byways from Myrtle Grove, Florida, to Atlanta. Myrtle Grove could be considered to be on the outskirts of Pensacola Florida and the former Naval air installation that was being rebuilt by Director Lloyd and the Tschaaa. This was why John Talbot, former outlaw biker and now head of his own gang known as the Krakens–the largest flying squad left in the Director's arsenal–was there.

The Squids had built a series of fences and electronic barriers that contained what used to be Mississippi, Alabama, and Georgia–give or take a few square miles here and there. Inside were those of sufficiently dark complexion as to be classified as cattle. To Talbot, they were all lesser men than himself.

As advanced as the Tschaaa were, no system is perfect. And since humans for the most part were now guarding humans, occasionally cattle got out, and contraband got in. That was where Talbot came in. Starting about a year prior, primary responsibility for handling border issues, jailbreaks, runaways and so forth, fell to John Talbot and his ilk. Cyborgs backed them up when it came time to harvest, so woe to the person who damaged "meat" without cause. The heavy lifting fell to John. He was a member of a vanishing special club; one of the some ten thousand humans who had aided the Tschaaa Invasion in the United States under the guise of the return of a master race.

When some of Talbot's supremacists had seen their first Tschaaa, and realized that the Squids were the race behind the invasion, they had breakdowns. Some killed themselves, others ran for the hills, and some joined the Resistance. Added to the ones lost in combat during and after the Strike, less than one in ten remained at the Director's—and the Tschaaa—beck and call.

Talbot didn't care. Hell, he had believed in UFOs and grey aliens before the first rock hit. Now, he got paid to catch and sometimes kill human dark meat and their cousins. He and his people—some two hundred men, women, and children—were paid in money, drugs, precious metals, booze, and whatever he could salvage. Part of that salvage was strange and exotic women. Talbot was in hog heaven.

Today, someone had whacked two good ole boy sentries for Cattle Country, blown a hole in the fence and now there was hell to pay.

He and his Krakens traveled as a group in a series of fancy SUVs, RVs, public transit and tour buses, and a couple of converted bank armored cars. They had two old cattle trucks as well, one for a few horses they kept, the other holding a few motorcycles and spare parts. A semi-tractor trailer with ATVs rounded out the transport. Talbot himself drove a Cadillac SUV, while a Jeep Cherokee driven by his old lady followed him, pulling his Harley on a trailer.

They had twin five-year-olds, one boy and one girl, who were the next generation. He had a half a dozen younger members who still rode Harleys all the time. The rest of the older members rode in the more comfortable transport. Traditional bikers were a thing of the past.

Talbot still remembered when he had officially adopted his new colors—the Krakens— some five years ago when Director Lloyd began organizing the remnants of the supremacists, renegades, and bikers who had helped support the invasion. Front men, grays and a few robos had used them to stamp out anyone who questioned the New World Order, but it was too hit and miss. They really did not know how humans thought, but instead treated everyone as disposable; probably the reason why barely one thousand members of the original flying squads that had supported the Invasion still existed.

When he had adopted his new colors, some old school bikers who hadn't gotten the word that the old way was gone tried to tell him that he couldn't have new colors unless all the surviving biker gangs voted approval. "Don't disrespect the old colors, there's a way things are done... yada, yada, yada."

Talbot, with the help of the Director's personal robocop, had offed some two dozen of the old school before they got the hint that the Krakens were the senior club in town. Hells Angels, Bandidos, Outlaws, and Pagans existed in small isolated compounds. Former skinheads and KKK members were still used in some areas to scare the locals and as sentries keeping the dark meat in Cattle Country.

Mostly, since everything was organized around local committees and overseer robocops, coordinated through Director Lloyd, the old boogie men had no mission. The Director was also forming military style security forces in San Diego, L.A. San Antonio, Houston, Pensacola, and, of course, Key West. Since last year, as power, food, shelter and medical care began to be provided again in an organized, almost national form, only Talbot's people were being used on a regular basis. They were also provided newer weapons and transport.

The Church of Kraken and the Reverend Kray had risen using the Kraken, a mythical tentacle giant squid creature, as a symbol not long after Talbot had made his presence known. Talbot should have been flattered, but in reality, he was irritated. He did all the heavy lifting, making the Kraken a symbol to be feared, and then this religious fanatic had stolen his idea. What really pissed off Talbot was when some so-called Krakens–"churchers" he called them– started eating other humans. What type of sick bastard did *that*?

Now Talbot's people were stopped along the main road, a mile down from the hole in the fence. Hopefully, surviving sentries had kept many people from walking all over the escape route. They had found one piece of discarded clothing, which Talbot had in his gloved hand. He walked over to Dogman, who was built like an Adonis, a solid, muscular man making women–and any gay men who might still live–drool with desire. Talbot did not know his original name, the man called himself Dogman for as long as he had known him.

Talbot handed Dogman the child's shirt that had been recovered. The man took it, gave it a momentary glance, and then immediately brought it over to the bus he had set up especially for him. Dogman had spared no expense or effort to create a state of the art mobile kennel, which resembled a dog spa in its luxury. Inside, he had a dozen dogs of various specialized breeds. He opened the rear door and quickly removed three Black Mouth Curs, a now rare breed from the Alabama area. Bred as hunting hound dogs, they had excellent noses to track prey, with jaws and teeth to back them up if the prey decided to fight them before Dogman got there.

The dogs sniffed the offered piece of clothing. Dogman said only one word, "Seek," and the three, heads to the wind, took off. The man jumped on a four-wheel ATV he had primed and ready and took off after them.

"Goddamnit. There he goes again," fumed Talbot. "Takes off without a word." Talbot signaled to three young bikers he had wisely standing by to follow Dogman, and they took off in pursuit.

Talbot got back into his SUV to wait for word from the dog handler. That S.O.B. talked more to his dogs than he did to humans, Talbot thought. Dogman had told him once when pressed that he believed dogs were morally superior, not to mention nicer, than ninety-nine percent of the people he knew, so why waste his time talking to humans? But Dogman had never let Talbot down. This time was no different.

A quarter of an hour later, and one of the bikers radioed back, "He's got 'em." And gave a quick location. Then, shots were heard.

"Fuck!" Talbot cursed. He yelled over his radio, "Assault team, follow me!" He took off like a proverbial bat out of hell, with three ATVs and a former border patrol Suburban inline. Thanks to the fact that the Director had gotten GPS up and running again last month, finding Dogman would be relatively simple.

An old former farmhouse and barn were off the main road by about a half mile. The young bikers were already involved in a firefight with the occupants when Talbot and the assault team arrived. With practiced ease, tear gas grenades were fired into the structures, as an old M-60 machine gun fired bursts at the firing points. Without warning, a bunch of humans came bursting out of the former farm structures.

"Look at those black bastards scatter. Just like a bunch of cockroaches!" somebody yelled. One fleeing man with a gun fired a shot from his pistol, and then was cut in half by the M-60. High-pitched shrieks were heard as more shots were fired.

Talbot's men were well schooled in leg shots. It took a little while longer, but some ninety percent of the adults were down with bullets in a leg, thigh, or knee. The rest, with the children, stopped and went to ground.

"Alright, you black mofos!" Talbot yelled over a bullhorn. "Hands on heads while you still have a head." A couple more shots rang out as someone still fought back, followed by a burst of assault rifle fire that produced more screams. "Cease fire! Cease fire!" Talbot yelled. The shooting stopped. Talbot waited a minute or two for the situation to sink in for the Cattle.

"If you want to survive along with your kids, do as we say, and do not resist." Talbot had already contacted a Falcon craft to respond and harvest the dead dark meat. Three adults had been killed outright. A fourth was dying from having parts of his body ripped off by one of the dogs. A robocop piloted Falcon could easily handle that small number. This had been arranged and accomplished many times during the last year. One just had to explain ahead of time the threat and to not indiscriminately start killing what the Squids saw as their Cattle, especially the young.

As Talbot supervised the rounding up of the rest of the rebels, and treatment of the wounded to keep them alive until they made it back to Cattle Country, one of his Lieutenants, Ray Sparks approached him.

"Bossman, Dogman has a problem. You should come quick."

Sparks was one of Talbot's more level-headed men, which was why he made him a Lieutenant. If he said Talbot should come, Talbot knew he had better. He found Dogman cradling one of his dogs. The Dark Mouth Cur was bleeding badly from a gunshot wound. Talbot knew it would die long before they made it back to their convoy vehicles, where there was a vet and a doctor.

"Sorry, Dogman. Didn't know one of the dark… "

"Don't," the large man growled.

"What? I just… "

"Just… don't."

Talbot made a lot of allowances for Dogman because of his unique abilities, but this attitude was getting old. Before he could say anything, Dogman turned and walked, carrying his dog to his ATV. On the back cargo rack he had made a padded bed area on which he could strap wounded dogs. With practiced hands he quickly secured his dog. But it was already too late. The dog gave one last sigh, and died.

Dogman stared at his canine companion. He bent over, whispered something in the dog's ear, and gently covered him with a blanket. Then, Dogman turned, and walked toward the crowd. Before Talbot realized what was happening, the big man approached one of the half dozen children, grabbed a fifteen year old boy, and producing a fillet knife, slit his throat from ear to ear all in the blink of an eye.

Talbot screamed, "No! Goddamnit. Stop!" But it had already happened.

The Falcon seemed to appear from nowhere. Dogman calmly walked to the ATV as the boy spasmed and bled out, adults screaming and crying around him. The robocop in the Falcon quickly took in the tableau, blue light alighting on Dogman as he now stood at the back of his ATV. He looked directly at the Falcon, as he rested his hands on his dead dog. The light went out. The Falcon, using its signature metal tentacles, picked up the dead dark meat, including the boy, and was gone.

"I swear to God, Bossman, those Squids might becoming more human. They understood about the dead dog."

Talbot walked over to Dogman, seething. Before he could say anything, Dogman stared at him with those cold eyes he had, and said, "They killed my child, I killed theirs." Talbot turned away. What could you say to a crazy mofo, who would get fried for a dog? Nothing.

He walked back to his Lieutenant, who had something long in his hands. A spear.

"Look, Bossman. Six guns, a bow and arrow, and a real life African spear."

Talbot took the spear, and examined it closely. On the shaft was a brass plate with the words: "Waziri, Property of Atlanta Museum of Natural History".

"Boys," Talbot said, "we may be taking a trip to Atlanta."

CHAPTER 5

To say Director Adam Lloyd was a bit like the mythical creature the satyr with its legendary sexual appetites was not far from the mark. For he had three full time "ladies" at his beck and call, as well as in his bed, when he located one Kathy Monroe, adult film star and an admitted fixation of his. However, he had another every important role for her to play, one that had little to do with her onscreen talents. It was a role Kathy Monroe would fill quite nicely, to the surprise of many. Belying the image of an out of control sexual beast, the Director also was adept at selecting people with specialized skills and talents to join him, and showed the humans he chose the advantages of a benign dictator. Adam Lloyd was trying to build a safe haven for humanity. It was assuredly not propaganda.

> —*The Great Compromise*, Appendix, item #7. Excerpt from the
> Sunday Supplement by Sally Reid, *Great Falls Herald*.

KEY WEST, FLORIDA

Adam looked at his watch. "It's almost 2:00pm. Who's up next for interview, Chief?" Chief Hamilton smiled. "Guess, Boss." "Hm. Judging by your grin... Kathy Monroe."

"That's why you're the boss, and I'm not. Can't hide anything from you."

"Have her come in, please."

"Private interview, Boss?"

"Yes please, Chief."

The Chief left to let Mary Lou know it was time to send in Ms. Monroe. Adam had actual jitters, like a nervous school boy at his first dance. Come on, pull yourself together, he told himself. He was possibly the most powerful human in the world, and yet he couldn't handle one attractive woman. There was a short knock on the door. "Come in."

Mary Lou entered first, announcing the visitor. "Ms. Monroe to see you, Director." Adam noticed that Mary Lou was shooting daggers at Kathy as she came in, as if she wanted to claw her eyes out. Damn, he did not expect that level of animosity. She, Jeanie, and Jamey had quickly bonded. Just another problem to deal with later. No rest for the wicked.

"Hello, Ms. Monroe. Please, have a seat. Care for something to drink?"

"Hello, Mr. Director. What can you offer... to drink that is." She flashed him her signature smile.

Adam took in all the details of the very attractive woman in front of him. Blonde, blue-eyed, with that smile that started in her eyes and then animated her whole face. Feminine, but strong-looking nose. She was wearing fashion designer jeans that were clean, pressed, but had seen better days. Even with the jeans, he could admire the shape of her legs from the top of her running shoes went all the way up, where they joined a perfect ass. A light blue blouse, with the top two buttons strategically unbuttoned, covered yet gave a hint at the sheer nylon bra beneath. He also noticed, quizzically, that she was carrying an Air Force flight jacket on her arm in a size too large for her.

"What would you like, Ms. Monroe?"

"Glass of water–with ice if you have it–and a shot of scotch, neat, please, Mr. Director."

"Coming right up."

As he took the ice and glasses out of the refrigerator, Kathy asked, "Bartender has the day off, Mr. Director?"

"No, simple tasks I do myself, saves wasted staff positions. And, I will make you a deal. If I can call you Kathy, you can call me Adam."

Kathy gave him an impish smile. "You can call me anything you want as long as it isn't nasty. Although I've heard it all in *my* industry." She added, "How about 'Boss', for you. I don't think I'm in a position to call you by your first name, even in private. Especially with your secretary giving me the 'stink eye'."

Adam paused pouring the drinks, and addressed Kathy. "It's that obvious?"

"Yes boss, it was. As soon as I walked up to her desk, I got the feeling she was ready for a good old-fashioned cat fight. I don't want one, but I won't back down if she tries."

Adam shook his head. "No, that won't happen. She knows that would definitely displease me."

Kathy shrugged, then took the two offered drinks from Adam. "Kempai," she offered in salute, and after tossing back the scotch, began to sip the iced water.

"Damn, I really missed ice cubes. Just like I really needed that scotch to settle my nerves." She set the two glasses down on the nearby end table and with a serious expression, added, "Like you said, Boss, I like to get to the point also." She took a deep breath, then asked, "Why me? Other than the obvious. I'm guessing you have a huge collection of my DVDs you want me to autograph."

Adam reappraised her. He should have realized that to survive the last six years and still be in one piece took someone with special qualities. Especially someone who, because of her reputation, could be in someone's private stable of kept women. Adam and the Chief had broken up several slave rings the past few years. Why humans, under the threat of extinction, couldn't stop from exploiting other humans he did not understand.

The Tschaaa enslaved humans because we were draft and food animals, a different species. Forced slavery of their own species was unknown to the Squids. Traditions and protocols let every being know their place in Tschaaa society.

"I would be lying if I said it had nothing to do with your career," Adam admitted. "However, although I must confess to having something of a schoolboy crush on you, your physical expertise is not the main reason I had the Chief look you up. I could have found enough of a lookalike to satisfy that urge."

"Well then, Boss, if it isn't just my good looks, or my talents in bed, what is it?"

Adam paused. "Remember an eternity ago when a porn producer said in an interview that your perkiness went a long way at five in the morning?"

Kathy smiled. "I thought I was the only human being who still remembered that."

"Well, there are two of us. You seem to have the unique ability to project a positive, upbeat... presence I guess I would call it, over radio, television, internet, even electronic media–you name it. Some people would say you are just a good actress. I say that you have the genuine ability to project your positive thinking, that inner you that really exists. You see the potential best in humanity, don't you? Despite the seedier side of life you've seen, and definitely all the crap you have been through in the past six years, you refuse to accept that things will always be bad."

Kathy gave a little snort. "Never give up, never surrender. That phrase was in a comedy, but I take it to heart. Also, *illegitimi non carborundum*– don't let the bastards get you down–in very bad Latin."

Adam smiled. "I like a variation of a movie quote, turned on its head. 'Positive Vibes, Moriarty, always with the positive vibes.' "

They both laughed, and again Adam saw that special spark Kathy had shine through.

"I need your ability, what one man called your 'perkiness at 5:00am'". Adam rose from his chair, and walked over to the large window overlooking the bay side of the Base.

"We are at a crossroads as a species. As nasty as things are, it could be worse. We could all be lined up tomorrow and shipped off to the harvesters. Every part of the world could be turned into a Dachau and an Auschwitz, a Pol Pot killing field, the ultimate Siberia."

He turned around and faced Kathy. "Our Lordship and a few others see potential in our species beyond being a piece of meat. The Tschaaa have the technology in a pinch to grow us in vats, similar to the grays." Adam gave a wry smile. "Lord Neptune said the result is the equivalent of Vienna sausage in a can, but it would still be edible with the Tschaaa equivalent of ketchup."

Kathy bit her bottom lip, then spoke. "You think I have the ability to help you keep things on an even keel, to help people keep on going on, day after day, working toward a positive outcome. Specifically, we are kept alive until we are seen as a needed, productive junior partner, so to speak, to the Tschaaa. And, my unique... 'perkiness' as you call it, is that unique?"

"Yes," Adam replied. "Yes, it is. I have made damn few mistakes in reading people's ability, how they can help us survive. And that's all it is about. Survival."

Kathy sighed. "Well, I have had stranger proposals. I guess, Boss, I could smile at you, bat my baby blues, and say…" At this, she adopted the voice of little girl. "Sure Daddy Warbucks. Whatever you say." She returned to her normal tone of voice. "*But*, we would both know I would be feeding you a load of horseshit. So, let me lay it out to you. You see this flight jacket, the one that's too big for me?"

"Sure," Adam replied. "I was going to ask you about it. The Chief and I are former Air Force."

"Well, I may have handled a lot of… joysticks in my former career, as it was, but I was never a pilot. My fiancé was."

Adam returned to his chair facing Kathy, and waited. He knew she would tell him the story in her own good time.

"He was a fighter pilot the day the first rock hit, the first strikes. He'd given me a ring the week before. Me, a porn star, barely beginning in mainstream films. Usually playing horny young things, only I wasn't so young anymore. He knew the Air Force brass wouldn't look too kindly at a wife who was in my line of work. The officers' wives club would have imploded. So he planned on getting out and, using a few connections I had, flying in Hollywood. Computer graphics can do wonders, but actual hotshot flying sequences are hard to beat. Not to mention ferrying execs around. The rocks hit, the Squids showed up, and he started fighting."

She gently patted the jacket. "This was his old flight jacket. He had just been issued a new one of some fantastic new material. There is–or was, I guess–some news footage made by a very gutsy photographer of an Air Force fighter with a wingman attacking a harvester ark coming in for a landing near L.A., on day three. The harvester was hit by a missile and went in. A delta went after the wingman and, somehow, was out maneuvered and shot down also by the same pilot that had hit the ark. A couple of minutes later a Falcon appeared. It hit the fighter with one of those 'tractor beams' they have. Apparently, the Tschaaa wanted to see who could take out a harvester and a delta with inferior technology." Kathy blinked back tears. "The fighter turned into the Falcon and rammed it before it was immobilized. The Falcon bellied in, pieces of the fighter imbedded in the body of the spacecraft."

Adam and Kathy both fell silent.

"How do you know… it was him?"

Kathy swallowed hard. "The wonders of digital film technology. A close up showed his tail number, with his handle and nickname painted in fairly small letters near the cockpit. 'Chubby' was his handle. And yes, he definitely had a large 'chubby'–at least large enough for this adult film actress. I should know, I'm an expert." A single tear rolled down her left cheek.

Adam looked at the jacket. "His name tag, is missing."

Anger flashed across her face. "Yeah. A bitch at the ranch house where I was holed up at didn't like the goo-goo eyes her so-called boyfriend was making at me. She stole the nametag, burning it to get back at me." Adam saw a feral grin on Kathy's face appear that he wouldn't have believed was possible. "She won't try that again with anyone anytime soon. I tore into her, tried to rip her tits off, which were definitely not as nice as mine. Here, look at this."

Kathy, with unexpected familiarity, opened her blouse and slid her right breast out of her bra cup. "See this? That little scar is from her trying to bite my nipple off. I returned the favor. She still had two when I left her, but I bet you she has scars." Kathy slipped her breast back into her bra. "So much for perkiness." She buttoned her blouse as she stood up.

"What do you think you're doing, Kathy?"

"Leaving, of course. Damaged goods, Boss. Who you think I was six years ago, that's not me now. Thanks for the hot showers, the trip, the scotch, but I think…"

"Kathy, sit down."

"No, I…"

"Sit. Down."

Kathy saw a hard look in Adam's eyes, and felt a cold rage behind the apparent calmness that scared her speechless. In another life, Adam might have become a hired killer, an assassin, a serial killer. That iciness was instead, here and now, from a man allegedly in charge of saving humanity as a species. She sat.

"This is not going to turn this into a pity party." Adam walked over to his bar, poured two glasses of scotch, put some ice and water in a third glass, and returned to Kathy. "Here."

"Thanks." There was a pause. "Boss?"

"Yes, Kathy?"

"Can we move over to that nice overstuffed sofa of yours? I could stand some more comfort. It's been a long time."

"Sure." They settled into their new seats and Adam began. "Everyone has lost someone. The Chief and I were having breakfast together in Atlanta one minute, all hell broke loose the next. But we survived. The Chief's wife and kids did not."

Kathy had the chance for a conversation with the Chief on the rather long trip back to Key West. He had felt her out, she him. She knew of the destruction that had happened around Atlanta, which had set into motion the chain of events that led them to Key West and Lord Neptune. The Chief had matter of factly talked about the complete strangers they had killed when certain people tried to hijack their vehicles, their equipment. No regrets, no emotions. And now the Director. The same, if not more, icy strength. Kathy shivered.

"What I said during the briefing was all truth, no bullshit. Everyone has to make the same decision. Can they survive here, or does this setup offend them."

Adam took a drink, then fixed her with his piercing blue eyes. "So, Miss Monroe. You tell me. I told you what I expect, what I want. What you need to do for me and the Tschaaa Lord. No more, no less. Your decision." Cold, almost a feral demeanor. Adam Lloyd was the alpha male, no question. Kathy kissed him. He kissed back. A quick fumbling and shedding of clothes followed.

"Wait, Kathy." He pulled his pants up enough to make it to his desk and retrieve a package of condoms. "You don't have to try to get pregnant."

She giggled. "That's nice. Now hurry up and screw me. It's been a long, dry spell."

Twenty minute later, the two satiated humans laid back on the sofa.

"I told you it has been a long time."

"I'll be honest with you, Kathy. I did not plan things to go this way."

She wrinkled her nose at him. "Doesn't matter, Boss. It happened. I liked it, you liked it. Both of us. A lot." She looked at Adam. "The question now is... what's next?"

Adam frowned. "Normally I have everything planned to a T. As much as I may have fantasized about you, I wasn't going to try and make you a concubine. The large part of what I told you about your abilities in communicating a special message *is* the reason why you are here. Seeing you on that local broadcast from San Diego was pure luck. It was just a test on connecting the west coast directly, real time, to here."

"And the rest of the reason was you had the hots for me."

"Alright, yes. Mea culpa. I've had the hots for you for years. But, remember what I said about the mission being *the Mission?*"

"Yes, Boss."

"That's true. No bullshit. I believe I can save what is left of the human race."

Whether he was mad, delusional, or both did not matter. Kathy saw in his steely eyes that he believed what he just said.

"So, what's next?"

"I set you up in a private apartment here. You are going to be a Special Assistant handling message and media communications. I came up with the title, so don't laugh."

"I learned never to laugh at the one who signs the check. I just laugh *with* them, not *at* them."

"And since we are dealing in truth right this minute, if things work out like they just did, you move in to my suite with me."

"Uh, Boss, don't get mad, but a fourth wheel is great on a car; a fourth for a game of bridge is okay. A fourth woman in your bed is a recipe for disaster."

"We'll discuss the future details later. I did have a suite planned here for you. Here is the key. The Chief can show you where it is. There are some clothes for work and some appropriate clothes for tonight… no protests. I provided all *six hundred* new arrivals with the right attire for tonight, no favoritism." He winked.

Kathy kissed him on the cheek. "I start work tomorrow? Where?"

"Report to Major Grant in Communications. There is a map in your room of the entire base. 8:00 am and don't be late. You may work directly for me, but Jane will not allow *anyone* to slouch on assignments I gave. She also helped me developed the program I have in mind."

"Then, I'll see you tonight?"

"Of course. It's my party! I also reserve one dance with all of the ladies I can handle, so be warned."

As Kathy finished putting her clothes back together in preparation to leaving, she turned toward Adam. "One last thing…"

"Shoot."

"I am nobody's bitch, unless I want to be. Threaten me, beat me, screw me over, and I still will not be yours, or anyone else's–even the Lord Squid's–bitch. I'll die first, after I cut someone's testicles or tits off."

Adam looked at her, saw the toughness in her. "If you think I'm trying to make everybody into someone's bitch, guess again. My survival plan involves humanity's lot improving, not being a permanent whipping boy. Or meatsicle."

In a flash, Kathy's famous perky smile returned. "Sorry, Boss, didn't mean to be such a downer."

Adam waved her comment away. "Don't worry. I wanted your honesty. You have my word, you are not going to be anybody's bitch. A nice squeeze maybe, but never a bitch."

Kathy giggled. "Aye aye, sir. See you tonight."

After she left, Adam sat down behind his desk. Life had just thrown him an unexpected curve ball. Kathy was just supposed to be a pinup with some excellent communication skills that would help the mission. He had fooled around with many women in the last few years. The closest he had ever come to the idea of having a long term relationship with was Major Grant, or Mary Lou. Even then, the spark wasn't there that could distract him from his ultimate goal.

In one face-to-face meeting, Kathy, a former porn star, had him thinking more serious thoughts about his personal future than anyone had in five years. At least any human. He shook his head. He had to be careful. He needed an honest-to-God love affair like a submarine needed a screen door. He called Chief on his radio phone. "Chief, so far so good. Check with Mary Lou, see if she needs any help rounding up the last few newbies I planned to meet with."

"Will do, Boss." Kathy's "boss" had a definite ring to it that the Chief's did not.

Professor Joseph Fassbinder sat in a comfortable chair in the waiting room. Ten feet in front of him was Mary Lou's desk. Although the chair definitely made his tired rear end feel rejuvenated, Professor Fassbinder was far from comfortable. He was as nervous as a high school Senior meeting his prom date's hardass old man for the first time.

The only thing that helped take the mind off his tension was Mary

Lou. She reminded him of some former celebrity beauty that he had seen in decades-old books or magazines his father had. Looking in those same books and magazines, Joseph had realized that he and his father both looked an awful lot like Charles Lindbergh, the famous pilot, skinny tallness and all. His father was long dead. Luckily, he had died just before the Invasion. His mother, however, wasn't so lucky. Don't go there, he reminded himself. That memory would only serve to royally screw him up right now.

Suddenly, it dawned on him. Bettie Page. Mary Lou was the spitting image of long dead Bettie Page, the pinup and bondage queen. Mary Lou caught him staring at her, and hers eyes met his with a quizzical look.

"Sorry." He mumbled and diverted his eyes.

"Just say it." It took Joseph a moment to realize that Mary Lou had spoken to him.

"Excuse me?"

"I *said*, 'Just say it.' I look just like Bettie Page."

Joseph blushed a bright crimson.

"Oh come on now, Professor. Do you think you're the first man who noticed that? Or who told me that? I take it as a compliment." Joseph was saved from further embarrassment by the loud ring of the telephone. "Right, Director," Mary Lou answered. She hung up the phone. "You're up, Professor."

As he unfolded his lanky frame from the chair, Mary Lou gave him a wry smile. "We can discuss your knowledge of pin up queens at a later date."

That didn't help his blush at all.

As the Professor walked into the Director's office, Adam met Joseph with his hand extended before he was halfway toward the desk.

"Professor Fassbinder. It's an honor. Glad you came." Joseph shook the Director's hand, stunned that he was being greeted like some long lost relative or celebrity. The Director acted as if he knew everything about Joseph that was important. "Please, have a seat in this incredible chair. Believe it or not, we make them around here."

Joseph sat, and immediately appreciated the effect the chair had on him. It was so comfortable that it seemed to suck all of his fears and insecurities from him. Was alien technology involved? Who cared.

He had been living on edge since the first rock came down. Somehow he and his wife, Professor Sarah Broadmore-Fassbinder, had survived in a small enclave in a state college town in California–a small community of intelligentsia, writers, professors, talking heads from the media, and a couple of former government officials that had bonded together and scraped enough food and supplies together to survive.

A week ago, out of the blue, Chief Hamilton had showed up on their doorstep. At first, it looked as if there was going to be a fight, as some believed they were about to be harvested. Although off the beaten track, everyone knew that the "eyes in the sky" could find most anyone if they wanted to. That, and the group had just started using the reconstructed internet the month before.

Chief Hamilton soon allayed their fears of being Cattle after all these years, though he had enough firepower, people, and a robocop that would have made any fight definitely one-sided. The Chief had specifically asked for Joseph and his wife to return with him, but Sarah did not want to leave. There was noticeable venom in her words when she told the Chief what she thought of quislings and anyone who talked to Squids. A Polysci professor, well-published before the first rock strike, she had been a central figure in many a controversial protest or movement to include television appearances. She had influence and when she spoke, people listened. Now, she had little, just enough to survive. But, she refused to give in on principle.

Joseph knew you cannot eat principle. Principle did not provide medical supplies for the few children in the group. When he realized that the Chief wanted him to come in the name of the Director, but was unwilling to force him, Joseph surprised himself with some hard-nosed wheeling and dealing. Before they left, a large amount of food, medical supplies, and fuel for their generators had been provided. Some toys and clothes appeared for the children. They were looked on as saints by those who stayed behind, principles or no. He somehow convinced Sarah that this was the chance to tell the Director to his face her opinion of him. Then, if still alive, they could leave. After living with death so long, the concept of it no longer scared him. After you are dead, being eaten or buried or cremated– *macht nichts.*

Now, he was face to face with the Director.

"May I offer you a drink, Professor?"

"Why, yes. I would die for a cold beer."

The Director laughed. "Well, that's easy. But I didn't ask you to come here to die for a beer. A cold one, coming up."

Joseph was surprised when the Director walked over to the bar near the large picture window in the office and drew a pint of ice cold beer from a hidden keg. He thought for sure the Director would have servants, underlings to do this. But, other than Mary Lou controlling entry, there was no one near his office. The cold beer was divine. He closed his eyes and almost cried.

"That, Professor, is locally brewed Conch Republic beer. Don't ask me how they make such good beer in such a humid climate, but they do. Here, while you enjoy your beer, let me show you something."

The Director went to his large desk and retrieved something. He walked back over to Joseph with a rectangular object that seemed oddly familiar. "Here, Professor. Remember this?" It was a bound copy of his self-published dissertation: *Star Trek, Star Wars, and Babylon Five: How Do We Really Get From Here to There at Greater than Light Speed.* Joseph was astounded. He turned the dissertation over, and then opened it to find numerous notes written in the margins.

"Where did you get this? I didn't print that many, and every one of them should have been burned up by know. I've heard they make good kindling."

Adam chuckled. "I found it at the University of Miami library, where it was probably on the road to a fireplace. It was said at the time of publishing this showed signs of becoming the next Einstein, or Michiro Kaku."

Joseph smiled sheepishly. "Well, it did get me a government grant and a security clearance."

"Even with the wife and all?"

Joseph knew then and there that the Director did know almost everything about him. His wife's political leanings had been a problem. A bigger problem was that she told him point blank that he was selling part of his soul if he took the money and position. But, positions in theoretical physics and space engineering did not come along every day. He soon found out he could apply for astronaut training as a civilian. So, even though his wife never really forgave him, he took the money and position.

Then the rocks hit. He and his wife hid out in a cabin in the Santa Fe mountains in California. The cabin belonged to a close friend who had come up with the plan that they would meet up at there should there ever be a large scale disaster that affected the social framework. Unfortunately, Joseph's friend and family never showed.

The nuclear, or long winter, caused by all the crap thrown up into the atmosphere caused one of the coldest winters on record. They barely survived in the cabin, although his friend had it well stocked. When a half-assed summer rolled around, he and Sarah dug their way out and headed down out of the mountains. They managed to make it to a state college to where some of his wife's friends lived, near an area she frequented in her travels for various causes. Hunkered down, they survived.

His wife and her friends spent an awful lot of time navel gazing, having grandiose discussions about political systems that no longer existed. They seemed to think that everything was temporary, that this was just a societal cycle like all the others. They failed to grasp the permanency of the Squids, as if they would suddenly disappear and humankind would argue politics again. Fat chance. He used his engineering background and some practical stuff he learned during summer jobs in school to keep things running and food on the table for the hundred plus adults and children. Then the Chief showed up. And now he was here. Joseph sipped his beer, then set it down.

"Director, I know you know all about me. And my wife. The chances of us ever agreeing on the path of humankind vis-à-vis the Tschaaa are slim to none."

"Then why did you come here? Curiosity?"

Joseph paused, sipped his beer again, and answered. "I wanted to see just how organized you were and yes, I wanted to see why you were interested in me. I was able to bargain for some supplies for the people I just left. If I never see another day, at least I have done something for some fellow humans. Not a bad epitaph, considering I could have been hamburger myself six years ago."

The Director surveyed him. It had not been a good six years. The Professor's slender build was now in desperate need of fattening up to keep him from looking like a poster child for anorexia research. He also had the beginnings of the proverbial thousand yard stare.

Adam tossed him a thin folder. "Here. This is part of the answer to the 'why me' question everyone asks."

Joseph opened the folder and examined two photos and a page of single-spaced type. "A flying saucer. So, the Squids have flying saucers. They also probably have unicorns for all I know. What does an alien flight system have to do with me?"

"Easy–they can't get them to work. There are two of them. They are not Tschaaa technology. Apparently they are some kind of interstellar or interdimensional craft that uses a propulsion system that is alien to them. Sounds like an attempt at a joke, doesn't it? Alien to the aliens."

"Oh come now, Director. How can I help a species that is light years ahead of us in technology? Why do they need some out-of-work Professor?"

"Now, look at this folder." Adam tossed another one at Joseph.

"This, I understand. Looks like a variation of one of those commercial space planes, pre-strike and Invasion that is."

"Well, Professor, you may not believe it, but The Tschaaa need help with both. And before you start pontificating on how much farther advanced the Tschaaa are than us; let me tell you a story."

"But first, another beer. And maybe some popcorn." The Director called Mary Lou on the intercom and requested some popcorn. Then he drew another beer for Joseph. By the time he handed the beer to Joseph, Mary Lou was walking in with a huge bowl of warm, fresh theater-style popcorn, butter and all. "Ah, the snack of champions. Beer and popcorn. Thank you, Mary Lou."

Joseph couldn't help but ogle Mary Lou a bit as she bent over with the popcorn. Damn, maybe she's Bettie Page's alien clone.

"Sir, how do you get fresh popcorn?" Joseph asked.

"Liberated a brand new machine from a brand new movie theater that was opening the day the first rock hit. Plus, a ton of makings. The theater opened and closed the same day. Hell of a spate of bad business luck." Adam sat down as Mary Lou left, closing the door.

He sipped at his own beer as he fed a handful of popcorn into his mouth. "One of my guilty pleasures. Now, where was I? Oh, that's right. Imagine, if you will, traveling on the Mayflower en route to the New World. But this Mayflower is the size of a large ocean liner, and the voyage takes a thousand years."

He took another sip of beer. "Now during this voyage, you have plenty of food, but it is rather boring. You have books, films, computers, libraries, theaters, sports. Not bad, so far. But the intellectual stimulation of the books, libraries, etc, is good for the first hundred years or so, as you eventually read, watch and enjoy what is available. Your fellow shipmates do create some new material, but there are thousands of people to share it with. Your scientific and educational studies are fine for the first hundred years, but, with limited resources, things become stagnant. And, in a closed society, no outside stimulation.

"We humans, about this time, would start trying to kill each other in competitive sports, limited war, etc. This might provide artificial stimulus for at least part of the population, so others would strive to come up with new ideas, equipment, and the such, to dominate the others, usually to obtain the best mate. After all, we are just nasty monkeys," Adam continued.

"As long as we limited our violence, at least some of us would survive, and we would not be brain dead with boredom. Well, the Squids aren't human. They do not war on each other. Their competition is limited so offspring have less of a chance of being injured. The breeding and birthing areas are large complexes along reefs and outcroppings in the ocean, so it would be simple to wipe out thousands if two Crèches went to war. That is an anathema to their culture.

Duels between individuals are few and limited in scope. They only become gravid every sixty days, and do not even think of having sex with a female that is not in the mood. They are as large as the male and just as nasty if they want to be. Breeding females have been selected through thousands of years of selection in each of the Crèches. Inferior females are sometimes sterilized. Young bucks compete in demonstrating accomplishments, in fighting other species, traditional predators, for a chance to mate with one of the breeders. Occasionally, a non-selected female is allowed to reproduce, just to keep a little biological diversity. But nowhere in their culture was a form of competitive warfare ever practiced."

Adam grabbed some more popcorn, as did Joseph. The Professor had forgotten how good simple pleasures were. Adam noted his expression and commented, "I claim popcorn is as habit forming as crack cocaine is, but it can't kill you. Well, unless your cholesterol gets so high that your heart explodes." Joseph laughed at the image, and then stuffed more popcorn in his mouth.

"Anyway, about one hundred years from Earth, the Squid's civilization started to become extremely stagnant. Intellectual development came to a near standstill. Young bucks took on very stylized form of competition, the equivalent of dance competitions or poetry readings. Some made a name by re-examining the work of some ancient brain, then memorizing it and reproducing by rote. They developed a bureaucracy along the lines of Ancient China, before the British came in and helped force opium on them. They managed to keep the breeders breeding, but only fifty percent of the offspring survived past the first year. Lord Neptune, who told me this, said it was as if the young never developed the will to live. Even though the breeders normally give birth from two to very occasionally eight to a litter, some during this period were lucky to produce one viable offspring that lived past the first year."

"Another beer, Professor?"

"I'm fine, Director. I have to watch it or I'll be loopy. We didn't get a lot of beer in California."

"Point well taken. Well, not only did the Squids have their own problems, but they also had trouble with reproduction of their grays, the clones, and the robocops. The clones in the vat became only about fifteen percent viable; the robocops were producing only fifty percent viable offspring. The genetic material of these species seemed to be wearing out. Whether cosmic or background radiation was leaking through to the occupants of the ships, no one knew, or seemed to care." Adam took another contemplative sip.

"Then, Our Lord reached majority. And, although some of the others think he is just this side of insane, a rare condition amongst Squids, he soon got a reputation for 'getting things done'." Adam looked at the clock. He still had time for the rest of the story.

"His Lordship monitored our TV and radio transmissions incessantly. This may be what helped keep an intellectual spark alive in him that was stagnant in others. He was the one who designed the Falcons, and the harvester robots–or robs. Hell, he basically developed the whole harvest ship system.

"Otherwise, the Squids would have just hit us, the young bucks slaughtering us the best they could in the first five years, then started getting ready to move on. At best, we would all be living in caves right now. Although Lords more senior than him got the plums, like Africa, everyone knew who was behind Cattle Country, and helping to organize large ocean breeding areas here on Earth. Most of the older Lords were afraid to let their breeders leave the ships."

Joseph raised an eyebrow in Adam's direction.

"You have a question that you are hesitant to ask. Spit it out. You're not going to the gulags–I've heard it all before."

Joseph took a drink of his beer, and then a deep breath. "So, Lord... Neptune helped make our slaughter efficient. Just like Himmler and company did with the Jews. Why would you cooperate with a butcher?"

"Because, Professor, the alternative–extinction as a species–is worse. If the Invasion had taken a turn for the worse... for us, that is. If the Squids had attacked as they originally planned, a disorganized mass, they would have been quickly frustrated. Then, instead of a thousand rocks, try two, three time as many, plus a few dozen nukes. They would have grabbed some breeding stock, and left us with a world freezing from the lack of sunlight thanks to a decade of nuclear winter. Instead of one segment of the human species–the darker-skinned races–being the major source of meat, we would all be. We would have no worth, other than as chickens in a factory farm."

Joseph shot a hard look at Adam. "That is an awfully cold and mean decision, Director. And selfish. We sold everyone else to save our own pale skins."

"No, to save the *human* race. Actually, human species as race is an artificial construct to explain local population variations due to environmental effects. We keep the genetic basis for our 'races' in the DNA of the survivors. But, at least we survive as an organized species, rather than maybe, small isolated bands at best. And, we rebuild our pre-strike civilization.

"Our Lordship has worked to convince the others of the idea of our long term benefit, not only as Cattle, but as worker bees like the grays, lizards and robos. It *is* the lesser of two evils. And remember, unlike the Jews in Europe, there are no allied countries to come to our rescue. Ever."

Silence. Joseph stared blankly ahead. Adam knew the Professor's brain was trying to come to grips with this. As was his heart. Adam continued with his explanation without waiting for a response. "Our Lordship realizes that the Tschaaa needs us, a young species with lots of potential, which is not stagnant. He has also persuaded the majority of the other Lords of our worth, at least in the short term. He has convinced them to give his Protocol of Selective Survival a chance.

"Because of that, in about two months, a revamped space plane will be launched to Platform One. I want you on it. You will look at those 'flying saucers' on board a Tschaaa generation ship."

Joseph's mouth dropped open. "Humans? Going into space, and not as a slab of beef? I don't believe it." He finished his beer in one final gulp. "I changed my mind. I need another."

Adam laughed. He stood up to get another beer. Joseph sat stunned. His mind was fighting a battle in which only he could decide the outcome. Now was his chance to go to space, to explore the universe from outside Earth's atmosphere. But he would be the equivalent of a trained service dog, of use only as long as his Master, the Tschaaa, had a purpose for him.

Adam returned and handed him his beer. Joseph sipped on it, silently staring. Adam waited calmly. He knew that Joseph had to get his mind around this. And decide. Finally, Joseph spoke. "Director, this is no bullshit, right? This isn't some cosmic joke? I know we are well past *The Twilight Zone's* 'To Serve Man' episode, but is there a hidden agenda?"

"No, Professor, there is no grand conspiracy. No hidden human experiments. The Tschaaa are really not that complicated. They are a species that developed due to evolutionary pressures and the occasional chance variation in their DNA, similar to humans. They just happened to develop earlier than we did, being an older species. And now, a stagnant species in this part of the galaxy."

"Director, can the Tschaaa keep their word? Is that a concept they have?"

"You mean honor? Yes, they do. But, we are still an inferior species, so it is complicated. They may use some of us as a food source, but they do not torture other creatures, like some humans have done. You are either a threat, a food source–or in the last thousand years or so–a client worker species that can perform a function that will help the Tschaaa survive and reproduce.

"We can be all three on Earth, but in space, all us live ones will only serve as client workers. The Tschaaa, as much as they like fresh kill, have limited space for live food animals on their starcraft. Fresh frozen and an amount of vat grown flesh will for the most part suffice until they reach another planet with a meat species. Except, of course, the huge ships taking the meatcicles, human sperm, ova and breeding stock back to their home world. All except what is important for the survival of the Tschaaa is left behind."

Adam raised his glass. "The one caveat to that is if you die in space and they have your body, you will be eaten as fresh kill. Nothing personal." He took a slow sip.

"What if we ate one of *them*?"

"They know we ate squid, calamari, octopus, all literal cousins to them. No problems as they expect one species to prey on another, ala Darwinism, if necessary."

The Director grabbed another handful of popcorn. "What they do not understand is the idea of cannibalism. The fact that we can eat our own species is the ultimate perversion. They do not have Jeffrey Dahmers. A Tschaaa who realizes he ate his own would go catatonic, then die.

"And before you ask, how do I know? Our Lord showed me a recording of a catatonic Squid. Killing your offspring, even by accident, or eating Tschaaa flesh causes them to go catatonic, then stop breathing. A disaster that wiped out a breeding area on their home world led to the surviving adults, who were the caretakers and mothers, to go catatonic. Out of twenty-nine adult survivors, all but one died within a week."

"How about the one exception?"

"A breeder. She became one of the few 'insane' Tschaaa around. They treated her like a shaman, or an oracle as was the case at Delphi. Happens once every hundred years or so." Adam chewed his popcorn while he let the images play in the Professor's head.

"Professor, we as a species have a wide range of behavior, called cultural variations. Maybe that keeps us vibrant, adaptable."

"The Tschaaa do not have variations. The Tschaaa have developed a very narrow range of cultural behavior, and definitely no equivalent to our idea of race. The homogenous nature of their culture probably resembles that of historical Japan, pre-World War Two."

"Then how do Crèches fit into things?" Joseph inquired.

"Strictly as extended families, all within a specific cultural norm. They form a hierarchy much like the traditional mafia families did. They ensure no one gets out of line, and reward success amongst the young males. Females are breeders and caretakers, only limited numbers become anything else."

Joseph sat silently again.

An old expression was that you could see someone's gears working in their head when they were deep in thought. Adam believed the expression fit the Professor to a T.

Finally, Joseph spoke. "There's a big chance that all this is a fantasy. But, I can't turn down the chance of seeing humankind in space again, even in a service capacity. We deserve the stars."

Adam smiled. "Good. You'll be given more details tomorrow, after this has all really sunk in. You can change your mind anytime before tomorrow morning. After that, you are literally under my control. Understood?"

"Understood."

"One for the road?"

"Yes, Director. I'll need to be well-lubricated to explain this to Sarah."

Adam looked at him intently. "Professor, if she wishes to leave, she may. If she stays, I will find her something to do to use her teaching experience. But, she follows the rules, like everyone else."

"Yes, Director. May I ask you one more question?"

"Shoot."

"Do you ever think of telling the Tschaaa to go to hell? To make one last stand at resistance?"

Adam smiled. "All the time. All the time. As does the Chief." He drained the last of his glass. "And you will not believe me, but I have told Lord Neptune on a regular basis that I still have those thoughts. His reply was laughter. Yes, even aliens have a form of laughter, and humor. Someday, I'll have to write a book on that subject. After he laughed, he told me—like the fictional Borg—that 'resistance is futile' unless I really wanted another thousand rocks to rain down on us.

"He knows that if the roles were reversed, the Tschaaa would have to accept or die. Once again, total acceptance of the rule of Darwinian selection based on some ancient religious belief, some protocol. Someone is always at the top of the food chain, and dictates to others who eats whom. As long as they can breed, the Tschaaa will do what is necessary to survive as a species."

"How many humans have died during the institution of these... protocols?"

"From what we can glean about the casualty rate for humans from the Panama Canal to the frozen north, today there are about one hundred million humans. That includes us in the occupied areas, the Resistance, some four million cattle, and an indeterminate number of Ferals still in hiding."

He let that sink in for a moment before he continued.

"Now if you will excuse me, I still have a few things to take care of before our Social tonight. Mary Lou will show you out." On cue, she appeared at the door.

"Thank you, Director," Joseph said, and shook Adam's hand.

"No, thank *you*, Professor."

Sometime later, the Chief knocked on Adam's door, then entered. "Boss, it's almost six o'clock. The Social starts at 7:00pm sharp." The Chief already had on his suit and tie, the Social being the only event that forced him to wear them.

"My suit takes just five minutes to put on, Chief. Take a seat and you can brief me on what else you found out there."

"Another poodle gun—sorry, M-16—with a complete military sight package. A small amount of ammo with it, including twenty rounds of match grade hollow-point. No other military stuff. Most places have been picked clean in six years."

Out of a small kitbag he seemed to always have with him, the Chief pulled a smaller-sized replica of a Colt Peacemaker. He handed it to Adam. "This is for you. Six shots of twenty-two magnum. It works. I tested and loaded it."

Adam frowned. "And this is for...?"

"Remember... Lord High Executioner?"

Then Adam remembered. He had wanted something smaller, but effective, in case he ran into any more baby-rapers in his midst. The 9mm he had used then had created a hell of a mess with a short range shot to the head.

He still remembered earlier today when he had told all the new arrivals that he was the Executive, Legislative, and Judicial branches all rolled into one. Then he had told them he was the Lord High Executioner as well, that he would handle in person any mistakes he let in. Like a certain serial pedophile. Judging by the silence and the looks on their faces, they believed him.

"Thanks, Chief. Here's hoping I don't have to ever use it." Adam slipped the gun into a drawer in his desk, and locked it. He raised his glass.

"I'll drink to that idea, tonight." Chief raised his in kind. Both men took a drink.

"Now, what about the air defense system I have you working on?"

"Four former ship-mounted Phalanx systems ring us, plus a five-inch and a three-inch gun. We have over a hundred Stingers on various mounts, and one old Chaparral system with Sidewinders. We are short ammo for the Phalanx, but I think I found some more in San Diego.

"Our gunship's about ready to fly. Plus, two GAU 30 ex A-10 weapons are en route, with over a thousand rounds of ammo. One 20mm Gatling gun is being recovered off of an F-15."

"Sounds like, short of a general war, I think we have enough firepower."

"Yes, Boss. We have enough for a *small* war. For land forces, Eglin will have four M-1 tanks up and running this week, added to a dozen Bradleys."

The Chief slapped his forehead. "I forgot. We have a hundred AT-4s, a dozen SWAWs and six Dragon anti-tank weapons coming, so we won't have to rely on those RPGs I 'liberated' from Cuba."

The Chief had done some wheeling and dealing with the small groups of survivors in Cuba. For food and other supplies, he had gotten a boatload of Cuban cigars, plus RPG launchers and a hundred grenades of various manufactures. By similar means, he had also obtained a thousand hand grenades, Claymore mines, and even a few anti-tank mines, from various sources in Central and South America.

"Find anything else interesting, Chief?"

"No new evidence of any cannibalism. I think we have pretty much nipped that in the bud. The Church of Kraken has helped, since His Lordship sent that recording to the titular head–the Most Reverend James Kray–explaining what being a Tschaaa really means."

Some humans had a unique ability to develop new belief systems at the drop of a hat, coming up with some new revelation to explain the meaning of everything. Creating a new religion based around the Tschaaa and some traditional Pagan beliefs was what the Church of Kraken was. The problem was that early adherents felt that to be a Kraken meant you had to consume human flesh like the Tschaaa did.

Lord Neptune, at Adam's prodding, had developed a filmed recording explaining that the eating of one's own species was an abomination that would result in a quick trip to a harvester–after Adam and Company were allowed to 'tenderize' the blasphemers. When your new gods' local representative tells you directly that you are screwing the pooch, you usually listen. At least in public.

On the base, there were some one hundred members of the new church. Amongst the Conch Republicans, close to a fourth of the some five thousand humans were converts. They bent over backwards if Adam mentioned that the Tschaaa Lord wanted something done.

"Well, Chief, let me put my party clothes on and we'll get going. I believe this will probably the last one of these we will be doing for a while. I think I need to get everyone settled before we bring anymore newbies in."

"What about the Cubans?" The Chief had recruited six surviving Cuban military members and their families who had helped him obtain some of the leftover hardware, Cuban cigars and–for the Tschaaa–sugar cane. Apparently, raw sugarcane was something that did not exist on the Tschaaa home world, although something similar but not as flavorful did. The Tschaaa here had suddenly developed one hell of a sweet tooth.

In the early days of the Invasion, when some ninety percent of the Cubans had been harvested due to the relatively dark skin of the populace, the survivors hid in the hills. Cuba had been split between the Tschaaa Lord that controlled South America and Lord Neptune in a resource sharing agreement. The South American Lord was not that interested in the Islands so he had let Neptune take over the Cuban area after a week of hectic harvesting. A small Crèche breeding area was set up in the warm waters.

When Adam and he Chief had come on the scene and made a foray looking for salvageable goods on a depopulated island, they had made contacts with the survivors and had brought back a bunch of raw cane, not only to satisfy everyone's sweet tooth but also in the hopes of possible ethanol production. By pure chance, the Tschaaa had also tried eating some of the cane as it resembled a bamboo like plant from their home world they used for medicinal purposes and "teeth" cleaning (The Tschaaa had their version of dental structures).

One taste and it was a match made in heaven. Now, a small group of humans tried to keep some of the fields producing, as well as harvesting wild plants. Adam had brought some plants back, and was growing them in their greenhouses. He was also trying to get some fields growing near Miami.

The Tschaaa young would eat all they could find, and the breeders claimed it helped during their pregnancy. Now there was another reason to look kindly at humans other than as a snack. The six surviving Cuban military members and their extended families–some fifty men, women and children–wanted to relocate to the Base. They were entirely beholden to the Chief for providing supplies that kept them alive, and would do anything for him.

"Well, let's bring the families over in a few months, with the caveat that they help us keep the sugar cane available. It gives us a nice bargaining chip with Lord Neptune and the Lord in South America."

"Yeah," the Chief said. "Lord Neptune acts like a kid a the candy store when you mention sugar cane."

"Then it's settled. Now, let me get ready for this damn Social."

At two minutes before 7:00pm, Adam entered the large auditorium, now reimagined as a large party room. A dozen or so round dining tables had been set up with multicolored tablecloths and decorations. As delightful as the surroundings were, they were not what truly set the festive mood of the event. It was the women. Every woman had been provided with a glamorous, formal dress that was tailored specifically for her.

Adam had found some dozen former dressmakers, designers, and tailors and convinced them to come to Key West. It was an easy decision for starving individuals in a currently underutilized profession. Not to mention some hairdressers and makeup artists, survivors of Hollywood. Additionally, he had several young apprentices gleaned from the children brought in the last four years to learn the ropes.

The transformations at these Socials were always surprising, and some simply astounding. Women, who a few days before had the beginnings of the thousand yard stare, were now alive, attractive, and sometimes downright ravishing creatures. As Adam began to make the rounds with the Chief, mingling, a woman would suddenly come up to him, grab his hand, hug him, or kiss him, usually speechless. The husbands of those married would be there, usually in the background, telling Adam and the Chief with a look, "Thank you for bringing back the love of my life."

A more than occasional tear would threaten to ruin makeup, and Mary Lou, Jeanie and Jamey would hustle the woman off for a quick repair job. Maybe it was a crass fantasy that he was perpetuating on some very vulnerable people, but Adam did not care. He could not save all humans, but he could make a difference in a small number, one day at a time. If some of them felt beholden over an act of kindness, so be it.

As he was extricating himself from a bear hug from a very small but very powerful woman, his gut suddenly told him there was someone behind him. Before he could turn around, he heard "Hello... Boss."

He turned, and there she was. Kathy. The long, midnight blue dress looked like it had been painted on her, hugging every part of her body just right. A slit up the left side showed an expanse of nylon-enclosed leg that took his breath away. Her blonde hair was up, showing off her exquisite neck, with a few long curls teasing her ears and shoulders. For the first time in a very, very long time the man with all of the words was speechless.

"How do I look? This is first new party dress I've had on in about six years." She twirled in her heels. "Well, what do you think? Boss."

He finally found his voice. "Kathy Monroe, you look absolutely stunning."

Kathy wrinkled her nose at him, smiling. "Aw, you probably tell all the girls that." At that moment, she glanced past him, and although her mouth was still smiling, her eyes were now wary. "Battle stations, Boss," she announced, and Adam turned to where she had been looking.

Professor Sarah Broadmore-Fassbinder, in a long burgundy dress, was coming at him like an enemy battle cruiser, full steam ahead.

Adam actually believed for a moment that she planned on ramming him. Sarah had always been attractive, with a slim but athletic looking body. She used to run pre-Squid and still had shapely runner's legs. But now, her muscular body was tense with determination, and her face reflected the difficulties of her past.

Years prior there was a female Representative from Colorado that was attractive, but she had a look on her face most of the time that looked like a combination of constipation and stick up ass syndrome, especially when someone disagreed with her strong feministic views. Men were physically stronger than women? Even when presented with scientific evidence to the contrary, women and men were the same, except men had the evil penis that must be controlled. And if they were not the same, dammit, she would *make* them the same by the power of law.

Sarah had the same intense, frustrated look, reflecting the belief she could change reality by sheer force of will.

"Good Evening, Professor. And if I may say so, that dress is quite becoming on you."

Sarah Broadmore-Fassbinder stopped just short of slamming into him, with a feral grin. "Well, Director. Glad that you recognized me. Though I might have expected to be introduced you earlier when you had that meeting with my husband."

"Sorry, but the meeting had to do with your husband's abilities, not yours." Adam saw her jaw tighten.

"So, your plans do not include strong, professional women? should have realized you have a stereotypical view of the female gender when you provided all the women with these clothes. Do you think you can disarm all women with a bit of frill, a piece of ribbon, so that we will conform and become the traditional 1950s housewives from *Leave It to Beaver*?"

"No, Ma'am. I thought everyone would enjoy a chance for a little 'dress up', men included, which is why every man also received a suit tailored for him. That's why *everyone* was measured before arriving. Not for a coffin, as some rumors have stated. A little bit of good old time Western Civilization does wonders for morale, in my experience."

"Do you wonder that we would have some apprehension, given the last six years?"

"No Ma'am, I do not. Contrary to popular belief, I lived through the last six years too. I am not some clone grown in a tank, which is another story circulating. To counter your statement about the role of women here, in this group of humans you see here tonight, you will find six medical doctors, ten nurses, five biologists, two agriculturists, ten security personnel, seven mechanics of various types, four computer geeks, a mathematician, two engineers and a theoretical physicist, all blessed with having been born female. I look at what you can do, not what gender you are. Trust me, with Tschaaa medical technology, if it were important, gender modification is a lot simpler than pre-strike. But it isn't important. What you can do for the human species is."

"But you still limited your one-on-one meetings to a few men."

"And one woman. Allow me introduce you to Ms. Monroe..."

The professor cut him off, purposefully not acknowledging Kathy. "You can't be serious. You compare a video whore to women with *real* accomplishments?"

Adam began to burn internally, though he did not show it. Dealing with aliens, you learn how to control your outward emotions. But before he could reply, Kathy did.

"Hey, lady. I'm right here. And yes I read, write, *and* understand English quite well. So, if you think I *don't* understand being insulted, guess again."

Sarah still refused to look at her. "As I just said, some tramp who showed her ass on film is hardly an example of professional accomplishment."

The Chief seemed to appear out of nowhere and stepped in between Sarah and Kathy. "Now, now ladies. This is fun time, not fight time."

"That's enough, Ma'am," Adam continued. "In street vernacular, don't let your mouth write a check your ass can't cash."

"Oh, of course. The savior of the human race. So where are all the dark faces, the brown faces? How many did you help slaughter?"

People were beginning to notice there was a conflict nearby, and were beginning to stare. Others moved to other side of the auditorium, glancing back nervously.

"Ma'am..." Adam began.

"It's *Professor*! Stop trying to pigeonhole and demean me with your chauvinistic titles. I earned my Professorship through hard work. Not by *screwing* someone."

"Ma'am." Adam's voice was solid ice. "Be. Quiet. Now."

Sarah, hearing something in his tone that sent a chill up the human spine, stopped and sputtered a bit.

"Chief, you have that picture of your family?"

"Always, Boss."

"May I have it please?"

The Chief produced a laminated photo that had been well worn. Adam took it carefully, and stepped in close to Sarah.

"First of all, Ma'am and Sir are honorific words that show good manners and respect. They were good enough for my mother and father, they are good enough for me. Second, who do you see in this picture?"

Sarah looked at it, and began to get a bit pale in the face. "A... dark-skinned woman of Middle Eastern descent and two children that look... mixed race."

"You see, the Chief's wife was an Afghani who he saved from being killed due to some honor-killing bullshit for being nice to Infidels. They got to know each other, fell in love, got married."

Sarah tried to look at the Chief. "I'm..."

"Be quiet." That icy tone again. "Guess what happened to them that first day?"

"I..."

"Be quiet. The question was rhetorical. A well-educated professor knows what 'rhetorical' means yes? Don't speak. Just nod your head if you understand."

Sarah nodded her head.

"Good. They were probably dark meat in some Squid's larder. And I know of former black friends from the Air Force who were probably some Tschaaa breeder's snack the first year."

"Yes, I made a choice to save who I can. Sorry that most of them have lighter skin. And oh, by the way, I was the Godfather to those kids when his wife converted to Christianity, which would have gotten her killed doubly by her own people. She survived all that, until an alien invasion. Bit of a cosmic fucking joke, don't you think?"

Adam leaned forwarded until he was nose to nose with Sarah.

"Don't *ever* accuse the Chief of being some racist asshole feeding dark-skinned kids to the Tschaaa. Ms. Monroe is here because she has a flair for communication and seems to brighten people's lives up a bit with her perkiness, some characteristics I think you lost well before the first rock strike."

The Director stood upright. "Oh, Mary Lou, glad you are here. Please join the Chief, Kathy and I for a drink at the bar." Adam took both Kathy and Mary Lou's arms and escorted them to the bar.

The Chief paused for a moment, putting the picture of his family away. Looking over the top of Sarah's head, he seemed to speak to no one in particular. "Too bad that some people walking and talking today are just as dead inside their heads as my family is dead for real." He left to join his friends.

"I'm sorry, Director," Mary Lou apologized. "I tried to head her off, but some young stud tried to pick me up and got in the way."

"No harm, no foul. She had her sights on me. Sometime tonight she would have gotten me." Adam paused to look in Kathy's direction. "By the way, Ms. Monroe, please accept my apologies for those boorish comments."

Kathy wrinkled her nose at him. "Boss, she was right. I did show my naked ass for a living. But, I think I am a bit too well-educated and classy to be a bimbo."

"Then why *did* you show your ass?" Mary Lou asked with a cocked eyebrow. She was wearing a dress that fit her body as nicely as Kathy's, slit up the side showing shapely leg.

"Needed the money, and found out this body could make a decent sum. Finally had enough cash to give up adult films to give mainstream Hollywood a go. The Squids showed up as I was on the way to an audition, and the rest is history."

"Oh," was all that Mary Lou could think to say in reply. She gave Kathy a look that meant she was sizing up possible competition. Why she seemed so protective when she was already occasionally sharing her bed with two other women puzzled Kathy, especially since Kathy had made it a point to stay in a separate apartment.

"Excuse us ladies, the Chief and I need a moment," the Director apologized, as he walked away from Mary Lou and Kathy, toward Major Grant. For once the Major had saw fit to wear an evening dress that showed off her well-endowed figure, slit up the side and all.

Kathy looked at her appraisingly.

"If you are checking out Jane for a possible roll in the hay, she is straighter than straight."

"Now, Mary Lou, why would you assume I like women that much?"

Mary Lou smirked. "I checked out your films."

"Well, you have heard of acting, haven't you?" Kathy gave Mary Lou a bit of a sideways glance. "But, you share your bed with the Barbie twins. So, female attraction isn't new to you, is it?"

Mary Lou responded abruptly. "What I do with Adam is private. I know that he has already 'tasted your wares'. But let me assure you that you're not the first, nor the last. The Director's appetite is legendary. I'd like to think it is a form of stress relief needed from having to watch people die, and knowing that each day you have helped condemn thousands of what were once called people of color to being pieces of meat, literally.

"But I'm going to be blunt and say that I don't trust you. My gut says there is a hidden agenda. I'm warning you, if you hurt Adam, I will mess you up."

Kathy stared back at Mary Lou. "If you want a fight, you've got one. I am willing to be friendly, but I won't be walked on. Not even by Bettie Page."

The two women, inches from each other, stared into each other's eyes. Mary Lou broke the gaze first. "Alright, now that we are both on notice, may I suggest we make the best of a bad situation. For the Director's sake."

"Agreed." Kathy replied. "Shake on it." She extended her right hand, and Mary Lou took it in a firm handshake. Both women held the handshake for a few extra seconds gauging each other's strength. Both quickly realized that neither one was a pushover. They released each other's grasp.

"Nice grip, Mary Lou. You're used to dealing in a man's world, aren't you?"

"Yes, Kathy, and I could say the same of you."

Adam returned at that moment. "My apologies again, ladies. Getting acquainted, are we?"

"Yes," answered both women in unison, each giving the other a knowing look and smile.

"Good. Because we will all be working together closely over the next weeks and months. Now, about those drinks."

Sarah was seething when her husband walked up. She was angrier with herself than the Director, angry for allowing the Director to so dominate her. She should have said more, she should have...

"Well, that was special," Joseph remarked sarcastically.

"Screw you, Joseph!" Sarah snapped. She was so goddamned *mad.* Her face was inches away from her husband's, their noses nearly touching, before she realized his right hand was digging painfully into her left bicep. He had never laid hands on her before. "Ouch! You're hurting me!"

"You just don't get it!" he hissed. "This is not some intellectual exercise. This is fucking *real.* The Tschaaa are real, human cattle are real, and the Director's power and mission are real. And he made me an real offer I couldn't refuse, to quote *The Godfather.*"

His hot breath was in her face. "Do you think I will die for you, now? Maybe six years ago, sure as hell not now. I have watched you and your pointy-headed friends perform intellectual masturbation while I and a few others scrounged the food and supplies needed to survive. I have put up with your artful disdain that I *dare* work with the

U.S. government, because I wanted the chance to travel to space."

Joseph was literally shaking with anger. Six years of stress and frustration, of listening to her sarcastic statements of intellectual superiority, of his physical love for her that was rejected, of barely surviving. And now, in this place, she dared to dictate what was right? "You can stay, you can leave, you can go fuck yourself. I don't care. You have burnt me out. I'm *staying.* I'm doing what is right for *me.*"

He stepped back, releasing her arm with a long sigh. "You used to be a beautiful, vivacious woman. I wanted children with you. Now, all I want is to be rid of you. Have a nice trip back to California. I need a drink." He turned and stormed off.

For the first time in a long time, Sarah's private thoughts were not enough company.

Adam and his small party had in drinks in hand from the honor bar that was pay as you go for scotch and other hard liquors. As Director, Adam had ensured that funds for a few drinks were provided in the pocket of every man's suit pants, and safety pinned to every woman's evening gown. He was a generous host, and knew his audience well.

Beer and wine were free, though seventy-five percent of it was Conch Republic locally brewed and vinted. The beer, especially the ale, was quite good. The wine varied from bottle to bottle. The bartenders on hand kept an eye on the patrons. They knew that many had only passing contact with alcohol in the past six years, so it was easy to drink too much.

However, most of the attendees made a beeline to the food that also offered free of charge. Several tables set up buffet-style provided cuisine from various Asian countries as well as variety of pasta dishes. Fresh fruit and vegetables from the extensive greenhouse and hydroponics area were often the first fresh food the new arrivals had seen in months, other than the occasional apple.

Once again, tears of gratitude were evident, especially those mothers with their children. Malnutrition was a thing of the past in the Keys. It was odd, but the most popular section was one that Adam had originally set up for arriving children. That was the hamburgers and hotdog grill. After the first run on this simple food, Adam had ensured that in all future Socials, there was plenty of good old beef and pork hotdogs and hamburgers. He had even added a large roast for french dip sandwiches. As usual, there was a bit of a line.

"Boss, where do you get the meat?" Kathy asked.

"We now have a herd of beef cattle and some pig pens here on the base. In addition, we obtained some cattle, especially some good old nasty Texan longhorns, and introduced them wild on vacated areas near Homestead and Miami. They are enough like African water buffalo that they quickly adapt to the Everglades and other rural areas. So, anyone can have some beef on the hoof if they hunt it. Plus, longhorns are big and tough enough to give anyone fits, including the 'gators. Oh, we do use alligator meat, as well, whiih tastes a bit like chicken."

He pointed to two long tables set off a bit by themselves, with a large flag above them. "And, Conch Republic seafood. Here, let me introduce you to someone."

"Then can I eat? I'm starving."

Adam chuckled. "Yes, this will only take a minute. He would be slighted if I did not introduce you to him."

They approached the seafood tables, and saw a tall, slender man with a large but well-trimmed grey beard. He was dressed in a caricature of a Military Class A Uniform coat, with oversized shoulder boards containing five stars on each.

"Kathy Monroe, may I introduce the Admiral, leader of the Conch Republic."

The Admiral broke into a large grin at the sound of his name and the sight of Kathy. Two gorgeous, rangy woman–for lack of a better description, real life Amazons–one blond and one brunette, flanked the Admiral, dressed in evening gowns that fit every bit as well as Kathy's. They were clearly much more than just eye candy, as they kept watchful eyes on everyone and everything around the Admiral. Both flashed smiles of familiarity at Adam, and the blond even winked.

The Admiral immediately took Kathy's right hand, clicked his heels in good German Kaiser imitation and pressed it to his lips. "Madam, it is indeed an honor. I probably have the largest remaining existing collection of your work, including your appearances on cable and mainstream television. Will you marry me?"

Kathy's mouth dropped open, but she quickly recovered and replied, "Why, we have just met, Admiral... ?"

"Just Admiral. I don't need another name. I know who I am, and so does every else in the Keys." Kathy wondered if the elevator in his head went all the way to the top, and if it ever had.

"Now, Admiral," Adam interjected. "Ms. Monroe just arrived here as my guest. Decorum requires some time for courtship before one pops the question, don't you think?"

"You are quite right, Director. How crude of me. But, please Kathy, remember me before you become betrothed to another."

Kathy flashed him her signature smile. "I certainly will, Admiral. I do have a weakness for men in uniform." The Amazons rolled their eyes at the comment, which the Admiral either didn't notice, or preferred to ignore.

"Now, Admiral, could you please show Kathy your excellent repast?"

"Of course. Cookie!" the Admiral bellowed, and a short man in a chef's hat appeared. He had a steaming plate of fish, crab, lobster, cornbread and silverware all ready to go.

"With compliments of the Conch Republic."

Kathy's eyes went wide, and she glanced imploringly at Adam.

"Thank you, Admiral. Now, if you will excuse us, Ms. Monroe needs sustenance."

"Only if you promise to bring her back."

"Of course, Admiral."

Adam escorted Kathy over to a nearby round table, and watched as she sat down and began to eat. A pang of guilt hit him as he realized that Kathy's diet had probably been hit and miss over the last few years, and here he was playing politician.

She ate in a concentrated manner, not sloppily, but like one who did not know when her next meal would come. It took her about five minutes to realize he was watching her, and she blushed, swallowed and put her fork down.

"Hell of a date I am. You buy me dinner, and I ignore you to stuff my face."

Adam looked at her intently. "Sorry. I forgot that this spread I take for granted is the first you have seen in years. I will admit I have a selfish streak in me that what I think is important is important to everyone. I'm fat, dumb and happy, and forget sometimes most people in the last six years are not."

Kathy took his right hand in hers. "Adam, you saved me and this whole auditorium of people from a continuous hand to mouth existence at best. And now I know you are working hard to provide this, 'spread' as you call it to as many people as you can. You need to apologize to no one. The Squids need to apologize. But I know that is impossible. It would be like me apologizing to a beef cow for eating meat." She sighed, let go his hand, and took up her fork again. "I am not going to let guilt about how I survived and others did not spoil my appetite. But, please, I hate to eat alone. Why don't you get a plate and join me? I have not had decent seafood in years."

Adam replied, with a flourish of his hand, "Your wish is my command. I'll be back in a minute."

The Director obtained a matching plate of seafood, much to the enjoyment of the Admiral and his cook. He returned to Kathy's table, sat down and began eating. Maybe it was the effect of his company, but the food seemed much more flavorful than ever before. He ate in silence for a few minutes, stuffing his face. Then he realized Kathy was now watching *him* intently.

"A penny for your thoughts, Ms. Morgan."

"You need to enjoy life more, Boss. I can tell that usually eating and drinking to you is just fuel for the engine, to keep you going. You need to enjoy the proverbial fruits of your labor."

Adam looked at her. This so-called porn star had wisdom and insight that was hard to ignore. And, he had a warm feeling in his lower body regions that wasn't just from the good food.

"Point taken, Kathy. But, I have to keep the eye on the prize."

He took another bite, chewed, swallowed, used his napkin to pat his lips and wipe his hands. He then stood up. "Please excuse me, but I must mingle. Everyone must have access to the Director tonight. A dance later, if you please?"

Kathy flashed her smile and wrinkled her nose. "Of course. But Mary Lou may fight me for it."

Adam chuckled again. "No need for that. Everyone who wants a dance gets one, even if I have to stay here all night. Although I try to get around the base, some people won't see me again for weeks. Now, finish your meal, and relax. I'll talk to you later."

He walked toward the other side of the auditorium, Kathy watching him the whole way. She took a deep breath, and slowly let it out. A lot of people believed Adam was just this side of Hitler or Pol Pot.

But he wasn't.

This was hard.

CHAPTER 6

Even as Director Adam Lloyd set up sanctuaries full of the formerly lost amenities and trappings of 21st Century civilization for his Chosen, others in the non-occupied or controlled areas of the world were getting by on their own. The inhabitants of the Feral areas, some near Tschaaa-controlled areas, tried to leach and scavenge what they could without drawing the attention of the cyborgs/robocops and other Tschaaa minions.

However, there still existed free-minded people who firmly remembered what the world had been before the coming of the Tschaaa. Some of these people set up Free States or Countries.

In the center of the former United States of America existed the Unoccupied States of America. Those who had fled there, away from Tschaaa control, had not just sought to hide.

As in days of the Swamp Fox Colonel Francis Marion during the American Revolution, they ran away and waited to fight again another day.

> —Excerpts from the *Literary Works of Royal Princess Akiko, Free Japan Royal Family.*

MALMSTROM ARMED FORCES BASE, MONTANA
UNOCCUPIED STATES OF AMERICA

Torbin Bender sat waiting for the Commander to finish speaking, literally twiddling his thumbs. The former Marine Sergeant, Navy Seal and Delta Force team member, now Field promotion Captain, was up next. He had a PowerPoint presentation that should knock the socks off all the occupants of the briefing room.

This was a big deal. In the room were representatives of Free Japan, as well as a few ragged representatives from former Russian-controlled areas now known as Free Russia, primarily from Siberia. This was a first attempt to organize a world-coordinated Resistance to the now firmly entrenched alien Tschaaa. He had to provide information they all needed and hopefully wanted to hear. The situation was still unstable, but Torbin felt his data was as reliable as possible. Six years of the Occupation had still left pockets of Ferals and Free Agents who provided information on the activities of the aliens. Torbin enjoyed the field craft, the nitty-gritty operations in the unsecured or Tshaaa-controlled areas. Sneaking around worrying about being discovered by the minions of Tschaaa brought back memories of his days in Delta Force and the SEALs. However, this Intelligence Officer role was giving him fits. He was a Field Ops man, not a POG, not a REMF. He had recently managed short field ops, permitted after he told the Commander he was getting cobwebs in his combat reflexes. He had been in on the first capture of a quisling renegade biker, one of three who tried to sneak into Montana by the back roads. This had been the first probe or enemy recon in months. Torbin was ordered to interrogate him after he had been softened up a bit, which had helped provide further information for this briefing.

As he waited for General John Reed, his Commander and former

U.S. Air Force pilot to finish speaking, he looked at his Captain's bars and still found them foreign. He was "enlisted material", never wanting to become an officer and a gentleman despite his four-year degree. But a well over sixty percent casualty rate in the lower forty-eight states, amongst surviving military of all branches after the first forty-eight hours of the Invasion, had led to some drastic promotions. Total casualties counts in this war usually meant ninety percent dead.

And then eaten.

Torbin was built like an Olympic athlete, just under six feet tall, brown hair, blue eyes, with a profile befitting a tv soap opera star. He had become a certified physical trainer in civilian life, after eight years of active duty, five of those in the SEALs and delta. His four-year degree was in Education, as he enjoyed teaching, so being a trainer combined his desire to instruct with his desire to remain physically active.

He had stayed in the Marine reserves, which led to his recall in the first forty-eight hours of the Invasion. Due to his SEAL training, he helped lead a hasty attack as the senior NCO in a thirty man assault platoon in the first seventy-two hours. The target, a harvester ark outside of what was left of Marine Corp Air Station Yuma, Arizona, would mark the last time the Squids tried to harvest in the desert.

The brass saw it as a chance to obtain some good intel, maybe some prisoners, as the Squids seemed to have landed in Yuma by mistake. They were proving to be fallible. The problem was, humans were much more fallible, and the Squids still had the "high ground"... space.

His memories quickly jumped from scene to scene. He had survived, but others, including a young Army Lieutenant, had not. A C-130 Special Ops pilot, an Air Force Captain, flew tree top level and dropped them off and picked them up in the middle of the night just outside Yuma, Arizona.

He had spent a night of passion with the female pilot after the mission. Both had needed the affirmation that they had survived by having a nice, warm human body to hold, and love. She had dropped off the face of the Earth after that, never to be seen again. As had millions of other humans.

The photos and video he and the others had provided, especially his up close and personal contact with a Front Man (the creature did not survive) provided much needed intelligence on the Tschaaa and their minions. But it was too little too late. And just afterwards, he found out his younger brother William, an Air Force pilot, had been killed. He had died a hero, but he was dead nonetheless. Torbin would trade ten heroes for the chance of having a beer with his brother again any day of the week.

What was now referred to as the Battle of Yuma Overpass had gotten him "noticed". So when he and numerous other military members fled to the Malmstrom Armed Forces Base, a certain newly-minted General John Reed found Torbin and latched on to him. It also eventually got him a battlefield commission, which stuck him doing briefings when he would much rather be kicking ass and taking names.

"Captain?" General Reed's voice cut short his reverie. "You're up."

It took a moment for Torbin to reorient himself from his past to the here and now. He stood up quickly.

"Sorry, Sir. Wool gathering again."

"Well, as they say, time's a-wasting."

"Yes, Sir."

Torbin scanned his audience. There were eight male representatives from Free Japan. Free Japan had embraced a return to a form of traditional pre-Commodore Perry code of Bushido infrastructure. This return to traditional Bushido culture was an attempt to deal with the horror of the demon-like creatures trying to kill and sometimes eat them, although the Japanese had been successful in keeping their 21st century technology intact.

From former Russian areas, primarily Siberia, the Russian military personnel were six in total, three of them were women. The women appeared to be all age thirty or younger, the Russian men well into their forties. Torbin thought the women were likely former Russian intelligence officials attempting to insert operatives using sexual attraction. All three women were highly attractive, but still retained the air of military training. Russian and Soviet spy habits die hard.

Three young "butterbars" from the U.S. were in attendance–one male, and two females–apparently ordered to get this updated briefing before going operational. Either he was getting older or they were getting younger, as the three young officers looked barely out of high school.

The two young women had darker complexions, probably part of the last group of humans to escape from Cattle Country about a year ago. They would definitely be motivated to get some payback.

Torbin began. "Good evening, ladies and gentlemen. I know it has been a rather long day, and it's getting late, so I will be as concentrated in my briefing as possible." He clicked the PowerPoint on, the first screen displayed showed North America, divided by color into Squid-controlled areas, Feral areas, and then the Unoccupied States of America (Montana, Wyoming, Colorado, the Dakotas, Nebraska, Kansas, parts of Minnesota and Idaho, and off by itself, the State of Alaska). Most of Canada was listed as either feral or unorganized, even though Torbin knew of some former Canadian military units that had fled to the Northern Provinces, the extreme cold keeping the Tschaaa out.

Both coasts, the Great Lakes, all of the Mississippi River valley, and the southern part of the Missouri River were under Tschaaa control, as was the Gulf of Mexico, Florida, Baja, and the Panama Canal Zone. The Columbia River area between Washington and

Oregon was shaded as in flux, the Tschaaa and their minions trying to reclaim the river from the horrible effects of the Hanford Nuclear Storage Area detonation, not to mention the volcanic activity of Mounts Rainier and Saint Helens. The oceans, other large bodies of water, and the areas of land extending about twenty miles from these water sources were firmly in alien control. Human naval vessels had almost ceased to exist.

The Japanese representatives had used low and slow aircraft to fly to Alaska. The Russians had crossed the Bering Strait in a Soviet-era hover landing craft, the Tschaaa disliking the cold winter seas and generally ignoring the movement of smaller craft. Humans could get away with limited sea travel, if they stayed away from Tschaaa breeding areas. The Russians had met with the Japanese and made the arduous overland trip in two weeks to get to this briefing. Torbin hoped they found it worth the effort.

Torbin pointed out the areas of interest. "Us, them, and No Man's Land, since about six years ago." He then pointed to the former states of Mississippi, Alabama, and Georgia. "Cattle Country. As far as we know, the largest human meat stock breeding and containment area the Squids have on Earth. Three to four million souls reside there. It is made up entirely of people with skin of a darker pigmentation, due to the psychological fixation that the Squids have. To them, dark meat is cleaner, safer, their best option for nourishment and survival."

Even in the darkness of the auditorium, Torbin could see the faces of the two young Lieutenants from the U.S. flush with anger, their lips tight across their faces. If he were them, he'd want to invade the area, tonight, and free their former friends and relatives. Torbin knew, unfortunately for all their sakes, that was not likely going to happen anytime soon.

He pointed to Key West, Florida. "The capital and control center of Squid-occupied North America. Home to what we believe is the most important Tschaaa Lord on Earth. Why so important, you ask? Because, although not the most senior Squid, his were the plans used for the Invasion. Specifically, he developed the technology, the tactics, and the decision for a long term stay.

"This has its positive and negatives. The worst case scenario, which nearly happened, would have resulted in a longer bombardment from space and more nukes. The Tschaaa would have left as soon as they had sufficient meat in their larders, and obtained DNA material as well viable breeding pairs for meat reproduction. We could be at the point of complete extinction, instead of just being temporarily beaten.

"We know this because we've managed to slip in a couple of agents down there. Plus, Director Lloyd, the Tschaaa puppet leader, tells everyone within earshot the alien 'master plan' whether or not they want to hear it. The Tschaaa, at least the Lord in charge of North America, thinks hiding anything from humans is a waste of time and effort. OPSEC and COMSEC are apparently foreign concepts. Where they come from, once they take control, the idea that someone would try and revolt or resist is an 'alien' concept." That got a few chuckles from the fatigued participants.

Torbin   continued. "This Lord, who apparently has a sense of humor as well as knowledge of human mythology, calls himself Neptune, after the Roman ruler of the sea. He was the one who finally convinced convinced the other Lords that our oceans were viable places to breed and to raise their young. Now, they have large, permanent 'nurseries' along all the coastlines in the more temperate waters of Earth."

"This is a good lead in to the 'know your enemy' segment of our presentation." Torbin advanced to the next slide. It showed a very dead young male Tschaaa, spread out on a large platform. The quality of the photo caused all of the personnel to lean forward intently, with some whispering in Russian between two of the male senior officers. Torbin knew what was on their minds. How did the Americans obtain such a prime specimen of Squid? The Japanese and Russians had only been able to obtain incomplete bodies due to combat damage.

"This not-so-little guy came into our possession much undamaged at the beginning of the second year of the Occupation. His delta fighter crashed in a corn field in North Dakota. Technically, it was what was *left* of a cornfield, because as you might recall, we had a bit of that nuclear winter going on at the time. A very nasty snirt blizzard–that's snow mixed with dirt blown about by high winds– seemed to have knocked him down, and interfered with the eye in the sky locating him. No one came looking for him until what passed as spring occurred a year later. A patrol of ours scavenging for food and anything else of use found the delta, saw the frozen body inside, and started screaming for attention."

Next slide showed a different angle view of the same Squid. "We now know Tschaaa are very closely related to our cephalopods here on earth in form and function. They possess combined characteristics of our giant Pacific octopus and larger squid species. They have a thick body, a rounded dome with ten appendages, consisting of eight arms and two specialized tentacles. They have a limited skeleton-like structure, a frame made of a type of cartilage. This prevents them from squeezing through small openings like a true octopus, but gives them extra body and frame strength that enables them to mobilize on land for short distances like a crab, rising up on their appendages supported by this frame. They have a combination gill and lung system that makes them a true amphibian, though they exist best in an ocean environment.

"Average weight is around one hundred sixty kilos, about three hundred to three hundred fifty pounds. So, as you can imagine, their appendages are rather strong in order to be able to support that mass while on land. There is very limited dimorphism in the Tschaaa, the males and females being about the same in size."

The next slide was a detailed illustration of the differences between male, female, and young Tschaaa anatomy. "Average appendage span is about six meters, their arms a bit stubbier than our octopi or squid as related to body size. The males have two longer tentacles, similar to squid hunting tentacles, with specialized grasping fingers, five per end. The females' two tentacles are shorter, with grasping appendages which are slightly smaller, almost 'dainty', if you will."

Torbin used the laser pointer to illuminate the tentacles. "Why the difference? Because the larger male tentacles, besides being used to manipulate tools as well if not better than our hands, are also used in mating. Although the males have fairly large external genitalia, for some unknown reason it is used only as the backup means to deliver their sperm. The Tschaaa seem to prefer implanting their sperm into the Tschaaa female with their strong, long and sensitive fingers. The smaller, dainty tentacle hands of the female, though capable of intricate tool use, are designed to caress, stroke, basically excite the male during the mating activity.

The three female Russian officers whispered something amongst themselves, then began to giggle until the senior Russian male gave them a dirty look.

"Now, after the two Squids do the 'nasty'–that is, mate–what happens next?" A fuzzy photo was shown of a female Tschaaa, with what first looked like four large buds or bumps emanating from her body.

"At first, scientists believed that they actually 'budded', that the young grew inside outward as buds, like on plants, then broke off to swim free. Now we know that, like marsupials (almost), the very tiny young are expelled from the birth canal, then attach themselves to some very small nipple-like structures in pouches near the base of the females' arms. There they grow in size, looking like large bumps, taking sustenance from their mother.

"At one year of age, they have the 'second birth', at which point they break free from their mother. Once free, they have the capability of swimming, both by arm locomotion and the siphon jet routine our native squid use. However, they stay near the birthing area for the next five years, tended by non-gravid females as the Breeders get pregnant again."

Torbin displayed a picture of several representative female Squids. "Females have limited options in Tschaaa society. Some ten percent are chosen, based on their genetics, to be full time breeders. Each breeder gives birth about every twelve to thirteen months, depending how fast a male can get his tentacles and sperm into the breeders' naughty bits after the second birth.

"They normally have from two to four young at a time, sometimes six, very rarely eight, and, once every one hundred years or so, a breeder has a litter of ten. This is a 'Big Deal', taking on basically religious and supernatural-like connotations. The easiest way to explain it would be if one human woman had a virgin birth in Christian belief every hundred years, producing several Messiahs.

"Eighty-five percent of the females spend their lives caring for the young of their Crèche. Before everyone begins to think this is a form of misogynistic slavery, know that in Tschaaa Society, the young are *everything* to the Tschaaa.

"All females involved in the production, care and maintenance of the young, both male and female, are treated with the utmost respect. They, after the young, get the bulk of the fresh cuts of meat.

A lot of that would be classified as 'veal'."

The Russian women, although professional military, became a bit pale when they realized what human veal was to the Squids. One of the Butterbars looked like she was having trouble keeping her last meal down.

"The last five percent are allowed to be warriors, technicians, scientists, whatever the males Squids do, and are treated exactly like them when it comes down to resource allocation. You see, males compete to climb up the social ladder so that they can mate with a breeder. Like alpha males in the animal kingdom, if you are not *numero uno* in a pack, the chances of having sex with a female are slim.

"Once in a great while, a regular female outside of the selected breeding lineages is randomly selected to be impregnated. This is to provide a little random genetic variance to prevent a line of royal idiots from taking over. There is no British royal family among the Squids." This elicited a few laughs.

"Now, why is all this is important in relation to the so-called Lord Neptune, you may ask? Well, his birth mother was one of the randomly-selected females to add genetic diversity. She then proceeded to give birth to ten Tschaaa."

Torbin let this sink in. "That's right. He and his brothers and sisters–littermates–were the closest thing to royalty, or supernatural leaders that the Squids have. He was told he was special, which may have led him to think in a special way, to our detriment. While the Tschaaa were getting stagnant in the thousand year long journey, Lord Neptune was just the opposite.

"Although the Senior Lords tried to limit his effect on the way things were done, he used his 'specialness' to push for new things. He found sufficient supporters so that ninety percent of the weapons and equipment used against us were either his new idea, or his modification of existing designs, including that equipment taken from the alien races the Squids ran into during their travel into space. He spent years studying our transmissions, and knows us possibly better than we know ourselves in some ways. He seems to be steps ahead of us on any given day. So, if any one Tschaaa is responsible for kicking our ass, it looks like him."

Torbin continued, "But, he is also the one pushing the idea that we are potentially of more use than just being a nice cut of meat. He seems to want to make us the equivalent of 'working dogs', allowed to coexist as long as we are both obedient and useful to our alien masters. He and the Director have outlined the Protocols of Selective Survival. These concepts have probably kept us from being nuked and rocked back to the Stone Age as the Tschaaa leave our solar system. The fact that their young seem to love our oceans probably doesn't hurt, either.

"Their home world seems to be almost eighty percent ocean, with ninety percent of dry land being around their equator. Although Squids can take cold water thanks to their copper-based blood, like our squids, they do not like it. Additionally, their young need warm seas the first few years to develop well.

"So, we get the Arctic and Antarctic oceans, parts of Alaskan and Canadian northern waters. They get the rest of the oceans."

Torbin changed slides. "Now, what and who else did the Squids bring with them? Let's look." Pictures of grays and lizards appeared. "Since the second week of the Invasion, we have seen few of them. Possibly because they make easier targets than they do soldiers."

The senior Russian Officer, a Colonel Antonov, cleared his throat loudly.

"Do you have a question, Sir?"

"My young Captain, you speak with an air of knowledge and experience in combat. But, I see large complexes in these northern states, and fair numbers of Americans. We Russians fought tooth and nail for our motherland. Now, three quarters of us are dead. How do we know that you are not just spinning tales to assuage your well-known American conceit and pride?"

Torbin looked to his Commander. General John Reed, though a former Air Force Puke and not a Marine, knew his stuff. Now, once again, they had to deal with someone playing power games when they should be thinking of killing Squids.

"Colonel," General Reed began, in a firm tone. "You have seen our photos from Yuma, Arizona, correct?"

"The Battle of Yuma? Yes, we have watched the DVD. It is like many combats we also had in the early days of the Invasion."

"Well, Colonel, Captain Torbin was an enlisted Marine then, and was the highest ranking person to survive. He got his people home after getting all that film evidence and destroying the harvester. I think he knows how to deal with aliens."

A young Japanese Lieutenant chose that moment to spring to rigid attention, began rambling in Japanese, then bowed to Torbin, as his Colonel Tanaka started to tell him be seated in Japanese. He sat down as quickly as he had risen. Then Colonel Tanaka himself stood, bowing slightly to General Reed.

"My apologies, General. Lt. Yamamoto was overtaken by the emotion of the moment. Please, Captain, continue."

Torbin looked at his boss. The General gave a nod. Torbin addressed Colonel Tanaka. "May I ask what the good Lieutenant was saying?"

The Colonel paused, and then answered in perfect English, "Captain, Lt. Yamamoto lost his family to one of the few harvesters that landed on Japan. They seemed more content to hit us with a few 'stones', and then strafe us from above. He has seen your film many times, and wishes that is what he could have done in Japan."

Torbin bowed to the Lieutenant. "Please, accept my condolences. My parents died quickly during a rock strike, and my brother died in combat. But I, too, wish I could have done more."

Colonel Tanaka asked Torbin, "You come from a military family?" "Yes, Sir. My father was a Ranger, my brother was an Air Force pilot. Past generations also served in the military, including World War Two, in the Pacific."

The Colonel drew himself up a bit, then, in a formal tone, "General, Captain, may I present Lt. Yamamoto, a descendent of Admiral Isoroku Yamamoto, who died fighting America in World War Two. The Lieutenant hopes to carry on the Yamamoto name with honor. He has done so thus far, in direct combat with the Tschaaa."

The Lieutenant snapped to his feet again and began to rattle off once more in Japanese.

"Yamamoto-San. English, please." Colonel Tanaka snapped.

Yamamoto took a deep breath, and then repeated in fluent English, "You do me and my family great honor, my Colonel."

"No Lieutenant, it is you who do us honor."

Colonel Tanaka continued speaking. "That family samurai sword the Lieutenant carries with him has already dispatched eight Tschaaa warriors."

Colonel Antonov snorted. "I am sorry, but do you expect us to believe he has killed eight Squid with a sword, when we only see them in aircraft? We fight robots and those giant warriors they have."

"Because, Colonel, the Islands of Japan have been selected for what we call special attention."

"How so?" asked General Reed.

"Because of the Fukushima nuclear plant meltdown and contamination we suffered after the tsunami. The Tschaaa seemed to be hesitant to eat us in the first few days after the Invasion, due to residual radiation that can still be detected in some areas with sensitive instruments."

One of the female Russians, a raven-haired beauty, seized that opportunity to chime in. "That is like Chernobyl. We've had no reports of aliens any nearer than two hundred miles from ground zero. They are afraid of radiation contamination." For this comment, she received another dirty look from Colonel Antonov.

"Yes, Ma'am," Torbin interjected. "The Squids are hyper sensitive about a contaminated food supply for their young." He turned to Colonel Tanaka. "What have the Squids been doing in Japan?"

"Their young warriors sneak ashore in ones and twos, sometimes in groups up to four. They hunt and kill, leaving the bodies behind, the only occasions in which we have heard of this happening. They seem to be testing themselves, bringing only handheld weapons with them."

Colonel Tanaka looked at his Lieutenant with the pride a father would have for his son. "Yamamoto-San has proven the superiority of traditional Nippon Bushido swordplay on land eight different times.

Tell them, Lieutenant."

"They seem to underestimate what a katana can do. Slash off a couple of appendages, and the aliens freeze for a brief moment, providing the perfect opportunity to impale the brain through their eye."

Torbin had once imagined himself 'Billy Badass' with a rifle. But a freaking sword?

"Gentlemen. Please," Colonel Antonov interjected. "Can we now continue with the briefing? I can assure you that everyone in this room has seen their share of conflict and deprivation. My staff and I are tired from a very long and arduous journey." It seemed now that the Colonel had lost his chance to one up everyone, he wanted to change the subject.

General Reed turned to Torbin. "Think you can finish expeditiously, Captain?"

"Yes, Sir. Now, let's look at the other players and their toys in this nasty game of death…"

Two hours later, Captain Torbin crashed on his rack. He had a private room, befitting his rank and accomplishments. He would gladly trade those creature comforts for a combat post.

There was a knock on his door. Now what? Reluctantly, he slow opened the door, and found Lieutenant Yamamoto standing on the other side, a bottle of scotch in one hand, and a bottle of saki in the other.

"Captain, please. I wish to share a toast with you."

Torbin smiled in relief. "Apparently, Lieutenant, you know my weakness. Any self- respecting Marine cannot turn down a drink offer, especially scotch. Do come in. Find a seat. I'll get the ice for the scotch. Do you want the saki warmed?"

"You have shared drinks with the Japanese before?"

"I have had a drink with just about every cultural group on Earth. I hope one day to have a drink with the Tschaaa. Just before I blow their brains out."

They were soon sitting down, enjoying the quality libations Yamamoto had provided.

Torbin noticed for the first time that Yamamoto seemed taller than the might have expected, 5' 10" at least. Torbin had previously accessed the limited internet they had set up using the military-based servers in the Unoccupied States and found a photo of Admiral Yamamoto. There was a family facial resemblance, but the Lieutenant was definitely leaner and taller than his ancestor. Probably inherited from the non-Yamamoto side of the family.

"What is your first name again, Lieutenant?"

"Ichiro. And yours, Captain?"

"Torbin. A family name. Tor for short, which is sometimes mistaken for Thor, but I am definitely not the God of Thunder. Marvel or otherwise."

"Ah. You read comic books."

"Ichiro, if I may call you that, ninety-nine percent of kids of my generation read comic books, of one kind or another. But your Japanese anime gave a kickstart to all future animated forms of entertainment… that is, until the Squids showed up."

They were silent for a few moments, musing about childhood joys probably gone forever.

"Are you a pilot, Tor-San?"

He snorted. "Not even close. My brother was, he came to it naturally. Why do you ask?"

"You had an accurate grasp of the Tschaaa deltas, the Falcons in the briefing. We know of the 32mm electromagnetic cannon, the three inch guided missiles used in actual combat. Although we now have limited fuel, we still intercept the odd delta that attempts to penetrate our airspace. Like the raids by Tschaaa warriors from the sea, they act as if it is a test, a game, a real life video game."

Ichiro continued, "But you Americans do not seem to have an operational Air Force of any capability. Is that so?"

Torbin chuckled. "Yes, that's true. We're trying to piece together aircraft as we speak, and we have maybe a dozen of all types available. The Squids targeted our airfields and airports, and were sabotaged by the Quisling Renegades, both which reduced most of our aircraft to scrap metal. We still have substantial ground to air defenses available, but that is good for point defense only."

Torbin did not mention the somewhat operational ICBMs that were still scattered around the former Northern Tier bases. But, even if they all still worked, they would only either cause another nuclear winter, or contaminate the living areas still under human control.

Humankind would be unlikely to recover from either one.

"However, we do have a good deal of intelligence assets. Because Lord so-called Neptune left so many pockets and centers of non-meat humans alone, to survive on their own largely unsupervised, we have a lot of sources of information that keep track of Tschaaa. Squid watching, Ichiro, is the only 'hobby' some humans have left."

Torbin looked at Ichiro. "You are a pilot."

"Hai. Yes, I was finishing pilot training when the Tschaaa attacked. It took me a few months longer to become fully certified, due to heavy aircraft and fuel losses. But, I saw my first aerial combat a year to the day after the first stone strike."

"What was it like?"

Ichiro gave a beaming smile. "Exhilarating. I knew I was born to be a warrior. There were two deltas, instead of the normal one." As innumerable fighter jocks before him, Ichiro began demonstrating the aerial combat with his hands.

"They came in at close to mach three, though we know they can go faster on their scramjets. But, they wanted us to intercept them, to fight. I and my three flight mates accommodated them." Torbin had never seen a more animated soldier or pilot. He also seemed to have a photographic memory, the way he demonstrated the entire combat, relating what each aircraft did and when.

"They fired their electromagnetic cannon, one round from each cannon, the finned shells traveling some two thousand meters per second. As you know, they have an organic limited artificial intelligence in the warhead that keys in on moving objects, using their fins and tiny maneuver jets to twist and turn after us."

Ichiro jumped to his feet, almost knocking over his drink. "But my Squadron Commander, Major Chiba, had planned for this. He had installed rear-facing, target-marking rockets on our jets. When we fired them, at the shells, their quick movement caused the finned shells to turn toward them. Chaff and flares traveled too slowly to attract the AI. Unlike those targets, our rockets were quick.

"The Tschaaa delta pilots seemed surprised by this tactic. They turned their now well-known fifteen plus gravity turns, boring toward the rockets.

"I turned my fighter around in the air, and was on the tail of one of the deltas for a moment. Before he could use his gravity pulse engine to accelerate out of the area, I fired every weapon I had. The tough skin and frame of the delta, though very strong, collapsed under my weapons. My first kill."

Ichiro paused, and then sat down, his demeanor suddenly becoming more subdued.

"The surviving delta did a 15 G turn, latched onto me, and shot me from the sky. I ejected, and my parachute opened. As I swung to Earth, dangling in my chute, the delta looked as if it would turn its gunnery run on me in apparent revenge for the loss of his twin. Then, it happened..."

Ichiro paused, and took a large gulp from his glass of saki.

"Major Chiba cut in front of the delta and turned directly into the craft, ramming him, as pilots in World War Two had sacrificed themselves for others, for Japan."

Ichiro was silent for another moment or two. Finally, he spoke. "On that day, I swore I would kill ten Squid for Captain Chiba. I have two more to kill."

The two warriors sat quietly. Torbin was the first to stir.

"A toast, Ichiro." Torbin interjected. "To all our comrades in arms, who have died, fighting the good fight. May their memory never fade, and our bravery do them honor."

"Hai. Kempai." They emptied their glasses, and Torbin refilled them.

"Before we are completely shit-faced, Ichiro, I must have you show me how you kill a Squid with your katana."

Ichiro laughed. "I am willing, but we are short a Tschaaa to use as for our demonstration."

Torbin slyly smiled. "Watch me work my magic, Ichiro."

He walked across the room, and pulled a large frame from the shadows into the room's center. At the top was a rather thick roll of unknown material.

Torbin took a quick step to one side. Ichiro, sensing something was up, stood up, right hand on the hilt of the katana that he carried by his left hip.

"Ichiro, please meet our special guest." Torbin pulled loose the restraining tie and a very exact 3D representation of the recovered Tschaaa, unraveled to the floor. Torbin had scarcely taken a breath to speak, and it was all over.

There was a blur of motion, the sounds of slashing. The Tschaaa model was sliced in three pieces, along the axis of the Squid's tentacles. Ichiro was now standing stock still, the katana he gripped in both hands still impaling the Squid's right eye perfectly.

Torbin gulped. "Well, so much for that training aid."

Ichiro smoothly sheathed his katana. "I am sorry if I destroyed something you need. It was an automatic reaction."

Torbin walked over to his desk and retrieved his Ka-Bar fighting knife.

"So, if the Tschaaa had a blade... "

The katana blade was already at his throat. "Remind me never to make you mad."

Ichiro sheathed his katana once more, and bowed. "I apologize, Torbin-San. I have maybe had too much to drink."

"Oh no you haven't. I wanted an example, and you gave me one. Have you always been this fast?"

"Yes, Torbin-San. Some medical specialists once said that I have the fastest reflexes in the Japanese defense forces. Why, I do not know."

"Hell, I do. It's called karma. You are destined to carve up Squids. Here, another drink, if you please."

At that moment, there was a light knock at the door. "Who the hell....?" Torbin strode over, and flung open the door, Ka-Bar still in his hands.

On the other side stood the three Russian female officers, a bottle of Vodka and glasses in their hands. The senior officer, a Captain, cocked an eyebrow, and looked at Torbin and his knife. "I see you are playing with your man toys. May we join?"

"I have never turned down three pretty women with a bottle of vodka in my life," Torbin replied. He stood aside, bowed, and swept his arm toward the center of the room, beckoning them inside. "'Come into my parlor,' said the spider to the flies." The three women laughed, and entered.

They wore matching fleece workout gear, as if part of a sports team. The sweats were baggy enough to conceal some of their fit curves, but not all. Aleksandra, the Captain with black hair, suddenly took notice of Ichiro. "Excellent. More company."

Ichiro stammered, and tried to move toward the door. "My apologies, Tor-san, but I must go..."

"Whoa, hoss. You cannot leave me outnumbered three to one. Even a Marine has his limitations."

"I... I...," Ichiro stammered again.

"Excuse us for one minute ladies." Torbin grabbed Ichiro by the arm and escorted him to his back bedroom.

"Ichi," he began. "Are you married?"

"Well, no, I..."

"Good. Then think of these ladies as three wandering geishas who have come to entertain the conquering samurai. "

"But..."

"Lieutenant. You still owe me for the training aid. It's also wise to accept an offer of hospitality. In the name of good international relations."

Ichiro sighed. "Yes, I owe you for the training aid. And for you, Tor-san, and for our countries, I will sacrifice myself."

Torbin wondered if Ichiro was bullshitting him with the last statement. But it did not matter. Three specimens of outstanding womanhood were in his room, and must be provided entertainment becoming of their ranks and positions.

"Good. Follow me." He returned to the main room, arms outstretched. "Ladies, in the name of full disclosure, there is absolutely nothing of any intelligence value in my room, so if you have any ideas..."

Three gorgeous women were standing in his living room, in their underwear.

Aleksandra caught his eye. "I think, Mister Spider, that the flies already have ideas of their own."

It was going to be an interesting night.

Torbin awoke with Afanasiy, a gorgeous blonde, gently kissing his back. He glanced at the clock. 5:00am. Due to the late night briefing, and trip fatigue on the part of the visiting military members, the General had told everyone that he did not want to see anyone before noon. This could not have come at a better time. He started to turn toward Afanasiy when another set of lips began to kiss his chest. Aleksandra, the Captain, was also demanding attention. He tried to position himself equally between the two women, when they became cognizant of what the other was trying to do. Rapid fire whispered Russian began between the two. Torbin did not speak Russian, but he could imagine, by the tone of voice, what was being said. Torbin decided it was time to stop them before things turned nasty. "Ladies. I have hot water in my shower, and plenty of high quality shampoo." At that, both women rose from the bed, and made their way quickly to the shower.

Inna, the third Russian, apparently watching the conflict, had untangled herself from Ichiro on the couch. The mention of a hot shower and soap apparently had magical powers, after a long and dirty trip. Torbin chuckled at the mercurial attitude of womanhood and stretched.

Ichiro was beginning to snore, so Torbin rose and tiptoed to the couch. He bent over and whispered in a high falsetto voice into Ichiro's ear, "Oh, my big Samurai, wake up. I must have more."

Ichiro smiled with closed eyes, muttering some pillow talk, and reached a hand upward which touched Torbin's beard stubble. His eyes popped open, and he began to curse in Japanese, as he tried to untangle himself from the blanket. Torbin jumped back, laughing. "Rise and shine sweetcakes, if you want some hot water in the shower."

Ichiro recovered quickly, and stood up with an embarrassed grin on his face. "You Americans. Always such jokesters."

"Oh come on, Ichi-san. I saw those Japanese game shows your people used to produce. You loved practical jokes. We even started copying them."

"You did say a hot shower?" Ichiro repeated.

"Yessir. You just have to share it with three Russians."

Ichiro's face broke into a broad grin, and he marched toward the bathroom in his boxers, showing off his muscular torso, and whistling a Japanese military tune. He must rise to the call of duty once more.

CHAPTER 7

My examinations of the workings of the Director's organizational skills revealed he had an excellent knack for finding people with the expertise he needed for certain specific projects and functions. Often, these people came with emotional and personal baggage that must be dealt with in order for them to fulfill the desired task. But of course, all surviving members of the human species at that time had psychological, social and emotional scars from years of the threat they or their children would be eaten by the Tschaaa, myself included.

One such married couple whom the Director had located, Professors Joseph and Sarah Fassbinder, would have much to work out before they played important parts in the history of the New Capital of Tschaaa-Controlled North America in Key West.

—Excerpts from the Literary Works of Princess Akiko, Free Japan Royal Family.

NEW CAPITAL KEY WEST, FLORIDA

While Torbin was waking up Ichiro, Joseph Fassbinder was also being woken up. But he was not in bed. Instead, he was propped up against a small tree about two blocks from the auditorium.

After his blow up with his wife, he had made a concerted effort to get shit-faced. He needed a good buzz, he deserved a good buzz, so he worked at and got himself a good buzz. He had used all his alcohol credits at the bar, just before being cut off by the bartender.

When the barkeep became distracted by a very attractive young woman in a revealing cocktail dress, Joseph had swiped a bottle of whiskey from behind the bar and disappeared toward the exit, bottle expertly concealed under his suit coat, which was a tad loose due to his undernourished frame.

The security troop let him leave, as they had been told some of the new personnel had assignments in the morning. Besides, this was a free twenty-four hour installation, with the perceived threats coming from the *outside*, not the inside the base.

He had wandered for a while, making a concerted effort to finish the near full bottle in the shortest amount of time possible, before being forced to use the tree as a support. He then passed out.

Joseph heard a male voice. "Sir. Sir. Time to wake up. The party's over."

He struggled to slowly open his eyes, and found himself looking into the face of one of the biggest men he had seen, in full battle rattle. He saw stripes on his arm that Joseph recognized as a Sergeant.

"Sorry, Sergeant. I guess I dozed off and lost track of time." He tried to stand up, and fell forward, caught at the last minute by the Sergeant.

"Whoa, Sir. Just sit there down for a moment until you get your balance. We do not need a busted face the second day here. Oh! Good morning, Ma'am."

The Sergeant tried to prop him up against the tree to free his right hand for a salute. Joseph proceeded to fall backwards. Someone caught him, and he heard a woman's voice. "Good morning yourself, Sergeant. It looks like my morning run is going to be interrupted." Suddenly, he felt another pair of hands support him, and the women's voice was closer. "And good morning to you as well, Professor. Based on the smell, I take it you did not make it back to your quarters last night."

Joseph managed to finally focus his eyes. He vaguely recognized Major Jane Grant in her sweatshirt and shorts. "Good morning, Major. Where am I?"

"You are a few blocks from my quarters, a shower, and a few cups of coffee. Sergeant, if you could help me with transportation, I will take this problem off your hands. I need to try and get him to work today."

"Yes, Ma'am. Thank you, Major. This saves me a ton of paperwork."

Ten minutes later, with the help of the two additional sets of hands, he was sitting on the Major's couch.

"Thanks for the ride, Sergeant."

"Oh, thank *you*, Major. Good luck." Joseph heard the front door shut.

He started to nod off again, but was woken up by two feminine hands unbuttoning his shirt. He started to protest, and then decided he liked the feel of the hands and the nice smell of the owner.

"Mm, I like your perfume, Major."

Jane laughed. "That's called 'eau du sweat', Professor. It's easy to come by around here. And, if you help me, this will be a lot easier and quicker. You desperately need a shower." With the Major's assistance, he was in the shower in less ten minutes.

Joseph leaned against the stall wall, cool water from the shower head beating on the top of his head, then running down his face and chest. He just might live. Suddenly, the shower stall door opened, and a face appeared. "Gangway, Professor. I need to clean up too."

"Wait a minute, Major. We haven't been properly introduced," Joseph protested.

"You don't have anything I haven't seen before," she responded. "But if you are going to be bashful, I'll give you a little more time. Then, out of the pool."

In five minutes, he was sitting on a clean towel in the kitchen. Another ten minutes later, and Jane came up and tossed him a set of boxer shorts and a man's undershirt. "Here, I wear these around my place when I'm relaxing. They should fit you. You're pretty damn skinny right now. You'll need some more meat on your bones if you are going to ride a rocket in a couple of month.

"Now that you are mostly sober and somewhat more presentable, allow me to formally introduce myself." She smiled. "I am Major Jane Grant, the Director's Operations Officer. You are Professor Joseph Fassbinder, who I am told will be helping us to obtain regular space travel again, with some additional help from the Squids, of course."

Joseph sighed, and said "Major, I wish to humbly apologize for this trouble. I owe you."

Jane handed him a cup of hot coffee, and two large donuts. "Here, this will help soak up the alcohol. No, you do not owe me anything, for two reasons. First, because we all work together here to survive in a crazy world inhabited by BEMs... that's bug-eyed monsters."

Jane took a sip of her coffee. "Second, do you happen to remember a Marcia Brand from your Mission Specialist Training for the Space Program, just before the rocks hit?"

Joseph got his wheels turning in his head, remembering a different time in a different place. "Yes, I do. She was one of the sharpest young ladies I have ever met. She was training as a spaceplane co-pilot, the youngest ever accepted."

"She was a cousin of mine, who was like a sister. She had the utmost respect for you. Had a bit of a crush on you as well. She told me you were one of the nicest people she had ever met, as well as the most brilliant. But in my book, nice beats out brilliant."

Jane took another drink of coffee. "She's dead now. Unfortunately, probably some Squid fed her remains to their young. I also help you in her memory, as she would have wanted it." Tears appeared in Jane's eyes. "Excuse me." She walked out to her bedroom.

Times like this reminded Joseph that just about everyone had been screwed over in one way or the other. They were all just making the best of it. The Tschaaa had changed human dynamics drastically, most likely forever. Now, they tried to keep a resemblance of humanity while trying to survive. Damn.

Joseph put the boxers and shirt on. They fit. Apparently, he had lost a lot of weight, and not in a good way. He wolfed down the donuts, suddenly starving. Jane came back with his suit pants that she was brushing out, and a windbreaker. "These will do today. We do not stand on formality, unless you're in uniform. Those standards are tougher. Ms. Monroe, because she will be in the public eye as a representative of the Director, will soon realize that's like."

At the mention of Kathy's name, the memory of what Sarah had done flooded back.

"Major, I need to apologize to Ms. Monroe for..."

"Never mind. Ms. Monroe is the proverbial tough cookie. It was water off a duck's back."

"Now, if you will excuse me, I need to finish getting ready." Jane walked back to her bedroom.

Only then did he realize she had been standing there only clad in her bra and panties. He had not been this relaxed with a woman in years.

Adam was moving slowly, recovering from a very late night entertaining the new arrivals. He had danced with every woman who had wanted to, more than one dancing with him just long enough to whisper a thank you in his ear, especially those who were mothers. And of course, Mary Lou, Jeanie, and Jamey each took a turn to trip the light fantastic. The highlight of the evening, however, was when Adam felt a tap on his shoulder, and turned to face Kathy, who said, "My turn, Boss. If you please."

She had a smooth rhythm and, as he held her, he noticed strong back and shoulder muscles he had somehow missed during their earlier encounter. She held him firmly, with strong fingers and arms that befit someone who worked at keeping in shape. As the song ended, Kathy kissed him on the cheek.

"Time for me to turn back into a pumpkin. I need to get a good night's sleep. I think Major Grant's going to try and work my ass off tomorrow."

Adam grinned. "I hope not. I rather enjoy your posterior where it is. I'm certain you'll do just fine. I'll be in contact when I can."

Kathy wrinkled her nose and flashed her signature smile. "I wouldn't mind some more dance time alone. Especially if is horizontal."

Adam laughed. "Don't worry. I don't think I could forget that."

Kathy squeezed his arm. "'Night, Boss." She slinked off, her sexy walk drawing many an appreciative stare from the males in attendance, and causing a few bruised arms for the husbands.

Now, 7:00am the next morning, Adam once again wished that he had a clone, so he could be in two places at once. The hard truth, however, was that duty called today. He had to meet the Lord.

His radio phone pinged.

"Yes, Chief."

"Boss, I have a Professor Sarah Broadmore who says she *really* needs to see you. Her husband is missing."

Shit. He needed this like he needed a hole in the head. "Send her up, Chief. Mary Lou has the morning off."

Adam quickly dressed in his tactical pants and shirt, which he wore when travelling to visit the Lord Neptune. He waited out by

Mary Lou's desk in the front office.

Sarah burst through the doors, dressed in slacks and shirt. She had her hair tied back in a ponytail that should have made her look younger. But her face was pale, and she looked like she had aged ten years.

"Joseph is missing." Her chin quivered while she attempted to regain some composure. "He never came back to the room last night. He started drinking, and then disappeared. He has never done this before. Ever."

Adam gave her a hard look. "Can you blame him? You've basically acted like you'd just as soon castrate him, than spend any time with him as his wife."

Sarah's chin quivered, and soon a tear appeared, running down her left cheek.

"Turn off the waterworks, Sarah. I'll help find him. I need him a lot more than apparently you do. Here's a box of tissues. Sit over there, next to Mary Lou's desk." He dialed Jane's phone.

"Morning, Sir!" Jane answered immediately. "If you are looking for a certain Professor Fassbinder, he is all cleaned up and headed toward the Science and Engineering Building."

Adam stared at his phone. "Major, have you been hiding the fact that you are clairvoyant all these months?"

"No, Sir. Just trying to anticipate your orders. Sir."

"Could you please stop by my office for a moment?"

"Yes, Sir."

Adam hung up the phone, and turned back to Sarah. She began sobbing. He stood where he was. He had never been married, never lived with a woman, prior to bringing his three ladies here to live with him. He knew that Joseph had loved her dearly once, but she may have finally killed that love.

Sarah finally stopped crying, and blew her nose. "Director, what will become of me?"

"I suspect that is entirely up to you."

She laughed harshly. "Really? I'm only here because of Joseph. Why didn't you just kill me and dump my body in the mangroves?"

"That seems a tad unnecessary. Contrary to what everyone believes, I actually do care about my fellow man... and woman. I did not lie at the briefing. You can stay or go this morning. We will provide transportation back to where you lived."

Sarah sniffed, blew her nose again. "What can I do here?"

"Well, Professor, you could teach. I was told you were quite the interesting lecturer in your early years. As long as you do not try to incite revolution by stirring crap up, you could help teach the younger folks. Most had their formal education interrupted. I do believe they are the future."

Sarah looked at him. "But I don't actually have a choice, do I?

"As I said before, yes, you do. I want actual volunteers. I'm working to turn North America back into a livable place again, not just a place where people survive in a hand-to-mouth existence. We have made great strides in the last year in the Tschaaa controlled area. Food is now being distributed. Hospitals have been set up. Televisions, radio, and the internet are all making a comeback. It takes time after an all out war. Look at World War Two and the Marshall Plan."

"What about the rest of the country, Director? What about the Cattle Country, the Unoccupied States?"

Adam shook his head. "I can only help those who I have the power to help. Frankly, the Tschaaa would just as soon let the interior states go to hell, as they have nothing the Tschaaa want. The Tschaaa leave them alone, and hopefully they leave the Tschaaa alone."

Adam continued. "I know that you are going to say things are unfair. The universe does not have a 'fairness doctrine'. Creatures are born, live, and die every day on various worlds, all subject to variations of Darwinian evolution. The strongest and fittest do survive to procreate, and work their way to the top of the food chain. Unfortunately, what we would at one time have referred to as people of color are currently at the bottom of the food chain. If we... if I am not careful, we could be right there with them."

Sarah was silent. Adam knew she was trying to resolve her inner conflict between her personal survival versus the unfairness of the situation. She did not want to admit she had no power right now to make a difference. Rights and fairness are concepts that work when all sides come from a framework of the same basic moral concepts. If the side with the power decides that your opinions do not matter, and they have no recognizable moral conscience, then the world turns to hell very quickly. The Squids were the Nazis, and humans were the

Jews, humans existing due to the sufferance of the Squids. Sarah took a deep breath, and let it out slowly.

"I suppose for once in my life, I will have to admit I am pretty powerless. That is a concept completely foreign to me."

"Believe me, Sarah, you are not alone. I had to come to the same conclusion five years ago."

"I will do as you ask as long as I can for my own, and Joseph's, survival. When feel I can no longer do so, you will be the first to know."

"Fair enough."

Major Grant arrived at that moment. "Director, you called."

"Good Morning, Major. Would you be so kind as take the Professor back to her quarters so that she can freshen up a bit, and then see that someone gets her to Training and Education?"

Jane smiled. "My pleasure, Sir." She addressed the Professor. "Ma'am, if you would come with me, please." She escorted Sarah to the winding staircase that led up to the Director's complex.

As they left, Adam sighed to himself. "I'm getting too old for this shit." He went back to his office and retrieved the satchel and briefcase that he needed for the meeting with Lord Neptune. This already had all the makings of a very long day.

Jane had a security troop drive her and Sarah to her quarters. She walked Sarah up to the door, where Sarah finally spoke to her. "Major, if I may ask, how is Joseph?"

"As well as can be expected." Jane paused. "Professor, I know little about you and won't presume to tell you how to live your life. But take this as friendly advice. Your husband is a fine man, well respected by some survivors here who knew him before the rocks. If you want to continue being his wife, please, cut him some slack. There are those here that would willingly swap places with you, and be his partner. I think you have another chance if you want it. He's a man of honor who loves you."

Sarah blinked back her tears. "Thank you, Major. I will strive to remember that."

"Please give me a call when you have a chance, Professor. I mean that."

"Thank you. I will."

Jane left Sarah and walked back to the vehicle. As she was driven to the Communications and Broadcasting Center to meet Kathy Monroe, she thought, What an idiot that woman is. I wish I would have been the one to meet Joseph ten years ago.

The aforementioned Joseph was in front of the Science and Engineering Building, trying to determine if it was too early to check in for work. He was still in the process of deciding when he was distracted by the most colorful former FedEx delivery truck he had ever seen. Written on the side in large red, white and blue letters was *"Conch Republic Eats. Drinks. Sundry Items. You Wants It, We Gets It."*

Joseph noticed that the driver's side had been modified by cutting a large access window with a small counter as the bottom sill. The window was open, though it looked like there were large fold down flaps inside to secure the opening. Emanating from the mobile kitchen inside were the most delicious aromas. His mouth watering, Joseph began checking his pockets for money. At first, all he found were some coins left over from his bout of drinking. Then tucked away in his wallet, he found something he had almost forgot he had, his lucky two dollar bill. The Director said they still used good old 'greenbacks' as tender, as there were now so many left in relation to the numbers of survivors. But, he had had this bill for so long. His stomach growled.

"Professor Fassbinder! Is that you?" A female voice called out. Perhaps his old two dollar bill would generate some luck once again.

He turned toward the voice, which belonged to an attractive young lady with red hair and freckles. Right behind her was a young man, red hair and freckles also. Instantly he noticed the strong family resemblance.

"It *is* you. My God, I thought someone was making it up. You *did* survive." The young lady started to throw her arms around him, but stopped when she saw the confused expression on his face.

"I'm sorry. Of course you don't recognize us. Remember Sandy and Samuel Olson, the 'Olson twins'? We were first year aeronautical engineering students in your class. We bugged the crap out of you until you let us help you with your research project."

He struggled to place them, and finally recognition kicked in. The Olson twins. They were young geniuses who had started college at age sixteen, and had managed to get assigned to his department. His eyes teared up as he realized there was another human being from his past that had survived. They were few and far between.

He threw his arms around her as he yelled, "My God! You both made it!" Soon they were both crying. People coming out of the building gave them space. Scenes like these repeated themselves all over the former U.S.A., as survivors found the familiar faces of family, friends, coworkers, and former neighbors. It was the new reality.

Next Samuel joined in, wrapping him in a bear hug. The group remained encircled for about another half minute, before they stepped back from each other. Joseph looked for something to wipe his eyes, and a voice from the food truck called, "Here. Just give it back." A rolled up towel hit him in the side of his head.

He and his newly rediscovered friends each used different corners to wipe eyes, and blow noses. The Olson twins gave him a quick update (without the gory details). They had somehow survived in the basement of a school dormitory that had been an old civil defense shelter in days gone by. It even had some old rations and survival hard candy that kept them alive for a couple of months. They emerged, bumped into a couple of other survivors, and headed for the hills.

After the first couple of months, the fact they were 'red headed white people' seemed to result in them being ignored by harvesters. Pale skin and freckles seemed to put them off. Living hand to mouth, three years later they bumped into one of the Director's foraging expeditions, saw what side of the bread the butter was on, and joined in. The former fresh-faced youngsters were gone, replaced by seasoned survivors.

"Are you hungry?" Samuel finally asked.

"Yes, but I'm afraid I'm short of funds. Maybe the Department will give me an advance…"

"Forget it. My treat and I'll order for us. The mystery meat burritos are to die for."

Joseph frowned. "Mystery meat?"

Samuel and Sandy laughed. "Don't worry. It's good quality meat. They just won't tell us all the different types of animals that are in it." They sat down at a nearby table, apparently provided to service the meal truck. Joseph soon had two large burritos, and a bottle of "near beer". To insure adequate and potable water, pasteurization of drinks in one way or the other was called for. Thus, the Conch Brewery made near beer–probably one percent alcohol on a good day–as a staple.

Joseph was about to wipe his mouth on the towel over his

shoulder, when he remembered. "Oh. Wait a minute, please." He grabbed the towel that had been thrown at him and walked to the truck.

"Excuse me. Here is you towel back, rather used. Thank you so very much."

A gorgeous woman with jet black hair locked her twinkling dark eyes with his, and grinned. "Don't mention it. Just remember the Conch Republic was there when needed, and *I'm* here every morning, rain or shine. Come and spend money, eat, get gas!" As she turned away, he saw her hair covered a large scar on the left side of her face. Even the scar did not detract from her extreme attractiveness. Sandy giggled as Joseph returned back to his friends.

"And Jolene, one of the Admiral's many daughters, captures another heart. Will the spell last? Or is the Professor able to break the magic that has enslaved so many. Including my own poor brother."

Samuel blushed a bright red. "If you weren't my twin... I'd make you regret those words."

Sandy laughed. "If I were not your twin sister, then the only fight I would be having is a good old-fashioned catfight with the local women for your attention! You see, my brother is seen as a very desirable catch by the local Conchettes. A couple have already come to face scratching and hair pulling over him." She snickered. "But not Jolene, much to his frustration."

Samuel kept blushing. "Just because I'm more attractive to the girls than you are to the guys isn't my fault."

Joseph broke in before he stuffed his mouth with burrito, "So, there's a lot of interaction with the locals?"

Sandy answered, "In a word, *hell yes*. They provide a lot of the local amenities, not only this meal truck but some general stores, restaurants and–my brother can attest to this personally–a bunch of bars and entertainment spots. Including at least two brothels."

Samuel couldn't stop blushing. He mumbled. "Just you wait. I might fight you yet."

Sandy continued. "After you get settled in, we'll take you on the grand tour." Joseph felt her hand on his thigh beneath their table. He suddenly realized that the former sixteen year old student was now an adult auburn-haired beauty, who was giving him smoldering looks. Did the heat in Key West make turn up everyone's personal temperature?

Samuel looked at his watch. "Eat up! Then we will take you in and introduce you to our Section Chief."

Still chewing on the best burrito he had ever tasted, Joseph managed to mumble, "Ours?"

Sandy smiled. "Yeah, you're going to be stuck with us again. We're assigned to the same project. We may even be going up in the space plane with you."

This day was getting curiouser and curiouser.

CHAPTER 8

Even in times of war, or in some ways, especially in times of war, close friendships are developed even as relationships with others on the proverbial same side become extremely acrimonious.

—Excerpts from the *Literary Works of Princess Akiko,* Free Japan Royal Family.

MALMSTROM ARMED FORCES BASE GREAT FALLS, MONTANA

Torbin was headed over to the main hangar on what was once Malmstrom Air Force Base, now Malmstrom Armed Forces Base. It was just before noon, and he had already been up for hours. At 8:30am, he had been the first customer at the Base Exchange, flying through the relatively well-stocked women's undergarment section.

Creative scavenging of abandoned towns in the surrounding former states, as well as into Canada, had produced a large supply of various and sundry items. The post-invasion decrease of the population of the Unoccupied States accounted for part of the surplus. Additionally, various cottage industries producing consumables had sprung up among the locals.

Torbin guessed the clerk secretly suspected he was some pervert when he bought a quantity of women's unmentionables, all of very similar sizes. A little prompting of Aleksandra had helped confirm his suspicions based on his, shall we say "sizing experience", and he had sought to buy everything he could. He then grabbed some feminine hygiene products, perfumes, deodorant, makeup, and frilly doodads.

His last stop was at the silk screening and embroidery shop run by his friend Mike, a disabled Gulf War vet. Torbin had provided him with lot of ideas for his products, including "I Kissed a Marine and All I Got

Was This Lousy T-Shirt." He bought three.

Mike used the "you've got to be kidding" look he often gave Torbin.

"Ask me no questions, and I will tell you no lies," Torbin responded.

"Tell me later, over a beer. You're buying," Mike retorted.

Torbin grinned, and then left. He put together three identical packages, then tracked the Russian female officers down at the chow hall, away from their male counter parts. He found the three women, and made his way toward them, wrapped gifts in hand. As he approached, he could tell something was wrong. The three women's bodies were tense and stiff. Then he noticed Aleksandra's black eye, which almost seemed to be getting darker as he looked.

"There you are, Captain." It was Colonel Antonov, walking up to him. His face was flushed, and looked a bit unsteady. As he neared, Torbin smelled cheap booze on his breath and exuding from the pores of his body. He came up and poked Torbin in the chest with his left index finger. "I will decide what my officers receive. You must ask permission before you attempt to buy their attentions and favors. Now, you will take the items back, or I will sell them when we return to Russia."

Torbin grabbed the Colonel's finger and bent it painfully back, sideways and down, all at once, nearly breaking it. He shoved the Colonel back. "Where I come from, *comrade*, you don't beat on women or junior officers just because you're drunk and pissed."

Antonov's face went white. He swore, and grabbed for a small pistol concealed under his fatigue blouse. Torbin saw red, and reached for the concealed Ka-Bar he always carried.

Ichiro seemed to appear from nowhere, and expertly tapped the Colonel's wrist with his sheathed katana. The pistol fell to the tarmac, and Ichiro then struck it like a hockey puck, sending it skittering away. He began to bow and apologize profusely. "Oh, many pardons, Colonel! I am so clumsy sometimes. Here, let me retrieve your pistol."

"*You slanty-eyed little ape!*" Colonel Antonov yelled it before he realized what he had said. A stone-faced Ichiro Yamamoto stopped bowing and stood up, his back straight as an arrow. In what was probably just a second but seemed like minutes as time perception slowed, Torbin saw Ichiro shift his feet and body. At the same time, his right hand grasped the katana's hilt, tensing for a draw.

"*Captain*! What is going on?" General John Reed's command voice cut through the tableau, freezing everyone at once. The General was not a big man, but some people have the ability to immediately take charge using only their voice and demeanor. Luckily for everyone involved, General Reed had this command presence.

Torbin turned toward the General and saluted smartly. "Sir. Just a little misunderstanding, Sir."

He then noticed that Colonel Tanaka was at General Reed's side. Ichiro saw his Colonel also and, before anyone else could speak, spat a couple of rapid sentences in Japanese to Colonel Tanaka. Immediately, Tanaka, stone-faced, stood ramrod straight and impaled Colonel Antonov with his stare.

"At ease! Everyone!"' General Reed commanded. "I do not know what happened, but this is *my* base. We do things *my* way."

He turned toward Antonov and sized him up immediately. "Colonel, you are drunk. That may fly in Russia, but not here. Go sleep it off." Antonov glared at the Russian females, and spat something at them in their native tongue.

"No, Colonel. You will *not* 'take care of them later'," General Reed commanded. "Do you think you are the only one here who speaks Russian? As I said, this is my base. Now, go to your quarters. Immediately."

Colonel Antonov stomped off.

"Captain."

"Sir!"

"Escort these personnel to the hangar. We need to get this show on the road."

"Yes, Sir." Ichiro and the female officers came to attention, saluted the General, about faced and fell in behind Torbin. With near practiced precision, the five officers marched in step to the main hangar. Colonel Tanaka gave a short crisp bow to General Reed. "General, I do not wish to intrude, but there is a matter of honor…"

"Colonel, with all due respect, after the Squids leave, you can have all the duels over honor you want. Hell, I'll probably volunteer to be your second. But right now, I've been tasked to form an alliance out of very limited resources, and since we here in the U.S.A. have a civilian government in control, I do what I'm told. So, sorry, everything else is on hold."

Tanaka took a deep breath then let it out slowly. "I understand, General. Please accept my apologies if Lt. Yamamoto has caused you any difficulties."

"Colonel, Lt. Yamamoto reacted the way any young man with a sense of decency would react. Yes, I saw the black eye. As the 'old fart in charge', I have to keep the men from fighting each other so that they may fight the real enemy. Agreed?"

"Yes, General. I will explain this to Lt. Yamamoto."

"Thank you kindly, Colonel. Now, I think you will find what is in that hangar very interesting…"

When Torbin and his little formation reached the hangar, they found that the rest of the personnel from the previous briefings were already in attendance, their attention focused on what was in the main hangar. No one else had seen the outside action, and Torbin was not about to share the situation with any of the others, including the three Butterbars.

The center of everyone's attention was a tall man hosing down a Tschaaa delta that was propped up and supported by a series of large jack stands. A large drainage tank set up around the aircraft was catching the run off. This was a different craft than the delta in the photos from the briefing the day before. Torbin told the Russians and Ichiro to find some seats in the small set of bleachers that had been set up, and he approached the tall man with the hose.

"Good afternoon, Pappy."

Without taking his eyes from the task at hand, Pappy responded, "Hello, Captain. Looks like a fairly large audience today. I hope everyone is ready to pay attention."

"As prepared as can be expected, Pappy. Are you just about ready to begin the dog and pony show?"

"Just as soon as I wash this thing off one more time. Despite all of our decontamination procedures, I keep getting fluctuating readings of high radiation. I can only surmise that the organically grown skin has pieces of radioactive dust and crap imbedded in the odd spot here and there, and that one more wash down will free up the crap causing the readings. As it is, I would limit direct contact with this bird to about five minutes. I have radiation detectors for everyone to attach to their pockets so we can keep track of their exposure."

"Thanks, Pappy. Let me get them handed out, and I'll introduce you."

Five minutes later, exposure strips handed out, Torbin began.

"Ladies and gentlemen, if I may have your attention. The tall man with the hose and salt and pepper hair is Peter 'Pappy' Gunn. Gunn is a former Army Chief Warrant Officer, who told our elected officials that he would not be re-drafted into the military when they tried to about five years ago. However, he hinted me might be able to convince him to work as a civilian consultant, as long as we keep him supplied with enough cigars to chew on and enough cold beer to drink." There was some light laughter. "Wisely, Madam President agreed, and he is here with us today, all six foot six of him."

"Oh, and for you history buffs out there, our 'Pappy' is related to another famous 'Pappy' Gunn of World War Two fame. That Pappy became famous for cobbling together various weapon systems to use on our aircraft in the Southwest Pacific, back when Japan and the U.S. were at war. I bet you that if we had known the Squids were nearing our neighborhood, the war would have ended real quick."

Torbin continued. "Be that as it may, our Pappy Gunn is carrying on a proud tradition of figuring out all things weapon related. He will therefore be able to go into much more detail concerning the threats and weapons I mentioned yesterday. Please pay attention. Pappy has a wealth of information to pass on in a limited amount of time. Pappy."

Pappy Gunn walked to the front of the bleachers, all six feet, six inches of him. Tall and lanky, he had a reputation of somehow twisting and wrapping his frame into and around the piece of equipment he was examining.

Perhaps that was part of the secret way he always managed to figure out to some degree or another how something worked.

"Afternoon. I know the good Captain gave you some information on who—or what— we are facing in this conflict. Here, in this hangar, I hope to pass on some more details on weapons and threats of the Squids. Hopefully you will also share some information with me. Every little bit helps, and even after six years of fighting with an enemy that has little concept of information security, there is still a lot to learn."

He turned and walked back toward the delta. "We obtained this little gem just two weeks ago. A survivalist from Idaho walked all the way from near the Washington-Idaho border to tell us about it. He is in the hospital being treated for radiation exposure, as he was in and around this delta prior to decontamination, as well as the Hanford mega explosion."

Pappy pointed to the starboard side. "This delta was apparently in the air when Hanford blew, and all this area here took some blast energy that fried the right ramjet and singed that area forward."

"The Squid pilot must have been a hotshot as he found a long stretch of highway in southwest Idaho and landed this bird." He pointed to the three large wheels, one in the nose, and one projecting from each wing.

"This landing gear–and I use that term loosely–is basically wheels that were added as an apparent afterthought. They only have large coil springs to absorb landing shock, and the brakes are comparable to a 1955 Chevy sedan. The Squid must have been good to keep from bouncing off the road into the ditch. This craft was clearly designed to operate from space and return to a low orbit station."

Pappy continued. "The Squid was nowhere to be found, so we assume a Falcon picked him up. How much radiation the body absorbed is hard to say, but since the geiger counters were having fits when we found the delta, there is a good chance he is buried in a lead box somewhere, if the Squids even bury their dead."

"The radioactivity is the reason, we believe, no one tried to salvage it. We know the Squids are sensitive about all types of contamination and poisoning, as they are afraid their young will be affected. The original plague that killed off much of their meat supply, their primary food, must have been devastating. The Squids left everything behind. We found in the craft the following."

Pappy motioned to an airman in a decontamination suit to wheel a cart close enough to the bleachers for the personnel to see. Pappy used a laser pointer to help in the examination of the equipment mounted on display boards.

"This medieval-looking thing is their equivalent of a crescent shaped sword or ax. See the thin wire or cable strung between the ends of the crescent? That is a monofilament, a monomolecular strand of condensed material that has the capability of slicing through all known metals when enough force is applied to it. We have one good report of a robocop using one to slice off the barrel of an

Abrams main tank gun. The curved blade on the other end of the four foot shaft has a point on it made from a tungsten alloy. Makes a dandy can opener on soft skinned vehicles."

Ichiro raised his hand. "Mr. Gunn. I have seen a cruder version of that, with a sharp blade suspended in place of the cutting strand."

Pappy shot him a quizzical look. "Oh really? What was the situation?"

"Young Tschaaa warriors are raiding our shores, coming from the sea, looking for individual combat."

"That's very interesting. I would like some more details when you get a chance."

"Hai! Of course, sir."

Pappy continued. "A large multi-charge pulse rifle. We usually see these in the hands of robocops, but, at least in the early days of the Invasion, the Squids seemed to have carried them also. They can penetrate the side armor of a tank at close range."

He then pointed out a long projectile, just under two meters long. "The three inch missile, launched from the delta, although some multiple ground mounts were seen at the end of organized resistance. The missile is guided by an organic based artificial intelligence seeker, which bore sights on anything moving. Once it gets locked on, the Rube Goldberg-looking mass of little holes–actually maneuver rockets openings–twists and turns that thing around like it was fluid. The warhead is equivalent to our old three-inch explosive shell, overkill on a jet fighter, somewhat effective on ground targets. Usually only one or two mounted per delta."

Pappy moved a bit closer to the aircraft itself. He used the laser pointer to outline the salient features of the craft. "That long thin nose contains a high energy plasma pulse weapon, the science of which we are just now figuring out. It can blast through a tank's armor at a thousand meters, no sweat. At longer ranges, even though the pulse or beam dissipates in atmosphere, it still contains enough oomph to fry electronic guidance and radio systems. Humans in the open are dead."

"The only good thing about this for us is that the amount of energy or charge for this weapon seems to be limited. We have reports of deltas using it at full power twice in one mission, no more."

"These two barrel-shaped protrusions near each side of the

cockpit are just that, barrels. These are the downsized version of electromagnetic rail guns, which fire 32mm long dart-like projectiles at two thousand meters a second. The kinetic energy is sufficient to blast most of what it hits. They also have an organic-based AI system that tracks motion, and small retractable maneuver fins that allow them to twist and turn after the target. When the velocity drops at very long ranges, there is still a small explosive charge in the warhead that goes off a second after impact. It's rather anemic, but can blow the head off an unprotected human, hole a thin vehicle body, and shatter cockpit glass."

"They are fired in pairs, with only ten in a drum per gun. No spray and pray for Squids, everything is based on guidance."

Pappy then pointed to openings near the cockpit. "As was mentioned before, two scramjet type engines that can propel the delta to at least Mach 3.5 by our radar track, but examination of the engines show a potential of Mach 5 or more. The rear nozzles can be tilted five degrees in any direction, aiding in maneuvering. The large center engine is a type of gravity or magnetic pulse engine, which is used to kick the delta into outer space, or accelerate from zero to five hundred knots in a second from a standing start. We are still trying to figure it out. The cockpit is a self-contained unit that is filled with heated water when a Squid flies, so the cushioning effect plus Squid body design means high-G, instantaneous maneuvers have little effect on them. The cockpit *is* the G suit. A small crude oxygen tank is used to keep the water oxygenated for the Squids. Their gills work well enough that they do not need a separate pressurized air system."

Pappy Gunn faced his audience.

"The delta, like most Squid machines, is some ninety percent organic in nature. This means, the outer shell is grown like a crustacean's mantle. This system makes for a very tough piece of equipment, like metal armor in its capabilities. We shape metal and ceramics to make our equipment, the Squids can grow theirs, then have metal and ceramic add-ons as needed. Small low orbit maneuver rockets are embedded in the organic body after the delta is grown. All of these characteristics result in an air and limited spacecraft built for hit and run strikes from low orbit. They land on Earth only rarely, or in this case, because the Squid flew too close to a nuclear blast."

"We have yet to recover a Falcon. We do have some jim dandy

news film of one being rammed by one of our fighters and going in."

Not again, Torbin thought. He tried to steel himself for watching the news footage once more. He should be used to it by now. But when a large television monitor was wheeled in front of the assembled personnel, and the footage began to play, Torbin stood up abruptly and walked to the latrine. He splashed his face with cold water, and stood by the sink, waiting. He had seen a lot of people die. But he would not watch his brother William die, over and over again on film. Not for anything or anyone. He waited while Pappy finished covering what was shown on the news footage, knowing it was over when one of the Japanese officers entered the latrine. He started to exit and almost ran over Ichiro.

"Torbin-San. Are you well?"

"As well as can be expected, given the circumstances."

He continued walking outside the hangar. He closed his eyes and let the sun warm his face, while taking slow, deep breaths. He felt a touch on his arm, and opened his eyes to see Aleksandra Smirnov, blackened eye and all, standing near him.

"You knew the pilot in that news footage, the one that rammed the Falcon."

Torbin took another breath and let it out slowly. "Yes, Captain, I knew him. Hell, Ma'am, I grew up with him! That was my brother, William." Aleksandra silently stood by his side. "He went the officer's route and joined the Air Force, I guess to show his Jarhead year older brother that he was better at something. And after all the shit I went through, the action I saw before he even got his wings, he goes and gets himself killed as a hero."

He then noticed Ichiro was also standing nearby. "Torbin-san, all Japanese pilots have heard about the American who took down the three alien craft from stories told by surviving American servicemen in Japan. But, we have never seen the recording before. Some believed maybe it was an exaggeration. Now, we know it was not."

"No, Ichiro, it happened. A day doesn't go by that I wish it was a myth, an exaggeration, and William will magically appear so that I can buy him a drink. But that's not going to happen."

Torbin took one more breath, and then turned to walk back into the hangar to complete the briefings. "Well, like my Grandpa used to say, daylight's a-wastin'. Shall we finish this?"

As they re-entered the hangar, Ichiro said a little prayer to himself, and thought what an honor it was to have met Torbin Bender. He prayed that his ancestors would help keep his new friend safe. He tightly gripped his family sword, the hard reality of the cold metal giving him a measure of comfort in an uncertain world.

It had been long day for the General. Another in a line of long days. He sat at his desk, wondering if he would ever have a "normal" day again. Then he realized he was having trouble remembering what a normal day was like. Master Sergeant Johansson, late of the Minnesota National Guard, knocked on his door jam, stuck his head in and announced, "Captain Bender here as requested, Sir."

"Good. Send him in, please."

Torbin marched in, saluted at attention. "Reporting as ordered, Sir."

"Thank you. Please, have a seat, Captain."

"Sergeant Johansson," the General called out. "Go ahead and take off. Please shut the door when you leave."

"Sir, I could stay, I have..."

"Sergeant, did I stutter?"

"No Sir. Have a nice night, Sir." After he heard the outer door shut, General Reed addressed Torbin.

"Relax, dammit. That's an order." He reached into his desk, and pulled out an unopened bottle of twelve year old scotch. He then stood up, glared at Torbin when he started to stand, and walked over to his small refrigerator.

"I guess that jerry-rigging the Sergeant did was good. It's making ice again." General Reed put ice cubes into two glasses, and walked back to his desk, setting one glass in front of Torbin. With practiced ease, he opened the bottle of scotch, and poured a good two ounces in each glass.

"This is single malt scotch. I never thought I would be pouring it for and sharing it with a mustang Jarhead Captain, but here we are."

"I never thought I'd be sharing twelve year old scotch with an Air Force Puke General. No offense meant, Sir."

General Reed chuckled. "None taken, Torbin."

They sat in silence for a few moments, sipping and enjoying the scotch.

General Reed reached into the left hand drawer of his desk and pulled out a double picture frame. He set it on the desk so Torbin could see it.

"Torbin, how long have we known each other?

"Almost five years, General."

"Ever seen these photos before?"

"No, Sir, I haven't."

"That is my wife, Ivana. Those are my two boys, Matt and Mark. She's the reason I speak Russian."

Torbin looked at the photo. The woman was a knockout with dark hair, a model's body and smoldering eyes. "You wife is beautiful, and your sons are handsome boys."

"Yes, they are. They *were*. I assume they are dead, as she was visiting relatives in Russia, outside Moscow, when the Squids hit us."

He took a large slug of his scotch, then refilled both glasses.

"I met her when I was an Air Force attaché at the embassy in Moscow. I was a young Light Colonel, never married, fast burner. I had been an A-10 driver, then a Special Ops pilot when I wrangled the Moscow assignment as part of an intelligence gathering effort. I wanted some career broadening and I wanted General's stars."

General Reed took another drink. "I met Ivana at some embassy function and fell madly in love. She was an interpreter, spoke better English than I did, and taught me Russian. I was told that marrying a Russian national, thanks to Putin and company, was probably not a good career move. But she was literally, no bullshit, my first and only great love."

"So, I set my horizons lower, married her, and got her to the U.S.

She became a citizen while pregnant. We had our sons, one after the other, and were talking about a daughter. I was going to retire and work for some think tank, as I had made some good contacts over the years. I managed to make Full Bird, was looking for a Reserve assignment so I could bow out gracefully."

He drank again. "Then, the fucking Squids showed up. Now, I have three stars, going on four, no family, and a near impossible mission."

He looked directly at Torbin. "This is it. I got this assignment because I speak Russian, can get things done, follow orders, and–if I do say so myself–I am one motivated individual. Torbin, if this fails, we putter along for a few decades, maybe a century. We revert back to a pre-industrial society, and all of 'this' becomes the stuff of legends.

That is, if the Squids just don't decide to hunt us all down. If we succeed and can really hurt the Squids, find some way to start wiping them out, the survivors will probably leave. Or, if we believe our friend the Director, they will accept us as equals or the top of the food chain again."

He paused for a moment, in reflection. "Or, we die trying. It isn't the worst thing that can happen. Existing as an intelligent side of beef, waiting for our slaughter, *that's* hell."

Torbin waited for the General to finish, then he asked, "General, why aren't you a Marine?"

General Reed laughed. "Funny you should ask that. My father told me he would be proud of me if I chose the military as a career. But, that he would kick my ass around the block if I joined the Marines."

"Why, Sir?"

"My Grandfather had been at Iwo Jima. He told my Dad stories that had a lasting impression on him about charging up the beach. My Dad said he did not raise a son to be cannon fodder." They sat and drank for a while longer. Finally, the General said, "Thank you, Captain, for the excellent company. Now, I believe it is time to turn in for the evening."

"Thank you, Sir, for the excellent scotch." Torbin rose, saluted. "General, I don't consider myself cannon fodder. But I will charge up a beach for you, for all the humans left. Just say the word, Sir."

General Reed looked at him. "I know you would, son. That is why you're here."

"Now, hit the rack, Captain. We have another busy day tomorrow."

"Aye aye, Sir." Torbin turned and left. General Reed sat at his desk for a few minutes, deep in thought. He then put his wife and children's picture away, finished his drink, and stashed the bottle.

He wondered again what a normal day would be like.

CHAPTER 9

El Segundo: "He is here, my Sire and Lord." Lord Neptune. "Good. Ensure the Director is brought here most haste. I have much to discuss with my most favored human."

—Excerpts from the *Literary Works of Royal Princess Akiko,* Free Japan Royal Family. Transcription of translated intercepted communications between Tschaaa Lord Neptune, Lord over North America, and his Tschaaa Second in Command, known as El Segundo.

KEY WEST, FLORIDA

As General Reed was preparing to leave his office, Adam Lloyd was just returning to his. He flopped lengthwise on the well-cushioned sofa. Damn, he felt tired. Maybe he was getting too old, though late thirties had not seemed old at all six years ago. The never-ending possibility of winding up as a cut of meat caused premature aging. "Director, are you back?" It was Mary Lou. She had the morning off, but trooper that she was, she came in and stayed around until he returned. She still had on her office attire of blouse, skirt and high heels.

"Yes, Mary Lou, I am. Finally. Murphy's Law was in full effect today. You can take off– I need to unwind and make some notes from my meeting with Our Lordship. But first, please come here." He stood up as she approached, and gently grabbing her shoulders, kissed her softly. He let her go. "Thanks for caring and checking on me."

Mary Lou smiled. "Any time, Adam."

Just then he heard a knock from the Mary Lou's office and heard, "Hey Boss, are you back?" It was Kathy.

Mary Lou started to say something, but Adam responded first.

"Yes Kathy, come in for a moment." Mary Lou immediately tensed up, and stepped back. Adam thought for a moment that she was almost getting into a self-defense stance. He would have to keep an eye on this "relationship" between her and Kathy. Kathy entered and shot Mary Lou a look of challenge before flashing her signature smile at Adam.

"Just wanted you to know, Boss. Major Grant tried to work my butt off, but I survived, and loved every minute of it."

Adam smiled. "I told you that you would do just fine."

"Well, thanks for the chance, Boss. I can tell you've had a long day, so I guess I will see you later. Goodnight, Boss. Goodnight, Mary Lou."

"Goodnight, Kathy," Mary Lou replied with a little too much syrup in her voice.

"Sleep tight, Kathy," Adam said. Kathy winked at him, turned, and slinked away.

Adam caught Mary Lou staring at Kathy's ass as she walked away. "A penny for your thoughts."

"She tries too hard. She wiggles her ass every chance she gets for effect. I don't trust her."

Adam gently put his left hand around her waist. "Hey, who's in charge here?"

"You are, Director."

"Have I done pretty well so far?"

"Adam, this isn't about you, it's..."

"It's about the competition, isn't it? Kathy isn't your biggest competitor, my work is. I care about you, and I'm still very attracted to you. But in the end, I still care about the mission most of all. I am still focused on what needs to be done, and no new sexual object–no matter how distracting you think she is–is going to change that."

Mary Lou blushed a little. "I'm sorry, Director."

"No need to apologize. Oh, and Adam, not the Director, will be in bed later on. I expect you to be there also. The sooner I can finish here, the sooner I will be there."

Mary Lou gave him a bit of an impish smile, and kissed his cheek. "See you later." She departed for the attached suite.

Adam sighed. Things seemed more complicated. Starting with the Professor's wife, continuing with his trip to meet their Lord, today had been one pain in the ass after the other.

The Chief had given him a ride to the small boat dock at the most southwestern point of Key West. Adam rode in the ex-U.S. Postal Service four cylinder Jeep in the left seat, steering wheel on the right. The Chief had the 50 caliber Sharps rifle he had recovered during his last scavenger trip, rounding up the most recent new human arrivals. After dropping off Adam, he was headed to the firing range to test out some Sharps reloads and plink a few practice rounds with his .45 automatic. They pulled up to the dock, and Adam got out, taking his briefcase and satchel from behind his seat.

For the umpteenth time, the Chief had asked, "Need me to go along, Boss?"

"No, Chief. Our Lordship still only wants one human at a time talking to him. If I get whacked someday, you'll get the chance to tell him the news. And then you get to do that until you get whacked."

"Well, Boss, I guess I'd better keep you breathing, because I have no desire to meet the lead Squid by myself."

"I guess that means I'm the one stuck for the time being, then."

The Chief put the Jeep in gear. "Be careful Boss. I'm not there to hold your hand."

"Loud and clear, Chief. I'll ping you on the radiophone when I head back. Have fun shootin'."

"Always, Boss. Always." With that, Chief drove off, leaving the Director to the business at hand. Adam carried his satchel and briefcase to the open fisherman tied up at the dock. The boat was supposed to be maintained by the Conch Republic as a symbol of their connection to the base. But one look at the boat and Adam knew that someone was either getting lazy or purposefully ignoring maintenance.

He opened his satchel again, checking the contents. It contained two bologna sandwiches, a greenhouse apple, two Conch Republic near beers, and a bag of stale pretzels (for seasickness nausea), just in case he became stranded. He'd eaten a leftover cookie and a couple of soda crackers, and drank a full glass of purified water before leaving, just enough salt and water to ward off dehydration or other heat-related problems.

Also in the satchel was a sawed off twelve gauge with two black powder rock salt loads. In a small shoulder holster he wore a five shot replica of a .31 caliber Colt Baby Dragoon pistol, also loaded by the Chief with five black powder loads.

The black powder was to create enough fire and brimstone to scare off any wandering Squid juvenile or early teen who felt a need to prove themselves with a human in a boat. The Tschaaa did not like sulphur and flame coming in their general direction, despite their transition to land, so it was used to scare off the young. Their early development in the ocean of their world was sans fire, other than underwater volcanic activity. Therefore, like most wet-skinned species, they did not like sources of heat too close. Despite their evolutionary development they kept some old intrinsic fear from their days as a more primitive species. The shot and rock salt was also effective for deterring anyone who might want to engage in some low level piracy.

Adam started up the open fisherman and soon realized just how rough the twin engines were running. He swore, and pinged up the Chief on his radiophone.

"Yeah, Boss."

"Chief, this so-called boat may make it there and but not back. I don't have the time to screw around, so if you don't hear from me in about five hours, send somebody out toward the Marquesas Keys looking for me. Otherwise, you're stuck with my job."

"Will do, Boss. I'll light a fire under the Admiral's ass as well. They get enough stuff from us that keeping the agreement about the boat should be a given."

"Roger that. See you later, Chief." The boat untied, Adam headed out with all the due speed he could muster. Marquesas Keys was at one time a series of tiny islands and reefs in a circle in a national wildlife refuge almost due west of Key West. Just a tad under twenty statute miles away, it was now a huge circular domed shaped complex of several stories, mostly underwater. It was nicknamed Squidville, as humans had seen few Tschaaa structures up until its building. Around it and the Dry Tortugas were a series of large Tschaaa breeding areas, crèches or beds in and near the many local reef structures. The domed complex itself housed Tschaaa versions of workshops, construction factories, laboratories, development centers as well as landing berths for both air and sea craft.

Here resided their Lordship, named by himself in homage to

human mythology as Lord Neptune, king and ruler of the great seas.

He had a great sense of humor, especially for the absurd. Adam wished he could pronounce his given Tschaaa name, but Lordship "Neptune" had insisted, stating, "Do not waste your time. Our translators work fine translating our voices to human speech. Your attempts to speak our language would just make us laugh so hard we would get nothing done."

Adam believed him. The one thing the Lordship had been from day one in their relationship was honest to a fault, no matter how cruel the truth can be at times.

Adam managed to make the trip in just under an hour, with the twin outboards badly overheating the last mile. He nursed the open fisherman up to the entrance dock he always used, and managed to get it shut down and tied off before the engines seized. Waiting for him was a young adult Squid Adam had named El Segundo, after a character in a western movie he had seen years ago. Adam was probably one of the few humans who had learned to tell Squids apart fairly accurately.

El Segundo had been meeting him for almost a year now, and had taken the human's nickname as his own. The Tschaaa wore no translator, just giving him a "welcome" sign with his two "social tentacles" that Tschaaa used in greeting. Since these two appendages were also the ones used for sexual intercourse/primary impregnation, Adam often mused what humankind would have been like if men waved their genitalia at each other as a form of "welcome". Then again, humans were far more concerned with sex and their sexuality, as they were far more driven by their perpetual base urges.

Humankind's attempts to deal through social mores with their three sixty-five day a year sexual "season" was a constant source of wonderment and mirth to the Lord Neptune. The Lordship believed the limited time that male and female Tschaaa were 'in the mood' for sexual relations gave them more time to deal with more intellectual pursuits. After all, they did achieve interstellar flight before mankind.

Adam stashed the sawed off twelve gauge under the boat seat, along with his small pistol. He kept a cheap but sharp knife on his hip, and brought the satchel and briefcase. He walked along the walkway constructed for items the Squids preferred to keep fairly dry, while El Segundo swam alongside. The Tschaaa could travel on land, but were so much more efficient in the ocean that there was where many preferred to remain. The fact that Earth's gravitational pull was about five percent more than their home world gave them another reason to prefer water locomotion as well.

He walked through the entrance way into what at one time would have been through the Keys' series of small land masses, but now was directly into a huge dome, ninety percent of it under water. The dome, "Squidville" to the humans, now covered almost all the above water reefs, mangroves and spits of the Marquesas Keys Refuge. How many stories were below sea level, Adam was unsure, but it was at least several. It was a good fifteen minute walk to the doorway into the Lordship's throne room and work area. Once he reached the doorway, he was on his own.

Adam walked slowly up to the Tschaaa Lord's receiving area. In a sudden flash of light, a large image was projected on the nearby curved wall. He heard a loud booming human voice.

"*I am the great and powerful Oz. Do not arouse the wrath of the great and powerful Oz.*" And there was Dorothy and company projected on the wall. Shit. He'd been watching old movies again. Lord Neptune loved to view, study, and just enjoy all forms of human pre-Invasion mass media. Tschaaa films, books, other informational media often resembled National Geographic travelogues and science tapes, with large historical musical dramas, similar to human operas, relating some of the greatest incidents in Tschaaa history. Fiction, other than the young's versions of Grimm's fairy tales and Aesop's fables (intended to instruct also) did not exist.

Making up stories for 'fun' was seen as a waste of time or mental aberration, which was why, had His Lordship not been so much more advanced than the other Tschaaa in his ability to handle Earth and its humans, he probably would have been sent to the Tschaaa form of a mental hospital.

Tschaaa did enjoy jokes and humor, but most of it was along the line of slapstick, practical jokes, and the occasional "your mama is so fat" street insults, usually by adolescents and to other adolescents. Adam just knew that if the Tschaaa had such a thing, His Lordship would have been a combination standup comedian and writer for situation comedies, and be very successful.

His Lordship was reclining in a large, modified hot tub. Though amphibious, the Tschaaa still preferred their original liquid environment. He was waving his social tentacles in signs of complete mirth and laughter. Adam knew he was also blowing bubbles from his gill slits, a sign of pure belly laughter. Adam approached him, smiling; palms open toward him in a sign of mirth also.

"Ah, Director! My favorite human. I see you noticed my new entrance images. I found that film of yours just the other day. Such a prime example of human fantasy."

The translator produced a human voice that reminded Adam of a combination of Shakespearean-trained actors from the London stage. Adam knew that Lord Neptune never did anything by chance, and probably spent many hours coming up with the right Lord voice. To human ears, Tschaaa speech itself sounded like a combination of porpoise clicks, sperm whale tones and hissing. Although reproducible with computer enhanced technology, human vocal chords were not designed for that type of communication, and there were a few sounds above and below the frequencies that human ears could not distinguish. As had been proven in the study of whales, certain of these frequencies and tones in ocean water could be heard for miles, resulting in excellent long range communication. Thus, when the Tschaaa adolescents and young left their Crèche birth areas to roam the oceans as part of growing up, were never really out of earshot of adults.

Adam chuckled. "Yes, your Lordship, *The Wizard of Oz* is a movie classic. Tell me, are you thinking of changing your 'human name' to The Wizard?"

The Tschaaa Lord laughed again. "No, my Director. Although I am great and powerful, I definitely have no need to hide behind a curtain.

Now, human, come closer and have a seat in the chair provided. I have much information to impart to you, and I imagine you have some updates for me."

"Yes, Sir. But first, I have something you will like." Adam reached into the satchel and produced a couple large stalks of sugar cane.

Tschaaa eyes were very large, and extremely sensitive. Lord Neptune knew what Adam was removing from his satchel before it was completely in view. "Ah. Some more of that delicious sweet cane. Please, hand it to me."

His Lordship reached out a social tentacle to Adam and gently took the sugar cane from Adams proffered hand. He placed one stalk up, out of the hot tub, and then gently fed the other into his mouth, hidden from view by facial tentacles. "If for no other reason than this delicious cane, I think I have convinced the greater majority of my fellow Lords that humans can be of greater service than just sources of meat."

"You could not grow sugar cane yourself?"

"Outside of the natural environment, it would probably not be the same. We can grow many things in our organic tanks and vats, but the results are never as good as those things produced naturally. It is also why we never grew any Tschaaa young in the tanks, not to mention it would seem... perverted I think is a good word. The grays, some bipedal warriors, those who you call front men, are the only higher life forms we have attempted. We eventually found or produced enough breeding pairs to result in natural growth of the cyborg warriors–robocops you call them–and other human relations, as natural growth produces a much better product."

"The same with your original 'meat' creatures?"

"Yes, Director. When the Plague hit, in order for growth in the tanks and vats, we eventually produced sufficient non affected sperm and eggs of our meat creatures to start producing fresh meat. The results, though edible in the strictest sense, were very... disappointing. This led to the Great Voyage here."

"Now, Director, onto other matters. How did your recent arrivals turn out?"

"Fine, Lordship. We now have over sixty-six hundred humans on base. And, I located Professor Fassbinder, that scientist I told you about."

"Excellent! I expect him on the platform when your new spaceplane flies. Hopefully, he can discover the secrets of those two saucers." Lord Neptune slowly chewed on the sugar cane. "Did you also obtain that blonde female you were looking for?"

Once again, he had no secrets from His Lordship.

"Yes sir, I did. She will be one of our primary 'faces' representing our human government in our mass media. I hope she will assist us in convincing the majority of humans that we, and by extrapolation you, as the face of the Tschaaa, are not bogeymen. The days of widespread harvesting is over and that we have a chance to become junior partners in your interstellar civilization."

"Again, excellent. Of course, being sexually desirable to you helps also, yes?"

Adam smiled. "You know me too well, Your Lordship."

Lord Neptune laughed. "Your species' constant sexuality is a source of mirth and wonderment to us. It is a mystery to the Tschaaa that you obtained the level advancement that you did, with you having constant sexual relations, or at least desires of such."

"Well, some of our human scientists believe that competition among us for mates actually spurred us to do great things."

"Like war on your own kind, Director?"

Adam sighed. "Unfortunately, some of our best advancements were sped along by warfare."

Lord Neptune's two social tentacles went high up in the air, denoting surprise or incredulous belief. "But you killed many of your own young."

"Yes sir, that too."

His Lordship was still and silent. Then he spoke. "Hopefully, our patronage will affect your behavior for the better."

"We can only hope, sir."

"Well, enough of that. Come, Director. Look at what I have been doing."

Lord Neptune slid out of the hot tub, and began to slither along the walkway like the oversized cephalopod that he was. He did not waste energy by rising up on his eight arms, to walk almost crablike, that Tschaaa could do if they were in a hurry. As always, he reminded Adam of a large, many legged bearlike creature, due to his size and weight. Even slithering, the Tschaaa could move quite fast, and Adam had to walk quickly to keep up.

The human and the alien were soon looking at a large bay where a Falcon was being worked on by Tschaaa grays.

"I obtained this from Europe. The Tschaaa Lord there is too lazy to repair it. I took it off his hands, as you humans would phrase it. Unfortunately, many of my fellow Lords have little foresight, have lost much of their drive to plan, to create. Too many elder Tschaaa are content to stuff their stomachs with the very available meat, with little concern of how it was harvested, who provided it."

This was a complaint that Adam had heard on many occasions.

Adam knew that if not for His Lordship, things would have been very different. The Tschaaa had no history of long term organized warfare among their species. They fought with other species on their home world for survival during their evolutionary climb up the development ladder. No other species had the level of intellectual development, so none had developed advanced tools or weapons. According to his Lordship, at some time lost in myth and history, the Tschaaa had evolved into an amphibious species, and expanded onto land. That had led to a great evolutionary change in diet, when the Tschaaa had discovered the species of meat primates.

Something about the difference in this protein, compared to the fish and sea creatures the Tschaaa had eaten for millennia, led to a change in eating habits, and thus in culture. Soon, the dark meat primates were the main source of protein rich sustenance of the Tschaaa breeders and young.

Despite their advanced development in all things organic and its uses, in all forms of biology and genetics, no Tschaaa scientist had ever bothered to see if the chemistry and the hormones in the primate meat may have had an effect on Tschaaa morphology and biology. Did the type of protein help give a boost to Tschaaa intellectual development? Adam thought it was fascinating that, just at the time the dark meat became available, the Tschaaa took a huge leap in evolutionary development. They became more organized, the size of Crèches increased, and they began to cooperate on a global scale.

Adam believed it was a definite cause and effect scenario. The fact that Tschaaa intellect suffered during the time the primate meat was very limited in quantity and quality was another strong indication.

"Come, my Director, I have some other developments to show you."

Adam followed him over to a table where a three foot object was covered by a tarp.

"Please, have a look " His Lordship said.

Adam removed the tarp. Underneath was a slab-sided object that was clearly a shoulder fired weapon. Adam looked at an 8x10 piece of paper covered in plastic that was attached with a large rubber band to the weapon. He read the clearly human printing. The author had excellent calligraphy. The document stated that the shoulder weapon was a downsized version of the electromagnetic rail guns mounted on the deltas. With a loaded magazine of forty fifty grain long nail-shaped hardened steel projectiles with tiny pop out fins for stabilization, total weapon weight was just less than twenty pounds. The projectiles were fired at a velocity of sixteen hundred meters per second, give or take a few, which caused devastating effects to soft targets down range. Recharging of the electromagnetic battery could be accomplished with a recessed hand crank, a photoelectric cell (more efficient than human photoelectric cells), or by plugging a pull-out charging cord into a standard 110 outlet.

"Please, Director, try it out on the piece of metal taken from one of your garbage dumpsters."

The target was some fifty meters away and already had been used for target practice, judging by the holes in it. The weapon had a pistol grip at the rear part, containing the magazine of .17 caliber ammunition. There was a large vertical handgrip set some six inches back from the apparent muzzle. Despite its bulk and weight, the basic super rifle was well balance and easy to manipulate. After following the directions to insure it was loaded and chambered, he mounted it to his cheek. A holographic sight was automatically projected in his line of sight. All he had to do was put the red dot on the center of the target and squeeze the trigger. He felt no recoil, just heard a supersonic crack from the high velocity round following a buzzing sound from the action. Even from fifty meters, Adam could see the near instantaneous impact flash. The hole produced was larger than the .17 caliber projectile. Adam looked down at the weapon.

"A human designed this."

His Lordship signed amusement. "Once again, my Director, you demonstrate your superior intellect."

"Now, watch what was designed to use it."

Adam felt rather than heard the Tschaaa verbal command given in a frequency beyond his hearing range. From the shadows came a six and a half foot figure. The biped looked like a human soldier, combat uniform and all, wearing a gas mask. As it walked up and stopped some six feet from the Tschaaa Lord, Adam saw that the figure was not wearing a uniform. Rather, the organic skin was molded into the shape of human attire, gas masked face and all.

Lord Neptune's octopus camouflage abilities demonstrated

themselves when his flesh began to automatically try to match the coloration of the approaching biped due to his excitement. "This soldier, as I call him, was developed at my behest by a human mated pair on Platform One. Another mated pair developed your shoulder weapon. The humans in space have produced great dividends for me. I am looking for more when others are sent up in two months in your spaceplane."

His Lordship signed for the soldier to leave. "They have the mental capacity of about a five year old human. They are designed for basic problem solving, but specialized for following orders. In addition to combat, they can also perform more mundane everyday functions. They will supplement the limited supply of grays and cyborgs. So far, one hundred have been produced in the growth vats. Now, if I can just convince my unimaginative fellow Lords to use them, my satisfaction will be complete."

He motioned Adam to follow him to the Tschaaa equivalent of a lounge. As they moved, His Lordship continued.

"I have also repaired five deltas, something no one else is doing. They are set up for ground launch using what humans call JATO rockets. Three are at Cape Canaveral, one here, one in the large Baja California Complex."

The Gulf of California had been literally closed off and connected from shore to shore in one huge complex, including a large breeding area and manufacturing section. Every other major port city up and down both former United States coasts and the Gulf of Mexico had some form of a Tschaaa complex. However, since the Marquesas Keys were His Lordship's base of operations, it had the most developed equipment and facilities, despite the two mile average diameter.

They arrived at the lounge, and His Lordship deftly obtained a drink for each of them from a refrigeration unit. His had a long tube, so that he could drink it with his mouth concealed by his face tentacles. Adam knew there were some teeth structures under there that made humans nervous. The Director's drink was a bottle of Conch Brew. The Tschaaa Lord clinked his container against Adam's bottle. "A toast to much more useful collaboration between Tschaaa and humans."

"I'll drink to that," was Adam's reply.

They each drank, the Tschaaa Lord reclining in the Tschaaa version of a lounge seat, Adam in a human chair.

"Director, I have often wished, despite what we have accomplished, that I had the power to travel back in time, to before the Plague, where things were simpler."

"Well your Lordship, there is an ancient Chinese curse–'may you live in interesting times'."

The Tschaaa Lord laughed, blowing bubbles thru his gill slits. "That fits the situation perfectly. In addition to dealing with stagnant elders, and the reduced ability of our tanks to produce viable grays and biped cyborg warriors due to worn out DNA, now I must deal with my own young Tschaaa demanding to go help the Asian Tschaaa Lord in his Japan 'operations'."

Adam looked at him quizzically. "You mean, harvesting operations?"

"No. Apparently, the young Tschaaa warriors are conducting what you humans term as 'raids' on the coasts of Japan, fighting with traditional blade weapons, as well as incursions by deltas, looking for aerial conflict. It provides thrilling experiences they claim they cannot have anywhere else." Lord Neptune gave the Tschaaa equivalent of a sigh. "I guess it could be worse. Too many Tschaaa had been satisfied with sitting around, getting fat on the over-abundance of food. At least they wish to do something.

"I have been given only limited resources for the production of replacement equipment. The new weapon I showed you, I can produce only one a day. I am repairing deltas in Baja California, after having produced only sixty new ones in the last six years. Using modified humans, we have created two hundred fifty successful new cyborgs since the invasion. Though superior in nature, these do not replace losses. The new soldiers, I can produce one a week after the initial production order. All because the stagnant Elders have no foresight."

The Tschaaa had no history or concept of long term wars or combat operations. Thus, the idea of a war production plan was unknown to them. It had taken Lord Neptune sixty years of wheedling, nagging, politicking, even actions nearing deception to produce the equipment for the initial invasion. This was managed with the reports from scouts and over sixty years of radio/television transmissions providing specific information on the threat humans could provide to any invader. The idea of real-time 'replacement equipment' was not a concept they had ever had to deal with. Things were used up, and then maybe a replacement was grown or produced, at a slow pace. Before the Plague, slow and steady won the race.

Afterward, it was still a challenge to convince the older Tschaaa to adopt new ways of doing things. Even competition for position in society had been stratified one way for so long that there was only so much upward mobility. Despite all this inertia, His Lordship had created a revolution, a firestorm based on his will alone. He had designed and implemented the organized, long-term invasion and harvesting plan, replacing the disorganized raiding plan originally agreed upon. Everything now flowed from His Lordship's concepts and ideas, no matter how slowly.

"Now, my Director, I must inform you of two very important matters." He took another sip from his drink. "Your amateur astronomers must have mentioned that our large Crèche ships are moving."

"Yes sir. Last week." Adam also had some professional people, with security, working at the McDonald Observatory in West Texas, but he did not advertise that fact. It was an island in a sea off a Feral area.

"Well, the mile-long Crèche Ships are moving to set up a dive into the gravity well of the sun to obtain a slingshot launch outside the solar system. This is to occur by the ten year mark in Earth years."

Adam fell silent for a moment. "So it is true. You plan to leave."

The Tschaaa Lord paused. "Only thirty percent of the Tschaaa, fifty percent of the grays and robocops, and one percent of the lizards are leaving. And, the ship of my Crèche will stay on the dark side of Earth's moon."

Adam looked at him. "So the Tschaaa will be here for the long haul."

"Yes, Director Adam, Earth's oceans have become our new home."

Adam sat silently for a full minute. He knew he must choose his words wisely. "This situation is going to cause a lot of fear when it gets out. Humankind has always kept a hope in the back of each person's mind that the Earth would be under human control again, at least during the next lifetime. It was a light at the end of a tunnel."

Lord Neptune signed regret and compassion with his tentacles.

"I hope that you can help convince the rest of humanity that it is in their interest to work with the Tschaaa, to be client species as our lizards, second only to the Tschaaa Lords in power and control."

He continued. "I have worked hard to put you in a position that, each day, Tschaaa become more beholden to what services and items that humans can provide, not just as Cattle. It has worked. In the next year, I will have either influence over or control of the Tschaaa dominated areas worldwide. All unrestrained harvesting that still exists in some areas will be gone very soon. Next week, I will begin providing you with the most advanced medical nanotechnology and organic medicine that will eventually increase human life spans by decades. I will turn over the rest of the near space communication grid, resulting in human life near to where it was six years ago. And more of you will have access to outer space."

Adam asked "What about the Feral and Rebel areas?"

"If I have learned anything from the study of humankind, it is that you can adjust your belief systems and morality when the proverbial grass is greener on the other side. Though the concept of 'lawns' is very strange to me. Just look at Nazi Germany, the Soviet Union, and Communist China. People adjust when it is beneficial for them, especially if the alternative is much worse."

"But the Jews and the dissidents go to the camps and the gulags," Adam stated.

"Yes Director, as you have said yourself, the universe is not fair. We will need Cattle, dark meat. Your so-called people of color will continue to be sacrificed."

Adam drained his beer. He had always feared that it would come to this. That he would keep millions alive with hope, to have the reality of the situation slapped in their faces. For those that made excuses in their mind that if you waited long enough, things would change better for the Cattle, that dream just disappeared. There would now be a permanent class of Humans, and one of Cattle, same species, different life. The Protocol of Selective Survival in its ultimate form.

"Well, Your Lordship, I guess I have my work set out for me. Hopefully you can support me in my attempts to control the situation.

There will be some strong resistance from a certain percentage of humans, and there may be an attempt at organized armed conflict from the Rebels. I may need some help from your Crèche."

"Of course, Director. We will make this work, as we have with all our endeavors." The Tschaaa Lord signed positive feelings and happiness with his social tentacles. "I have one lesser item of possible conflict. Please look at this picture." He handed a photo to Adam. The creature on it looked like someone's idea of a sci-fi nightmare. Six limbs, four of them long thin legs that branched several inches from the bottom into two long toe like structures each. The front two limbs were arms with large five clawed hands. Long hair like structures run up and down the arms. The face was basically two huge eyes above a large teeth filled mouth, with an extremely long tongue. The body was circular and resembled an Earthly crab's domed shape.

"What is this?" Adam asked.

"It is a beast from our home world. We used to hunt it for sport. It is about five of your feet tall when its legs are extended, and is about one hundred twenty to one hundred forty pounds. The hairlike structures on the arms are very similar to your porcupine quills, and just as sharp. The closest name we could translate it to in Earth English would be 'Eater', as that what it does for most of its existence. Its stomach can stretch and extend some two feet below its body when full, at which time the Eater prefers to fall into a deep sleep like state so that it can completely digest the prey.

"It eats almost anything, and its very strong gastric acids can break down anything short of depleted uranium. It reproduces asexually. After it has stuffed itself several times in a row, it buds two young from its back, which 'hatch' about a week later. The young remain around the adult just long enough to see it feed. After they comprehend the concept, they are capable of hunting for their own food. They will not eat their own kind."

Adam kept examining the picture. "Why are you showing me this picture, your Lordship?"

The Tschaaa Lord wiggled its arms in a sign of consternation and embarrassment. "Some Lords had brought examples along with them, trying to hunt them in specially designed areas on our large ships. The limited area greatly reduced the sport to a quick one on one fight, so that the activity soon fell out of favor onboard.

"It was decided that releasing them on Earth would result in two things. One, there would now be room for the traditional hunts. Two, the Tschaaa Lord that made the decision saw it as a means to displace some of the Chinese populace, which had displeased him in the first year after the rock strike by refusing to cooperate and harassing his coastal breeding areas."

Adam knew that harassing breeders and young was a death sentence. Now, it appeared as if an entire culture might be sentenced to death, not for meat but for revenge.

Lord Neptune sighed. "Unfortunately, Eaters breed like your rabbits, and are constantly on the move. It has been an Earth month since the introduction of a dozen or so. There are reports of sightings in Eastern Russia, and they seem to be moving toward Europe and former areas of Korea."

Adam knew the Korean peninsula was almost barren of life, thanks to the North Korean resistance. The Eaters would soon move on.

"Can they swim, Lordship?

"Yes, they can, although they are land creatures. They seemed to have originated in our ocean."

"Well, I suppose I now have an interesting and unique subject for Kathy Monroe to discuss during a broadcast," said Adam.

"Excellent!" His Lordship exclaimed. "The primary subject will be the Crèche Ship movement?"

Now it was Adam's turn to sigh. "I will start with a story that the Tschaaa are exploring the solar system and asteroids for usable resources. I will hold off on mentioning the sun dive for as long as I can. I need time to get set up for panic and violence."

His Lordship gave a sign of compassion.

"Director, Adam, I have one more question. It is rather... theoretical in nature."

"Like we humans say, shoot."

The Lord paused for a moment. Then he asked, "Could you be my friend?"

Adam was caught off guard. What brought this on? He had to be careful in his answer or he may suddenly disappear.

"Well, we refer to our dogs as 'man's best friend'. Most humans stopped eating dog meat decades ago, and we bred them to be our companions. Dog and man both greatly enjoy physical contact with the other. But that took many thousands of years of development, of change from wolf to dog and primitive man to Homo sapiens."

He could tell that Lord Neptune was in deep contemplation. Then, his Lordship spoke. "I hope you and I can find a way to speed up the process. Thousands of years is much too long a time. Once your species can accept the division between client and cattle, man and meat, dog and wolf, I think the next step will result in humans being the Tschaaa's best friend."

The rest of the conversation was small talk. Adam did say that Talbot and his Krakens had asked to go to Atlanta in Cattle Country to see who was behind the organized breakout that had just happened.

"I will leave the details to you, My Director. Just ensure they have communications with a Falcon or two in case some... harvesting takes place. I dislike wasted meat."

"Yes, your Lordship."

The Tschaaa Lord looked at Adam intently. "Just for your information, I contemplated at one time making Talbot a Director."

"Oh?" Adam said.

"Yes, I held that idea for a brief time. He lacks what you humans refer to as finesse, what we Tschaaa refer to as 'gill cleaning', the ability to clean another's gills quickly and efficiently with pleasure, not discomfort."

"Yes, your Lordship. It goes without saying that I am glad you chose me instead."

"As I am glad, Director. As I too am glad."

Adam left soon thereafter, with assurances that Andrew, the robocop assigned to Key West, would soon be by with new nanotechnology, and to assist in beginning preparation for the dissemination of information about the sun dive and its aftermath.

As Adam left, he thought of Andrew. He was one of two hundred fifty successful modifications of more recent Earthborn humans to what was almost a total cyborg interface. Of the two hundred fifty-four volunteers selected, two hundred and fifty were successful, an extremely high success rate. As far as Adam was concerned, the end results were superior to the original cyborg warrior, developed from Gigantipithicus and Homo Erectus DNA. Not only did Andrew and his brothers have higher natural cognitive ability, independent of computer interface, but as having grown up as a human child, he had the natural understanding of the human experience on Earth.

Did Andrew see Adam as a "friend"? Now that was an idea to ponder. Andrew was still basically human, though the computer brain interface produced a very fast and varied mental process, the abilities to handle various tasks and different lines of thinking all the same time. Adam wondered if he still really 'thought' like a human. It was surprising that only four of the human/information system interface attempts failed. His Lordship said all four went insane and had to be 'dismantled'. Adam believed it was due to a tight selection process from thousands of applicants, and that volunteering to become something both less and more than human led to an initial good mindset for success. All the applicants also had to accept the fact they would be completely subservient to the Tschaaa, twenty-hours a day, no private life. They were literally 'wired in' to the massive Tschaaa information, communication and data processing system, with instant contact. This meant they could have no secrets. They also had to accept harvesting dark meat personally. Therefore, a large percentage of applicants must come with a preconceived notion of racial superiority. Due to the size requirements, close to a seven foot minimum upon complete modification, most were of Nordic stock from Northern Europe and the former U.S., with a few tall Irish, Scottish, and light-skinned Spaniards and Italians. Adam had gotten word that a call for more volunteers had just been released in Europe. Knowing the rather limited amenities and creature comforts, especially decent food, Adam was pessimistic they would find a dozen applicants who could meet the size and health requirements.

Maybe they would extend the call to North America.

Adam was escorted by El Segundo back to the dock. The Tschaaa offspring of His Lordship gave him a respectful wave of his tentacles and disappeared beneath the waters. Adam sat in the boat for a few minutes, eating one of his sandwiches and drinking a bottle of near beer. Out here was one of the few places left where he could be truly 'alone'. He still needed private time, wrapped in his own musings, which hard to find at the Key West Base, the New Capital of North America.

Adam stretched, looked at the abused boat engines and shook his head. Well, here goes. He turned the blowers on, which sounded as if the fan bearings were shot, then waited. After a couple of minutes, he cranked the engines. They started up, and then the port one literally burst into flames. Luckily the fire extinguisher still worked. He shut everything down, and sat on the bow. He looked at his watch. He was already past due for contacting the Chief, so he reached for his radio phone.

Then he heard an engine. It sounded like a Sea-Doo, or WaveRunner. He shielded his eyes from the sun and caught sight of the sea craft approaching from about ten o'clock to his reference. It was a large two-seater, with one figure on board. He stepped to the stern of the open fisherman and waved to the Sea-Doo. At that, the driver accelerated toward him, cutting the engine back to idle at just the right moment so that the craft coasted to a near stop next to Adam's boat. Adam used his boat hook to hold the craft near.

"Ahoy, Captain. I guess you must be the Director." A slightly sultry and strong-sounding female voice emanated from the pilot's seat, and told Adam the operator was a woman.

"Yes, Sailor, I am the Director. You must be my ride." Adam looked at the young lady. She was a strong and curvy woman, with dark brown hair tied back in a bun.

She flashed him a small smile. "Begging the Director's pardon, but I'm a Coastie, so I prefer Guardsman. We are bit sensitive about being lumped in with swabbies."

Not only fit, capable, but a bit feisty. Adam smiled back. He did not readily recognize her, but he knew he would soon come to like her.

"Sorry, Ma'am. I'm a former propellerhead, Air Force. We get confused on the water."

Her smile disappeared as her gaze traveled past Adam. "We have visitors." It was then that Adam noticed the Coastie had a Beretta M-9 in a shoulder holster, with a magazine pouch and large fighting knife balancing the opposite side of the rig. She reached for the pistol as Adam turned and saw two adolescent Squids pop out of the ocean, each having a large-edged weapon pointed at the humans. Adam knew the two Squids were doing the equivalent of demonstrating their 'maleness' by challenging a couple of humans near a Tschaaa breeding area, authorized or not. And sometimes, like human teenagers, they acted out with violent results.

"Stop right there, fishheads!" the Coastie bellowed, quite authoritatively. The Squids stopped, moving their arms to stay afloat and in place. Their eyes focused on the Coastie, ignoring Adam. He had the boathook in his hands, still hoping the situation did not come to blows. Once before it had been necessary for Adam to let fly with a black powder load in order to scare an agitated Squid away. He knew injuring one could lead to problems. But he was not about to be slapped around, or watch one of his people get skewered. Adam thought he heard some Squid clicks, a couple of low tones. The two youngsters then blew their gills in the Squid version of a belly laugh, and flipped a sign with their social tentacles that Adam had come to understand. Adam snickered as the two Squid disappeared beneath the waves.

The Coastie looked at him quizzically "What was that about, Sir? Was something funny?"

How not to offend a professional woman? "What is your name?"

"Heidi Faust, Petty Officer First Class, Sir." She smartly saluted him, her hand no longer on her pistol.

"Petty Officer Faust, please do not be offended, but the Tschaaa think that all... well-endowed human females are breeders. They do not understand our sexuality. To them we are a bunch of randy monkeys. The sign they gave meant something similar to apologies for interrupting mating."

Heidi's face flushed. "I should have shot the assholes. I was born with big breast genes. What's their excuse, asshole genes?"

Adam began to laugh, and after a couple of seconds, so did Heidi. He did not get a reason to laugh like this very often. It felt good.

"I take it, Petty Officer, that you are my ride."

"That would be me, Sir." "Well, let me stow my briefcase and ditty bag, and we can get moving." Adam, while Heidi held onto the side of the boat for stability, secured his items in a hatch beneath the rear seat. "Here, Ma'am, have a near beer. Not enough alcohol to worry about."

Heidi flashed Adam a smile that lit up her eyes. "Thank you, Director. It is getting warm out here."

Adam clambered on behind her as if it was a large motorcycle. Heidi began drinking the near beer. "So tell me, how did a former U.S. Coastguardsman get here?"

"The Chief, Sir. He found me up the coast by Miami, trying to survive by fishing where the Squids would let me. A couple of swabbies and I, plus some civilians, hooked up after everything fell apart, staying where it was warmer when the nuclear winter kicked in. I had my Coast Guard cutter blown out from beneath me by an underwater mine the Squids were so nice to place. I was the one and only survivor."

Adam watched her profile as she finished off the near beer. "So why work with the creatures that killed your shipmates?"

Heidi tossed the empty bottle purposefully at where the Squids had been, a sign of protest. "They stopped eating us, I got tired of living hand to mouth, and the Chief made me an offer I couldn't refuse."

Adam grinned. "He has a way of doing that. Can you use that knife?"

She gave him a sideways grin. "My folks ran a gym and dojo outside Palm Beach. I was doing judo and Gracie Jiu Jitsu from the time I was five. I met my boyfriend there later. He taught me Filipino eskrima knife fighting. We joined the Coast Guard together." Suddenly her face and eyes clouded. Adam had seen that look a thousand times before.

Everyone she was talking about was dead.

"Sorry. Didn't mean to pry."

"Not your fault, Sir. Every survivor I've met has lost someone. After a while, you are just glad to be alive."

Heidi had an attractive face, with full lips and a strong German nose that looked good on her. She had hazel eyes that flashed when she laughed. How had he not noticed her before? The base wasn't that crowded.

"I do not remember meeting you, Petty Officer. Why not?" "You were supposed to, right after the Chief recruited me. That was a bit over a year from me losing my cutter. You were really busy then..."

"Well, it was my loss. It's one of the reasons I instituted the initial briefings and socials, so I could meet everyone. Somehow you slipped through the cracks." Adam grinned.

Heidi grinned back. "So, Director, I think we need to head back before the Chief thinks we are goofing off."

"Hell, the Chief knows I goof off every chance I get. Let's go, then,

Petty Officer.

"Aye aye, Sir."

Adam wrapped his arms around Heidi's waist to hold on. He felt the strong, supple strength in her stomach muscles. She accelerated and they were soon hauling ass back to the Key West base.

The close proximity of an attractive woman and the vibration of the Sea-Doo, soon produced an embarrassing reaction that Adam attempted to hide from Heidi Faust. However, he had to hold tight as she was hauling ass with a competency born of experience. Adam kept hoping that the Petty Officer would not notice. He was wrong. Just under an hour later, as they were about a mile from shore, Heidi cut their speed to an idle. She turned her head back toward Adam. "Director, if I may be so bold, is that a gun in your pocket, or are you just happy to see me?"

Adam then did something he did not do often. He blushed.

"Please, don't take it the wrong way, Petty Officer. I don't take advantage of my position..."

Heidi let loose with a strong, throaty laugh. "With all due respect, then you are the first person I have ever met that hasn't at one time or another, including me." She winked at Adam. "I'm not offended, Director. A good man is hard to find. Or is it a hard man is good to find?" She laughed again.

Adam laughed also. Damn, she had a good sense of humor.

"Seriously, Ms. Faust, if you are as good as you say with that knife, I could use the lessons. Chaperoned, of course."

"Anytime, Director. But just remember, I'll be one of the most dangerous things to a man with an erection–a woman with a sharp knife."

With that last comment, Heidi accelerated again suddenly, Adam grabbing on tight to keep from falling off. Smart ass Coastie.

Back in his office, Adam found himself alone, grinning like an idiot. He would definitely would take Heidi up on her offer, if for no other reason than she made him laugh a lot. He needed the reminder that he had a sense of humor these days.

He looked at the time, and headed to his quarters. He turned and quietly walked out the door, down toward the suite where Kathy resided. He lightly knocked on the door, and she opened it immediately, dressed in a short, sheer robe and nothing more.

"Adam, I thought you would never get here." she whispered. She pulled him in, and quietly closed the door behind him. Placing her arms around his neck, she leapt up and wrapped her strong legs around his waist.

"Come here, you," she ordered.

An hour later, he extricated himself from Kathy's arms, kissed her cheek, and quietly padded to the apartment door. He put his trunks back on, and returned to his office. As quietly as possible, he went to his private bathroom and took a shower. He made sure he washed all of Kathy's scent off him, then got out and dried off. He then walked nude back to his master bedroom.

Mary Lou was sleeping in the oversized bed alone, slightly snoring. He slid into bed, and spooned up next to her. He kissed her shoulder, and fell into a deep sleep.

CHAPTER 10

Whether they resided in the Feral areas, Tschaaa-controlled areas, or the Free States and Countries, humans still discovered or rediscovered the concepts of love and of family. This is a constant of the human condition, sometimes resulting in often strange and stressful situations.

> —Excerpts from the *Literary Works of Royal Princess Akiko,* Free Japan Royal Family

MALMSTROM ALLIED ARMED FORCES BASE, MONTANA

Torbin was tired. These long days, in addition to some of the recent emotional upheaval, were finally getting to him. Despite his excellent physical shape, everyone had their limits. He was beginning to suddenly feel old. However, when he approached to the door to his quarters and found it unlocked, a jolt of adrenaline woke him up. He unscrewed the nearest hallway light. Then, his Ka-Bar in his hand, he pushed the door open, and low rolled into his darkened front room. "I am unarmed, Captain." It was Aleksandra. He stood up, and saw the Russian sitting on his sofa in the dark. "How, may I ask, did you gain access to my quarters?"

She sighed. "I am a trained intelligence operative. Of course I was trained in how to get into locked rooms."

Torbin re-sheathed his Ka-Bar. "So, what's next?"

"Come here, my Torbin, and find out."

An hour and a half later, he was holding her close in his bed. She was gently caressing and scratching his chest with her fingernails.

"Thank you for defending my honor, my Captain. It has been ages since a concept like honor has been part of my life."

Torbin stoked her lush hair. "You deserve better, Aleks. Life since the first rock strike has made things hard enough, without us humans treating each other like bovine excrement."

"You mean bullshit?" Aleksandra replied.

Torbin chuckled. "Here I am, trying to be all gentlemanly and correct, and you go all earthy on me."

Aleksandra raised herself up from Torbin's shoulder and looked into his eyes. She kissed him on the lips, slowly and sensually. "You deserve better also, Torbin. Give me a chance, and I will show you 'better'."

"Promises, promises." Torbin mumbled as he put his arms around Aleksandra and pulled her close.

Suddenly, there was a loud banging on the front door, and someone called his name.

"What the hell?" Torbin exclaimed as he rolled out of bed. He grabbed his Ka-Bar, and padded naked to the door. "This had better be good," he yelled as he yanked it open.

Two large Military Police Officers were at the door. They took one look at Torbin's state of undress, and the Senior Sergeant asked "Are you alone, Captain?"

"No, he is not," Aleksandra called from the bedroom door, sheet wrapped around her.

"Sorry, Ma'am, but I must ask how long you have been here with the Captain."

"An hour and a half at least. Why, Sergeant?"

The second Military Policeman was relaying the information on his radio. He informed the Senior Sergeant, "It happened within the last half hour. Even Captain Bender can't be in two places at once."

What happened, Sergeant?" Torbin demanded.

"Ma'am, Sir. The Russian Colonel was found dead with a broken neck. It looked like it just happened."

Torbin was stunned. Aleksandra broke the silence first.

"The General is at his office?"

"Yes, Ma'am.

"Come, Captain, we must go there. Thank you, Sergeant."

"Yes, Ma'am." The two MPs left. Five minutes later, after some rapid dressing, the two Captains were en route to the Commander's Office.

The other Russian officers were already present when Torbin and Aleksandra arrived, as was Colonel Tanaka. Torbin entered, and saluted. "Sir."

General Reed saluted back. "I understand you have an ironclad alibi, so there is no reason to ask you what you've been doing." He gave Aleksandra a knowing look, which she returned with typical Russian stoicism.

"Now we need to start a full investigation."

The Russian second in command, Major Romanov interrupted. "With all due respect, General, that is not necessary. We have more important things on which to focus."

General Reed looked at the Major like he had lost his mind.

"Major, how in the hell can I explain to your government what happened without an investigation. My own Madam President will have my ass if I don't and dot the I's and cross the T's, so I can imagine what your government will want to do to me."

Major Romanov sighed. "General, they will say nothing. My cousin was a pig, always had been a pig. Yes, he was my cousin. But he was a pig who survived because he knew where the skeletons were hidden, and he abused his underlings. No one in my family liked him. He was sent here hoping he would screw something up so badly that he could be shot before he could use his information to blackmail his way out. So trust me, General, you will be doing everyone a favor by agreeing that the drunken ass fell and broke his neck."

The Major paused. "Or, you can start an international incident by accusing foul play and setting back plans for a counterattack on the Tschaaa back months, if not years."

Silence. General Reed then let out the air had been holding in his tight chest. "Major, I do not usually agree to not searching for the truth. 'The Truth Shall Set You Free.' I believe that. But, the Mission takes precedence over my belief. I agree with you. I ask that you communicate directly with your government."

He turned to Colonel Tanaka. "Any problem with the Major's proposal, Colonel?"

"No, General. You both have more say in this matter than I. I yield to your decision."

Major Romanov then spoke again. "I do have one favor, General."

"And what is that, Major?"

"The three young female officers will need to stay here on detached duty indefinitely. I know my pig cousin has already communicated via our secured radio relay some remarks questioning their loyalty. They will be, shall we say, pressured, about his death, whether they know anything or not. I do not want them harmed unnecessarily."

General Reed rolled his eyes and sighed again. "What in the hell have I gotten myself into? All right, that's it. No more deals. Now, shall we all go back to bed? I'll have my mortuary officer prepare an accidental death finding and prepare the body for shipment back to Russia."

As everyone began to leave, the General called Torbin back. "Captain, since you have such a way with women, especially Russian women, your additional duty is to get the three young officers integrated into our command structure and mission. They will also need to be quartered near other women, if possible. But bottom line is this: everyone works. Hard. Capisce? Clear?"

"Crystal clear, *Sir.*"

"Now, get some sleep. That's an order."

Torbin saluted smartly and left. General Reed sat in quiet contemplation for a few moments, then removed the picture of his wife and son from the desk drawer. "Darling, days like this, I wish I was with you instead of here. I miss you, and the presence of all these Russians makes me miss you more. But I know you would want me to fight the good fight. So, I stay." The General kissed the photo, and put it back in his drawer.

Time for rest. Tomorrow was going to be a long day.

CHAPTER II

Joseph Fassbinder woke early, before the sun had risen. He was surprised to discover Sarah, sleeping next to him, in the darkness of their shared quarters. It took him a moment to recover, and to recall the events leading up to their reunion.

The previous day, Joseph had stayed at his new office until almost 6:00pm. His new boss, Mike Jones, had been incredibly generous to him, letting him know that whatever he needed he would get, no questions asked. Mike had given him the distinct impression that if Joseph wanted to take over as supervisor of the Aeronautical Physics, Engineering, and Space Travel Section, he would be on cloud nine. Like Joseph, he was a scientist first, and administrator second. Joseph did not rise to the bait.

After work, he dreaded the walk back to his quarters. He had no idea what Sarah had decided, or if he would see her again. No matter what happened, he was not looking forward to the possibly that his relationship with his wife would probably never improve. As angry as he had become, he still loved Sarah.

Joseph passed a large food van, known around the office as the "roach coach". He remembered seeing some signage that beer and alcohol was available starting at 4:00pm, aka Happy Hour. He decided he would need some liquid courage.

He walked up to the serving counter and saw the comely Jolene sitting on a chair on the other side. She was holding a large bag of ice on her scar. Joseph had started to retreat to the front door, when she spotted him.

"Good afternoon, Professor Fassbinder. Can I get you something?" Jolene stood up, still holding the bag of ice to her face. Joseph tried to avert his eyes, feeling that he was staring at her injury.

"My crystal ball tells me that you might in need of a stiff drink. It also says that you are wondering about my scar but are too polite to ask." Joseph only managed to clear his throat in response. Jolene laughed; hers was a pleasant and gentle sound. "First, a shot of home brewed whiskey on me. Then, the story you want to hear."

Joseph blushed. "How did you know my name?"

"The three of us 'roach coaches', as we are called, have free access to the base. We Conchies hear and see everything. But, we are friendly and respectful, so no dirty laundry will be aired. Here, take your drink."

Joseph took the highball glass containing poured brown liquid over ice. He sniffed, and then sipped. It was surprisingly smooth for home brew, and still had a good kick.

"This is quite good for homemade whiskey... Jolene, is it?"

Jolene smiled. "Distilling secrets of the Admiral, my adoptive Father. Actually, he calls all us young 'Conchettes' his daughters, and treats us like we were his own. Woe to the person who disrespects one of us."

Joseph sipped his drink. "I'm not in the habit of disrespecting young ladies."

Jolene flashed a wide smile at him. "I like being called a lady. I think I'll like you, Professor."

Joseph started to blush again, and Jolene gave a bit of a belly laugh at his discomfort. "Relax, Professor. You'll get used to normal human interaction. You don't have to look over your shoulder here, contrary to rumors."

Jolene held the ice to her face again. Joseph sipped his whiskey, enjoying the simple pleasure of a pre-Squid normal activity.

Jolene then put the ice bag down. "The ice is to stop phantom pain I get sometimes. Doctors tell me there is no reason why my pain still occurs, other than nerve memory of some type from my original injury. I'm still lucky. I should be dead."

Joseph raised an eyebrow. "Dead?"

"Yes, dead. About a year after the first rock, a member of the new Church of Kraken decided that he wanted a piece of me, both sexually and literally. The early members decided that they needed to eat human flesh like their new demigods, the Tschaaa. They wanted to *be* a Squid."

Jolene poured herself a shot and freshened up Joseph's drink.

"I owe the Director my life." She threw the shot back. "Whoa. That *is* smooth, isn't it? Just as the asshole was beginning to cut me, hence this scar on my left jaw line, the Director showed up out of nowhere. He had apparently just been contacted by His Lordship Neptune a week or so prior, here in the Keys."

Jolene's eyes had a bit of a faraway look to them. "I have never seen anyone so angry before. But it was a good anger, the kind the heroic have from seeing the weak and innocent being hurt, and then they step in to stop it."

"Anyway, Director Lloyd wound up hacking the asshole to bits with a machete. He took him apart piece by piece. Then he and the Chief bandaged me up. The Admiral showed up, saw what had happened, and he has respected the Director ever since, Tschaaa or no Tschaaa."

Jolene stared into Joseph's eyes. "The Director has saved everyone he can. He saved me, he saved many others in similar situations. All that shit about him being a monster is just that. Shit. He saves who he can. And I am living proof.

"He offered to fix my scar once the Tschaaa started providing their superior medical supplies. I said no. It serves as a reminder of what could have been. Besides, I think it gives me character." Jolene laughed.

"Now, Professor, one for the road, take a couple more beers with you, and go make up with your wife."

Joseph's mouth dropped open. "How…"

"I told you we hear everything. I'll see you here tomorrow."

Sarah was waiting for him when he arrived at their quarters. There had been a sea change in her. She now had a job, was determined to stay, and almost begged him to forgive her. There were some more tears, from both Joseph and Sarah. He realized that he still loved the woman he had married.

Ten minutes later, after such a long dry spell he couldn't remember the last time, they made love. Afterward, he stayed awake and watched the sleeping woman next to him. They were quite good together in bed, always had been. Life had just gotten in the way. Now, it was changing.

After everything that had happened today, he was beginning to wonder if maybe there was something in the water.

CHAPTER 12

While some groups of humanity attempted to retain or re-discover basic cultural norms and morals, others sank into a morass of depravity and bizarre behavior that is hard to comprehend by many. Possibly a citizen of Ancient Rome from the reign of Emperor Caligula could more readily accept and understand what occurred on parts of 21st *Century Earth.*

—Excerpts from the *Literary Works of Princess Akiko,*   Free Japan Royal Family.

ATLANTA, CATTLE COUNTRY

A couple of days had passed since his meeting with Malcolm whatever the hell his real name was. The Mayor did not care, for tonight was Fight Night.

In an old sports auditorium, Mayor Johnson's version of bread and circuses was about to begin. He had soon realized after he took over as acting Mayor that base entertainment helped take people's minds off of reality. Fights and violence seemed to attract the populace more than most things. Add alcohol, fresh from the monthly supply drops, and he put on quite the party.

The last three fights had shown a pattern of success. Mayor Young had found that catfights floated everyone's boat. And the prize for winning was the almost irreplaceable. The woman who won obtained complete protection for her children. No chance of any veal being seized from her family. Thus, there were no shortages of volunteers.

Tonight, two small, but apparently fierce women were fighting. Their only protection was eye goggles to protect them from gouging each other's eyes out. Blind women did no one any good. The referees would keep them from actually killing one other. But, Mayor Johnson knew that this fight, like the previous ones, would be a bloody biting, scratching, hair pulling, kicking, punching and screaming bitch fight. And it was the first of a three fight scorecard.

He tried to keep the fights within ethnic groups as there was enough animosity already without adding to it. His technicians had managed to get the jumbotrons to work, so everyone could have a good view of the gory details when the women went after each other. He was also burning DVDs for sale to the highest bidder. The winner received freedom from having family members eaten, as well as a few bucks and other incidentals. The loser met whatever fate the Mayor was in the mood for that evening.

The roar of the crowd told him that the two combatants had entered the arena. The two women were so evenly matched they could have been twins. They both were rather good looking, so he hoped his medical staff could keep them from suffering any permanent scarring.

The two attractive women entered the arena from opposite ends. Other than the goggles, the only other adornment was a red or blue thick ribbon tied on their left arm. This was to help in identification, primarily for betting purposes. No one really cared about their names. The announcer ran through the standard litany of their respective sizes, weights, etc, as well as general rules, which were almost non-existent. Then, in the time-honored tradition, he yelled over the PA system, "Let's get ready to rumble!"

Both women, their black, shoulder-length hair thick and loose, charged each other like two wild animals. They slammed into each other in the center of the arena, breast to breast, clawing their sharpened fingernails into each other's faces and necks. They screamed and cursed as they tried to kick each other, and fell to the soft grass as their legs became intertwined. Clumps of hair were ripped from each other's heads as they rolled around on the ground. The crowd roared with approval as the fight intensified. Blue managed to use her legs and feet to flip Red up and over her, resulting in a short break in their grappling. Both women sprang to their feet, then began to circle each other with clawed hands.

Red lunged and dug her nails into Blue's shoulders. Blue screamed and began kicking Red to make her let go. Red slapped Blue hard across the face with her right hand, and tried to follow up with her left. Blue tucked her chin to her chest and began throwing hard punches into Red's tanned body, smashing her fists against the woman's breasts and ribcage. Red backed up, covering her chest with her arms, and then lashed out with her feet, aiming at Blue's crotch. Blue wrapped her arms around Red's right leg as she kicked, digging her fingernails into the soft skin of the shapely thighs. She pulled the leg up, throwing Red off balance. They tumbled to the grass, Red clawing at Blue's soft skin as they fell.

They began to roll on the ground again, arms wrapped around each other in bear hugs, clawed hands gouging and scratching each other's backs as well as buttocks. Suddenly, Red let loose with a high-pitched scream. It was soon evident that Blue had clamped her teeth onto Red's left breast, and began to worry it like terrier with a rat. Red screamed again and dug her fingernails into the neck and throat of her rival, tried to force her to release her bite. A trickle of blood was evident from Red's breast, as she clawed at Blue's face with her free hand. Red hooked her nail into Blue's left cheek, which finally resulted in release of the bite. Otherwise, Blue would have had her mouth ripped open.

Blue managed to dislodge Red's finger, and bit the offending hand. Red cried out and began beating Blue on her head with her free hand, the hammer-strikes eventually resulting in the hand to be freed.

Red pushed herself back from Blue with her legs and feet, and tried to stand up. Blue threw herself at the other woman, her hands again clawed. She raked Red's breasts, now smeared with blood. But Red was still in the fight. The two battered and bloodied combatants managed to regain their feet, but were clearly winded. The red bloody scratches and gouges on their bodies were mute testimony of the sharpness of their fingernails and the savagery of their attacks.

They circled, cursing at each other. In a sudden move, Red made a dive for Blue's legs. She managed to dig her nails into the other's thighs for a moment. Then Blue smashed her elbow down on the back of Red's head. The stunned woman went to her knees. Blue trapped Red's head between her strong, shapely thighs, rolling to her side. She bent over and reached down to claw at the undefended thighs and crotch of Red. Red, still partially stunned, tried to pry herself loose from the trapping thighs. She regained enough of her senses to use her own teeth as she clawed at Blue's buttocks. Blue yelped as Red sunk teeth into the inner thigh area. Blue responded by hammer fist blows to Red's back, until the pain and damage to her thigh forced her to release the other woman's head. They rolled apart, both clearly the worse for wear.

The crowd began going completely nuts. The Mayor grinned, and then guffawed. Damn, what a fight! This would be talked about for months to come.

The two combatants rose slowly, on wobbly legs. Both had tear-stained faces from the effects of the pain they had inflicted on each other. They circled again, trying to regain their breath.

Red sprang a kick to Blue's crotch, but she caught it on her outer thigh. Then Blue lunged forward and drove a combination of fists to her rival's stomach and chest. Red tried to cover up with her arms and hands. This left her face unprotected. Blue closed on Red and sunk her teeth into the woman's jaw line on the left side of her face. Red screamed and again tried to claw herself loose from the damaging bite. Blue shifted her bite to the neck, drawing blood.

Red sagged, and Blue let her fall to the ground. Blue then straddled and sat on the stunned Red in a classic schoolyard pin, her knees holding Red's shoulders to the ground. Blue cursed at Red, and then, to the howling appreciation of the crowd, spit in her face. Twice. Blue used her hands to smear the spittle all over Red's face, as the defeated woman's heels beat a powerless drum beat on the ground. Blue rolled off Red, and somehow had the energy to stand up. She placed her bare right foot on Red's face and pressed it into the grass. Blue raised her right fist in the sign of victory.

The crowd went wild. Coins began to be thrown at the victor, as bills would not have reached the arena floor.

"Where in the hell did you find these two, Joe?"

The former professional football player gave the Mayor his signature grin. "Oh, you know Boss, word gets around to me. Seems that Red tried to steal Blue's husband. They were going to fight in the street when their people told them to fight for something real, not just sex. So, here we are."

"Goddamn. I *knew* there was something to why they seemed to hate each other. Well, get Blue and Red cleaned up. I want to speak them both about their futures."

Mayor Young was already sizing up the next competitors for the next match when Red and Blue showed up in his box suite. Both had cleaned up rather well, aside from some swelling and bruising. Red would not look at Blue, and instead looked at the ground.

The Mayor a large envelope to Blue. "Your reward. Certificate stating you and your family are exempt from harvesting, unless you or your kindred commits a felony crime. There is also some money and chits you can use. You are one tough woman. Care for a drink?"

Blue not only looked at him and *through* him as well. Damn, the Mayor thought. I don't envy any man who steps out on a woman that ice cold.

"No, thank you, Mayor. May I leave?"

Mayor Johnson sighed. "Yes. Good job. You're going to be something of a legend around here." She did not reply, just bowed and turned to leave. She glared at Red. "Leave my husband alone, or I will gouge out your eyes." Blue hissed at Red. Red kept looking at the floor as Blue left.

The Mayor looked at Red. "Well, you lost. But the fight was so good, I decided to find something for you." He tossed her an envelope. "You have dispensation for one year. Then your family can be harvested."

She looked at him for the first time, surprise in her eyes. "Thank you. Oh, thank you!"

"There's a little cash there too. Given your impressive performance, I think we might be willing to offer you a second chance. Maybe you can fight someone else for permanent status if you'd like." He took a closer look at her. He found her strikingly beautiful, damage and all. "Unless you might be willing to offer another barter of some kind for my consideration…"

It was early the next morning when Mayor Johnson awoke in his suite, Red cuddled up to him. He did not know her real name and did not care. She had quickly decided what side of the bread the butter was on, and, for that matter, who supplied the bread. Red let him know that she had nothing to return to, she had no children yet. So, for now she was the Mayor's main squeeze.

She had made herself available and willing all night long, knowing that for a man like the Mayor, that attitude cemented the deal. If she performed like this on a regular basis, hell, she could stay forever.

The mayor kissed her firm curved figure, and extricated himself from her grasp. He took care of his bathroom needs and was getting dressed when he heard a small knocking on the outside door to his suite. He went to the door and peered through the peephole. It was Joe.

"What's up, Joe?"

"Mayor, we have a problem headed this way, fast. It's that crazy ass Talbot and his Kraken Flying Squad. They're on the outskirts of Atlanta."

"*What*? Coming here? What the fuck, is he nuts? There are a half a million brothers just waiting to kill his sorry pale ass. Nobody has that many bullets."

"Well, Boss, he already kneecapped two young men that got in his way, and a Falcon traveling with them harvested a third. After that, everyone scattered."

Most of the survivors the Squids classified as dark meat had begun to centralize around the major pre-rock strike population centers in the former tri-state area, because that was where the food and other supplies were first delivered to by Director Lloyd and his people. Attempts to organize some type of subsistence farming on earlier fertile lands were mostly failures. During the past year, instead of Falcons dropping supplies, large balloons and dirigibles were being used for the supply drops. Definitely not as accurate, they made up in tonnage. As long as he and the other "Mayors", representatives of the major population centers, supplied a monthly quota of "meat" to the gigantic harvesting center in the former port of Savannah, Georgia, the food and other supplies kept coming.

When in the beginning, organized resistance to the "quotas" was attempted, a few things happened. Initially, food and supplies stopped and people began starving, fighting, even eating each other. Robos and their Falcons then began random harvesting in the middle of the night. This was usually initiated with the demolition of buildings while people were still inside. Finally, as they fled the fire and destruction, people of color were unceremoniously snatched up and slaughtered, sometimes while suspended overhead. There was nothing like blood raining on someone's head to create a quick attitude adjustment.

The survivors chose the "Mayors" to talk to the Tschaaa. In a flash, agreements were made, and once again the age old process of basically buying and selling people so that others could survive began. Now, an average of five thousand Cattle were required delivered to Savannah for "processing" each month, including a substantial number of veal units. Most of the fresh meat went to feed the Squid's young. The Mayors and their helpers had to insure delivery, or else the Falcons came looking, with the help of the Krakens. Sadly, some individuals were willing to sell their own young. But, since abortions were common place in some communities pre-strike, it wasn't that difficult a leap.

Talbot and Company never came this far into Cattle Country. Not ever. Talbot must have suicidal thoughts, robocops or no robocops.

"How close is he?"

"Within the hour, he should be here, barring a major firefight."

"*Fuck!*" the Mayor exploded. "Just when I start enjoying myself, this shit happens. Get the office ready, Joe, for their arrival. I'll be there shortly."

"Sure, Boss." Joe left. He knew the drill.

Martin Luther returned to Red and woke her up.

"Honey, something's come up. Stay here in the suite. There is some food and drink in the refrigerator, some DVDs near the TV, some women's clothes in the closet. Just do not leave. In fact, lock the door when I leave. Understand?"

Red could tell he was worried. She had no desire to screw up a good thing. She had found a protector and sugar-daddy and did not plan on blowing it.

"Anything you say, Mayor."

Mayor Luther stroked her cheek. "When we are alone, call me Marty. I like you, Red. Like me back and we will get along just fine."

"Yes, Marty." She reached up and kissed him. Maybe he wasn't so bad after all.

Mayor Luther quickly dressed and recovered his Luger from beside the bed. He had decided a long time ago that if Talbot and company came for him, he would fight. Tonight might be the night. Or maybe not. He met Joe at the office. He had a couple of his security people standing at the door to the office, each with sawed off double-barreled twelve gauges, obtained by Joe from God knows where. The Mayor poured himself a shot of bourbon and tossed it back. He needed it to help settle his nerves. Then, he sat back to wait in silence.

About a half hour later, they heard a large number of engines in the streets nearby, followed by some shouts and a single gunshot. The Mayor sat frozen, staring at the door to his office. He could hear the loud hoots and howls of Torbin's men, along with the thunder of their heavy boots, coming up the stairs and then down the hallway.

"Hey, *boy*! Watch where you point that shotgun unless you want it up your ass."

Mayor Luther had encountered the voice before on the telephone and recognized it as Talbot, public enemy number one.

Talbot and company burst through the door using the two security men as battering rams, sending them sprawling at the foot of the Mayor's desk. Joe stood with his hand on his great bowie knife, standing still but ready to explode into action if necessary. Talbot regarded the Mayor's aide. "Joe. Long time no see. I still say you would have been one of the best players in the NFL if not for the Squids. But then again, we wouldn't be having all this 'fun' now would we?"

Talbot turned his attention to the Mayor. "Hey, Marty. Sorry, but we had to gut shoot some meat outside that got too close. The Falcon has already harvested him, so there's no mess to clean up. But I digress. Lieutenant Sparks." Ray Sparks handed Talbot an object, which he took and tossed unceremoniously on the desk with a resounding clatter. "Look familiar, Mayor?"

Martin Luther saw it was a spear. He picked it up and examined it. It took him only a few moments to notice the information plate on the shaft. "Property of the Atlanta Museum of Natural History" it read.

"I never was one to hang around museums, Mr. Talbot."

Talbot grinned. "I never thought I would see the day when homegrown badasses carried African spears in America. I mean, we used to call you 'spearchuckers' but I never saw one of you actually have one, a spear that is. Until the other day, when we tracked down the meat that broke through the fence in the Florida Panhandle. And now, the question is how an African spear from a museum in Atlanta, Georgia, wound up in Florida."

He glared at the Mayor. "Any ideas?"

Without missing a beat, Martin responded. "I suspect someone stole it from the Museum. The place has been closed since just after the first rock strike, six years ago." Sweat began to bead up on the Mayor's forehead. He had no idea what else to say.

Talbot broke the silence. "I know you don't know. Hell, you're too busy porking the losers of your catfight extravaganzas." Talbot chuckled. "Yes, we have heard all about your little circuses. Wished I could have gotten here sooner to watch the last one. I heard you record them, right?"

"Yes, we do."

Talbot slapped his hands together. "Good. I want a copy sent to me. As well as a dozen of your good-looking brawl babies. Well, at least as good looking as a female bruiser can be."

Talbot walked over and sat on edge of the Mayor's desk. "We won't stay long, as the 'natives' are getting restless. Sounds like an old Tarzan movie, doesn't it?"

"After we leave, you have seven days to come up with the women, the recording of the fight, and seven young livestock who get to accept responsibility for the breakout. Send them to Savannah with notes pinned to their asses stating they are the seven who planned it, and we will call it even."

Martin Luther hesitated. The populace would know what was happening when seven men were suddenly grabbed, above the quota they had just filled.

"I said, capisce. Understand?" Talbot roared.

The Mayor jumped in his seat. "Yes, I understand."

"Good. Now, as much as I enjoy your company, time to go. Make sure you deliver on time. Otherwise, we'll have the robos start harvesting at random."

Talbot jumped off the desk and strode to the door. "Goodbye, Joe. See you next time. Hell, you might be Mayor then." He began laughing at his joke, joined by the other Kraken Squad Members as they all barged out the door. The two now empty shotguns were tossed into the office by the Tail End Charlie.

"Don't forget the DVD of the fight!" Talbot called once more from the hallway. The Mayor was shaking with anger and fear.

"You okay, Boss?" Joe asked.

"Fuck. As good as I can be. At least I'm still alive." He used his shaking hand to pour himself another drink.

Talbot and his Krakens clambered down the stairwells to the street below, bellowing and laughing. They just loved to mess with anyone they could intimidate. As they joined the security team guarding their transportation, Talbot noticed a tall, muscular, very dark skinned man leaning against the wall of the building across the street. He seemed to be watching them without a care in the world, ignoring even the Falcon circling the city overhead.

"Hey, dark meat. What are you looking at?" Talbot yelled.

"Just some white meat fooling around with the His Honor, the Mayor."

Talbot laughed, and walked toward the young man with the big mouth.

"My, my, we have a set of balls, don't we? What's your name, meat?"

"I go by Malcolm these days. And you, what name do you go by?"

"Talbot of the Krakens, and no, not that Church. In the old days we would be a biker gang. Now we're the biggest son of a bitch in the valley." His men laughed. "Don't you know you could wind up dead if you piss us or that robocop flying around off?"

Malcolm gave one short laugh, then responded. "We are already dead. We were dead the day the Squids showed up. It's just a matter now of when we stop being the walking dead and truly die."

Talbot examined him more closely. This man, with his very dark skin, was one of the smartest humans Talbot had met in the last few years. How had he stayed alive?

"Pardon me for asking, but how did someone who looks like you not been harvested by now? The Squids, you know, love dark meat. The darker the better."

Malcolm shrugged. "Just lucky, I guess. Mind if I ask you a question?"

"Go ahead. This is one of the most interesting conversations I've had in a long time."

"Did you have fun with His Honor, the House Nigger?"

Talbot stared at Malcolm. Then he started laughing, as did all his men. He laughed so hard that he almost fell over. As he wiped tears from his eyes, he told Malcolm. "You know my man, I sure hope you're around the next time I have to visit the Mayor. You're a hell of a lot more fun than he is."

"Who knows, Talbot of the Krakens, I may be the Mayor when you return."

Talbot laughed again. "Well, Malcolm of the walking dead, your luck is still holding. Most folks like you standing around eyeballing us would be dead by now. So, yeah, you could be Mayor soon. If you are and I have to look you up, you can buy me a drink." Everyone laughed, including Malcolm.

"Sounds like a deal to me, Talbot of the Krakens."

Talbot signaled it was time leave. "Time to leave, Malcolm. See you next time, I hope." He climbed into his SUV and accelerated down the street, his units soon falling in behind.

As the sound of the vehicle engines began to fade, Malcolm straightened up from his position on the wall. He looked up to a fifth story window in a building two blocks away. He gave a high sign to the sniper manning the homemade 50 caliber bolt action sniper rifle. Malcolm knew that if he had taken Talbot out, all hell would have broken loose. The 50 probably would not have taken out the Falcon. But man, it would have been a fun few minutes.

When you're already "dead", it's the little fun things in life that get you through the day.

CHAPTER 13

The Director Adam Lloyd became quite adept in his special form of propaganda. With the assistance of Kathy Monroe, the perfect on screen image and messenger for the Protocols of Selective Survival, the Director began spreading the word about the New Age the Tschaaa were bringing to humanity, at least part of it. But not everyone who received the message accepted it. This was especially true of those humans residing in Unoccupied States of America.

> —Excerpts from the *Literary Works of Princess Akiko,* Free Japan Royal Family.

KEY WEST, FLORIDA

The past few weeks had been very busy for Adam, Kathy, Mary Lou and the Chief. The whole base had become a literal beehive of activity. Knowing the information he had just received from his Lordship, Adam lit a fire under all departments and sections, in an attempt to get things done as quickly as possible before the inevitable pushback from the populace. Only he and the Chief knew the full story of the Tschaaa ship movement, although he knew scientists and astronomers involved in the project could easily extrapolate the ships' destinations from the angles of trajectory. When the truth of the Tschaaa plans was discovered by other individuals clever enough to put the pieces together, the information would spread throughout the general populace like wildfire.

Before that happened, Adam needed to have a buffer in place to mitigate the effects of the knowledge that the Squids were here to stay in large numbers indefinitely. No small centralized colonies, the Tschaaa breeding areas would be huge and worldwide. He began instructing Kathy to broadcast all of the benefits the Tschaaa were graciously providing. Cell phones, the full internet, a national power grid, superior nanotechnology, and medicine for everyone in the Tschaaa controlled areas, as well as fresh food and produce being readily produced on restructured farms.

Kathy was the perfect spokesman, just as Adam had believed she would be. Her looks attracted those men, and a few women, who wanted to watch eye candy on the reconstituted nationwide broadcasting system. Her proverbial and legendary–at least in the old adult movie industry–'perky' demeanor woke many households in the morning with a smile. She always managed to soften the blow with her delivery of the sometimes difficult news. People soon found out when she interviewed people she was not an emotionless airhead, but instead, a woman who actually cared about her fellow humans. A prime example was when the first Eaters, who reproduced and traveled at an unexpected exponential rate, hit the west coast. Despite Adam's specific instructions to the contrary, Kathy had finagled a security team and air transportation to the Oregon coast, near where the Columbia River met the Pacific, behind his back. Adam was furious when he was informed that she was near the radioactive contaminated Columbia River, but it was too late to bring her back. Kathy had an ability to persuade others of the validity of her plans, whether or not they had been cleared with the powers that be. In service of the truth, permission and caution be damned.

Near a small active port created by the Tschaaa, Kathy had interviewed some of the first humans who had encountered the Eaters and survived. They were with Tschaaa and robocop overseers to salvage materials from the abandoned structures, vehicles, and boats left up and down the Oregon and Washington coasts.

Somehow, some Eaters made it to mainland America, possibly on an abandoned former Chinese barge that seemed to belong to some smugglers.

China, now run by warlords, knew that the Occupied States were creating disposable goods and wealth once again, as well as providing surplus food. The surplus was both fresh and leftover canned and dry goods salvaged from abandoned buildings in harvested areas. And the surplus also gave rise to a thriving smuggling industrial. While the Tschaaa surveillance system noticed the slow moving surface vessels, the aliens did not care as long as they stayed away from breeding areas and Cattle Country.

Adam watched the taped interviews with a mixture of pride and seething anger. One minute, a young couple of humans, with two young children, were talking about these weird creatures they had seen. Then, without warning, a couple of Eaters had attacked. Kathy continued to broadcast as she pushed the husband and wife to safety, putting herself between the Eaters and the kids. The attack had happened so fast, and the threat was so new, that the security team was flat-footed for a few seconds. Kathy screamed at the creatures, waving her arms to distract them. It worked. She was seconds from death, but the kids had escaped. Assault rifles and shotguns, finally on target, blasted the two creatures to bloody bits six feet from Kathy, on camera.

As the security team approached, Kathy was heard to say off camera, "Whoa! That was kind of scary, wasn't it, boys and girls?"

On camera, Kathy was seen being hugged by the mother of the two children, who thanked her between sobs for saving her children. It was great footage that showed, Squids or no Squids, humans still cared about other humans. Basic humanity could still exist.

Kathy's perky smile returned, as she chatted with the security team while they did a quick examination of the remains. It soon occurred to security that where there were two creatures, there could be more, they quickly bum-rushed the survivors off the beach. "Hey, guys, it's hard to run and broadcast at the same time, you know," she quipped, and giggled.

Adam personally reamed the security team a new asshole for letting Kathy convince them that a several day trip to the West Coast was somehow authorized, and almost getting her killed. Then, he gave them medals and bonuses for courage in face of a new and very dangerous enemy. Kathy became the symbol of what was right with the government. After all, if she worked for the Director, and she put herself in harm's way to save others, especially children, then it was logical that the Director and his people must still have a strong spirit of humanity. They care. This broadcast also reached the Feral and Unoccupied States of America.

Feral areas began to have access to power and the grid, as they tapped and hacked in, with Adam's people intentionally looking the other way. If the so-called "enemy" is actually helping make your life easier, it is harder to convince people to risk their lives to attack it.

Adam repacked his ditty bag and briefcase. His team and a small security detail were to fly to Cape Canaveral for a nationwide special broadcast about the pending spaceplane launch. This was one subject that seemed to generate a lot of positive feedback from the surviving populace. It pointed to the fact that, at least for the people outside Cattle Country, the Tschaaa were trying to better humanity's lot in literally astronomical proportions. Why would they do that if they planned to eat them?

Mary Lou entered his office. "Ready, Boss?"

"Finishing touches, Mary Lou. Is Kathy here?"

"Yes." Still with the cold demeanor whenever he mentioned Kathy. Like oil and water, those women did not want to mix. The fact that Kathy was now becoming a household name did not help the relationship.

It had gotten to the point that both women made blatant attempts to show off their physical assets when they were around Adam in his office, or in the broadcast studio. This was bizarre because he was having sex with both of them behind closed doors, whenever time permitted, so he already had intimate knowledge of both their bodies. And both knew he desired them. It almost seemed like they were showing off more to each other, than to him.

Today, for example, they were wearing almost identical blue pants suits, tailored to accentuate every feminine curve. They kept glancing in each other's direction, occasionally locking eyes.

Adam knew people–women in particular–were sexually competitive, but this was beginning to get ridiculous. He was thinking of having a lengthy discussion with them after work someday. That was, when he had the time. Right now, he needed to complete this broadcast.

He rounded up Kathy and Mary Lou and they headed down to the main building entrance. The Chief met him curbside in front of the building, a look of frustration on his face.

"Boss, two of our three security troops are down for the count with some nasty food poisoning. I can find two more, but it will just take a few."

"Are the pilots armed?"

"Yes, Boss."

"Well, grab a couple of your special briefcases for us, and let's hit the road. The trip is going to take a while as it is, and we have a busy schedule. I don't need more delays. The pilots and flight engineer will just have to do double duty, if necessary. Besides, Cape Canaveral has Tschaaa security out the ass, several robocops and even some lizards floating around."

"Okay, Boss. Let's head to the airport."

The lone remaining security officer was a Sergeant Jackson, a tall, sandy-haired man who had come in the last group of new arrivals. Chief Hamilton had told Adam that he had an extreme gung ho attitude, having been the child of a white Supremacist that hated those of a darker complexion even before the Tschaaa appeared. He thought the Squids had been a godsend. Adam never really trusted fanatics. It had been his experience that people of extreme views were hard to control, and it was not unknown for one to suddenly become just as fanatical about a view once held as opposite. People such as these seemed to just enjoy being fanatics, the basis of their fanaticism being secondary to their enthusiasm for holding opinions contrary to the majority of the population.

Yet, Jackson seemed to be completely beholden to the Chief, who he appeared to treat like his long lost savior. And because the Chief was loyal to Adam, Adam thought Sergeant Jackson also must be loyal to him by default.

They arrived at the Key West Airport, where the re-engined DC-3 Gooney Bird was being prepped for takeoff. Part of a small fleet that had operated out of the Florida Keys pre-strike and infestation, this plane had the original Pratt and Whitney engines replaced by a more modern TurboProp, which upped the top speed and load carrying capability. It was set up to carry some twenty passengers quite comfortably, some of the seats modified to face each other over small fold down tables.

Mary Lou and Kathy intentionally sat opposite one another, which piqued Adam's curiosity. After a smooth take off, he began doing some subtle people watching as the Chief played a game of solitaire with a well-worn deck of cards.

Sure enough, periodically, the two women were giving each other incredibly dirty looks. Adam was also fairly certain he saw a couple of single finger salutes flashed at each other when they assumed no one else was watching. He clenched his teeth. This had to stop. Without warning, the plane lurched. At the same moment, Adam heard a loud "bang" from the port side engine, which belched smoke, then stopped.

"Ladies and gentlemen, this is your Captain speaking. The port engine just shit the proverbial bed, so I will be looking for a field to set down on. Please fasten your seat belts. Thank you."

The pilot and co-pilot were both former Air Force and airline pilots that had survived the last few years by being very good at what they did. After thousands of hours of flying, this was the first serious in-flight emergency that Adam could remember.

An old civil aviation field, only just cleared off by the locals at Adam's behest and payment, was found north of Miami.

"Director, do you have anyone following us?" the pilot asked over the intercom.

Adam unbuckled his belt and went to the cockpit. "What do you have?"

"We have an old Cessna 172 shadowing us all of a sudden, ever since the engine blew. It's making me very nervous."

"You and me both, Captain." Adam quickly returned to his seat with the others. He noticed Sergeant Jackson was staring at Kathy, like he expected her to say something to him. "Alright people. You know the drill. Rig for possible crash landing, seat backs up, tables stowed, put you head down on your knees, hands on the back of your neck just before landing. Kathy, Mary Lou, quit screwing with each other."

There were two surprised looks. "Don't say anything. We have a Cessna 172 behind us, which may have up to four people jammed in it.

Chief, Sergeant Jackson, prepare to repel boarders when we roll to a stop."

"Yes, Boss." The Chief checked the special briefcases he had stored under the seats.

The approach the Captain made was flawless, and he greased the DC-3 onto the runway with one engine. Adam planned on giving him a bonus. As the plane was braked to a stop, Adam and the Chief were already out of their seats. Sergeant Jackson was still staring at Kathy with his bright blue eyes.

"Care to join us, Sergeant?" the Director asked, his hand on the Sergeant's shoulder. The Sergeant rose from his seat quickly, and suddenly Adam found himself staring down the barrel of Jackson's M-9 Beretta. Jackson then spoke the first words anyone had heard from him the entire flight. "Goodbye, traitor."

Adam's peripheral vision caught a blur of movement, as the Chief threw himself at Jackson. Then the Sergeant's head exploded and Mary Lou screamed, as she and everyone else was splattered with Jackson's blood and brains. It took all a few stunned moments to register that Kathy was the one holding a large caliber two shot derringer in her hand. No time to ponder. The flight engineer hauled ass back to Adam, who waved him off.

"Problem taken care of. Get ready to help us with the Cessna."

Adam and the Chief each popped open a briefcase. Adam pulled out an MP-5K sub compact submachine gun with a twenty round magazine.

The Chief pulled out a sawed-off double-barreled twelve gauge from his case, and grabbed up the M-9 Beretta the dead assassin had dropped. The flight engineer had a well-used M-2 Carbine with a thirty round banana clip he had kept stashed onboard somewhere.

"Stay here ladies, and get down." Adam, Chief and the Flight Engineer made their way to the rear hatch door.

Mary Lou stared at Kathy. "Where in the hell did you get that?"

"Around," answered Kathy. "A girl has to keep her secrets."

Mary Lou grabbed Kathy's left bicep, digging her sharp fingernails in. "I told you not to fuck around when it concerns Adam."

Kathy raised her Derringer, and pointed it at Mary Lou's face. "Let go of my arm, bitch."

"This isn't over!" she hissed, backing away quickly.

"I know," Kathy hissed back, lowering her weapon to her lap.

Adam, Chief Hamilton, and the flight engineer scrambled out of the Gooney Bird and used the tail plane as cover. The Cessna was taxiing toward the DC-3 and began to slow some fifty yards back.

"Shoot first, ask questions later," Adam ordered, and he began to empty his weapon's magazine into the Cessna. The flight engineer opened up also with good accuracy. Some forty rounds later, the Cessna, its gas tanks unprotected and its body unarmored, began to fall apart and burst into flames. A figure bailed out of the passenger side door, rolled, and popped back up, firing some kind of assault rifle. Adam pulled his Glock 26 and began firing as the flight engineer fired the last rounds in his Carbine magazine. One of the men hit the individual and he went down.

"Damnit! You didn't let him get close enough for my twelve gauge," the Chief protested.

"Well then, go ahead up and check for survivors, Chief, if you want something to do."

"Okay, Boss, will do." Chief Hamilton swung wide and came at the Cessna from a ninety degree angle.

"What's your name again, Sergeant?" Adam asked the flight engineer.

"Forrest, Director."

"Well, Sergeant Forrest, your shooting just got you a healthy bonus. Thanks."

"Thank you, Director. I haven't had this much excitement in ages."

Chief Hamilton called back. "Everyone in the Cessna is toast and dead. The guy on the runway bought it also. Shot to the head."

"Damn. No one to question. Chief, come on back."

Adam quickly turned around and climbed back into the plane. He found Mary Lou and Kathy seething in complete silence. The pilots had un-assed the plane and were making sure the fire was out on the port engine.

"All right, ladies. All is secure. Kathy, where in the hell did you get that gun?"

"I brought it with me. No one asked, so no one knew."

Adam interrogated Kathy further. "I don't know what was going on between you and Sergeant Jackson, but for someone that didn't seem to have a lot of contact with anyone other than the Chief before, he seemed especially focused on you. Any ideas?"

"Christ, I don't know. Look, I just blew someone's brains out. You may be used to that, but I sure as hell am not. I get stares all the time."

"Maybe if you kept your legs crossed and your chest in your dress, you wouldn't get stares," Mary Lou snarled. Kathy and Mary Lou lunged at each other, each going for the other's face.

Something seemed to click in Adam's brain, a threshold had been reached, and passed. Kathy felt steel trap fingers around her throat, with a duplicate grip making Mary Lou's eyes bug out. Both women had their heads shoved hard against the bulkhead.

"That's it!" growled Adam. "This shit stops *now*. I have more important matters than to referee a catfight. Understand?" He was squeezing their throats so hard all they could do was croak. Adam released his grip and the two women almost fell over. "I *said*, understand?"

Both women managed to hoarsely whisper, "Yes."

Kathy, for the first time in years, began bawling in pure rage.

"This is just fucking great!" she bellowed. "I save your ass, my ass, even *her* ass, and I get *choked*. I almost get eaten by some six legged freaks on a beach and I get shit." She sucked in another breath.

"Fine. Well, fuck you all! I quit! Go ahead and shoot me. Otherwise, I'm fucking gone!" Kathy stormed off the plane, almost bowling the Chief over who was just about to re-plane. Mary Lou started to make a comment, but a cold, icy stare from Adam shut her up. Adam took a deep breath, and followed Kathy.

Sergeant Forrest was standing outside, examining the assault rifle the Chief had recovered from the body on the tarmac when Kathy stormed up, grabbed it from him, and began marching down the field. She did not care where she was or where she was going; she just had to get away. She had never felt so betrayed, nor so rejected. Years of pent up emotions now poured out of her. The image of her dead fiancé flooded her mind, and she sincerely wished that she had died with him.

Strong arms wrapped around her and lifted her up off her feet. She began to kick, to struggle. Adam whispered in her ear, "Kathy, I'm sorry. I owe you my life." Kathy's body went limp, and she dropped the rifle from her hands. Adam put her back on her feet, now having to hold her up as the shock of what had happened began to finally penetrate her anger. He spun her around, and she buried her face in Adam's chest and she sobbed.

"Listen to me," Adam explained. "First, I don't make it a habit of laying hands on women, in a way that's aggressive, not sensual. Second, whether you want to hear it or not, I love you. I love Mary Lou. Hell, I love Jamey and Janine in my own way. But I love the Mission, my Mission, to save as many members of the humanity I can, first and foremost."

Adam sighed. "This is not the first time has infiltrated my team and tried to take me out. It just hasn't happened in quite a while." He gently tilted her face up and met her tear filled eyes. "It is not the first time someone got close to me, to try and kill me, then changed their mind."

Kathy started to speak, but Adam put his fingers on her lips. "Hush. Jackson believed he had a connection of some sort with you. I believe you may have also been contacted by someone after the Chief contacted you. You still love and miss your hero fiancé and hate Squids, who I am working for as much as I'm working for my fellow humans. So, you have entertained some ideas of revenge on the nearest, biggest target. Me.

"Then, for whatever reason, that idea changed. I'd like to believe it is because I am such a sterling example of humanity. But I know it isn't. I don't need a reason. Things have just changed. As things change in this screwed up world, I have learned to accept them and move on. I have to."

He gazed deeply into her eyes. "I need you. The people need you. Whether you like it or not, you are becoming a symbol of hope; hope for a better tomorrow for at least part of mankind. But if you want to leave, I understand. You just saved my life, so I owe you yours."

Kathy's mind was trying to go in several directions all at once. Somehow, she refocused her thoughts, got past the awful hurt and feelings of loss. She sighed. "Adam, my fiancé's name was William. I miss him so much it still feels like a piece of me is missing, even six years later. Maybe it's because I have an idealized memory of him, frozen in time. Hell, I'm no psychiatrist. I don't know. I just know how I feel."

She swallowed the lump in her throat. "I also love the hell out of you. You remind me of William, and yet you're different. I was ready to hate you, to play you. Now, I can't." She was shaking, some from the post shooting shock, some from fear of what she was going to say.

"I knew that someone like Jackson existed. I did not know it was him. I have not had contact with anyone since just before I arrived. I was supposed to contact someone by passing a note through a mailbox in the Conch area of Key West. I never did. That is the truth, Adam. If you wish to kill me, I think you'd be doing me a favor. It would end the pain."

As Adam often had to do before, he made a decision, and there was no turning back. "Kathy, this stays between us. It ends here. If you want to kill me later, I will probably even help you. I suddenly feel very old, and very tired. I will not give up on the Mission. But, I may not be able to see it through to the end."

Kathy kissed him. "Don't give up! No, you're not perfect, but you're here for a purpose, otherwise you wouldn't have been able to save so many people, and delay the end of us all."

"Yes," she continued. "You have done that, somehow. Don't forget that, whatever your failures." She wiped her eyes, smearing makeup. Then, she flashed her signature perky smile. "It's showtime again, Boss. I'll swallow the pain if you will."

Adam thought for the thousandth time what cruel God had thrust this role on him. Why had he not been killed six years ago in Atlanta?

He walked Kathy back to the plane, and straight to where Mary Lou's was sitting. He knelt before her seat. "Mary Lou, please forgive my physical abuse. I lost my temper and should not have. I am sorry. Please forgive me."

Mary Lou took his face in her hands, and kissed him. "Boss, you did what you figured was right. I owe you too much to hold a grudge. May I speak to Kathy, alone?"

"No fighting?"

"No fighting, Boss."

Mary Lou found Kathy outside the plane, staring at the burning Cessna. She stood beside her. "Kathy, I owe you for saving Adam. I was completely helpless, and you were not." She sighed. "I still don't trust you, and I don't know if I can like you. But, as we agreed that first night we talked, we need to call a truce for Adam's sake."

Kathy continued to watch the flames as she responded. "Yes, but we are going to have accept the reality of the situation. We both love Adam, and he loves us both. Equally. So, sure, truce."

"Truce. But my original warning stands. Don't screw Adam over, or I will mess you up."

The two beautiful women regarded one other. There was still a part of them that wanted to beat the crap out of each other. But, that would cause pain to Adam, and distract him from his Mission. So, truce. For now.

They returned to the plane, as the two pilots tried to obtain alternate air transport. The port engine was scrap.

"Someone placed an explosive charge on the engine, so small it wouldn't be noticed," the Captain informed Adam. "I don't know if the dead Sergeant planted it, or someone else did. It was enough to really trash the engine, though."

Adam grunted. "Well, I guess my Security Chief has a sabotage investigation on his hands. Thanks, Captain. By the way, the way you and your co-pilot greased this Gooney Bird onto this field with only one engine did not go unnoticed. Look for a bonus."

The Captain shrugged. "Comes with the job, Director. Besides, you don't know it yet, but I owed you big time since that last group of newbies came in."

Adam looked at him quizzically. "How so?"

"You and the Chief found my daughter and son-in-law. I've discovered that I'm going to be a grandfather. Now, Sir, excuse me while I get you another plane to ride." He turned to radio Key West.

Not for the first time, Adam allowed himself a small feeling of self-satisfaction. Three more lives in the plus column. If only he could reduce the minus column.

CHAPTER 14

Aleksandra was helping Torbin put his Marine Corps dress uniform together, something he had not worn since being commissioned. He and Aleksandra looked over the details in the full length mirror.

"Torbin, yours has to be the most colorful uniform I have ever seen. I must admit, I am jealous," the Russian Captain teased as she brushed off pieces of lint.

"Yes. Don't you think I fill it out nicely? Especially the pants?"

She playfully slapped him. Then she kissed him. "You are a typical crazy American Yankee. Why did I have to fall in love with you?"

"Fate, kismet, whatever. You are a hard ass Russian. Why did I fall in love with you?"

Aleksandra grabbed his right hand and pushed it to her left butt cheek. "Squeeze it. It is not hard. It is firm, but soft and sexy. You are wrong again, Americanski." They kissed. Wartime romance was rough and dangerous, especially when both people involved went into harm's way. But, when you found someone who fit you, who completes you, danger be damned.

Aleksandra gently pushed him away. "Let me finish helping you, Torbin. You must look perfect for your Madam President. Tomorrow, the rest of us meet her. Today, it is your time." Torbin felt embarrassed. The General told him the President, who had somehow managed to sneak onto the base without any fanfare, had specifically asked the General for his presence ASAP. She apparently had an award or medal to give him, and then wanted one on one time with him, about what, no one knew.

A few finishing touches and he was a handsome Marine in traditional dress blues. Aleksandra squeezed his arm, and sent him on his way. Torbin marched smartly to the General's office some blocks away, the light exercise helping to quiet the butterflies in his stomach. Rubbing shoulders with a combat team was his idea of fun, not rubbing shoulders with the upper Chain of Command, especially the President. He quickly covered the distance, and his NCOIC waved him toward the door. Torbin Bender sharply knocked on the door, and entered upon hearing "Enter." He stopped in front of the General's desk, smartly saluting. "Reporting as ordered, Sir."

Out of the corner of his eye he noticed the President, Sandra Paul, sitting alone in a comfortable chair. No staff, no security. Noted for her attractiveness, she had a firm chin, straight yet feminine nose, and a full head of shoulder length brown hair with small streaks of gray. Even well into her fifties, she had a young, vibrant demeanor. She was a very fit woman who had engaged in multiple sports, including judo. Probably the most famous woman in North America, she was a legend.

Her pre-Squid political critics had written her off as a conservative bimbo because of her good looks, Midwestern demeanor and her uncompromising politics when it came to a strong, moral America. She had weathered many a political caricature of her, her family, her background, her residence in Alaska. Now she had the last laugh. Ninety-nine percent of her critics were dead, many eaten. She often joked afterward, "They were right. I was too tough. Yes, too tough to eat."

She stood up and approached Torbin. He turned toward her, still at ramrod attention, and snapped a parade field perfect salute. To his surprise, Madam President returned it with the same parade field precision. "Madam President. Reporting as ordered, Ma'am."

"At ease, Captain. And I do mean at ease. Relax. You Marines seem to be unable to relax past a stiff Parade Rest. Now, *relax*.That's an order."

Torbin tried to let his spine relax. He managed to obtain a five percent decrease in his stiffness.

The President chuckled. "Well, I guess that is all I am going to get. General, let's all have a sit down around your coffee table. And break out that bottle you have hidden in your desk. The good Captain and I could both use a drink."

Torbin took the glass offered, found a chair, and finally began to relax a bit. President Paul produced a very normal large female purse that matched her dark blue skirted business suit. "After reading your file, Captain Bender, I know you hate pomp and circumstance. So here." She pulled some small objects out of her purse, and reached out her hand to pass them to Torbin. "A Distinguished Service cross, a special medal and citation from the Japanese government, and a Hero of Free Russia cross. Congratulations. And I do mean congratulations. Your country recognizes your unique abilities. You have managed to cobble together an alliance between three remote countries."

"Begging your pardon Ma'am, but it has been the General..."

"Stow it, Marine," General Reed ordered. "Accept the fact that, despite your expertise in resolving conflicts at the tbarrelend of a gun, you now have a new skill set. You are also an excellent diplomat."

Torbin blushed. The last thing *anyone* had ever said about him was that he was diplomatic. His idea of diplomacy was a two by four to the head to get the attention of the other parties involved.

Madam President continued, "The Japanese government left Lt. Yamamoto, soon to be Captain, here in your tutelage in order to assist Pappy Gunn in adapting Tschaaa technology to our uses. Now, we have a nearly operational delta. The three Russian officers have been a godsend in developing trusted relations with the Russians. You were instrumental in keeping them productive and happy. Every time something improves, your name is involved somehow."

She took a large sip from her drink. "Good scotch, General. My husband was a scotch drinker, and he taught me to appreciate the difference between the good stuff and swill. But I digress... I don't know if you were blessed or born with the talent, but all I know is that, every project you touch becomes golden. Don't argue with your President."

Torbin took a drink rather than answer. He had difficulty accepting compliments.

"Now, Captain, the bad news. An attempt we orchestrated to assassinate Director Lloyd recently failed. All of our agents are dead, except for one that was apparently was turned by the Director. Again."

General Reed snorted in disgust and frustration. "Lloyd must be a combination of Svengali and Rasputin. No one seems to be able to keep focus on the mission against him once in his company."

"Especially women, General. Captain, the woman we inserted into Lloyd's inner circle was Kathy Monroe. I believe she was your late brother's girlfriend."

Torbin froze. "Actually, Madam President, they were engaged to be married."

"An Air Force Captain was going to marry a porn star? I can't imagine his commanders would have approved."

"He was going to resign his commission, Ma'am."

"Why, in all that is holy, would he even entertain that thought?"

Torbin slowly stood. He felt a white hot anger that surged through his entire body. "Madam President, General, with all due respect, they were madly in love. I know. I met her. War or no war, that's my younger brother we are talking about, and I can't stand here and allow you to question his honor. I request that you take back your comments, immediately, or I will be forced to resign my commission."

He knew he was probably looking at the end of his career, but fuck them. Family was family, dead or alive. You do not disrespect them.

The President observed Torbin in contemplation for a moment. She turned to Reed. "You're absolutely right, General. Captain Torbin has the requisite toughness and intensity. Captain, I apologize for the crass test, but I needed to know just how much of a spine you have."

She stood up and extended her hand. "Please accept an old, tough broad's heartfelt apology. I know what it is like to have your family besmirched. And then to lose them."

Torbin knew she had one daughter still living. Her husband, son, and another daughter were dead. He took her hand and had to control himself from crushing it. His brother was one subject that was still very raw to him, even six years later.

"Captain, we have a very tough and classified mission for you. This is why only the three of us are here right now. Director Lloyd and his Tschaaa Lordship seemed to have the unique ability to figure what we are going to do before even *we* know what we are doing. You will pick the team that you will use. Everyone will only know what they need to know to do their job. Only we three will have the full mission plan.

Understood?"

"Yes, Ma'am." He met the President's eyes. "What do I have to do, Madam President?"

"You, Captain Torbin, are going to help me capture or kill Director Lloyd, and nuke that Squid."

CHAPTER 15

Even at this much later date, some twenty five years after the events, there are still those who find it difficult to understand why very highly educated and scientific-minded individuals bought into the Protocol of Selective Survival's promises made by Director Lloyd.Some say that, much like those who aided the Nazi's Final Solution or the racism based greater East Asian co-prosperity sphere of Imperial Japan, anyone who aggressively helped Adam Lloyd in his projects must have been evil or deranged.

However, I do believe there is one extremely salient difference when you compare the events of World War Two and those of the Tschaaa Invasion and Infestation. The Tschaaa threatened to kill and eat everyone, if humans were not found worthy of client status.

So, despite the Tschaaa preference for those of darker skin, many members of the alien species would just as soon feed humans to their young as to wait for us to prove our worth for something greater. Thus, a select few humans, as well as Tschaaa, believed they had to prove humanity's worth as being more than just tasty protein.

At one time, horses were treated as wild game. Then, the Mongols and others found they could be ridden and pull war chariots

Suddenly, they had a much more important role than being just another source of meat.

But of course, in a pinch, horses could still be eaten.

> —Excerpts from the *Literary Works* of *Princess Akiko, Free Japan Royal Family.*

CAPE CANAVERAL SPACE CENTER FLORIDA

It had been a tense day for Professor Joseph Fassbinder. When word had come that the Director would be delayed due to the failed attack, Joseph's initial fear was that everything would be delayed. He had busted his butt to get himself and the space plane ready for launch and he did not want the launch date to be set back, for fear that it would be cancelled.

So, when he heard that Adam Lloyd and company were again en route, he breathed a sigh of relief. His wife Sarah had remained at Key West, as she was involved in setting up a truly adequate education system for the increasing population. Now that she had a function that actually helped people, she was much happier. She still had her basic beliefs concerning the unfairness of it all, but she was making the best of it.

Joseph had been in a crash course of physical fitness and nutrition to get him ready for space. Lots of food, lots of exercise, and many long hours as he prepared everything technical for the launch. He had filled out some so he did not have the look of a walking cadaver, but he would never be fat. He still had the slim build and physical resemblance of a World War II-era Charles Lindbergh.

The meeting scheduled with the Director and Kathy Monroe was for a broadcast showing everyone in North America just how close they were to launching back into space. Security was tight. How many robocops there were, he had no idea, only that there were more than he could count. There were also lizards and few of a new soldier class of artificial beings, grown in tanks like the grays.

Human security was rather slim, but there were a couple of people who had worked at the Cape pre-rock strike, so they had intimate knowledge of the set up. The Cape had largely been spared. One small rock hit the administration building and that was it. Strikes at Homestead Field, Miami, and other parts of Florida had led to the area eventually being pretty depopulated. Only within the past year had Director Lloyd located enough human scientists, engineers, and support personnel to start full operations again.

The numerous Tschaaa breeding areas along the Florida coast, ensured that the Director always had access to a substantial amount of alien support. Many younger Squids were seen both in and out of the water, working around the Cape. They provided all the sea-based security. Needless to say, any human wanting a swim had better find an inland pool.

Joseph was meeting the Director's party at the base of the main launch gantry. The size of the structure made the humans and even the Tschaaa in the area appear ant-like in comparison. Standing next to Joseph was Andrew, the robo assigned directly to the Director. "The Director should have let me escort him here, Professor," Andrew said in his signature baritone. "Then no one would have considered attacking him."

"Well, Andrew, you know the Director wants to appear as independent as possible. But you could have forced him to accept your security presence, couldn't you?"

"I have been directed by his Lordship to follow the Director's directions as long as he isn't trying to commit the equivalent of suicide. Otherwise, he can make as many mistakes as he wishes, as long as the ultimate desired results are eventually reached."

Joseph mulled that over for a minute. "And the ultimate desired result?" he asked.

"Full integration of humans into Tschaaa operations, especially in near Earth orbit," Andrew replied. A thrill coursed up Joseph's spine. So, the Director hadn't been exaggerating. He glanced at Andrew. He knew that the robocops were completely integrated into the Tschaaa computer and communication system, knew everything the Tschaaa knew, and were incapable of lying. The Tschaaa had infused them with the same inability to deceive in communications that the sea creatures had. This, in Joseph's opinion, was weird. The Tschaaa, like their Earthbound cousins, had the ability to change their skin into camouflaged colors in order to blend into their surroundings. Yet somehow, the idea of deception, of using lies and equivocation to hide ideas, had never developed in their society. Physical concealment was one thing, maybe even physical ambush of prey.

Intellectual concealment was another matter.

The sun was low in the sky when the Director and his party arrived. Joseph and Andrew met them as they exited the Humvees that had picked them up at the nearby airfield.

"Professor. Good to see you."

"I am much more pleased to see that you got here in one piece, Director. This type of excitement is not the type an astrophysicist prefers."

"But being launched on the end of a roman candle in a new, untested aircraft, is the type of excitement you do like, right, Professor?"

The Director had a point. What he was about to do was not exactly safe. "Well, Director, I guess one man's refreshment is another man's poison."

Adam turned to the cyborg. "Nothing to say, Andrew? No lecture, no I told you so?" Andrew turned his head ever so slightly toward the Director.

"Would it do any good? I have given you numerous reasons why you should be more careful. I have offered you time and again my services as transport. Yet, you refuse."

"Now Andrew, you know I must be approachable. I must appear very human to those around me. Flying around in an alien aircraft with a huge cyborg makes me appear to be less than human, and definitely not approachable."

"I believe you are just stubborn, Director," the robo replied. "Why should I waste my breath on a man who is as stubborn as a mule? I believe I shall ask the new information database to include a picture of you in the definition to the term 'stubborn ass'."

Nobody else said a word, but the Director immediately erupted in laughter. "I forget that under all that hardware is still a man with a sense of humor, albeit a damn dry one. Someday, when stand up comedy makes a comeback, you might want to take your act on the road."

"Why, Director, when I have a ready made audience already?" Joseph would later swear he saw a twinkle work its way from Andrew's eyes, from beneath the robocop's protective visor. At this, the rest of the laughed party laughed as well, which helped release some of the tension from the failed attack.

"Come, Professor, let's head toward the administration building. A bit of planning, then everyone needs to rest. You and Miss Monroe will be broadcasting live tomorrow from here in front of the gantry. At that time, everyone will see for themselves that yes, we are really about to return to space."

CHAPTER 16

Professor Sarah Fassbinder, now primary teacher for some two dozen children, ages six to sixteen, had all of her students on the main athletic and parade field at 8:00am. She had decided that a few calisthenics and a walk around the track every morning would help get the children's blood flowing. It also might help use up some of the children's excess energy and relieve their stress. Six years of living hand to mouth, under constant fear of being eaten and with little or no structure, made it difficult for the young humans to sit still in a traditional classroom setting.

The older children were also given the responsibility of helping and keeping track of the younger children, both in and out of the classroom. Sarah was trying to reintroduce basic human interaction among non-related youngsters, many of whom had no contact with other children while in hiding.

"All right, young ladies and gentlemen. In the immutable words of our military, 'you know the drill.' Robert, lead the others in a few calisthenics. Then we take our walk around the track. I want you older ladies and gentlemen to review with the younger children what the assignments are today. Let's get started."

Sarah had forgotten how much fun it was to teach, to help educate young minds to bloom and grow. She was finally doing what she had originally trained to do in university. Somehow, she had been sidetracked into philosophical navel-gazing and fighting the establishment rather than establishing the future.

When the first rock hit, everything was frozen in time. Now, thanks to the Director, she had a chance to live, to teach again. She hated what he was doing, picking who lived and who died at the behest of the Tschaaa. But she could not hate *him* anymore. She could tell he did care about his fellow humans, and did what he could to help as many as possible to survive. She often wondered if he bled inside every time he thought about the human cattle he helped condemn to the slaughterhouse.

Suddenly, a blurred form entered her peripheral vision. At first, her mind said "dog", but then registered the six-legged horror. It must have been hiding in the drainage ditch on the edge of the field. It did not really matter where it came from. It quickly reached an eight year old girl and literally clamped its wide mouth over the complete upper torso. Sarah screamed and charged the creature. Without any weapons to fight a clawed and toothed predator, she did not even think. She was a mother cat protecting her young. The screams from across the field immediately drew Major Grant's attention, as she was cutting across en route to a meeting in a nearby office. She was trying to get caught up on a few small projects while the Boss was away, as the Director could be a major distraction. Instantly, everything else was forgotten, except for the word "Eater". The creature was a duplicate of the two that had been filmed trying to attack Kathy. Six limbs, two ending in clawed hands, with a huge, oversized mouth full of teeth; they got their name because they lived to eat. And now one was eating a young girl.

Jane automatically ran toward the danger. She was military, it was her job. The survival part of her brain scolded, "You dumb bitch, you have no weapons. What are you going to do?" The soldier portion replied, "Bitch, find a weapon."

Between her and the children was a five foot tall metal fence stake, the type used to secure temporary wire fencing. It was still stuck in the ground, apparently used to mark some pre-measured distance on the field. She grabbed it and tore it from the ground. By rights, that was physically impossible. Even a fit, one hundred thirty-five pound zaftig female should have had difficulty pulling a metal rod out that had been pounded over a foot into the ground.

Whether it was divine help, or just the biological response that causes the overproduction of adrenaline in times of crisis, Jane had it. The Major grabbed and yanked the fence stake out in one motion, just as Sarah threw herself at the Eater. The Professor screamed, scratched and clawed at the body of the horror, until a blow from one of the limbs caught her on the edge of her jaw, and cold cocked her. Two of the older boys then rushed the Eater. A flick of one of the creature's forelimbs flipped quill-like hairs off its forearms, and impaled the skin of the approaching boys just as porcupine quills impale an attacking dog. They screamed in pain, temporarily halted in their assault.

One of Jane's old boyfriends, dead some six years, had competed in the javelin throw in college. He had taken her to the sports field when he practiced, and she had tried it a few times. While not good enough to compete, she hadn't been bad either. Now, everything he had showed her came back. The Eater, eight year old girl stuffed into its expandable stomach, was looking for a place to escape so that it could digest its meal. Just as it began to move, the fence stake pierced its large right eye. It let out a howling scream no one at the scene would ever forget. A second later, Jane was on top of it. She threw her whole weight onto the stake, driving it through the eye into what passed as its brain.

It shuddered, regurgitated its last meal, and died. Jane started to grab the girl's lifeless body, and screamed in pain as her hands were seared by stomach juices from the Eater. One of the older boys ripped off his sweatshirt and tried to wipe off the girls face. Her flesh began to slough off the skull. The boy turned around and vomited. Jane grabbed her radio phone from her pocket and began screaming into it. "*Eaters!* At the sports field. Everyone get here... *Now!*" She heard Sarah behind her scream, "Susie!" Somehow she tackled Sarah and held her down, keeping her from the acid covered body.

The hazmat team carefully washed and cleaned the area around the dead bodies of the Eater and the girl, making sure the very corrosive stomach acids were neutralized. Jane had her hands treated. Luckily she suffered the equivalent of first degree chemical burns, nothing more. Sarah was sitting in the back of the ambulance, sobbing. Jane went to her. "Sarah..."

"It's all my fault. They were under my care. I'm no fucking good!" Jane grabbed and shook her, painful hands and all. "Sarah. *Look* at me!" Sarah's eyes finally focused on Jane. "There was nothing you could do. Eaters are a force of nature. Like a pissed-off bear in the woods. Hell, I saw you jump on that damned thing. You're lucky it didn't rip out your throat."

Sarah managed to catch her breath. "I should have..." "You should have nothing. You were doing your job. Which does not include taking on alien life forms. That's *my* job." Jane began to tear up. "Christ! It was *our* job–my and the other soldiers' job–and, we let it through."

Suddenly, Sarah was calm. With steeliness in her voice she responded. "Now look here, Major. You're a *hero*. That *thing* could have killed others. *You* killed it with the equivalent of a spear. A spear! And you beat yourself up? What are you, nuts?"

The two women stared silently at each other. Jane rested her sore hands on Sarah's shoulders. "Maybe I am a little nuts. But, I'm sane enough to know you have a class full of students that really need their teacher now. The teacher that almost sacrificed her life for them."

Sarah took a deep breath, and then let it out. "You are right, the living need me. And, Major, they need you also. No recriminations, no guilt. Just help us prevent this from ever happening again. Deal?" Jane managed to smile. "Deal." She yelped when she tried to shake Sarah's hand, "Damn, this is going to hurt for a while." "Yes, Jane, it will. It will hurt. But, I think we can get through it, with a little help from our friends." Sarah stood up and hugged her. Then, she stepped back, and wiped her face with the edge of the blanket the paramedics had wrapped her in.

"I guess I need to go to the kids. Thank you again, Major Grant... Jane. Oh. Can someone contact my husband and let him know I'm alright?"

"Done and done, Professor. See you later." They both turned to leave when suddenly Jane turned back.

"Sarah."

"What is it, Jane?"

"Joseph is one hell of a lucky man."

Sarah smiled. "Thank you." She returned to her class. Their parents would need a lot of help getting through this.

CHAPTER 17

The Director stood by the launch gantry, giving Kathy and Joseph some last minute instructions for the upcoming broadcast.

"Joseph, just relax and follow Kathy's lead. Not only is she a natural, but she has a lot of experience in this type of broadcast. We went over the basic questions, but I want this to be real and genuine, not some canned crap. I need people to see your true feelings, your beliefs about this space mission. Just relax and act like you're having a conversation with me. Or better yet, imagine that you are in bed with your wife, having a nice talk about the business of the day."

Kathy giggled. "I think the Professor would have something on his mind other than what is going on here if he was in bed with his wife. At least I hope so." Joseph blushed.

Adam gave Kathy a small glare. "Now see what you've done. I can't have him blushing during this broadcast. He is going to be one of the new heroes of humanity." Joseph blushed more. Kathy began to laugh. "Boss, I know you are used to running everything, but trust me. I'll make sure this goes smoothly. The Professor will do just fine once we start talking."

"Damn, I sound like an old woman, don't I?" Adam sighed. "No, don't answer that. I'll leave this in your capable hands, Kathy."

Without warning, Andrew the cyborg appeared, seemingly from nowhere. How a being so large could move in such a quiet and unobtrusive manner was a mystery. "Director, an Eater attack just happened on Key West. I have Security Control on the line." He pulled a handset from a hidden recess in his chest plate and handed it to Adam.

"This is the Director. Report." Adam stood silently, listening to the controller on the other end. Kathy was frozen with memories of her close call with the Eaters in Oregon, all caught on camera. Joseph stood in shock. This was out of his expertise and experience.

"Thank you. Keep me posted." Adam addressed Joseph. "An Eater attacked your wife's class. She's fine, but one of her students is dead. You are going to fly back with me on Andrew's Falcon, immediately. Andrew?"

"Of course, Director. I am at your service."

The Director now turned to Kathy. "I really need you to use your ability to communicate over that big eye we call broadcast television. This is going to be breaking news, no copy. Quick transition from the original subject to the Eater threat. Use film from your attack. You have more experience dealing with them than anyone else around. I need you to prevent panic, and prevent *anything* from derailing this space mission. People must know that things are getting better, that we are in control, that they are safe under Tschaaa oversight. Understand, Kathy?"

"Understood. I'll handle it, Boss. I'll make you proud." Kathy refocused on Joseph. "Take care, Professor. Make sure your wife is safe and sound. I'll take a rain check on this interview." She kissed Joseph's cheek. "See you later."

Kathy dashed over to the production and broadcast technicians and began to brief everyone on what was going on.

"She's definitely not a dumb blonde, is she, Director?"

"No Joseph, she's anything but. Come on, you get your wish. A ride in a Falcon."

Joseph had always wanted to get on board a Falcon, but not for this reason. The loss of anyone at Key West Operations Base was painful, the population was still small enough that most people had at least a passing knowledge of everyone else. The child and teenaged population was still more limited; everyone recognized each and every one of the young humans by name. And now one was dead, killed in a horrible fashion. While getting settled onboard the Falcon, Adam Lloyd gave him a quick rundown on what had happened. An Eater had caught Sarah's class completely flat-footed. Sarah had almost been killed trying to defend her charges. By pure chance, Major Grant had been nearby. "Let me get this straight, Director. Jane

Grant killed this creature with an improvised spear?"

"Yes, Joseph, she did. Only our security police and soldiers normally go armed. I think that policy changes as of now. Having a feral population of very dangerous creatures on your doorstep requires drastic measures. I'm going to have as many people armed as possible. Everyone is going to be required to help provide for their own defense."

"I think you have a bonafide hero on your hands, Director. Killing a nasty alien with a spear is not something people, even the military, train for."

"Yes, I know. I knew that from the first moment, when the Chief and I recruited her, she was special and was capable of great things. She definitely just proved it in spades."

"Time to strap in, Gentlemen." Andrew's voice boomed over the speaker system. The Falcon was not set up for comfortable passenger travel. Andrew occupied the pilot's chair, with another similar chair just behind it. Behind those were four very basic 1950s-style airline passenger seats. The cargo hold was just for that–cargo–which usually included collected meat.

Adam and Joseph strapped themselves in. The Falcon levitated and shot straight up, reminding Joseph of a high speed elevator suddenly rising. They accelerated straight ahead in the proverbial blink of an eye. Joseph felt a slight acceleration, but not to the extent he believed he would. Before he could comment, the Director explained. "Acceleration dampening system, Professor. This craft can create a small field that counteracts gravity and acceleration, at least in the passenger area."

Joseph was bemused. "And they need me to give them advice on spacecraft? I think they have sold themselves a bill of goods."

"I disagree, Professor, if for no other reason than the Tschaaa have become rather stagnant. Even before the long trip here, they lacked the true hints of genius that often fuels great discoveries. Humans still have that spark."

"We have arrived," Andrew announced.

"My God!" exclaimed Joseph. "How fast were we going? I felt virtually nothing."

"Over Mach 3, Professor. Give or take a couple of decimal points," Andrew answered over the intercom.

"It was smoother than riding in a luxury car. I sure would like to have one of these. This Falcon makes our spaceplane look like a Model T. I understand you could fly to the moon and back in this."

"You are correct, Professor," Andrew replied. "Falcons can fly between planets. Maybe someday, Professor, you will have that chance. But right now, one step at a time. Prepare for debarkation." Andrew had landed them in the middle of the sports field where the attack had taken place. Two vehicles were there to meet them. No sooner had they cleared the Falcon than Andrew launched, out of sight, with little or no noise. Even a delta, superior to human fighter aircraft, still looked like an also ran when compared to the Falcons. Joseph wondered what other marvels he would discover when he took the spaceplane up to Platform One.

"Professor, your wife is in her classroom. She has an overdeveloped sense of duty. Please take her home and help her rest. That's an order," Adam said it calmly but with a bit of steel in his voice.

"Yes, Sir." Joseph answered.

"Tell Sarah we know how she tried to defend her wards like a she bear defending her cubs. That will not soon be forgotten by me or the parents of the children."

"Yes, Director. I will be certain to tell her that. I don't expect my wife to almost get her killed on a normal day in school."

"Please also let her know I would like to see her after she has rested and recovered. Now, I must track down Major Grant." The two men took the separate vehicles and went their separate ways.

Joseph found Sarah in her main classroom, reviewing the class roster
when he walked in.

"Joseph! What are you doing here? How did you get here so fast?"

"A quick ride in a Falcon, thanks to your heroics. I have orders from the Director to take you home to rest."

"I... I can't do that Joseph. I still need to talk to all the parents, to explain what happened. They need to hear it from me. The children were in my care. I am responsible." As Sarah spoke, her tone began to take on a shrillness that told Joseph one thing. Traumatic shock was beginning to set in. He went to her as she stood up to argue with him. He threw his arms around her, kissed her on her forehead, and then hugged her tight.

"I thought I had lost you."

Sarah sputtered, then grabbed him tightly and began to sob into his chest. They stood that way for what seemed like an eternity, as Sarah poured out her fear and frustration in tears. When she was finally finished, she looked up at her tall, still gangly husband.

"You have always been too tall to kiss right. You should have married an Amazon, not a woman like me."

"You, my dear, are far from normal. I know that, the Director knows that, and now the rest of Key West knows that."

"All I did was get myself knocked silly, Joseph. Jane Grant is the real hero. She killed the fucker. Pardon my French."

Joseph took her face in his hands, and kissed her long and deep. "Dearest, you put yourself in danger with little or no hope for success. With no training of any kind to fall back on. That takes true courage."

Joseph kissed her again. "I have been ordered to take you home. Right now, the Director is in no mood for disagreement. Wipe your eyes. Then we go. There is a car waiting for us outside."

"All right, Joseph. No argument from me today." Sarah took a deep breath, and then she sighed. "I'm too tired."

She looked into his eyes. "I love you, Professor."

"I love you too, Professor. Let's go home."

The Director growled at Major Grant's staff when they tried to snap to attention when he entered the office. "At ease, damnit. I'm not a four star General."

He barged into the Major's office, shutting the door behind him just short of slamming it. Adam found Jane Grant at her desk, trying to compose an after action report, typing in on her computer with her injured hands. "Director, I'm just trying to get this done while it is fresh in my mind," Jane explained as she jumped to her feet.

"Go home and rest, Major. *That* is an order."

Jane froze for a moment, and then her shoulders slumped a bit. "Yes, Sir. I'm leaving."

A moment later, the Director was hugging her. "If you ever get yourself killed pulling a stunt like that, I will be royally pissed. Trying to break in a new Ops Officer *and* Jill of all trades, master of most is too damn hard."

He let her go and stepped back. "By the way, I already heard someone refer to you as Wonder Woman. Being a hero is going to be a pain in the ass for you."

Jane began to tear up. "I was a few moments too late, Director. I had to watch a young girl being slaughtered." Adam produced a silken handkerchief and handed it to her. "Here, Major, wipe your eyes and blow your nose. Then, go to your quarters and let your hands heal. The fault for the girl's death stops at my desk. I have gotten way too complacent. An assassination attempt, then a young girl is eaten in front of her classmates. Time for me to buckle down and do my job."

"I started a formal inquiry into the assassination, Director. The investigators are working on it as we speak..."

"That is enough, Major. Go home and rest. Let the rest of us earn our pay. Okay?"

Jane smiled. "Yes Sir. Heard and done." She winced when she picked up her cover.

"Hurts?" Adam asked.

"Yes Sir. My hands and my gut. I keep wondering if I had been walking just a bit faster, been a few minutes earlier, I could have been between that bastard Eater and that little girl."

"Then you would have been out of position to do what you did, and you and Sarah Fassbinder would be dead along with that little girl. Plus, maybe that thing would have killed other children, who knows. I don't know its mental processes. What I do know is that you used a metal fence post to make a throw which would have made an olympic javelin thrower envious. Everything happens for a reason. Don't second guess yourself. You did what you could, and killed that horror. That means a lot. To the people here and to me."

Jane suddenly kissed Adam's cheek. "Sorry to violate protocol, but thank you, Sir. Your opinion means the world to me."

Adam smiled. "Thank you, Major. Now, please. Rest."

"Yes Sir."

After viewing the remains of the Eater at a special room at the Biology and Animal Husbandry Section of the Dept. of Resources, Adam called Chief Hamilton on a secure line. "Chief, thanks to Major Grant, we have one dead Eater here. The question is, how did it get here so fast? The last report was a sighting near San Francisco a week ago. A couple may have moved down the coast from Kathy's contact in Oregon. But, all the way across the continental U.S.? I don't buy it."

"Well, Boss, we did just have that first convoy of trucks from the west coast to the east coast, containing surplus and salvaged material. Maybe one stowed away."

"No, Chief, that trip took eight days. After spending that many days cooped up, from what I understand, an Eater would have burst out of the truck trailer like a bat out of hell. Someone would have either been eaten, or at least have seen it."

"Then Boss, I'd go to the source. Ask the Tschaaa how this could have happened."

"Excellent idea. I'll get Andrew to get me a secure video link with our Lordship. I'll brief you later."

"Sounds good. And Boss, when you have a moment, watch our broadcasts. Kathy is creating newscast history for a new generation to follow. Fox and CNN would both be eating their hearts out if they still existed."

Adam always thought Kathy would work out. Now, he knew for sure. "Will do. Gotta go Chief."

The Director contacted Andrew, who met him at his office. Andrew pulled a small monitor screen connected to a video phone, directly from his cyborg body. He silently made contact to the Tschaaa Lordship though his personal interface. The image of the Tschaaa Lordship known as Neptune flashed onto the com screen.

"Director. Andrew told me what happened. You lost a young one to an Eater."

While the Tschaaa Lord's translator broadcast his language into English, he manipulated his social tentacles to communicate extreme sorrow and distress. Adam had been given a video dictionary of Tschaaa sign speech, as important to Tschaaa as facial expressions and voice inflections were to humans.

Adam had never actually seen a Tschaaa demonstrate extreme sorrow and distress. Now he saw the waving, twitching and shaking of the tentacles, so unlike the smooth, flowing movements the Tschaaa normally exhibited. It was almost like he was sobbing.

"Yes, my Lordship. We lost an eight year old female child to an Eater. Now I have a large favor I must ask. A huge favor. I need to know how the Eater got from the west coast to the east coast in such a short time, with no sightings in-between. It seems impossible." His Lordship paused, its tentacles frozen in signs of sorrow for a few moments.

"Unfortunately, I was afraid you would ask that question so quickly. There are times when I think a less perceptive Director would make my job easier; fewer difficult questions. But then, we would not have made the progress we have today."

The Tschaaa Lord paused. "Unfortunately, in some ways, I already have what I believe is the answer." What appeared to be a Tschaaa version of a radar track showed the large unmistakable outline of a Falcon meeting with what looked like a large Go-fast boat off of the Florida Keys. The two vehicles stayed together for about ten minutes, then the Falcon disappeared in the blink of an eye. The Go-fast made its way to Tavernier Cove.

"That, my good Director, was a Falcon from the Lord in control of Africa. I was only notified of this meeting by our surveillance system because I specifically asked for the information. We Tschaaa do not conduct what you humans call espionage against one another, so no one pays attention to our comings and goings, or the movements of air and spacecraft unless there is a danger of collision. Protocol dictates we contact each other when a Lord enters another Lord's area. It has been followed in the past."

"But not now, my Lordship."

"No, Adam, not now. I am certain, as you are, that one or more of the Eaters were transported by that Falcon. Next week is scheduled a meeting of all the Earthbound Lords. This will cause a serious area of contention."

Adam paused, weighing how he was going to ask the same question. "If I may be so bold My Lordship... Tschaaa rarely, if ever, conspire against another Crèche, correct?"

The Tschaaa Lordship Neptune signed resignation with its tentacles, almost like a human sigh. "Yes, my Director that is so. But now, it appears as if your human foibles are beginning to infect some Tschaaa Lords. In the past, conflict involving areas and populations of food stock would be handled directly and dealt with. A worst case scenario would involve a duel between individual Tschaaa. No lies, no attempts to damage another's possessions by subterfuge."

Adam remained silent. Tschaaa interrelationships had just entered a new phase for them.

The Tschaaa Lord continued. "Rest assured, I will have an answer or I will challenge this Lord to a duel. Maybe even both. This is the first time such a situation like this has happened in several millennia. It approaches what you humans would refer to as insanity."

Adam stayed silent for a moment longer, unless he could no longer contain his curiosity. "Sir, Lordship, I must ask. Why the distress over the loss of one of our children? Sorry if I am blunt, but are they not used like we use veal?"

"Because, my Director, as I have often said, you are not meat. That is what the so called dark ones, those individuals rounded up in Cattle Country are for. I ask you, if a young canine–a puppy–died, would you not feel sorrow?"

"Yes, My Lordship, I would. But prior to the invasion, there were people in parts of the world that ate dogs. They may feel sorrow about a personal pet, but not specifically puppies."

"Well, then, My Director, I guess I am beginning to look at your young, your children, as you look at puppies. Your continued presence may be starting to influence my feelings and beliefs. Is that good, or bad?"

"Your Lordship, with respect, I think it is a good thing."

"So do I, my Adam, so do I. And, hopefully, I can convince the other Lords that to embrace the idea that violent and deceitful parts of human nature is an aberration. But the love of puppies, of young non-Cattle humans, is not."

"Yes Lord, I agree."

"Good." The Squid Lord signed fellowship with its tentacles. "Now, I will have what you call the eye in the sky present me with a workup as to where the human seacraft went. Then, I will let you know. You may track them and the Eaters down. The humans will be harvested. You may kill the Eaters. Agreed?"

"Yes Sir."

"Excellent. I will have Andrew give you the information once we have completed our investigation. Now, I must go. Please extend my sorrow to the birth mother of the young one. All Tschaaa grieve when our young are lost."

"Yes, my Lordship, I will tell her."

Lord Neptune ended the connection. Andrew stowed his equipment in his secret nooks and crannies that were his man-machine interface.

"You will have the necessary information as soon as I do, Director. Then, we go hunting."

"Thank you, Andrew. May I ask a personal question?"

"I have no personal life. I am interfaced twenty-four hours a day. Go ahead, ask anything."

"Did you have children before your... change into a robocop?"

"No, I did not." Andrew paused in thought for a few moments. "But I would have liked to have some, I believe. That is almost impossible now, of course. However, although I am part man, part Tschaaa machine, I can still feel for the young. Both the Tschaaa connected side of me and the human connected side of me agree... the young, children, are of primary importance."

CHAPTER 18

As events transpired in the Tschaaa controlled Reconstructed States of America, they did not go unnoticed by those outside the occupied areas. Nor did they distract or deter the citizens of the Unoccupied States of America and their allies from their primary mission: Freeing the human species from the yoke of Tschaaa oppression.

  —From the *Literary Works of Princess Akiko,* Free Japan Royal Family

MALMSTROM ARMED FORCES BASE, MONTANA

Lt. Yamamoto, the three Russian female officers, "Pappy" Gunn, General Reed, and Torbin were in a conference room at the Headquarters Building for a special ceremony. Only Torbin and the General knew what was about to happen. All four foreign national officers were dressed in their equivalent of dress uniforms, something that Torbin had commissioned. Torbin had provided the photos of Russian and Japanese dress uniforms to a group of tailors, and the sizes of the four officers.

A week prior, the General had told him to arrange all the foreign national officers to have dress uniforms befitting their station. Torbin, being a good Marine, immediately got to work with no questions asked. Then, Madam President showed up out of the clear blue sky and he now knew the reason. All four officers had tried on the uniforms the day before, and with a couple minor alterations, soon all had dress uniforms their own countries could not provide them in a foreign land.

Of course, none of them held a candle to Marine Corps Dress Blues.

The officers snapped to attention when Madam President entered the conference room. Following her was one of the broadest, most muscular black men that Torbin had ever seen. He was a tad over six feet, but his mass made him look much bigger. He looked like ninety-nine percent of his body mass was muscle.

"At ease, ladies and gentlemen. I know we are all very busy, but sometimes a little recognition, pomp and circumstance is required. Afterward, I will be giving everyone in the room a little briefing about a project for which I need your help."

"First, a quick introduction. The rather large African-American man behind me is former Chief Master Sergeant George Williams the Fourth. He now serves as my bodyguard, special assistant and troubleshooter when I need to ensure something is done. You may think of him as a Special Assistant to the Office of the President. He was also an Air Force judo team member who made the U.S. Olympic team a while back, when there *was* a U.S. Olympic team. In the heavyweight division, of course."

Madam President smiled. "He will be staying here, General, in order to ensure you receive all the support you need. "

"Yes, Ma'am." General Reed acknowledged. He was also acknowledging that he knew Mr. Williams was the eyes and ears of President, to ensure the General did what he was required. Or else. Ichiro showed signs of recognizing Mr. Williams, and had a look in his eyes that Torbin had come to understand was one of utmost respect. Torbin would have to inquire later about how Ichiro's connection to the President's distinctive assistant.

"And now for the pomp and circumstance. Ladies first. Captain Aleksandra Smirnov, Lieutenants Afanasiy Kozlov, Inna Popov, front and center."

The three Russian Officers marched up to the front of the room and formed a line, Captain Aleksandra saluting as ranking officer.

"Personnel reporting as ordered, Madam President."

The President inquired of Torbin, "Have you been trying to turn them into hardass Marines, Captain Bender?"

Before he could answer, Aleksandra piped up. "Begging your pardon, Madam President. We are Russian. We were born hard."

The President chuckled. "I suspect that is true. Captain, you and your comrades are hereby awarded the brand new U. S. of A. Tschaaa Campaign Medal for your efforts fighting our common enemy.

Congratulations." She shook the hand of each of the Russian women, and then smartly saluted them. The Russian officers stepped back, and assumed their prior stances.

"Captain Yamamoto. Front and center."

Ichiro was momentarily confused. Should he correct the President about his rank? He smartly stepped to the front of the room and saluted. "Lieutenant Yamamoto reporting as ordered, Ma'am."

Madam President saluted back, and added, "That's *Captain* Yamamoto. As of last week. I have here your promotion orders, as well as a Japanese Distinguished Service Medal. You should know better than to disagree with an older woman." She smiled at her own comment. Ichiro's registered shock, and then pride.

"In our tradition, mothers and wives often pin on our men's new rank. Would you mind if I filled in for them?"

Ichiro looked into the President's eyes. "I would be honored, Madam President."

After she had deftly pinned on the new rank, she handed Ichiro two wrapped packages. "Your Commander also asked me to deliver these packages from your aunt. He said you would know what they are."

Ichiro took the soft packages reverently from Madam President. He touched them to his forehead as he bowed to the President. "You do my family honor, Madam President."

"You do our citizens honor by helping us free our country from an occupying enemy, Captain Yamamoto. It is an honor to stand in for your family." Captain Yamamoto came to attention, saluted, did an about face, then returned to his seat.

"Now that we have concluded the fun portion of our business, let us address the serious part," announced the President. "Mr. Williams, the PowerPoint, please." The lights dimmed, and enlarged images of an area map and military base appeared on the screen. "Ladies and Gentlemen, Key West Operations Base and new capital of the Occupied States of America. Home to Director Lloyd and his minions."

A second image appeared, showing a huge installation ninety percent underwater. "Marquesas Keys, once a National Park. Now home for His Tschaaa Lordship, who adopted the Earthly name of Neptune from our human mythology."

Madam President turned and looked at her small audience. "This is our target. We need to plan a strike at these nerve centers as soon as possible. After six years of occupation, resistance from the general population outside of the Unoccupied States has all but disappeared. The only attempts at defying Tschaaa control have been breakouts from Cattle Country and failed attempts at assassination of Director Lloyd. We just lost five operatives. Director Lloyd has a very charmed life."

She continued. "Captain Torbin is putting together a very highly classified attempt at a major attack against Key West and the Tschaaa installation. You all will be involved. You will know only what you need to know. Captain Torbin will be the *only* one with the complete picture."

Madam President clicked to the next slide in the PowerPoint presentation. A series of pictures of men and women appeared. "Here are photos of the Director, his right hand man Chief Hamilton, and various members of his inner circle. As you can see, many of them are female. Adam Lloyd seems to have a way with ladies, and has been able to 'turn' all the female operatives we have slipped into the area. For you Russian officers, General Reed thinks the Director is a modern day Rasputin." Aleksandra raised a respectful hand. "Yes, Captain."

"Madam President, it is commonly reported in Russian history archives that Rasputin was able to hypnotize, to take mental control of those around him. Do you and the General believe that the Director has such power?"

"Yes, Captain Smirnov. He either has some ability to exert mental control on all those around him, or he is just plain damn lucky."

The President suddenly displayed a small smile. "Now is as good a time to mention Mr. Williams' source of expertise of this subject.

George, care to elaborate on the subject?"

George Williams stood up, and sighed. "The Director, Chief Hamilton, and I served together in the U.S. Air Force prior to the first rock strike. Both were commensurate professionals and Adam Lloyd was one of the nicest people you could meet. Not a racist bone in him."

"Before someone asks what happened, I do not know. I think he actually believes that he is insuring the survival of at least part of the humanity by sacrificing another part. Intelligence we have obtained is that Adam Lloyd and the Chief have personally saved dozens of people. And when I mean personally saved, I mean they have killed some real assholes, pardon my French, to save other humans. They have even taken out some harvester Robs with no ill effects on them. His Tschaaa Lordship has given him unprecedented power and latitude under the so-called Protocols of Selected Survival, and so far it has worked. Every day, the Director broadcasts over his reconstituted mass media new successes, new advances. They are about to launch a Tschaaa supported space launch from Cape Canaveral. Bottom line, he gets things done."

"But," George Williams continued. "There has appeared a chink in the armor. This morning, while we were getting ready for this meeting, an alien lifeform known as an Eater appeared on Key West and ate a child."

There was a sharp intake of breath from the Russians.

"Yes, I know. The Eaters have already appeared in substantial numbers in East Russia, now Free Russia, after being dumped in China. However, it is physically impossible for an Eater to travel unnoticed from the last known location on the U.S. west coast, all the way to Key West in just over a week, unless it had help."

The former Chief clicked to a new screen. "We have some excellent computer and communications hackers, former Homeland Security and U.S. Customs cyber agents, who hacked this picture of a meet of a Falcon with a human go-fast boat just off the Key Largo area. The hacked information points to the fact that another Lord is screwing with Lord Neptune."

The President chuckled. "The fact is, the Squids have no concept of communications and signal security. Only those systems that Director Lloyd has put in place have any security or anti-hacking software. However, the Tschaaa do talk over secure lines maintained by the new crop of robocops, which are more difficult to hack."

The officers watched the short surveillance video, and then the Kathy Monroe broadcast of the complete story, gory details and all, minus the secret meet between boat and craft. Seeing his brother's former fiancé on the broadcast made Torbin do a double take. The last six years had been kind to her, or she was just very tough. She still looked great.

"The Eater slaughtered a young eight year old girl before being killed by Major Jane Grant," Kathy reported. "Major Grant did this using an improvised spear. To say she is a hero is an understatement."

A woman identified as Professor Fassbinder was then on camera. "Major Grant saved my life and the lives of my other students. If the Medal of Honor still exists, she deserves it."

Back to Kathy. "Our Lordship, Lord Neptune, personally provided this reporter the following audio recording."

A generic photo of a large Tschaaa was displayed as the Shakespearean voice he had created for human contact proclaimed, "To all the humans in the Tschaaa controlled area of North America. Rest assured that the Eater threat will not be allowed to continue. And, to the parents of the victim, the little young one, it is a source of pain that I, with all my resources, was unable to prevent this death. The young are of supreme importance, for Tschaaa and for humans equally. My sorrow is great, but my resolve is greater. The young will be protected."

The video ended. Captain Torbin spoke up. "Is that statement from the Squid Lord for real, or just so much bullpucky?"

Madam President looked toward George Williams. He answered, "Yes, Captain, believe it or not. The Squids have an extremely developed sense of duty toward their young. Now, this Lordship is apparently beginning to extend that sense of duty and protection toward human children associated with those under his direct control. This may be a potential weakness that we may use against him."

"And how would that work?" General Reed asked.

"Threats of attacks on breeding areas may distract the Tschaaa, and get us a chance to hit them in their main command and control centers. Failing that, an actual capability to interfere with their breeding on a large scale basis might force them to deal with us an equals, rather than as chattel."

"Or, it would cause such a massive retaliation that all of us will be living in caves as they take breeding stock and leave," pointed out General Reed.

"We have considered that. It is our assessment that the Tschaaa are becoming much too attached to our oceans. We think our planet is a bit younger than theirs, and our oceans are a reminder of younger, happier days that the Tschaaa will have difficulty leaving behind. Or destroying."

General Reed grunted. "I certainly hope you are right, Mr. Williams."

The President interrupted. "Since everyone in this room has been cleared both by us and their respective countries, and the room has been secured from eavesdropping, let me cut to the chase. We, and by *we* I mean all resources of the U.S.A., have been working on multiple scenarios by which we might attack and expel the enemy from our country, and eventually the entire Earth. This includes biological and chemical attacks." She paused a few seconds to let that sink in. "We have even looked at trying to replicate the disease that made the original prey creatures–the meat primates on their home world–poisonous and infect us with it. If it won't kill us too, that is.

"We are looking into specific attacks against the Squid's breeding Crèches. But that is taking time. We need to make a strike soon, to show the world that the human race has not just rolled over and acquiesced to being food for an alien species on a daily basis. Inertia is beginning to set in, people. The idea that people of a darker skin pigmentation are just fine as sacrificial lambs is becoming commonplace...

"...And that is *unacceptable!*" Madam President slammed her fist on the table. Torbin saw anger in her eyes that brought him a new level of respect. It appeared that, given the chance, she would gut a Squid herself with a dull blade.

Madam President drew a deep breath. "The idea of an alien invader occupying much of my America makes my blood boil. I am an old-fashioned patriot. Death before dishonor. If anyone here isn't willing to buy a ticket for this ride, it's time to get off the train."

No one spoke. Then Ichiro slowly stood. "Madam President, if I may."

"Of course, Captain. You have certainly earned the right to be heard."

He began. "In my country, my people have accepted the possibility of death since the first day the Tako–Squids–arrived. Through an accident of history that resulted in high radiation levels in parts of my country, we were spared the harvesting the rest of the world has suffered. Although we have had to work hard to feed our people, we have suffered only limited physical attacks. The spirit of Bushido is now strong in our people. Not the Bushido depicted in your

Hollywood, but what Bushido, the way of the warrior, was originally meant to be. Be honorable. Protect the weak, the old, and the young. And fight and die if necessary, for our country, our people.

"My government, my people, want all to know... this fight is also *our* fight. Everyone, every human, is now an honorary Japanese. We will fight and die rather than let another person be used as a meal for a Tako."

The President looked at Ichiro. She thought what a fine young man he was. He reminded her of her son, but her son was dead. She was the President of many, not just a mother of a few.

"Now I know why you were just honored by your countrymen, my new Captain. I think you just put into words what everyone has been thinking for a while. We are honored to be considered your countrymen and countrywomen."

Ichiro bowed. Madam President bowed in return. What she did not realize was that Ichiro had just adopted her personally as well, a long lost relative now reunited, a family member to be honored... and protected.

"Back to brass tacks. As of this moment, attack planning begins, with each of you as representatives of your respective countries. Yes, this has all been coordinated with your respective leaders and commanders. Captain Torbin will work out more of the details with each of you. Much of the information will be compartmentalized, built into an organization of cells, each with a specific duty. As we reach D-Day, then everything will be put into the big picture and communicated in total. This extreme caution concerning specific details is because our so-called Lord Neptune seems to ferret out things even before we realize what we are about to do."

The President continued. "I will say two specific things about assignments now. Captain Yamamoto, you and Mister Gunn will have the task of bringing a Squid delta up to flying status in record time. Just imagine that it needs to be done as of yesterday, because it does. The Japanese government is transporting more pieces and a couple of fairly complete deltas to us. Thanks to the numerous dogfights the Squids seem to be enjoying having with the Japanese Air Force, rather than just bomb it out of existence, quite a few deltas have been lost over and around the Japanese islands, one credited to Captain Yamamoto. We need an operational delta, to be flown by the good

Captain here. Clear?"

"Hai. Crystal, Madam President."

"Now, Captain Smirnov. You and your Lieutenants, all trained intelligence operatives, spies–let's just air that dirty laundry now–get to figure out how to successfully infiltrate Director Lloyd's inner sanctum. Preferably, by one of you three attractive ladies. If not, we need you to find a another likely candidate, as soon as possible. Mr. Williams can assist with details about who Director Lloyd and the Chief really are, and what they really believe."

The President looked directly at Torbin. "The General and I have details to share with you. Right now, we need you to start planning how you would attack Key West and bring down the Director."

She paused. She knew she was about to send many people to their deaths, possibly people in this room. Tough as she was, she was still human.

"As I have said before, acceptance of the status quo is unacceptable, especially when it means quotas of humans being sent to slaughter. We have to shake things up *now*. I know you have heard that the Tschaaa have removed most of their large generational star craft from Earth orbit. Our scientists surmise they will eventually attempt a Sun Dive Maneuver to slingshot themselves out of the solar system. Sounds like good news, right?"

She gave a wry grin. "The problem is, they are leaving most of their brethren behind. Once they are gone, the Tschaaa won't be able to leave, even if they want to. So, we have about four years at most to make Earth so uncomfortable–maybe even deadly–that they will want to leave on those ships. If not, it will be a species fight to the death.

"Now, time for me to go to the General's office. It has been a pleasure to meet you all, and it is an honor to serve with you. You are the future for humanity. So, as we progress, go with godspeed. Thank you."

The sun was setting when Torbin headed back to his quarters. Aleksandra would meet him there later. He frowned. The concept of her being sent undercover was not a pleasant one. However, they were soldiers, and were paid to head to the sound of battle.

He heard a cry of greeting. It was Ichiro. "Torbin-san! A moment please."

He stopped and waited for Ichiro to catch up, which didn't take long. Damn, he could move fast when he wanted to. Apparently, Ichiro's slender appearance belied the fact that his body was a coiled spring of energy. "What's up, my new Captain?"

Ichiro grinned a bit self-consciously. "I did not expect that, my friend. There are so many more qualified Japanese officers…"

"Oh, bullshit. Ichiro, there are times when you are just too self-deprecating. You deserve whatever you get, if for no other reason than you've managed to stay sane after dealing with me and the other crazy gaijin."

Ichiro gave a short laugh, before returning to a more serious expression. "Torbin-san, I have… something for you. From my home."

Torbin was about to respond with a typical smart ass remark when the look in Ichiro's eyes told him this was very important to the young Japanese. "Go ahead, Ichiro."

Ichiro handed over one of the wrapped packages that had been given to him by the President. "Please, Torbin-san. Open it."

Torbin carefully unwrapped the package. Inside was something he, being an amateur military historian, had read about but believed was a thing of the past. "Is this a thousand stitch belt?"

"Hai, a senninbari haramaki. A belt for eternal good luck in war, for protection. My Aunt had two made. This is for you. I am wearing mine already." The thousand stitch belt was literally, a cloth belt made up of one thousand french knot stitches, and not just by one person's hand. Ichiro's Aunt had one thousand different Japanese women add a single stitch to the belt, one at a time. She might have stood on a street corner, asking passersby to each sew one stitch in the belt, in the traditional way. Or maybe she took it to work. However she did it, this belt represented a way of life not seen in the west. The stitching was interlaced with red color, and what appeared to be human hair. Torbin touched the soft cloth of the six inch wide belt.

"Ichiro, I can't take this. I am not Japanese and I am… unworthy." He stammered the last word of the sentence. He was a man never at a loss for words. Until now.

"Torbin-san, now it is time for me to tell you not to be so humble. First, as I said to Madam President, you are all honorary Japanese. And, you are my brother, from this day forward. No, do not argue. You have the spirit of the Samurai in you. You must have been Japanese in a past life. There is no other explanation. You have shed blood and given your own blood as a warrior. You *are* worthy."

Torbin had an unfamiliar lump in his throat. Damn. No one had ever done something like this, other than his late brother William. Quickly, he unbuttoned his uniform blouse and his shirt, and wrapped the belt around his waist. It felt like it had always been there, like it belonged there. He buttoned his uniform back up as a smiling Ichiro looked on. Then, from under his blouse, he removed his Ka-bar that he always carried, even when wearing his dress blues.

"Ichiro, some of our Native American tribes had an ancient ritual." He slit his left palm. "Please do the same to your palm." Ichiro produced a tanto knife and slit his left palm. Torbin reached out and Ichiro, seeing what was needed, clasped his cut left palm to Torbin's left palm. "Ichiro, we are now blood brothers. Our blood has mixed. We are now brothers here, and in death, when we pass on to the next realm. This bond cannot be broken by other humans... or aliens."

Ichiro beamed. "This has been a good day. We are now brothers in blood. We will now be invincible. We will slay the Takos in numbers that will be as numerous as grains of sand on the beach. Now, we need a drink, a toast. I have sake in my room."

"Okay, but just one drink. I need my rest. I have a shitload of things to do."

"Hai. Of course... brother."

Early the next morning, Aleksandra and Torbin were sharing breakfast in his quarters prior to setting out for another long day of work. She had chewed his ass out in both English and Russian when he had been delayed at Ichiro's for more than just one cup of sake. Then, they made up with some raucous sex, after which they had lain together in bed, Aleks snuggled up on his chest, gently running her nails across his body. And, as countless humans before had done, engaged in a little serious pillow talk.

"Torbin, did you know that Mr. Williams had him meet his family, had him over for meals?" They knew who "he" was without mentioning the name.

"Well, Aleks, sometimes people change. Sometimes, seeing too much blood, too much death can corrupt a person's ability to make a rational decision. They choose what they believe is the lesser evil, without being able to admit to themselves that their choice is still evil."

"I do not know what to think, Tor. He seems to really believe he is helping most by watching some being sacrificed. He apparently is a very nice, helpful, even loving person."

Torbin grunted. "People say the same thing about psychopaths, sociopaths, serial killers. Many charm their victims, and lull them with a false sense of security. That is, until their own brutal instincts kick in, and they follow their own dark and disturbed desires. So, sorry if I don't propose a certain individual for a Citizen of the Year Award."

"Well, Torbin, my love, if he is a sociopath, is psychotic, he still is able to function without killing people other than in self-defense. And women just love and worship him."

Torbin chuckled. "Women always like the bad boys. Nice guys finish last." Aleks pinched him. "Ouch, woman."

"Is that why I love you, because you are a 'bad boy'?"

"The baddest," Torbin answered.

Suddenly, Aleks rose from his chest, and stared directly into his eyes, just inches away. "My Captain, I love you because you are the most honorable man I have ever met. You are the one I desire to spend the rest of my life with… if you will have me."

Torbin had been feeling a warm glow for quite some time whenever he was near Aleksandra. Hell, whenever he thought of her. It wasn't just sexual. For what was probably the first time in his life, he was head over heels in love. Based on the look in Aleks' eyes, she felt the same. The last time he saw anything similar was the look Kathy Monroe had given his brother William, and vice versa.

Aleks' brow furrowed. "I just saw a dark cloud pass your eyes. What is it? Do you not want me?"

Torbin put his finger to her lips. "Hush. That is farthest thing from the truth."

He took her face in his hands. "Aleksandra Smirnov, I love you more than you can imagine. I wake up every day, happy that it is another day that I will see you. Will you marry me? I don't have a ring; I can't ask your father for your hand…" Aleks stopped his rambling with a deep passionate kiss.

"Is that a 'yes', or were you were just trying to get me to shut…" Another kiss from Aleks.

A minute later, Aleks pulled her lips away. "Torbin Bender, of course I will marry you. After this war is over, I will give you many fine Russian babies."

"Does this mean that you do not want to cuddle up to a certain sociopath we were just talking... Ouch! You bit me!"

"I will do worse things to you if you ever mention that idea again." Aleks then gave him an evil little smile. "Besides, you are lucky. His 'harem' already has a black-haired woman, as well as blondes. We have decided he would be attracted to a red headed woman. So, you are stuck with me."

Torbin covered his eyes with the back of his arm and spoke in a falsetto voice. "Stuck with you. Such torture..." Aleks distracted Torbin once more with a kiss, and a few other things she had in mind.

It was an hour or so later, they were eating an American-style breakfast Torbin had prepared. Ham, bacon, eggs, and toast, with dark Russian Caravan tea as the only concession to Aleks.

"You will make me fat, Torbin my love," Aleks protested.

"Then I will just have to work it off you, my dear," Torbin answered with a wink and a grin.

She smiled back. "Promises, promises."

The secure line telephone rang, a recent addition to his quarters. It was still early, with nothing scheduled until later, but Torbin decided to take the call. "Captain Bender here." It was the General. "Good. I see you're up already. I know you have some training plans in the works for the selection of the personnel you will need, but we have a real time problem that may be used as part of the selection process. Eaters have miraculously appeared near Montana and in Alaska, along with reports of so called Kraken humans. They may have been seeded like the one down south. In about a week, I need to you to start picking a team to take to the field for some real world action that will double as training and selection. Nothing like the actual fear of death to see how someone acts under pressure. See you in the training section later." "Yes Sir." He hung up the telephone, a grin on his face. He pumped his fist. "Yes!"

"What is it?" Aleks asked.

"Action. A chance get to go to the field to hunt Eaters and Krakens. It will be used as part of my selection process for assault team members. I won't be stuck in the Training Section." "I am happy for you, Captain. It will free me and give my fellow officers more time to develop our on infiltration strategy." She stood up stiffly and began to take her dishes to the sink.

Sensing that something was amiss, Torbin stepped over and grabbed Aleks around her waist. "Sorry I sounded so excited about leaving the base. It has nothing to do with you." Aleks set the dishes down and turned in his arms to face him. She put her hands on his shoulders and looked into his eyes. "You American men are just as stupid as Russian men. You do not understand women at all. Of course I know it has nothing to do with trying to get away from me. I can tell by the way you look at me and touch me that you are, in the American vernacular, 'hooked'." Torbin noticed her eyes were beginning to moisten with tears.

"But you men think you are indestructible. We women know different. So we are fearful that you will return injured from playing with your man toys." Her voice caught. "Or maybe not return at all. "Torbin, you are first man I have truly loved. You are the first man I have allowed myself to care for since the Squids arrived. I have seen too many people killed and eaten, to not have developed a tough, steely shell. I am *hard*." A tear rolled down her cheek. "Now you have softened that shell and I am feeling again. Damn you." She kissed him hard. He kissed her back. They stood hugging each other for a while. Finally, they separated.

"Now I must touch up my makeup so that I look as a Russian officer is expected to." She looked into Torbin's eyes. "You have my heart. Please do not break it."

The next few days became a blur of preparation activity. Torbin put together two teams of possible applicants for his Special Unit, twenty each, forty total. He knew Ichiro was actually part of the air assets part of the mission, but in the back of his mind he was scheming to have him with the assault unit if that fell through. With the son of Nippon's combat skills, he knew no one would question his presence. As Torbin readied a trip to the field to go after the Eaters, Krakens, and maybe Ferals, Ichiro demonstrated his abilities to everyone in a most unusual way. All forty of Torbin's applicants were present in the gym, where he was busting their asses with calisthenics, sprints, push ups, trying to put as much pressure on them as possible. His years training to be a certified physical trainer as well as his SEAL experience gave him a one up on his personnel. As the saying goes, "You train like you fight, you fight like you train." That afternoon, they would go to the "shoot house" for live fire drills. Thanks to some help from the base training technicians, he had come up with some realistic and very nasty simulations and mannequins of Eaters. The film of Kathy Monroe's attack provided real world images of what Eaters were really like. "Alright, troops. Take a break. Get some water. I don't want anyone falling out due to dehydration. *Clear?*" "*Crystal.*" As one, the forty applicants responded. He did not let on but the quick bonding they exhibited gave him a warm, feral feeling. Like a pack of wolves, they were quick to learn how to work as a close knit group of predators. Wolves. That was a good symbol, especially in Montana, where wolves were making a comeback, thanks to the reduction of human presence in their traditional hunting areas. Even man's best friend, the dog, started as a wolf. He suddenly had an idea for a special unit patch.

Ichiro walked in. Instead of a combat fatigue uniform, he was wearing a traditional judo gi. He had no belt on yet, but was carrying something rolled up in his hand. Torbin knew he had the thousand stitch belt on underneath, just as Torbin did. It was a bond they shared that could not be broken.

George Williams entered from the opposite end of the gym. He had a newer looking gi on, with a slightly used black belt in his hand. He stopped short of some mats that had been set up for combatants.

He turned toward the fifty star American flag that still resided in a place of honor in the main entrance of the gym. He bowed, then quickly wrapped and tied his belt on in the traditional manner.

Ichiro approached the mats. He knelt, bowed and touched what Torbin saw was a rolled up belt in his hand to his forehead. He quickly rose up on his knees and wrapped and tied the belt around his waist. This belt had not been commercially dyed to black, it was actually a white belt that was now very black from years of use. Torbin whistled low to himself at the realization.

After he had received his thousand stitch belt, Torbin had asked Ichiro over cups of sake how the he knew Mr. Williams. Ichiro had replied, "He had competed against my uncle and I in the Olympics, in judo. In the heavyweight division. My uncle had to, how you say, 'bulk up' to try and get closer to the American weights. Even then, Mr. William still was bigger, though within standards. "My uncle told me during my training that Mr. Williams was as skilled as he. But his superior size, weight and muscle mass gave him an advantage. Judo and jiu jitsu are said to be able to allow the small to defeat the large. That only works if the large does not have the same skill as the small."

Now, looking at Ichiro, Torbin saw he had been trained in a very hard, traditional manner. No wonder he was so skilled and so focused. He had been raised to be a Samurai from childhood.

Ichiro stood and approached the mats, bowing before stepping on them. He then stepped forward and bowed to Mr. Williams who had also entered the mats.

"Captain Bender, may we borrow you for a few minutes?" Mr. Williams asked in a loud voice.

"Of course, Sir. As long as you don't mind my guys watching."

Mr. Williams nodded in assent, and then motioned him over to the mats. "If you could please let us know when to begin and keep an eye on us so that if one of us misses the other one tapping out, you stop the match. We don't want anyone to be choked out unnecessarily."

"Will do, Sir." The two protagonists approached each other, and then bowed. They were standing arm's length apart, facing each other.

"Captain Yamamoto, are you ready?"

"Hai."

"Mr. Williams, are you ready?"

"Yes Sir."

"I am not going to waste my time asking two black belts if they know the rules. So, upon my mark, you will begin. Alright, gentlemen... begin."

Both men grabbed each other's gi, trying to get a good grip toward the back of the judo gi top collar, sleeve, belt, or front. At the same time, they slid on their feet, moving, shifting, and almost dancing with each other. Each man was trying to throw his opponent ever so slightly off balance, to gain an advantage so that he could get a good throwing technique applied. Suddenly, Mr. Williams went for a traditional uki otashi–floating hip throw–the one often seen in movies. A man with superior muscular power could definitely make this throw look easy by literally overpowering his opponent. It looked like he had, as Ichiro began to be thrown over George's left hip. As Ichiro went over, he twisted in a blur of motion so that he literally landed on his feet before the throw seemed to be complete.

Dropping down to his knees, he used some of the bigger man's momentum to pull him off balance, causing him to literally trip over Ichiro's now lower body. George went into a forward roll and was able to roll free, winding up in a standing position facing his opponent.

Ichiro rolled backwards, kicking out with his feet so that he rolled back on his hands. He rose into a handstand, followed by handspring to his feet. Torbin's mouth dropped open. He thought he was a prime physical specimen, but he suddenly felt like a slug.

The large black man gave a broad grin. "Captain, I heard you were as fast as greased lightning and as flexible as a snake. Now I know there was no exaggeration."

Ichiro made a slight bow to acknowledge the compliment, and then reengaged his opponent. For the next ten minutes, the action seemed to repeat itself. Mr. Williams would seemingly have Ichiro in a foot sweep, a leg tripping throw, a stomach throw, a shoulder throw. In each case, Ichiro would either slide out of it, twist out of it, or go with the move and quickly flip onto his feet, then using the bigger man's momentum to push, trip or flip him toward the mat, making George roll out of his own technique. Torbin had never seen this extreme degree of judo play. He was used to clean throws, slaps to the mat, then some ground grappling as the opponents tried for a collar choke or submission hold. But Ichiro never had to break his fall; he seemed to always land on his feet. And the older man, though in excellent shape, was beginning to breathe hard. Ichiro, on the other hand, had barely broken a sweat.

"Looks like it's time to try something else," declared Mr. Williams. As the two men closed, George went for a standing collar choke, grabbing the lapels of the gi, crossing them and trying to twist the collar into the side of Ichiro's neck. He was going to use his brute strength to overpower Ichiro and make him submit, since blows were not allowed in judo. Ichiro, in a sudden move, pulled his chin down to his chest between his shoulders, the gi collar now sipping up toward the top of his head. He went limp, collapsing backwards and downwards while grabbing the sleeves of the bigger man's gi sleeves. Ichiro seemed to roll his long, muscular body into a ball. In actuality, he was bringing his feet up into the large man's stomach as he rolled backwards. Caught by surprise and off balance, George tried to go into a forward roll in order to roll through the technique and out the other side. No such luck.

Two strong legs attached to the feet on his stomach sprang out like released coiled springs. The large black man was propelled like a rocket upwards. With Ichiro still holding on to his sleeves, he was rotated up and over the Japanese warrior, being kicked so that he came crashing down on his muscular behind. A blur of motion followed and George Williams the fourth found himself so wrapped up by Ichiro's arms and legs, it was as if Ichiro had morphed into a Squid. He felt the gi's collar pressing onto the side of his neck where the main artery carries blood to the brain. A few moments of pressure, and it would be lights out. The former Chief tapped out. Ichiro untangled himself in, stood up, and extended his hand to help up the larger man.

During the match, there had been a level of silence among the observing military men that was unusual in a gym setting. Now there was a roars of *"Oorah!"* and rebel yells, followed by deafening applause.

Torbin had to yell, "At ease!" several times as loud as he could to stop the display of exuberance. Finally he gained control. *"Fall in, dammit!"* he bellowed. All forty men fell into two twenty man

groups, ten men to a rank.

"Alright. At ease." He turned toward Ichiro. "Did I ask you to remind me to never piss you off?"

"Could you remind me also?" George Williams interjected. He reached out to shake Ichiro's hand. "Captain, you are definitely your uncle's nephew, and then some. Even at the height of my judo career, I would never be able to move like you did. Did you study some new form of martial arts I don't know about?"

Ichiro gave him a shy smile. "No, Mr. Williams. I just studied with my uncle, and did what you Americans say comes naturally." "If I may be so bold to express an outside opinion," Torbin began. "I believe the reason that my friend Ichiro is blessed with his abilities is karma, pure and simple."

"Karma? What do you mean?" George asked. "Easy. Captain Yamamoto was put on this Earth to kill Squids. His ability with a Katana is supernatural. He has reflexes that that are unbelievable. A higher power must have sent him here to take care of Squids. There is no other explanation that fits. He appears at just the right time, is trained just the right way. He is meant to be here now." Torbin knew that they probably considered he was nuts. He didn't care.

George hesitated for a moment before responding. "I'm a God fearing Christian, Southern Baptist. I guess you could be an old testament Warrior of God. But in the greater scheme of things, whatever the reason, you have skills we need and can sure use. I am glad I have had a chance to meet you and compete with you." Ichiro bowed to the large man. "You do me honor, Mr. Williams" "Hell, son, call me George. You're the first man to beat me in years." Ichiro smiled. "Okay, George-san. If you wish to workout again, it would be my pleasure."

"I bet it would. Let this old man rest up a bit, before I take you up on it. Now, before I leave, I expect you two Captains to meet me for drinks at the club at say, 7:00pm. I'll buy you each a steak dinner, if you wish."

"Yes Sir. See you at seven."

He returned his attention to his forty troops. "Alright, gentlemen. Now that we've had our entertainment for the day, two sprints around the inside track, shower, change, grab chow, then meet me at the range in full battle rattle at 1:00pm. The rest of the day, we'll get to bust a bunch of caps, one of my most favorite activities."

"Are we *clear*?" he bellowed.

"*Crystal!*" they yelled back.

"Formation, atten*hut*! Fall out." The forty men took off, running the two laps on the track as fast as they could. The faster they were done, the more time for chow. Eating, fighting and fucking. That summed up the favorite activities of a combat troop. Torbin knew he had a good core of volunteers. He would have to narrow it down to a twelve man assault team, and two security rear guards. He would have a twelve man backup team if something happened to the primary prior to S-Day.

S-Day. Squid Day. His choice of terms. Screw D-Day, A-Day, whatever. The enemy were Squids. Everyone needed to remember that. They were not humans, though they would have to fight some humans along the way. Especially when he went in for the Director. He looked at his watch. Time to grab a sandwich at one of the Conch roach coaches, then change into his battle rattle.

CHAPTER 19

As a trained scientist and medical professional, I should have seen the signs of what was being done much, much earlier. My failings may have led to permanent damage to our species. I may not have tried to perform some of the perverted acts similar to those of Joseph Mengele, but I still bear the responsibility of blinding myself to realities. I was blinded by the promises of Tschaaa medical science. I ignored the signs of extreme dysfunction and damage. May God forgive me.

> —Excerpts from the "Great Compromise" by Princess Akiko of the Free Japan Royal Family. Appendix 15, Recovered Notes from Doctor Brigitte Fredericks Private Diary, Key West, Florida

KEY WEST, FLORIDA

While Bender was working hard to put an assault team together, Professor Joseph Fassbinder and his wife Sarah were taking a break from their duties, visiting a combination restaurant and bar in downtown Key West. Called *The Admiral's Cabin*, it was owned by the Admiral and operated by many of his daughters, although he stopped in often to ensure everything was going well. Had anyone remembered the Admiral's true name, they might have recognized him as the former manager of one of the largest former resort hotels in the Keys. Therefore, running a commercial establishment came second nature to him.

His odd uniform and rough-looking, sun bleached demeanor was an affectation that had occurred since the Tschaaa occupied the Keys. His appearance may have been a bit bizarre, but a quick mind still operated under his white, sun bleached hair. Today he made sure he was present when he heard that Joseph, a new class of rocketman soon heading off into space, was present.

He had arranged a special table in a side enclave, with a waiter and hostess standing nearby to serve just the Fassbinders and their young guides, the Olson twins. Sandy and Samuel led them there, espousing the charms and excellence of the establishment, especially the drinks. Joseph was surprised to find that they were expected, and even more so when they were shown to their seat of honor. He asked the twins, "Did you tell them we were coming? I thought we came here to have a drink at the bar and admire the history of Old Key West. I did not expect a private table, private service staff. This is embarrassing."

Before the twins could answer, the Admiral appeared from nowhere. "Professor. And Mrs. Professor. Or should I call you Professors One and Two, as I understand *both* of you have doctorates well above my level of understanding."

He then belted out a hardy laugh. The Admiral always seem to chuckle a lot, even when he was angry. "And yes, of course I knew you were coming here. You see, I have the most well-developed informal intelligence establishment in North America, probably the world. The Conch Republic knows all and sees all. I dare say, I knew you were coming before you did."

Joseph did not know what to make of the odd character, and smiled cautiously. The Admiral began to guffaw and slapped him on the back. "Relax, Professor One. You and Professor Two are here to have fun. You are my guests."

He grabbed a menu. "Please, allow me to order for you. Garçon. Garçon, attend please." The dedicated wait staff hurried to the table. The Admiral soon ordered "surf and turf" combination platters, Long Island iced teas, and key lime pie for dessert. The Olsons ordered their own stews and boilermakers. Joseph could tell by their demeanor that they had been here many times before.

After he left the area, Joseph inquired of Sandy, "Is he always so... unusual?"

She laughed. "Yes, for as long as we have been coming here. Almost three years. He *is* the Conch Republic personified. Brash, independent, tough, but fun-loving. And a bit eccentric. He's extremely protective of his people, especially his daughters. Don't ask me how many he's 'adopted', but they must be in the dozens.

Everyone here seems to love him like the crazy Uncle that brings the dangerous fireworks for the Fourth of July." Joseph noticed Sam was looking around, searching for something or someone. "Looking for something, Samuel?" Sam suddenly stopped and blushed.

"He's just looking for Jolene. She works here sometimes." "She must be quite a woman if he is so smitten with her," Sarah interjected.

"The Professor has met her," Sandy remarked with a sly grin. "He can tell you all about her."

"Oh, really?" Sarah replied. "Tell me about this femme fatale, Joseph. What makes her so special?" She cocked an eyebrow, a warning that Joseph had better give a good answer, or suffer the consequences. Before he could answer, Jolene appeared from the back of the establishment, making a beeline toward their table. Joseph started to stutter and blushed. He was still a bit of a blockhead when it came to interpersonal relationships.

"Uh, honey, let me introduce..."

Jolene didn't even acknowledge the presence of Joseph or the Olsons. She went straight to Sarah, threw her arms around her, and kissed her on the cheek. Sarah began to sputter, as Jolene began in explanation, "Professor, I have a niece in your class, Mary Ann Lane. You helped save her from that damned Eater. I owe you and Major Grant big time. Your money's no good when I am here. Put it away." She turned to Joseph. "Hi, Professor. Glad you finally brought your wife here. I see Sam and Sandy came along too. Looks like you're up for a fun evening."

Sam managed to say, "Hi, Jolene!" to her before Jolene turned and hugged Sarah again.

"It was Major Grant that killed that thing. I was just knocked on my ass." Sarah finally confessed.

Jolene brushed aside her protestations. "Oh hush! You threw yourself on that thing, distracting it so the Major could kill it. Just accept my thank, and no more arguing."

Sarah, a bit teary eyed, finally said, "Oh alright. You're welcome." Jolene then turned her attention to Joseph. "You'd better treat her right, Professor, or else I'll take a dull fish knife to you." Joseph could tell she was dead serious.

"Yes Ma'am."

Jolene patted Sarah's shoulder. "I've got to go now. See you later. If the Admiral doesn't get you good service, come see me in the main bar and I'll fix you up." Then, like a force of nature, she traveled back the way she came. Sarah was still dabbing her eyes with a napkin, when Joseph asked, "Are you okay, honey?"

"It's just my waterworks seem a bit sensitive lately. You'd think I'd get used to this show of gratitude, but... Damnit. Jane did all the heavy lifting."

Joseph put his arm around her. "Darling, I love you. Just accept the fact that people care that you even tried. Most people would have run screaming. It looks like our drinks are coming. That should help." The Long Island iced teas helped to lubricate Joseph and Sarah, as Sam and Sandy's drinks helped relax them. They were soon involved in small talk.

"Professor, I am jealous," Sam interjected. "Jolene kissed you the first time you met. It took me a month to get to first base." His sister slapped his arm. "Quit talking about your sexual frustration. You have women hanging all over you."

"Yes, but not Jolene," he shot back.

"She seemed quite the woman," Sarah stated. "How did you meet her, Joseph?"

He took a drink of his cocktail. "I met her my first day of work. She was running the Conch roach coach outside my building. She knew who I was already." He paused and looked at Sarah. "She gave me the beers I brought back to our room. She said I had to go home and make up." Sarah suddenly kissed him, a kiss that lingered a few moments longer than was comfortable for their dining companions. Sandy interrupted them. "I'm going to the ladies room. Would you like to show you where it is, Sarah?"

"Yes, I think that might be a good idea," Sarah answered. She kissed her husband once more on the cheek. "Don't start flirting while I'm gone."

"No worries. I think your friend Jolene would cut my balls off." Everyone laughed, and the two women headed to the restroom. Joseph watched Sarah walk away. He felt a stirring in his loins as he watched his wife slink off in the black cocktail dress she had found. She seemed to look and act years younger, and her body seemed firmer, rejuvenated. He had a strong urge to run after her, grab her, and show his firsthand appreciation for her sensuous form. Joseph shook his head to bring his thoughts back to the table.

"Professor, I don't mean to speak out of line, but your wife is *hot*. You are one lucky man."

Joseph looked at Sam. "This I know. But tell me, where are all these young women who are throwing themselves at you?" Sam laughed. "A couple are in the bar as we speak. I just really wished Jolene wouldn't play so hard to get." They both laughed. "Well, young sir, you have lots of time ahead of you. Enjoy the attention you get now. As you age, the number of those desiring you decreases."

"Let me warn you, Professor. My sister has the hots for you. I guess in your case, you must be like fine wine. Better with age." Joseph laughed the comment off, but he knew it was true. Sandy sometimes would bump her firm body into him. He was sure she was doing it on purpose. He made a mental note to make sure she did not get him cornered alone. He didn't need any problems, now that Sarah and he were acting like newlyweds again.

Sarah was touching up her makeup in the ladies room. She thought to herself that she seemed to look younger. "This is weird," she mumbled to herself. Must be because she felt like a young schoolgirl with Joseph these days.

"You have a great looking husband, Sarah." Sandy was standing next to her. She was about an inch shorter, but was just as shapely.

Sarah had noticed her nice legs, and she could swear she had nothing on under her shapely night dress. "Yes, I know. I'm lucky. To be honest, I almost lost him."

Sandy then said something that was completely from left field. "Would you fight to keep him?"

Sarah sputtered a bit. "Wha... what do you mean?"

"If you think he's worth keeping, you'd have to hurt me pretty badly to make me give up trying to have him for myself." Sandy had an intense look in her eyes, and seemed to be breathing a bit harder. Sarah began to have an odd, almost feral feeling herself. She started sizing up Sandy. She was younger, but no bigger or stronger-looking than Sarah. A momentary image of her yanking on Sandy's auburn hair flashed through her mind.

"Yes, I would," she snapped.

"You would fight me?" Sandy asked again, meeting her eyes.

"Yes," she hissed. Where that answer came from, Sarah had no idea. Other than a couple of schoolyard scraps in junior high, she had been decidedly non-violent. Now, she was thinking she had nice manicured sharp nails, which could do a number on Sandy's face and body. The two women started to close the space between them. Jolene chose that moment to walk in. "Evening ladies. Everything okay here?"

It broke the moment. A few more seconds, and they would have been rolling on the bathroom floor.

"Just fine, Jolene," Sandy answered, and went to the mirror to check her makeup and hair.

Sarah reached over to Jolene and kissed her cheek. "Thanks for sending my husband home with the beer that day. I owe you." Jolene broke into a big grin. "I just did what was right, Professor." "My friends call me Sarah, Jolene." Sarah noticed the large scar on the left side of Jolene's face that had been covered by her long hair and paused.

Jolene said. "Okay, Sarah, it's a deal. And that scar was a present from an asshole who was tried to kill me."

Sarah blushed a bit. "I didn't mean to stare..."

Jolene waved her off. "The Director offered to have it fixed with Tschaaa nanite technology, but I turned it down. I think it gives me character."

Sandy took the opportunity to leave. "Excuse me, ladies. See you back at the table." Sarah glared a bit at Sandy as she swung her hips out the door. Jolene grinned after her. "You two were about to get into it with each other, weren't you?"

Sarah looked at Jolene. "How could you tell?"

Jolene laughed. "It's been happening with increased regularity.

Almost every night, two girls get into a hair pulling contest. Unless it's broken up, they end up like two alley cats, all scratched, bruised, and bitten."

"Any idea why?" The scientist in her felt an urge to ask more questions.

"Nope," Jolene answered. "Must be something in the water." Sarah seemed concerned. "What about you? Any desire to scratch my eyes out?"

"Hell, no!" Jolene chuckled. "I have no desire to battle anyone. I'm a lover, not a fighter."

Both women laughed. "I'd better get back to my table before that redhead tries to put the moves on my husband. See you later, Jolene." Jolene laughed again and waved goodbye.

Sarah hurried back to the table, and sat down next to her husband. Sandy had not arrived yet. Then Sarah saw her at the bar, chatting up a couple of good looking young men. She turned to Joseph, grabbed him, kissing him passionately.

"My, my, aren't you feisty tonight," Joseph smirked.

Sarah leaned close and whispered into his ear. "Just wait until later, when we get home." She reached under the table and ran her hand up his thigh. Their food arrived at that moment, as did Sandy. For the rest of the evening, Joseph noticed an odd tension between Sandy and Sarah. They kept giving each other little smirks, twisting their bodies to emphasize their curves in some type of weird competition.

Eventually, he whispered to his wife, "Darling, what is going on?" His wife squeezed his thigh under the table. "I'll tell you at home."

Over the course of the evening, conversation included talk about "the good old days", before the Tschaaa appeared. Sam made a startling comment. "Sometimes, I think the Squids' coming is a godsend."

Both Joseph and Sarah were taken aback. "How can you say that with the number of people killed? And people of color becoming?" Sarah was to pounce on Sam with questions. She may have controlled her old radicalism, but she wasn't dead.

Sam answered defiantly. "How can I say that? Easy. We had a black President who did more to institute class warfare and divide the nation, after claiming he was the great unifier, than anyone in history.

Africans practiced genocide on their own people just because they were of a different tribe. The Cambodians slaughtered a million of their own people in the name of Communism. Even "white people" lost out on education and jobs due to affirmative action because we were blamed for slavery and segregation. Hell, I wasn't even born until the Millennium, yet somehow it was my fault." He took a slug of his drink.

"All of the secular socialists and atheists were promoting Darwinism and evolution. Well, guess what? The Tschaaa are proof of Darwin's theory of the survival of the fittest. It's not my fault either that people of color lost out in the cosmic crap shoot of evolution. It's just that the Tschaaa find them tastier than us." Sarah continued, "But you lost family and friends. Don't you wish that you had them back?"

"If wishes were horses beggars would ride," Sam mumbled. "Of course I miss my parents, my cousins, my friends. But Darwin won. Now, we have to make the best of it, and climb back toward the top. Hell, our early ancestors were meals for leopards and hyenas. But we worked past that, began to top them in the food chain. Eventually, we'll be equal to or on top of the Squids in the food chain again, just as we beat out the all the other predators." Samuel's face was flushed by the end of his speech. The fresh faced student Joseph had known years ago was long gone.

"Pardon my brother," Sandy interjected. "He wonders why Jolene and other women tend to shy away from him. It's because he always carries a soap box around with him."

Samuel waved at his sister in a sign of dismissal. "You're just like the other women. You don't want to admit the unpleasant truth. I need another drink." He stood up and wobbled toward the bar, where Jolene was tending.

"He is very angry, isn't he?" Joseph asked.

Sandy sighed. "He's just frustrated and self-centered. He is my twin and I love him, but he seems to want what he can't have. Primarily Jolene. And to change the past to what *he* wants." Sandy gave Joseph a bit of a smoldering look. "I know what is obtainable, and what isn't. Therefore, I'm less frustrated."

Sarah glared at Sandy. "Sometimes there are obstacles that are greater than you realize."

Both women began to lean in toward each other. Joseph jumped in. "Hey, Sandy, can you suggest some other establishments to visit in the future? My wife and I have some fun to catch up on." He squeezed his wife's hand.

Sandy saw the gesture and sighed. "Yes, Professor. Let me write on this napkin..."

The evening was becoming curiouser and curiouser. Finally, they had all eaten, drank and laughed enough. Various men and women kept coming over to strike up a conversation with the Olson twins, all unattached singles. Two young ladies in particular kept glaring at each other as they vied for Sam's attention.

Joseph glanced at his watch. "Come on, time to go. I'm about to fall over." He and Sarah got up to excuse themselves. Surprisingly Sarah and Sandy hugged each other. Then he noticed that they purposefully pressed their breasts together and squeezed each other in a short bear hug, as if checking out the strength of the other's body.

After tipping the serving staff handsomely, they left the establishment, waving at the Admiral as he was coordinating something with his staff. Outside they jumped on a Conch trolley, the local efficient transportation system. Aboard was the recent addition was two armed guards, one Base personnel, one Conch Republican. They were the result of the Eater threat.

Unfortunately, the Director's Security Forces had been unable to locate any of the other Eaters that had been transported into the mangroves. There, thanks to their voracious appetite, they had begun to eat the local fauna, and were soon reproducing like rabbits. At least a couple of the aliens, close to giving birth, had apparently been released. Within a day, there were four young. Then, within a week, four more, with four more on the way. There were few gators where they had been dropped, so there were no large predators to compete. The local manatee population, having made a big comeback because of few humans in boats to run over them, began to suffer. More food, more births. Sightings began in the mangroves, and a few were shot and killed. Then, a couple of the creatures arrived during the night in downtown Key West, eating a dog and its owner. All hell broke loose. The two were quickly tracked down and shot, but the damage had been done. No outside security presence meant that few people ventured out. Soon most of the population had a gun, leading to some shooting at shadows and one death from gunshot. The next day, armed trained personnel appeared on the trolleys, as well as on walking patrols and on a couple of jeeps running around. Joseph and Sarah found a seat toward the back of the trolley in order to be alone. There they kissed deeply, fumbling with each other's clothing and bodies like teenagers. The fifteen minute trip to their quarters seemed to pass in a few moments. The trolley driver rang the bell when they reached their quarters, as the trolleys allowed on the base with no restrictions. Joseph slipped a tip to him as they exited, the two guards having purposefully ignored he two lovers in the back.

The professors had first floor quarters in what was basically a two bedroom duplex. After some six years living either in a cabin or modified offices on a college campus, this was like a palace. Joseph did not let Sarah reach their bedroom. He unzipped her dress, pulling it over her head. With practiced ease, he unclipped the back bra clasp, and let her bra slip off. She giggled. "You always were good with clasps and hooks."

"It must be my engineering background," her husband deadpanned. He scooped her up into his arms and carried her to the marital bed.

An hour later, Joseph was spooned up against his wife's warm body. Already, the contact was causing warmness in his loins and he began to have another reaction. Damn. It must have been the years of sexual drought that was causing his horniness. Sarah made a nice humming sound of satisfaction as she stirred, touching his body. "I love you, Sarah. I always have, I always will," he whispered into her ear. "I love you, Joseph, my husband," she whispered back. "I thought you should know that after tonight, I might be pregnant." Joseph had thought that might be the case when she refused him the time to put on a condom. Suddenly, he wanted a child by her. "While I have your complete attention, you gorgeous creature, come here one more time..."

Joseph was glad today was Saturday, a day off. He had literally screwed himself silly, and his lower regions ached a bit from an unknown number of orgasms. He heard the toilet flush. A moment later a nude Sarah walked from the bathroom, heading back to the bed. "Hungry?" She asked. Joseph looked at her. Her body was almost back to its firm, sensual form that had been his wife during their college and early marriage days. His tall, lanky frame seemed to offer a unique challenge to her, and it seemed she was always trying to climb him like a tree. He gently smiled. "Well, are you? A smile is not an answer. I'm famished. Want to join me in the kitchen?" He stood up silently and walked to her. Bending over, he took her face in his hands. "Sarah Ann Broadmore Fassbinder, I love you. Would you marry me?" She gently removed his right hand and kissed it. "Silly, we are already married. I think I have a copy in the stuff we saved after the rocks hit." He looked into her eyes. "No, I want to marry you again. I want to take the vows again. I almost lost you. I want you to know how much I love and need you, especially as we are about to start a family. Please, it can be a small service if you want, just…"

Sarah began to cry. She threw a her arms around him and squeezed so hard he wondered if perhaps he had done something wrong. She kept crying, and he just held on to her, gently stroking her hair. Finally, she stopped. She tried to wipe his eyes with her hands, then turned and found some napkins they had appropriated from the chow hall. She blew her nose, wiped her eyes. "Sorry, those damned waterworks again." She turned her face up to his, and made direct eye contact. "Joseph Fassbinder, I will marry you again–any place, any time. I almost lost you. Before, I didn't know what I had. Now I do. I'm alive today because of you.

"Just before the invasion, I was thinking divorce. I was a goddamned snob, and I thought you were a dolt holding me back. The rocks hit, and I went numb. Then I turned bitter. I believed the whole invasion was the universe's way of screwing up my life, and my career. Next the Chief showed up, we came here, I made an ass of myself to the Director, and you left." A tear ran down her cheek. "I still need to apologize to the Chief. Right now, I need to apologize to you, my dearest. Can you forgive me?"

Joseph thought how lucky he was to get a second chance. "Sarah, if you want me to formally accept your apology, then consider it accepted. But it isn't necessary. We have been through hell. I love you more than life itself. When I heard about the Eater, I realized how close I had come to losing you forever. There is a part of me that only you can fill. So, are you going to marry me, again, or not?" "Yes, my love. I will marry you nude in the town square if you want me to."

Joseph laughed, "As interesting as that might be, I want to keep this gorgeous body to myself." Then they were quiet. Sarah whispered in his ear, "Please make love to me, Joseph. I know I've probably worn you out last night. But, please."

He made slow love to her there on the carpet in front of the bed. If asked, they could not answer as to why they did not go back to the marital bed. It just seemed right to do it on the floor, to satisfy their more primal urges. After they were both finally satisfied, they gently kissed again. "Still want some food, Sarah?" Joseph finally asked.

"Yes, I'll fix it."

"No, you won't. You will take a nice warm shower, or bath, which ever you want. I will then wait on you. I think I may have just given you a child. You need to rest and relax." He gently untangled himself from her and went to the kitchen. Sarah laid there for a few moments.

Her face broke into a broad grin, as she murmured to herself, "Twins. I will have twins."

CHAPTER 20

"Space, the final frontier..."
> —*Star Trek*, the Series. Gene Roddenberry. Footnote, Chapter Five, *The Great Compromise* by Royal Princess Akiko, Free Japan Royal Family.

THE CAPE, FLORIDA

The space shot had been postponed for a couple of weeks following the first Eater death. Now the launch time was rapidly approaching. Joseph was at the Cape, reviewing last minute details. Andrew had taken on the job of zipping him back and forth on his Falcon. Joseph had asked him why, when the Director had dedicated aircraft.

"My independent evaluation is that it is safer and faster," answered Andrew. "The Director is hard-headed about his autonomy, his independence. He does not like to depend on anyone more than absolutely necessary. Unfortunately, his idea as to what is necessary is not always in congruence with the facts of the situation. I have been directed to let him do what he wants, unless he is about to get himself killed. With you, I have complete autonomy. Thus, you travel with me."

Joseph had to admit that he was getting spoiled flying in the Falcon. He sat in the co-pilot's seat and watched Andrew fly. The cyborg had a direct interface, so he did not need to touch the controls, which had a hand shaped recess where a joystick would have been. A normal humanoid would put its hand into the recess. Sensors interfaced with the hand and enabled the pilot to operate the craft based on finger and arm movements. By watching Andrew, he believed he could figure out how to use the hand recess to fly the craft, as long as the craft would interface with his hand.

Andrew landed within walking distance of the launch control building. Joseph walked down the small entrance ramp and was met by the Olson twins. Their genius had been indispensable in getting the spaceplane ready for launch. Now, it was just seven days until launch. Seven Days. Just seven months ago, Joseph was worried about where Sarah and he would find their next meal. Now, he had finally begun to fill out with lots of good food and exercise. And he was about to take the next small step for a man, but a giant leap for humankind. He had asked Andrew why it was so important that humans used their outdated technology to launch into space once again. Why not use a Delta or a Falcon?

"Humans must prove to the other Lords that they can be more than just meat. They must do it on their own, with only limited support from Tschaaa or the other species' technology. Some Tschaaa think you are the equivalent of a fairly smart parrot. Able to copy what others say and do, but with limited problem solving capabilities."

Joseph had been surprised. "Where did they think we got our aircraft and other machines from? I realize they may seem crude compared to your Falcons, but they still function." Andrew replied, "They do not care where your technology came from. Someone else could have left the items. As the Tschaaa discovered on a few ruined planets not long after traveling outside their solar system. Everyone is automatically assumed to be inferior to the Tschaaa. Your worth must be proven positively, rather than demonstrated by existing products. Once the Tschaaa get an idea in their heads, it is difficult, if not impossible, to remove it."

Soon Joseph was in the launch control room, looking over the final plans and details.

"Well, Sam and Sandy, it looks like everything is ready to go. Let's go up the gantry and check our transportation."

The twins formed one part of his crew, with one additional former astronaut rounding it out. Former lieutenant Colonel Bettie Bardun had trained in the old shuttle program, and when it was cancelled, managed to finagle a trip on a Russian capsule to the International Space Station, to begin training on the commercial spaceplane project. The Tschaaa came, and everything went to hell in a handbasket.

Bardun had actually survived at the Cape, where she visiting when the rocks fell. Along with some technicians and security personnel, she had barricaded herself in the administrative offices, living off hurricane supplies. They made a few forays into the surrounding communities and managed to stay alive and in control of most of the launch area, until Director Lloyd showed up some four years ago. Cape Canaveral was one of the first places he and the Chief had established control after the Florida Keys and Miami. A nearby Tschaaa breeding area had been established along the shallows, but they had ignored the launch area after a short penetration by a bunch of young warriors. They harvested a couple of humans, and then took the meat back to the newborns. They never returned. Cattle Country had been established by that time.

Colonel Bardun could have been a sister to the tall female lead in series of sci-fi movies involving a nasty species of aliens with acid for blood. She had been nicknamed "Rip" after the name of the protagonist, but she had never gotten angry over it. A good sense of humor helped keep her alive and relatively sane. And now, she was going back into space.

"Ready for a final interior check before we seal her up?" the Colonel asked Joseph.

"Might as well do it. In seven days we make history."

"Alright, then let's give her a close look. Get up in every nook and cranny and made sure we don't miss a thing. I want her to go off without a hitch."

"You can say that again." Sandy chimed in. She had been giving the Colonel some once overs lately, almost like she was imagining what was underneath her flight suit, and not bothering Joseph. He wished she would calm her lust. He knew she already had a string of "conquests" among the young males at the Cape. He was a bit surprised that she now had suddenly started paying close attention to Colonel Bardun.

They took the elevator up to the spaceplane perched on top of the equivalent of a giant roman candle. A conventional-looking delta winged large aircraft; two engines perched on top of one another would boost them into orbit after the original large rocket booster kicked them up to the edge of the atmosphere. The new engines made use of a very dense organic fuel the Tschaaa had literally grown in some of their vats. The energy available was immense compared to human fuel types. This enabled the spaceplane to make do with less on board fuel and thus more room for cargo, in a smaller craft than the shuttle. Two hours later, after going over the craft with a fine toothed comb, Colonel Bardun had the launch technicians seal the spaceplane.

"Well, lady and gentlemen, seven days from now we launch. What are your plans, Professor?" the Colonel asked. "Andrew offered to give me a ride back to Key West for tonight and tomorrow. Anybody else need a lift? I can probably convince Andrew to find room aboard his Falcon."

Bettie Bardun smiled. "Thanks, Professor, but I have no people there, so it would be a wasted trip. I think I'll stay here and relax, review a few procedures for launch."

Sandy piped up. "I'll second that. Care to join me for dinner, Colonel? A girl's night out?"

The tall woman paused, and then answered. "Sure. I haven't been able to do that in years."

Sam frowned at his sister. "I guess I'll find my own entertainment for tonight. Don't keep the Colonel out too late, Sis." "Don't worry, brother, we'll be back in quarters at a reasonable time." She gave Bettie a wink and a smile that was a bit confusing, but Bettie shrugged it off. A little bit of relaxation would do her good. "Okay," said the Professor. "I'll see you all day after tomorrow." He headed out to meet Andrew.

"Well, Colonel, I'm going to change into something a bit more comfortable and frilly. How about you?"

Bettie had to think for a moment. She had a black cocktail dress she had picked up in the last few months, with a few other odds and ends. She wore flight suits or a former USAF uniform most of the time. Social time was not something she experienced very often these days.

"I have a basic black number that will suffice, I think. We can eat at the All Ranks Club, if that's okay."

"Fine by me." Sandy flashed a big grin. "Meet you at the Club in an hour."

An hour later, Bettie was just getting the hang of her high heels after near six years of non-use. She had felt an unusual desire to be as feminine as possible, so that even though she normally towered over most men, she wore her black four inch heels. Her smooth, fit and long legs were further emphasized. A sheer black bra and matching underwear, items she had forgotten she owned, completed her ensemble. Bettie saw Sandy approach, wearing a dark blue cocktail dress and matching high heels, her long auburn hair shone with golden highlights. Even by her standards, Bettie classify her companion as 'hot'.

Sandy seemed to read her mind. "Well, look at you, Colonel. Aren't you the hot one?" Sandy smiled, and Bettie blushed a bit in reply.

"This is the first time that I've dressed up in ages. I guess I still clean up pretty well."

Sandy giggled. "That is an understatement, Colonel. Since it is girls' night out, can I call you Bettie?"

"Of course. You're a civilian, so rank doesn't apply. Just remember who's boss when we are underway."

"Aye aye, Sir." Sandy giggled again and gave a sharp salute, which surprised Bettie. "Come on, let's hit the bar for a quick drink." As they passed through the cocktail lounge to find a table, men's heads turned. Bettie felt a little thrill at being admired for her body as well as her mind. She had been so busy with her scientific work, any idea of sex had been suppressed. Now she knew she was still desirable. At the table, a waitress came over and took their drink order, giving the two women a once over as well. As she walked away, Bettie noticed that Sandy was admiring the waitress' backside.

Sandy seemed to know that Bettie had caught her looking. "I like women, although I usually prefer men."

Bettie shrugged. "Sexual identification didn't matter in the Air Force after they did away with 'Don't Ask, Don't Tell'. Regardless of your preference, just don't get caught screwing a subordinate." The drinks arrived and they relaxed. They chatted about the Cape, Key West, and recent history. Most people tended steer away from in-depth conversation of pre-invasion days, as most had lost family and friends. Sandy and slid her chair out to the near side of the table. Before Bettie could respond, Sandy reached out and caressed her thigh. An electric shock went through Bettie. Then she surprised herself by reaching her hand out to Sandy's bare knee. The younger women smiled at her. "What say we get dinner to go and head to my place?"

"Yes," was all that Bettie could answer.

The two women wrestled on the queen-sized bed of the suite. Sandy let out squeals of frustration as Bettie Bardun kept overpowering her nude body. Finally, Bettie was straddling the redhead, pinning her hands near her head. Sandy, breathing hard, glared up at the tall, lean woman. "You have to be so goddamned strong. It's not fair."

Bettie laughed, then bent down and kissed Sandy. Sandy did nothing to resist. Instead, she was soon making little noises of pleasure at the back of her throat.

An hour later, Bettie lay on her back. Her body smelled of sex and sweat. Sandy was snuggled up against Bettie, her head on Bettie's left shoulder. She was caressing Bettie's left breast with her hand.

"So, Colonel. How do I compare with other women you have had?"

Bettie looked down at her. "Honestly, I fooled around once at a sorority function in College. We played a bit of drunken feeling each other up. Nothing was mentioned after that night."

Sandy laughed. "Well, I guess making love to another woman must just come naturally to you."

"So, Sandy, how many women have you... slept with." "Quite a few since coming to Key West. There must be something in the water, as I have discovered I am an equal opportunity sex partner. Man, woman... doesn't matter, as long as you attract me."

Bettie kissed Sandy's forehead. "So I attract you? Well, you definitely turn me on, the first time a woman has to this extent."

"Previous love affairs with men, then?"

Bettie's expression turned dark. Sandy noticed the change and rose up on her arm so she could look down at her.

"Hey, sorry if I said something wrong. I don't want to ruin the moment."

Bettie smiled at her, then rose up and kissed her. "Sandy, I was in love with a man, a pilot, when the Squids attacked. He was a Colonel by the name of Clifton Hunter. Neither one of us were spring chickens. He had a previous wife and kids. I had put my career first, so my lovers I had were not serious... until Cliff." She sighed. "He was sent to Area 51 during the first days of the invasion. That is the last time I heard from him. I assume he is dead, since I imagine he would have tried to contact me by now. My face has been on the television for over a month."

"So why me, then? A woman, years your junior?"

"Hell, I don't know. Maybe there is something in the water. Look, I can't make promises. This is new to me."

"How I feel about you is new to me as well. You aren't like my other lovers. I have real feelings for you." Sandy looked into her eyes. "I could love you, Bettie. I hope that doesn't bother you."

They kissed again, passionately, and Bettie separated from the embrace to lay head to head next to her lover. "I don't know why, but this relationship feels like something I've needed for a long time. We have to fly a mission together with me as the Command Pilot. I won't have time to love you. And, you cannot treat me any differently. If you can't accept that, you stay behind."

"You are tough, aren't you? Good. I like strong people, not pushovers." Sandy smirked. "I'll agree. Just don't expect me to ignore it if some other woman starts sniffing around you. I'll mess her up."

Bettie, moving quickly, had Sandy pinned to the bed, hands on Sandy's wrists. "This is how we started. Two falls out of three?"

CHAPTER 21

Adam Lloyd sat at his office desk, watching the live feed from the Cape. Launch Day. Now, humans made one more relatively crude attempt at spaceflight to Platform One. Buried in it were the remains of the International Space Station. The launch was being broadcast all over North America, and parts of the rest of the world.

Ever since they began broadcasting the accomplishments of the occupation administration, especially the space program, a steady stream of people from the Feral areas–those areas not occupied or part of the Rebel areas–had begun to move to the occupied areas. After some six years of hand to mouth existence, the medical care, food, power, shelter, and amenities like television and the internet were a huge incentive to "reconnect" with the coastal areas. More ex-technical people, aircraft mechanics, pilots, police, EMTs, you name it, were checking into the major ports up and down both coasts. The Vigilance Committees, small groups of humans under watch by a robocop, were now tasked with the inserting and inclusion of the new arrivals into the existing framework. Already, a dozen pilots and two dozen maintenance types were up at the former Eglin Air Force Base, working on getting an air fleet together. Other maintenance types were hard at work on equipment and infrastructure. A half dozen new medical centers were being brought online. Agricultural crops were being grown in the fertile valleys of Southern California, fruit crops in Florida. Other groups of humans were traveling along the Gulf of Mexico and salvaging the remains of crops and fruits that had gone wild but still existed.

With the help of the Tschaaa, manufacturing plants were being set up around San Diego and Los Angeles to produce traditional consumer goods. Others were popping up in Florida, Louisiana, and Texas. Because of this, people had real jobs again, instead of subsistence living and scavenging. Recycling of usable goods had been increasing during the last three years, helping to provide raw materials for new goods to be manufactured. Adam was trying to reopen mines in Mexico, and in small areas in Nevada and Arizona with the help of the lizards, who thrived in the hot, dry climates. Yuma, Arizona and Twentynine Palms, California, as well as Area 51 in Nevada, were now the home of lizard settlements. They in turn were breeding another generation.

He stretched, and rubbed his eyes. His body was worn from working long hours the past week, waiting for the launch. As he took a short break his thoughts returned to a virtual meeting he had with Lord Neptune some two weeks after the Eater attack on the base. He had asked about the recent meeting of all the Lords. His Lordship's tentacles seemed to indicate a bit of agitation before he answered.

"My Director, to be honest, the Lord of Africa is…no more."

"No more? Does that mean what I think it does, my Lordship?"

"I believe so. The Lord's body has been recycled into Mother Ocean."

Adam fell silent. He did not see the Tschaaa as having mafia-like sensibilities.

"I sense surprise, my Adam."

"Yes, I did not think that you…summarily executed your own kind."

Lord Neptune signed resignation. "The first time in centuries, and we have had to terminate the life of a senior Tschaaa. Usually, someone conducting such aberrant behavior would become catatonic after being forced to acknowledge what they have done. Our species does not have a history of lying or espionage. By smuggling those Eaters into your area, he not only committed a form of humanlike spy-craft, he also endangered young Tschaaa. An Eater can be dangerous to an adult, and have preyed on our young since we first migrated to land on our home world."

His Lordship began to display rage. His body changed to a dark camouflage, the digits on his social tentacles clenching and unclenching like a human's hand would. "He endangered the *young.*

Just to seek revenge upon me, and upon my 'pet' humans. He was either insane or evil. Maybe both." The artificial voice did a bang up job registering humanlike emotion.

His Lordship's body began to shift back to its normal color, a light aqua. He was calming down. "I apologize for the display of anger, My Director. But to threaten our young is the ultimate crime."

"Will this action affect us, Your Lordship?"

"Human reactions to the loss of a young one to an Eater forced my fellow Lords to admit that at least non-cattle may have Tschaaa like sensibilities and intellect. Your launch will hopefully help them to further recognize your useful abilities."

Joseph paused. "Your Lordship, I hope that soon we can have a relationship with the other Lords similar to the one we enjoy with you. But, who will take over Africa?"

"One of my distant Crèche members, Director. I have been tasked with trying to reorganize what is left of the meat resources. And, to be completely honest, thanks in part to your efforts of showing what Tschaaa and human coordinated actions can accomplish, I am now considered what you humans would call the Senior Lord here on Earth."

"Congratulations, My Lordship. Won't this limit your time you can spend directly with us here on North America?"

"Never, My Director. I have become an expert in what you humans call 'delegating authority and responsibility'. I am also grooming the Tschaaa you know as El Segundo for additional duties. In the very near future, you will also be dealing with him."

"He will have a distinctive human voice?"

"Yes, he will create one much as I have. I will help him chose a voice that matches his Tschaaa personality. However, I will still spend much time with you, if for no other reason that I obtain a level of intellectual stimulation I have trouble finding with my fellow Tschaaa. Part of that is due to your alien outlook on things, and part is due to the change in my outlook that has come about through contact with you humans, especially you, My Director."

"So, you believe we, an alien species, are affecting how you think?"

"You specifically, Director, you affect me. Our conversations have enabled me to see an alien viewpoint. The lizards did not have that effect on any individual Tschaaa, nor any other prior race or species with which we have come in contact. Maybe it is because, on one hand, you are prey. On the other, you are entering into a cooperative relationship, where you assist us and we assist you. Your relationships with your dogs are one of profound affections as well as a symbiotic relationship that is mutually beneficial. That relationship developed over thousands of years. Possibly because our intellects are so much closer to equal, a similar relationship is developing many times faster."

His Lordship signed the Tschaaa equivalent of a shrug. "As some of your Humans say, it is what it is. Now, we must get back to the business at hand. Tell me about how close you are to launching…"

Now, Adam was watching the real-time broadcast from the Cape, listening to Kathy Munroe's commentary.

"In less than fifteen minutes, the first humans to be launched into space for many years will be headed toward Platform One, a supersized space station. Colonel Bettie Bardun, Commander and Pilot, will guide the spaceplane to dock with the platform. Professor Fassbinder has been trained as a co-pilot should the Colonel become incapacitated. Mission Specialists Sandy and Samuel Olson round out the crew, and will remain on Platform One for at least a month, assisting in ongoing projects."

The cameras cut away from the launch gantry and focused on Kathy. Damn, she was gorgeous. Her sex appeal seemed to translate, even over the airways. At least it did to him. Kathy had become The Symbol, the face of the future. Even threats, like the Eaters, seemed less insurmountable after she had explained the situation. Her calm demeanor and signature perky smile communicated, "Don't worry. Things will be alright. We can work this out together."

Kathy continued. "Twelve other humans, including four Chinese nationals, are currently residing on Platform One. The Chinese astronauts have been there since when the Tschaaa first arrived." No mention of invasion. That was unspoken. Rather, it was arrival, as if the aliens had been anticipated and welcome visitors. "They will return to Earth when Colonel Barden and Professor Fassbinder navigate the spaceplane back to Earth, in about a week or so. They are waiting to be reunited with their countrymen at the first opportunity."

In reality, they would likely stay in Key West and raise families, if they hadn't been exposed to too much radiation. Former Communist China had been broken up into warring municipalities ruled by warlords. The chance the Chinese astronauts could locate any surviving relatives and get to them in one piece was very remote.

Internal strife, nuclear winter brought on by the rocks, and the breakdown of central control within a month of the invasion had reduced to Chinese population to five hundred million. Still a sizeable population, but nowhere near the one and a half billion former residents of the Celestial Kingdom.

"The voice in my ear says we are now going to cut to live audio feed from launch control and the spaceplane crew." What followed was a fairly mundane exchange reminiscent of pre-strike and invasion days. However, with the six year gap since the last launch of any spacecraft or satellite, the event took on greater significance.

The final countdown began. "Twenty, nineteen, eighteen,..." interspersed with comments from both Colonel Bardun and the Launch Control crew notifying each other of actions taken, equipment status. It was "zero" and the main thrusters began boosting the whole shebang skyward. The Tschaaa fuel in the pocket boosters led to a quicker and more powerful burn rate, so the complete launch vehicle looked like it was running in fast forward. Some of the launch gantry appeared to have been damaged due to this additional power, and Adam held his breath when he expected to see pieces start flying. The structure held together for the most part and Adam began breathing again.

What Adam couldn't know was that on board Bettie Bardun was trying to adjust to what felt like being hit by a giant fist while on a bucking bronco. "Fuck!" she exclaimed, as she struggled to adjust to the unexpected thrust and Gs. She had visions of the human designed spacecraft crumbling apart under the extra acceleration. However, as any good engineer will tell you, a "fudge factor" is often built into any design to take into account unforeseen forces and Murphy's Law. The spaceplane and rocket boosters held together. Before she knew it, she felt and heard the "bang" that indicated the first stage had separated. Much faster than expected, the small second stage booster kicked in, then quickly expended itself. Bettie was on her own now. The unexpected acceleration kicked them into the beginnings of a low orbit without any use of the spaceplane engines. Bettie, recognizing the change in the flight characteristics, quickly overrode their automatic activation.

The G forces had been reduced so Joseph could now focus on what Bettie was doing. Bettie looked like a one legged man in an ass kicking contest, flipping switches, checking gauges, talking to Mission Control. Joseph heard the rising fear in the Mission Control specialist's voice when he realized that things were happening a lot faster than planned. Colonel Bardun's voice was cool and calm, like she was in a kindergarten classroom rather in a speeding craft. She turned her head slightly toward Joseph.

"Professor, keep an eye out. We are travelling a lot faster than was expected and I do not want to collide with something that sneaks up on us." She began to use the attitude and steering jets, making sure the craft was adjusted to the correct attitude. Finally, they had completed almost a full orbit and could see Platform One. "Station Control, OSA Spacecraft *Hope* approaching from course 100. Do you have me on scope?"

The calm, mostly monotone voice with a slightly odd accent came back. "I have you, Colonel Bardun. Please release control of the craft." Joseph recognized it as one of the original robocops, which had learned modern human language recently. Grown from proto-human DNA, every bit of their demeanor was different than other cyborgs. Human, but not quite human. They felt a slight jolt, and then the craft seemed to be pulled toward the space station on a leisurely yet straight course. "Holy Captain Kirk! It's a tractor-beam," Bettie exclaimed.

Joseph checked in on the Olson twins, located in seats behind them.

"Fine, Professor," Sandy answered.

"Are we about to dock with the platform, Professor?" Samuel asked.

"Yes, we are. Ahead of schedule. That Tschaaa fuel was a hell of a lot more efficient than anything we have."

The robocop brought the spaceplane into a large docking bay as effortlessly as placing a plate on a table. It seemed so anticlimactic. Joseph turned to Bettie. "Thanks for saving our asses in the first part of the flight. A lot of pilots would have lost their heads."

She shrugged inside her protective suit. "I was just doing my job. Not a big deal."

"Colonel, that was a huge deal, and you are one impressive pilot."

She smiled. "Oh, all right. I'll accept a compliment, Professor. By the way, have you noticed that we have a bit of gravity on board?"

Joseph tried moving his arms and felt the difference from weightlessness. "You're right! So soon."

"They can generate a gravity field, but if you remember our briefings, the Platform has a slight spin on it as well." Colonel Bardun hit her intercom connection with the Olson twins. "Just as a reminder, we have a substantial gravity field as of now. Don't trip and fall, it will hurt. Keep your helmets secured until we make sure the docking bay is pressurized."

About five minutes later, someone knocked on their small airlock door. Sam went in, locked the inner door, and opened the outer one. It was a gray. The large expressionless eyes scanned Sam. "Humans... please follow."

Five minutes later, after informing Mission Control they had arrived safely and would broadcast more details once they were officially received, the four humans followed the gray out of the docking area. The whole structure looked like a classic sci-fi space station, a huge wheel slowly turning, but with a shot of steroids. Over two miles in diameter, with each of the eight mile-long spokes containing three stories, the available capacity was breathtaking.

They had been told one of the humans would come and take them to the head office to meet the senior Tschaaa in charge of the Platform. As they proceeded into one of the main corridors running through a large "spoke" that connected the outer ring to the center of the superstation, Bettie saw a figure approach slowly. An odd and unexpected feeling of both excitement and fear went through Bettie as she thought she recognized their human contact.

"Im-fricking-possible," she muttered under her breath. Then she heard a familiar voice she had not heard for over six years.

"Welcome aboard, Bettie Bardun. It's about time you got here." It was Cliff Hunter. *Dead* Cliff Hunter, apparently very much alive. Bettie stopped dead in her tracks, her crewmates nearly running into her.

"Anything wrong, Colonel?" Joseph asked.

"It's okay, Professor. Bettie has just seen a ghost," Cliff replied.

"Come here and give this old specter a hug, Bettie. To hell with protocol." In one quick motion, she was in his arms. He was only about an inch taller, but his broad shoulders and chest engulfed her small frame. Bettie used to kid him about looking like a cartoon character, with his v-shaped chest, chiseled features, and slender waist.

Bettie began to simultaneously laugh and cry. "You son of a bitch! You're supposed to be dead."

Cliff winked. "The stories of my demise have been greatly exaggerated, my dear."

Bettie pulled back enough to look at his face. A few more lines, some hair now white, but it was still Cliff. "Why didn't you tell someone?" she demanded. "You're not even listed among the human staff up here."

"Sorry, darling, I couldn't. I was put on ice, and told that if I pissed off the Lordship in charge here, I would have a quick trip out the airlock. I guessed the way I got here pissed off some beings."

He glanced at Bettie's companions. "Pardon me while I completely destroy any semblance of good order and discipline and kiss the woman who was *supposed* to be my fiancée." He kissed her deeply, and she automatically responded. It was like they had only been apart for six days, not six years. Bettie and Cliff finally separated, and Bettie asked, "Did I hear the word 'fiancée'?"

"Oh, almost forgot. I've been carrying this around for six years." Cliff pulled a small beat up ring case from his patched up flight suit, with may have been dried blood on it. "Here. It's been too long for me to get down on one knee. You can't say no to marrying me."

She smirked at him. "How do you know I'm not already hitched, you conceited bastard?"

"Good intelligence. Now, are you going to say yes, or am I going to have to take this thing back to where I bought it?"

It was gorgeous. A huge stone surrounded by a starburst of others. A ring like this had not been manufactured since the first rock hit.

She started to cry. "Damn you." She heard her shipmates behind them begin to applaud.

"Congratulations, Colonel," Joseph declared. "Now, I hate to be a party pooper, but please. Say yes, kiss him, and let's go check in with the powers that be. I have a broadcast to make." Bettie did just that. They slowed their walk to the Central Control Room so that Cliff could explain to Bettie and company how he came to be on Platform One. "It started with a launch of our one and only space interceptor from Area 51. I had been helping test various systems on that craft when the 'balloon went up'. Or, actually, the rocks came down." He squeezed his new fiancée's hand. "I couldn't even tell the good Colonel here what I was doing. Need to know crap and all.

"Anyway, on day seven of the invasion, they managed to get what looked like a cross between an SR-71 and one of those spaceships from a Saturday morning cartoon show up and running. It had an experimental pulse generator engine, two to be exact, and we cobbled a few weapons onto it. There was a 30 mm cannon from an A-10, two Sidewinders and two AMRAAM air to air missiles, and a tactical suitcase nuke hooked up to a small cruise missile."

He sighed. "Man, were we rushing around like our hair was fire. Before I knew it, I was strapped in, doing some half-assed systems checks. Then, they told me I had to act as a delta was approaching the area. We didn't know it was just running a recon flight. They launched me using some Jato rockets, so I got off the ground. Then, a thousand feet up, I fired the engines." He chuckled. "What a kick in the ass! I managed to get the interceptor pointed straight up and away I went. I was slammed into my seat by I don't know how many Gs. Somehow, I managed to shut the engines off after a few moments before I blacked out. After that, I restarted them and used them in small bursts of power by throttling up and down. The engineers had built one hell of a strong craft, or else I would have broken apart due to the unexpected power of the two experimental engines."

"Before I knew it, I was in near orbit. I saw the huge asteroid that is Base One and decided it made a hell of a good target because it was so big, even I would have difficulty in missing it. I used the gyros and maneuver rockets to line up my nose on the target, and then hit my main engines."

"Were you scared?" Samuel interjected.

"Frack yes! Oops, sorry about my language. Anyway, there I was, hundreds of thousands of feet in altitude, flat on my back, and barrelling toward the target. No shit."

Bettie jabbed him in his ribs. "Please, stay focused. I know this is fun for you, but it's still a shock to me."

"Sorry, Bettie. I haven't had a new audience in years. I'm almost there... I was lining up, accelerating toward this huge rock when suddenly, deltas were in my flight path. They must have launched from Base One at a near right angle, and did not even see me. I knew it was only a matter of time before someone noticed me. So, I started firing."

His eyes had faraway look to them as he continued. "I hit the 30 mike-mike first. In outer space, there's no air friction to affect the trajectory, just Earth's gravity, which at my altitude was reduced. I was basically weightless, so the rounds were too. Straight line of shot, over a mile away, I hit the first one. A satisfying plume of water shot out as the cockpit was penetrated. Then, the cockpit itself disintegrated, and pieces of craft and Squid joined the rest of the space junk orbiting the Earth."

His voice took on a new intensity. "Other deltas began to notice something new was in orbit with them. I was soon the proverbial one legged man in an ass kicking contest as I quickly had a target rich environment.

"The Squids had more experience in operating their craft in space and I was definitely learning as I went. Maneuver jets, vectoring the main engines, using the gyros, I was trying to twist and turn and shoot all at once. I hit two more deltas with the 30, and watched as they turned into space junk. I hit the gun one more time and it fired a couple of rounds and quit. I hit a delta with at least one round, and it started to leak water from the cockpit system into space. It broke off the attack on me, but was quickly replaced with another, that started firing rounds at me."

He squeezed Bettie's hand again. "I cooked off one of the sidewinders and the damn delta started tracking it instead of me. I found out later that the Squids and their systems latch on to whatever is travelling fastest or maneuvering sharpest, much like predators like T-Rex apparently did.

"I cooked off the second sidewinder, which tried to track the ambient heat the delta still had from its rockets. The sidewinder's maneuver fins were worthless in airless space, but its gyro and the missile vectoring engine trying to jerk it around caused it to kind of skid toward the delta. Once its internal 'brain' said that it was going to miss, it self-detonated. That peppered the delta with some debris, but also threw some in my direction. So, I almost shot myself down. One decent chunk cracked the delta's cockpit, releasing more frozen water in Earth orbit.

"The Squid pilot must have been pissed as he turned toward me and started shooting. So I launched an AMRAAM missile at him. They have directional engine thrust so it was able to redirect toward the delta after I skidded my nose to point in the general direction. The delta fired at it at point blank range, so when the warhead exploded, it shattered the cockpit and nose cone. I saw the Squid in its cockpit seat zip by me. Then I took more hits from shrapnel. My cockpit was holed, but since I was in a suit, I still had pressure and oxygen. The straps in my seat held me in. The interceptor held together, and I tried to line up on the asteroid again."

He swallowed. "More deltas came at me. I fired my last missile, armed the cruise missile with the nuke, and pushed the throttles forward." Everyone continued to walk slowly, waiting for Cliff to finish.

"Something hit my spacecraft and it came apart. I remember trying to eject, and I blacked out. When I regained consciousness, I was floating in space. I saw a delta tumbling end over end nearby, spewing the water atmosphere of the cockpit out in every direction. It smashed into another craft and they both started tumbling toward Earth's atmosphere. I said a prayer and tried enjoy the view, as I knew my air would run out before I was pulled into the atmosphere. And swore because I couldn't leave Bettie here a note told her how much I loved her." Bettie leaned in a bit closer to Cliff.

"What happened next?" Sandy asked.

"A large Falcon spacecraft latched onto me and pulled me in. The robocop piloting the Falcon was one belonging to his Lordship Neptune. He grabbed me and pulled me in on direct orders of the Lordship. I wound up onboard Base One with the four Chinese astronauts. Because I had destroyed at least five deltas, my existence was hushed up. His Lordship, being a student of human nature, knew he needed another hero like Captain Bender stirring up resistance like he needed four more arms."

"Captain Bender?" Joseph asked.

"A young pilot who died while taking down three Tschaaa craft, including a Falcon, near San Diego." Cliff answered. He continued, "The nuke warhead on the missile did not go off, so no major damage was done to Base One. The Chinese and I were told, after over a week of isolation, we could cooperate, or be slaughtered and eaten. I figured if I stayed alive long enough, I might be able to contribute somehow to long term human survival. So, here I am, six years later."

Bettie squeezed his hand. "We're glad you are."

"In my experience, the Tschaaa rarely do things without a reason," Joseph explained. "I suspect I will receive some special directions when I talk to the Director about you, Colonel Hunter. Let's head into the main control room and find out, shall we?"

Bettie whispered to Cliff, "If you can't come back to Earth, I'm staying here. I take it you have been exercising under Earth G in case you can go back?"

"Affirmative. Between the slow spin and the artificial gravity field on most of this station, I think I've been able to keep my bone and muscle mass up. But like they say, nothing is like the real thing."

He put his arms around Bettie one more time and gave her one more a hug. "Damn, you feel good. Now, let's go meet the Wizard."

The Tschaaa Lord in charge of the station was younger than Lord Neptune. Cliff had called him the Wizard, after the character in the Oz books, a nickname he had come up with because he was always behind a curtain of bulkheads and doorways in the central section of Platform One. He communicated through grays and robos, or occasionally as a disembodied voice. Like his Lordship in Key West, he had created a human sounding voice to emanate from his translator. This voice sounded like a broadcaster from the 1980s. Plain, clear, easy to understand. No apparent emotion. But, surprise of surprises, the Wizard came from behind his curtain. He lounged in a large sling like hammock affair, his eight arms hanging down loose, suspended about twelve feet in the air so the humans had to look up at him. He was of average size, and the humans would be hard pressed to differentiate him from other Squids.

"Welcome aboard, humans. Colonel Bardun? You are female, yes? Your accomplishment in piloting such a crude craft from the atmosphere into space gives other humans—male and female—a goal to meet. His Lordship in Key West sends his congratulations. I wish to add my own."

"Professor Joseph, I have a direct secure line open to your Lordship. Approach the console where the gray is standing."

"Thank you, your Lordship," a nervous Joseph replied, walking to the console. He still felt very uneasy anywhere near a Squid.

"Colonel Hunter, I will share with you one thing the Lordship in Key West will inform the Professor. You will be headed back on the spaceplane in about one Earth week. To say that I will be sorry that you are leaving would be a falsehood, something we Tschaaa, unlike humans, have trouble uttering." The Wizard held his tentacles loose, not using them to sign any emotions. "One of the Tschaaa pilots you destroyed six years ago shared both birth mother and sire with me, though a more recent birth group. That did not please me."

Cliff replied, "Well, your Lordship, I would be lying if I said I was sorry that I sent your sibling to the ocean for disposal."

Bettie froze. What the hell was he trying to do? Get himself spaced, now, after they were just reunited?

But the Tschaaa Lord did not react at all. "I respect you as a warrior, Colonel. That is why you were not harvested and eaten. However, I have heard you that would be tough and bitter tasting had I eaten you."

The Tschaaa faced the other members of the group. "The two Olsons will remain here for at least one Earth month to help the human scientists, as well as our own, on engineering projects. I expect excellent things from you. Please do not waste time, air, or other resources here on Platform One."

"Yes, your Lordship," Sandy and Samuel answered in unison.

"I see the Professor has completed his conversation with Earth. The Colonel is returning with the spaceplane, yes?"

"Yes, your Lordship. And I will be helping you with the examination of craft you have here. After we set up the study, Sandy and Samuel Olson will be doing most of the work on this project. I expect they will learn and accomplish much."

The Tschaaa Lord shifted his body slightly. "Good. Now, I will allow you humans to depart to your living quarters. Tomorrow, you will all begin your assistance of the personnel on this station."

Joseph saw Cliff give a slight tilt of his head toward a side exit, and guessed they had just been dismissed. "Thank you, Lordship." He departed where Cliff had indicated, the other humans quickly catching on.

The exit led directly into what had been the International Space Station, with a couple of large compartments added. Cliff gave them a brief tour. "Here is where we sleep, bathe, eat, crap, and do whatever we humans do when not working with the Tschaaa."

Joseph interjected. "Is the Wizard always so... animated?"

Cliff laughed. "To say he exudes the charisma of a rock is an understatement. Just imagine having to put up with this for six years. Anyway, over there in that added compartment are sleeping quarters for you. There are functioning airplane type toilets thanks to the gravity provided. The other large added compartment is the kitchen, dining, and social recreation area. We are provided with an odd assortment of food, whatever an occasional Falcon brings up, plus a food synthesizer that produces soup and tofu-like foods. The soups are not bad; the fake tofu is not edible in my humble opinion. But, it will keep you alive."

He led them into a part of the original space station. "That area is my crib. It's cozy enough for me. I've managed to scrounge a lot of stuff, including a few books that somehow made it up the gravity well. Plus a Tschaaa version of a laptop, which is actually quite fun to use."

"So, Cliff, just how is this place set up, vis-à-vis the other humans and the Tschaaa?" Joseph inquired.

"Well, Professor, we work in person primarily with lizards, grays, an occasional robo, and online with the Tschaaa. The Tschaaa give us general instructions, or a project or idea they want us to work on. We then run with it. It soon dawned on the Tschaaa that we could come up with a lot more original ideas than they could. The lizards are brilliant, but slow and methodical. The grays are just plain weird."

He shook his head. "If they are told to do something, they will do it or die trying. I don't know if they have a true sense of individual self. They can talk and reason, but sometimes it seems like they are working off a collective type brain. They do not show emotions. Believe it or not, lizards show emotion, once you know how to read their expressions and body language. They have a very droll sense of humor."

"We humans are divided into two groups. 'Old hands', the original four Chinese astronauts and myself, all taken into captivity within the first couple of weeks. The four Chinese are pair bounded, two women, and two men. Then, two years ago, fourteen volunteers showed up. Director Lloyd and the Tschaaa selected these people out of a group of scientists that had jumped at the chance to go into space, Tschaaa control or no Tschaaa control. Twelve still remain alive."

"What do you mean, still remain alive?" Bettie interjected.

"One, a man, committed suicide two months after arrival by a large overdose of a synthetic painkiller he was working on. Apparently the stress got to him. The other, a woman, died a year ago. She was caught trying to sabotage the Tschaaa living quarters with some biological agent. The Wizard had her hacked to death by a couple of young warriors as we humans watched." There was an audiable gasp from the four new arrivals.

Cliff shrugged. "Hey, this may sound crass, but we are still basically at war. You get caught as a saboteur or as a spy, you die, just like in past human wars. Her death let us know that if we got caught, screwing something up on purpose, we were next."

Bettie asked, "Then why were you baiting that Tschaaa Lord? Arguing with them like that seems like a good way to get a quick trip out the airlock."

Cliff chuckled. "Oh, that. We have been talking like that for almost six years. I am like a spirited horse or dog to him. He likes the fact that I make him think sometimes." His expression changed. "While we are on a serious topic, do not forget one important fact. To His Lordship in Key West and the Tschaaa over whom he has influence, we are seen as pets or useful beasts of burden, for now. But, no matter our current role, the bottom line is that we are expendable. Cause too many problems, you wind up as meat. Therefore, everyone here does enough to stay alive, and tries not to do anything that may harm another human. The Tschaaa do not seem to worry about us plotting a revolution. I know they listen in on us periodically, even when we are cursing them. However, they seem so sure of their position of power that short of trying to build a secret nuke they let us accomplish our assigned tasks in whatever way we want."

Cliff sighed. "It's not easy for an old soldier like me *not* to fight them, to go out in a blaze of glory. But I decided after seeing what happened the first month or so, that I could be cannon fodder now, or work to help humans survive until things get better. Until the day our own Moses comes, says, 'Let my people go,' splits the Red Sea, and leads us out of bondage. As unrealistic as it may seem, I chose the latter."

"Hope," Bettie said.

"Come again?" Cliff asked.

"Hope. That is how our spaceplane got its name. Hope for a better future for us, and maybe later those humans classified as Cattle. I came up with the name. The Director approved it."

Cliff smiled at her warmly. "That's why I love you. You're definitely a thinker and a romantic, all rolled up into one."

"One last little set of factoids," Cliff continued. "Over the last six years, the Squids have been sweeping the various Earth orbits of all the space junk. Dead satellites, pieces of rocket boosters, dropped wrenches and hammers from various space walks, pieces of asteroids caught in Earth's gravity well. Guess what they did to all that stuff?"

"Boosted it toward the sun?" suggested Sandy.

"Naw, that would be a waste of resources. They brought them to Base One, melted and welded them together, and have these objects sitting by the mass drivers. That way, if they wanted to, the Tschaaa would have a ready made batch of rocks to sling at us. We'd have another nuclear winter if they ever do it. I don't believe they'd do that because it would seriously affect their breeding Crèches, but they could sure smash a few population centers as a reminder to not piss them off. So, we have a sword of Damocles above our heads. Well, not *our* heads, because we are up here, but everyone else's."

Cliff then flashed a smile. "Come on, let's get you settled."

A few hours later, the four new arrivals had their cubicles and sleeping quarters set up. Cliff had grabbed Bettie's gear and stowed it in his quarters. "I can rig another hammock for you, or we can sleep on the floor. On the floor, we can wrap around each other, though I don't have a lot of padding."

Bettie slyly smiled at him. "You forget I'm a pilot too. And what are aircrew good at? Scrounging." She quickly pulled two plastic wrapped bundles out of her equipment bag, and threw them to Cliff.

"Air mattresses. How did you think about packing two? Plan on finding a boyfriend?"

Bettie blushed a little. "Actually, now that we are alone, Sandy and I had a little... something going on very recently."

Cliff raised his eyebrow. "I didn't realize you were interested in other women."

"I wasn't. It just… happened. Literally. One minute, I am straighter than straight, next minute…"

Cliff's brow furrowed. "Hmmm. I have something to show you in the labs later. The Tschaaa have us working on some human biology experiments that seem fairly benign. Now, I wonder…"

Bettie blushed more. "Are you… angry?"

Cliff stepped forward and kissed her. "You love me; I love you. We were supposed to both be dead; we are not. The past is the past. Now, we can at least try to start over where we left off." Bettie grabbed him and hugged him as tightly as she could. Cliff was slightly taken aback. "Damn, woman! What have you been doing, powerlifting?" Cliff hugged her back, but definitely not as tightly.

Bettie slowly released her squeeze. "I thought I was dreaming when I saw you. I grieved when, after a year, I had not heard from you. I was certain you were dead. I was surviving hand to mouth until about two years ago, when the Director and his people first showed up at the Cape. We have been slowly rebuilding ever since. Now, I am here."

She kissed him slowly, nibbling on his mouth. He kissed her lips, and then her throat and her neck. Bettie began to breathe harder. She ran her long fingers through his hair as he embraced her fully for the first time in six years. Finally, she slowly pushed him back.

"One moment, please darling. I think we have a few moments for personal time."

With practiced ease, she unzipped her flight suit. Underneath were green panties and bra. Not exactly fancy lingerie, but to Cliff they were the sexist things he had ever seen.

"Still remember how to unhook a bra?"

"I think so, Bettie. If not, I suspect you will help me."

"Darling Cliff, I will help you with anything you want."

"Anything?" He asked, with a bit of a leer.

Before he knew it, she had shucked her bra. "Guess," she answered.

About a half hour later, they were laying on their flight suits on the hard floor. Bettie felt like she was in a dream. She suddenly pinched herself, hard. "Ouch!" she exclaimed.

Cliff looked concerned. "What are you doing?"

"I had to make sure this wasn't just a dream."

"It's real enough, alright. What is going to be dreamlike is when I travel back to Earth with you."

Bettie kissed his chest. "I'll get you there. I'm also sure I can help you find something to do."

Cliff frowned. "What if I want to go to the Unoccupied States?"

Bettie contemplated his question. "I don't actually know. The Director says that everyone is free to leave within the first twenty-hours after they arrive. I have not heard of him stopping anyone."

"Would he tell people if someone left?"

"I think so. The odd thing is that neither the Tschaaa Lordship nor he makes any attempt to hide things from us. He allows people outside the Tschaaa controlled areas to hack into the new internet. He has provided medical treatment to people who just showed up from the Feral areas, then let them leave. I saw that happen more than once when he took control of the Cape."

"He hasn't tried to take out the Unoccupied States?"

"No, Cliff. Even after quite a few assassination attempts. The last one was close, too."

"What about Cattle Country?"

Bettie sighed. "Yes, he keeps the people designated as meat contained. I know that he looks at it as the lesser of two evils. The alternative is to put everyone on the menu."

"What do you think, Bettie?"

She paused. She had to admit to herself that this was a subject she tried not to think too often about. "Cliff, the idea that any human is being eaten makes me ill. I have to admit, however, that I am not ready to attempt a suicide mission to stop it. Because that is what it would be, a suicide mission. I know that, as a military member, I should have resisted to the end. After everything fell apart and I had no real way to carry on a war against occupation, I entered survival mode. The Director found out who and what I was, and offered me a job and a chance to travel back into space. I took it. Is that selfish? Yes. I only hope that someday I am in a position to help those people I left behind."

Cliff kissed her. "I guess all we can do is what I have been doing for the last six years. Take life one day at a time."

He stood up. "Come on, I think we need to find the others and try to put a meal together. Then finally get some sleep. Lord Wizard is a hard task master. He'll keep us busy until we leave. I just hope the Olsons know what they are getting into by volunteering to stay."

CHAPTER 22

The Director sat quietly after speaking with Professor Fassbinder. The short conversation after the arrival of the spaceplane at its destination had been broadcast live, with Kathy providing an introduction and conclusion. He had congratulated the crew on their achievement, and mentioned in passing that one of the more permanent human occupants of the Platform would be returning to Earth, but he did not specify the name. It was only the previous week, that Cliff Hunter and his history had been revealed to Adam. He was beginning to realize that, although the Tschaaa had a cultural aversion against outright lying, his Lordship had developed a good ability to remain silent about something until he was ready to reveal it. Perhaps it was a form of purposeful ignorance. If his Lordship did not admit to it, it did not exist yet.

Adam stood and stretched. He was going to head to the gym in about an hour for another workout with Heidi Faust, the former Coastie. She had demonstrated an excellent working knowledge of all things martial arts related, and had begun instructing him quite in Filipino knife fighting techniques. Heidi possessed a physical speed and strength beyond any normal human her size, especially most women he had known. The tricks she had shown him with a balisong folding knife that were a blur when she performed them.

His radio phone pinged. "Director here."

"Director Lloyd." It was Andrew. "I will be at your office within ten minutes. The Lordship wishes to speak to you on a secure line."

"I'll be here."

The Tschaaa Lord had provided a recorded message for the successful spaceplane mission that was played as if it were live at the end of the broadcast between Adam and Professor Fassbinder. Now, he wanted to speak with the Director, subject unknown. Adam sighed. Colonel Hunter posed enough of a pain in the ass; Adam did not need any further unforeseen complications.

Promptly at the ten minute mark, he heard Andrew greeting Mary Lou in the outer office. She did not bother to buzz Andrew in, because if he showed up, Adam was already expecting him.

The very large cyborg, part man and part mechanical entity, walked effortlessly into the office. The original movie character for whom cyborgs had been dubbed "robocops" thumped around. Andrew could walk stealthily in a gliding fashion that belied his four hundred pound weight. "Good Day, Director."

"Good Day, Andrew."

Andrew produced the familiar combination handset and screen from the concealed location in his frame. Adam took the device in his hand and announced, "Adam here."

"My Director. How are you today? Such a glorious day it is." His Lordship was in one of his very enthusiastic moods. "The spaceplane mission has shown what humans can do, after recovering from much destruction some six years ago. My fellow Lordships are pleasantly surprised, and greatly impressed. Following the unfortunate forced demise of the African Lordship, I have been able to convince them to follow my lead more each day. Much of this is due to your direct efforts."

"Thank you. I am but your humble servant."

"Nonsense," Lordship Neptune answered. "You have taken a small idea from me and built it into a successful mission. As a positive result from your efforts, I have been given complete control of all manufacturing resources. My new soldier class individuals will be grown in large vats at the San Diego/Baja California Complex, at least one being delivered for service each day, with new weapons to match. Other vats are being set up around Earth. I also have been given control of the manufacturing and organic growth resources aboard Base One. Six new robocops, as you call them, are being finished from some human stock from Europe, and six from America. Finally, new deltas and Falcons are being scheduled for manufacture, along with new weapons that have been developed. With the help of you humans, new interstellar craft will be developed and built to replace the inefficient Generational Ships we use now." Adam could tell by the actions of Lord Neptune's tentacles that he was very happy.

"Our participation has that much of an effect, my Lordship?"

The Tschaaa Lord made a sound the Squid equivalent of a chortle. "Yes. As I have said before, many of my fellow Tschaaa have become lazy and stagnant in their thinking. Because of my success, and continued success of my humans, the Lords are only too are willing to let us perform what you, my Director, would refer to as the 'heavy lifting'."

Adam was pleased. "I hope this will assure the continual survival of my fellow humans."

"Of course, Director Lloyd. You and your fellows are rapidly becoming an essential part of the continual healthy existence of the Tschaaa species on this planet. There is an increasing belief that the Earth Mother Ocean is somehow directly connected with our original Mother Ocean at our home world. I do not concern myself with such theological discussions, and I do not see how there could be an actual connection. But, I must admit that I have no explanation as to how your giant squid creatures developed so closely parallel to us, and even larger in size. Your seas and oceans seem to support our way of life even better than our original Mother Ocean, even despite the pollution and abuse you humans inflicted upon the environment."

His Lordship could tell by his expression, that Adam was considering whether or not to ask a question. "Present your inquiry, my Director. You cannot anger or offend me. Your loyalty and assistance have me, as your saying goes, 'on the top of the world'."

Adam cleared his throat. "My Lordship, with the increases in technology and biological sciences since your arrival, is there a chance that someday you may be able to produce sufficient dark meat artificially, of sufficient quality that not another human will be harvested?"

His Lordship signed compassion. "Your concern for your yet unborn young does credit to your species. There is always that possibility. Some of your human scientists on Platform One are involved in some experiments that may bear results helpful to achieving that result. But, I must be truthful. My fellow Tschaaa have been accustomed to consuming fresh meat for millennia and may not accept a replacement, unless it is indistinguishable from the original."

"Speaking of the Humans on Platform One, are there any... restrictions concerning Colonel Hunter?" Adam asked.

Lord Neptune's tentacles ceased their movements for a minute. "I am sorry I could not inform you about him before. Colonel Hunter was almost successful in attacking Base One some six years ago, shooting down several of our deltas. One was piloted by an offspring of mine."

"Please accept my condolences, my Lordship."

The Tschaaa waved his tentacle in dismissal. "She died as a Warrior, one of a minority of female Tschaaa that achieved success in that distinguished role. She served and died with honor. Colonel Hunter was a worthy opponent. It is what you humans call 'ancient history'.

"But to answer your question, you may utilize the Colonel in any way that is productive in achieving your aims with one restriction... please keep him away from any armed space interceptors you may have hidden away."

Adam laughed, and his Lordship signed amusement. "You may also discover, my Director, that Colonel Hunter may be distracted at the moment from doing anything complicated. You see, he is a pair mate with your spaceplane pilot, Colonel Bardun."

Adam was surprised. "They are a couple, as we humans would say? How did you discover that when he has been incommunicado for some six years?"

"Some of my secrets must continue to remain so. Now, Adam, I must go. With my new authority comes new responsibilities. Again, congratulations and thank you for your efforts. I will speak with you later."

Adam signed off and handed the communicator back to Andrew. "Did you know about the Colonel?"

"Yes. He is in the Tschaaa databases. But no mention had been made over clear air communication."

"Hm... And now I must find a position for him."

"If I may suggest, Director, what about spaceplane pilot? You really only have a single experienced one. And a mated pair may work hard for their continued survival."

"Very true, Andrew."

"Now, you must excuse me, Director. His Lordship has other tasks for me."

CHAPTER 23

One of the concepts that seems to attract and fascinate historians of all types, from armchair to chairs of University departments, is the apparent congruence and confluence of many of the main characters and participants in what we now call the Infestation and the Great Compromise. By some trick or quirk of fate, the working of the Universe, or some invisible hand we have yet to discover, individuals with positions of extreme importance in how things progressed seemed to be destined to come in contact with each other at just the right time, under just the right circumstances. For this was destined to be their future, but is now our realty. One such incident involved two of the central characters instrumental in the future Great Compromise. Who could have foreseen the wide reaching ramifications from the meeting of Torbin Bender and the then Abigail Young, the Avenging Angel, my dear friend?

—Excerpts from the *Literary Works of Princess Akiko*, Free Japan Royal Family.

WYOMING/UTAH BORDER, UNOCCUPIED STATES OF AMERICA

While the Director was handling the successes associated with the launch and its aftermath, Torbin Bender was coping with a dangerous situation that was rapidly turning to shit. He had begun the morning running training maneuvers with the forty soldiers he was preparing for S-Day. Meanwhile, Malmstrom Operations Base had received a panicked hotline telephone call from Evanston, Wyoming near the Utah border that they were under attack, followed immediately by silence.

Torbin and his unit were patrolling for Eaters and Krakens along the Montana/Idaho Border, using the limited mission as a way to shake out the assault unit members, see who worked together the best for the final team. The Unit had already intercepted three Krakens trying to use motorcycles on back roads to infiltrate. A short chase and about a dozen rounds fired, there were three dead Krakens. The base called and directed them to respond.

They hauled ass down the roads in their Humvees to Evanston and found... no one. According to information based on a limited census conducted some five years ago, there should have been one thousand men, women, and children. They had guns and other arms, so they clearly had some means of self-defense. However, as Torbin and his personnel entered the town, they found nothing moving, not even a single stray animal. Their vehicles crawled down a main street, as they scanned from the side to side. The Tschaaa said that Eaters very rarely attacked in anything larger than a pair. Yet, where was everyone?

They stopped completely, and dismounted. As they turned off the vehicle engines to listen, they heard a scrabbling sound, growing louder and apparently headed in their direction.

"What the..." Torbin started to say.

The Eaters seemed to come from every direction. None had the distended stomach of a recent meal, but some had the beginnings of the two buds that signaled that two more creatures were on the way. There were dozens.

"360 perimeter! *Fire at will!*" Torbin yelled, and began firing his assault weapon at one target after another. A couple of Ma Deuces opened up, as well as a M240 medium machine gun. A Mark 19 began shooting 40 mike-mike grenades into the buildings along the side of the street from which the Eaters were exploding. Torbin fired at one rushing at him, stitching rounds thru both large eyes. The Eater's legs collapsed and the creature pancaked as rounds penetrated to what passed as its brain. He fired at the second Eater that passed into his sight area, putting it down like the first. Next a third. Then a fourth. His weapon ran dry.

"Reloading!" He yelled, swapping for a new mag. Another Eater was almost on top of him.

Several shotgun blasts from a drum fed Saiga semi-auto twelve gauge, courtesy of the Russians, tore the guts from the Eater. It collapsed sideways, and Torbin jumped back, managing to dodge the corrosive stomach acids which were splashed from the ripped intestines.

"Thanks, Sergeant Washington."

"I aim to please, Captain." Sergeant Washington quipped.

Torbin heard some screams that told him they were taking casualties. He kept firing.

He cut the legs out from under another Eater, which then tried to use its arms to crawl toward him. Torbin fired a single round through each eye, and it finally stopped. The mad minute was over. It was quiet, except for the sound of moaning and cries of pain from the troops.

"Gunny. Status report!" Torbin commanded.

Gunnery Sergeant Greg Smith, late of the U.S. Marine Corps, began a head count. Right then Corporal Black, manning a Ma Deuce on the front Humvee, called out. "Contact, twelve o'clock, one hundred meters."

"What've we got?" Torbin asked.

"Two Eaters just entered the street, and looks like they're facing this way. Wait, now one is taking off. The other is headed straight toward us."

"Take it out, Corporal."

"Yes, Sir!" A couple moments later, a single round of 50 caliber between the eyes flattened the Eater.

"Well done, Corporal Black."

"Thank you, Sir."

"Gunny. Got the numbers?"

"Yes, Captain. Ten casualties. Seven minor, one serious... two dead, Sir. Sorry."

'Fuck', Torbin thought. He had lost men before, but this had been entirely unexpected. He had lost men to wild alien animals.

"All right troops. Listen up! I screwed up, and underestimated the enemy. That ends now. Everything gets checked out by the numbers. Stay frosty. Understand?"

"Oorah!" came the response. Lessons learned from these deaths would ensure they did not happen again. Just then, Torbin could have sworn he heard a cry for help.

"Captain. Up there. The steeple of that church, where the bell is."

Torbin looked up, and then grabbed his binocs. "Well, I'll be damned. Survivors." He spotted a single adult female, and what appeared to be three children. "Corporal Tatupu, take a squad and rescue those civilians."

"Yes Sir." Corporal Tapua Tatupu was a huge American Samoan, noted for his unnatural strength. He took a look at his rifle, which looked small in his hands. He laid it in the back of a Humvee, and grabbed the M60E1 they had brought along as spare firepower. He threw a couple of ammunition belts across his chest, Pancho Villa style, then called out, "Squad One. On me. assault formation. Let's go!"

The Corporal and ten troops quickly made their way to the double doors at the entrance of the church. A large building, the Church was also fairly old, apparently having been part of the original town. The troops lined up, breached the doors, and went in by the numbers, the Corporal in front. The M60 boomed. Then silence.

"One Eater down. You and you. Get up those stairs and get the civilians," the Corporal ordered.

"Yes, Corporal."

In five minutes, the woman and three children were down in front of the Church, the EMT checking them for injury. The soldiers also brought out a very injured male, his right arm severely burned from what looked like Eater stomach juices.

"Sir, the lady said the man here was jumped by an Eater that tried to eat his arm. He managed to blow its brains out, but received some stomach acid for his efforts," Corporal Tatupu reported.

"I think this is a good time for a chopper dust off," Torbin replied. "Private Hagel. I need the tactical radio."

"Here Sir." Torbin took the handset of the backpack radio, a modification that tried to bounce waves off of both cell towers, as well as off of the ionosphere. He soon had Malmstrom Security Control on the line.

"Yes, that's affirmative. Need chopper support for four civilian survivors, one serious injury civilian, one serious military, and one moderate military. Yes, ASAP. Roger. Over and out."

He cautiously approached the civilian woman, a thirty-something year old frontier type that was still attractive even in her disheveled state. Her hair was pulled back in a ponytail, and she was helping the three children, ages six to twelve, drink from water canteens. "Excuse me, ma'am."

She smiled in reply. "No need to stand on ceremony, Captain. You saved us. Just tell me what I need to do."

"What's your name?"

"I'm Heather O'Hara, teacher and librarian of this town."

Torbin saw she had the frontier toughness of two centuries ago, when the American People were expanding Westward. She also had a lever action rifle in her left hand.

"Well, Ms. O'Hara, two helicopters should be here in about an hour to airlift you, the children and the gentleman to Malmstrom Operations Base. There you'll receive food, quarters, and medical aid. Right now, this town is not secure. Can you tell me what happened?"

Heather paused. "Yes, I can. Hell visited us here. Pure and simple."

It seemed that about two weeks ago a large herd of feral pigs, well known by the townspeople who hunted them for fresh meat and sport, had suddenly disappeared. An unofficial dump about two miles out from the town had been used as an additional food source for the pigs in order to fatten them up. Then, no pigs. A hunting party went out and saw the first Eater, which they promptly shot. It was decided that the Eater and maybe a sibling or two had scared off the pigs, who would come back once the Eaters were gone. So, the townsmen started sending out hunting parties to rid the area of Eaters. Being an independent and self-sufficient lot, they informed no one. Near a farmers feed lot where a calf had turned up missing, two hunters were jumped by an Eater and injured before they killed it. One of the men was bitten and burnt by regurgitated digestive juices of the creature, an unpleasant characteristic of contacts with Eaters.

The badly injured man was recuperating in his home near the edge of town three days later when Eaters broke in and dragged him away, long with his wife, his dog, and his cat. People responded to their screams but it was too late. Tracks indicated at least four Eaters, in spire of prior stories indicating that Eaters sometimes attacked in pairs, but nothing more numerous. A good old fashioned posse was formed–two dozen armed menfolk–some with military combat experience. A couple of good old bloodhounds were used to help track, as it had been established that dogs *hated* Eaters, and would attack them on sight. A few hours later, about a dozen shots were heard. Then, nothing. No one returned. No one answered the radio calls.

They had a Town Hall Meeting. It was decided to start moving everyone to the Town Hall and the Church on the main thoroughfare. As this was taking place, some two dozen Eaters attacked. Once again, no one expected such pack behavior. The creatures immediately ravaged anyone they could latch onto. Crossfire also hit a few town residents, adding to the confusion.

Heather grabbed three children she knew, having lost her own family in the first days of the invasion and harvesting. She took them to the church, where the Assistant Pastor Randolph, the injured civilian, was trying to fit as many people inside as possible. Another half dozen Eaters then struck from the other end of the main street, scrambling directly for the moving figures in and around the church. The barrelled in through a back door of the church. Randolph shot a couple before he had his arm almost taken off. Everyone scattered. Heather grabbed the kids and headed up the steeple to the church bell tower. Somehow, the Pastor followed before he collapsed at the bottom of the steeple stairs and ladder. Heather climbed back down and managed to get the access door locked and barricaded with a bunch of boxes of bibles. She had her own rifle, a Marlin 30-30, that she fired through the door when one Eater began tearing through to get to the Pastor.

She heard shots and screams echoing from all over town. After binding Randolph's wounds as best she could, she joined the children at the top of the steeple. From there she watched the surreal tableau below. Eaters were being shot and killed, but were quickly replaced with others. Panic set in, and people began fleeing from the center of town. A fire somehow started in the basement of the Town Hall, adding to the fear and confusion. Heather watched as people tried to get into vehicles and flee, only to have some of the vehicles mobbed by Eaters. Eventually, a window would be smashed in and the occupants mauled.

Within about a half hour there were no living humans within sight of the church. When silence had settled in, Heather made quick trip to the church kitchen and grabbed as much water and canned goods as she could, as well as a couple of fresh loaves of bread. She returned to the Steeple and secured the door once more.

While Heather recounted her story, she also shared that she believed the Eaters were attracted to people whom they had wounded due to the digestive juice/saliva smell they left on the wounded, in addition to the smell of fresh blood. Torbin believed that jived with reports he had gleaned. It was much like Komodo dragons in the Southwest Pacific.

Someone must have made the telephone call from the town hall to Malmstrom just before the fire started, as it had been about an hour later when Torbin was contacted and told to respond. It took Torbin and his unit just under twenty-four hours to finish the patrols they were on in Western Montana and haul ass to Evanston. And now, they were here, with dozens of dead alien bodies that needed tending to.

"Well, Heather, we'll bring you to Malmstrom with the children and the Pastor. When this area is secure, we'll bring you back."

Heather looked at him. "Thank you, Captain, but I think it will be a while before I'll want to come back. Think they can find me something to do near the base?"

"I'm certain of it. If nothing else, you have a lot of hands-on experience in survival."

Just then, he heard a single shot that sounded like it came from a large caliber firearm.

"Anybody see where that came from?" He bellowed.

"Out to the south of town, Captain," someone yelled back.

"Gunny. Take a squad out and sweep the area south of here."

"Aye aye, Sir." The Gunnery Sergeant began yelling for Squad Two to fall in behind him. Within a couple of minutes, the troops were moving out in loose column formation.

"Ma'am, please stay behind cover with the kids until we figure this out."

Corporal Black manning the Ma Deuce on the forward Humvee called out, "People approaching from twelve o'clock Sir."

Torbin jogged up to the Humvee and looked through his binoculars. He saw three smallish adult-sized figures in some kind of camouflaged uniform approaching in a loose diamond formation. They all had long arms slung, but were pushing two ragged looking figures before them. The front figure held its hands out, palms up, to show that they were empty. Torbin unslung his rifle and placed it on the hood of the Humvee. "Got me covered, Corporal?"

"Of course, Sir. This is close range for my Deuce."

"Don't fire unless I go down. Clear?"

"Crystal, Sir."

Torbin walked out to meet the three humans. About thirty yards away, Torbin noticed two of the figures had feminine curves that the camo pants could not conceal.

"Captain Torbin Bender of the Unoccupied States at your service. To whom am I speaking?"

"Avenging Angel Abigail Young, Nauvoo Legion, State of Deseret, formerly Utah." It was a young feminine voice, but one which spoke with authority. Sixteen, seventeen years of age? The figure to her right was definitely a female also. The one figure to the left rear looked like a young male.

"So, how do I address you, Ma'am?"

She was close enough to speak in a normal voice. She took off her Fritz helmet that was adorned with a large set of painted on wings. She had naturally blonde hair, braided up into a bun, and flashed a genuine smile. "You can call me Abigail, Sir, being my senior."

The Captain chuckled. "Hey, I'm not that old. Call me Torbin. I take it you are in command of this small Unit.

"Yes sir. Torbin. I am an Avenger First Class. To my right is Ruth Young, Second Class. The young man is Mathew Young, Third Class."

"You all related?"

She shook her head. "No. We Avenging Angels all take the Prophet Brigham Young's name to show we operate in his name and spirit."

"Is this it? Kind of sparse in the numbers department to be leaving your borders. And I see you have a couple of prisoners." Abigail frowned. "We started with six. Two are dead, passed on to glory. One is wounded in a cave a few miles away. That is why I am approaching you. Can you provide us with some medical help? He is bitten and burned. Plus, we have these two... scum." The one called Mathew had forced the two handcuffed miscreants to kneel during the conversation.

Torbin regarded the young woman. Five foot seven or so, a hundred thirty pounds on a good day. Yet, she had the air of an efficient soldier and killer. "Would you consider air evac? I have two choppers in route."

She glanced back at her fellow Avengers. They each gave a slight nod. "I believe, given the circumstances, that would be a good idea. You are non-believers, but not heathens as the Ferals are. Or evil ones like these Krakens." Abigail spat the name out as she spoke it.

"No, Ma'am. I may be a bit rowdy at times, but I definitely not like a Feral." Ferals to the Tschaaa meant all humans not under their control. Ferals to everyone else meant humans that had basically reverted back to a primitive concept of behavior; anyone not part of the Group was potential Prey, in every sense of the word. Abigail pointed due South. "We came straight north the last few miles, crossing the border over a day ago, while tracking Demons that had killed some of our people."

"Demons? You mean Eaters?"

"Yes, I guess that is what you call them on your broadcasts. They are Demons to us, brought here by the Antichrist and the Evil One."

It took a moment for Torbin to translate. "Director Lloyd and the Tschaaa Lord."

Abigail spat in a very unladylike fashion. "Yes. His name is a curse. The Evil One the curser."

"Cthulhu, the ancient Evil One," Mathew suddenly spurt out.

"Stop that!" Abigail yelled at him. "This is not one of the fantasy books you read."

"H.P. Lovecraft," Torbin commented.

Mathew's eyes widened. "You have read his stories?"

"Yes, young man, at about your age. I looked them up recently. It's funny, isn't it, how they match much of what is happening today. An evil in the form of a Kraken like species. Go figure."

Abigail glanced back at him. "Whatever his name, you agree as to his evil nature. Our mission is to destroy his minions, send them back to *hell*."

'This is sick,' Torbin thought. 'A young girl coming into womanhood in a world where she is killing monsters instead of going to Senior Prom.' He was going to mutilate the Tschaaa Lords the first chance he got.

"If you three will walk back with me, I will introduce you to the men and make arrangements to retrieve your fellow soldier." As they approached his troops, Torbin noted that the three teenagers were on relaxed alert status, walking loose but not missing anything. Some of his men took a break from dragging Eater bodies into a large pile for burning and walked over to get a look at the three newcomers. The female form even in a uniform attracts males like honey attracts flies. Soon, several soldiers were buzzing around Abigail and Ruth.

"At ease, troops. These soldiers are from the former State of Utah. They are military members so treat them with the commensurate respect." There was a little bit of grousing, but everyone kept a respectful distance.

Torbin marched over to the lead Humvee. "Ready for a little trip, Corporal Black?"

The young dark-haired soldier gave a slight smile. "Of course, Sir."

Torbin returned to Abigail and the others. "You can jump in the Humvee there with me. I'll drive, the Private will man the 50. We should be able to get close to the cave and recover your teammate. Sound good?"

"Yes, Captain Bender. Thank you."

"Gunny, get the people ready for the medivac. We'll take the prisoners with us in the Humvees, unless Abigail disagrees. I'm going to take a little trip."

Large, broad-shouldered and deep-chested Gunny Smith commented, "Sir, if something happens to you, the General will have my balls."

"True, Gunny. But I'll not put anyone into a risky situation that I am not willing to face. I underestimated the Eaters here. I owe the men not to do it again until I figure out what is going on." He handed the NCO his assault rifle. "Hang onto this. I'll take the 1897 pump twelve gauge we found. I don't want to give someone a full auto weapon. I'll also have my pistol."

"You're the boss, Sir. Just make it back in one piece."

"Don't worry, Gunny, I'll be careful."

He turned and directed the three Avenging Angels. "Mount up. Let's do this quick."

The three had apparently previous ridden in a Humvee before. They quickly found seats and belts. Torbin started the engine, pulled out the line of vehicles, and then made a ninety degree turn to due south. "Just indicate where we need to go, Abigail. You're the navigator."

"Yes, Sir," came the reply. Abigail was soon giving clear and concise directions. Torbin had noticed that she carried a Remington

Pump .308 rifle with an extended ten round magazine. Ruth had an M-16 clone, and Mathew had a bolt action scoped .308 Remington. The two ladies also carried sawed off double barreled shotguns, shoved in the pack on their backs. Mathew had a Hipoint 9mm carbine slung in his.

"Need some ammo later, Abigail?"

"If you have some to spare, yes... Torbin. We have only a dozen or so rounds left per weapon."

"The Corporal up top should have more than enough firepower if we need to bug out fast. But maybe I should ask how you young people ending up with a dangerous job like this?"

"We all came down from Idaho. We were irradiated when the Hanford Nuclear Plant Complex blew and we fled south through the fallout area to Salt Lake City, as some of my family was Mormon. The Church decided it would not be a good idea if we found husbands or wives, too much chance of serious birth defects from damaged DNA. So, we serve the Prophet and God the best way we can; killing Demons, Evil Ones, Ferals, so that others may live."

Torbin was silent. Abigail had become mature beyond her years, but not by her choice. The Tschaaa had a lot to pay for.

"You are betrothed, are you not, Torbin?"

"Why, yes. Who told you?"

Abigail shrugged. "It is a gift from God. I can see into a person, feel what is inside. You have a love inside your rough exterior that is connected to another. I hope your children are all healthy."

Children? How in the hell did she know that he and Aleks just started trying to make a baby? "Thank you, Abigail. Now, it looks like we are about a couple hundred yards from where you said the cave was located. Time to stop and go on foot.

"Leave your rifle here. Take only your shotgun. If we have to shoot our way in it's going to be time to leave. I have this pump and my pistol to slow them up if we have to run from the Eaters. Do you have a pistol as well?"

"Yes." Abigail pulled out a little top break .32 revolver. Torbin frowned. "Kind of small, isn't it?"

"I carry it for two-legged Demons passing as men who try to abuse me. Nothing more."

"Well, it might mess up a man's plumbing at point blank range, but won't do us much good in a firefight. Let's leave it behind for now." He called over to Corporal Black. "Keep your hands on that Ma Deuce. Our job is to keep the other two Avengers here in one piece, and ready to cover our retreat. Clear?"

The Private grinned. "Crystal, Captain."

Torbin signaled to Abigail and they began a quick walk down the animal trail that Abigail said led to the small cave in which her comrade was hidden. It took them just a few minutes to travel some two hundred yards to a small clearing. A fairly substantial brush-covered hill rose near the small clearing in the forest. Abigail pointed to a spot that looked like every other. Torbin was impressed when she deftly moved some strategically placed branches and revealed a small opening. She entered, and Torbin followed. He had a small LED flashlight that revealed the injured man. The man looked a bit older, maybe twenty years of age, and was very pale. His left arm and side were heavily bandaged, with blood seeping through.

"Here is some help, Peter," Abigail whispered.

"You came back." Peter slowly raised his eyes to glance at Torbin. "Heathen?"

"No," Abigail answered. "Just a non-believer from the Armed Forces of the Unoccupied States."

"Captain Torbin at your service. I am now going to pick you up onto my shoulders in a fireman's carry. It may hurt, but we have to move. Understand?"

Peter nodded yes. "Good, here goes." Torbin easily positioned the wounded man on his shoulders. "Abigail, grab his rifle, and let's go."

They were met by an Eater at the opening. Before Torbin could react, Abigail raised the lever action she had retrieved from Peter and fired a round right between the large eyes of the alien. The creature collapsing where it had stood. Quickly, Torbin passed the body and started striding up the trail.

Fifty yards up the path, an Eater came rushing up from behind them. Abigail turned and tried to lever a fresh round and fire. The round she had just fired had apparently split, bulged, and jammed itself in the chamber. Abigail reefed on the lever action and ripped the case head off the expended round. "Shit!" The unexpected curse from the devoted Mormon caused Torbin to look back and catch a glimpse of their pursuer. In one smooth motion, he turned and fired from the hip with his pump shotgun. The heavy shot struck the alien in its eyes, at least one buckshot penetrating to its brain. Its body slumped to the trail.

"Ditch the rifle, troop. Take my shotgun." Abigail reacted to the orders automatically, easily bowing to his seniority. She grabbed the shotgun, ejected the spent shell and chambered another twelve gauge, the rifle forgotten on the trail. Torbin began jogging easily with the extra load. The man was a slender, probably no more than one hundred fifty pounds. Torbin was strong for his relative size and weight, and easily hustled along the trail toward the Humvee.

"Eaters moving in the brush," Abigail warned.

Torbin attempted to increase his pace to a full run. He had to be careful that he did not trip on the rough ground. He did not want to end up in a firefight, even a one sided one, with an unknown number of Eaters.

Moments later, they emerged from the brush near the Humvee. There were looks of relief on Ruth and Mathew's faces as Torbin brought the injured Peter up to the vehicle, just as the fifty caliber spoke. He glanced back over his shoulder in time to see three Eaters dissected by the heavy machine gun rounds. "Eaters still in the bush, Captain. I also thought I saw a human figure take off. Couldn't get a shot."

Abigail shook a fist in fury toward the underbrush. "Kraken scum! I know they are inserting the Demons into this area. I feel it in my bones."

Torbin nodded in assent as he laid Peter on a stretcher. "That fits what we know. It appears the Director and the Tschaaa Lord in Key West have decided to start harassing us." "I know of only one true Lord, and that is Jesus Christ," Abigail commented.

They strapped Peter to the stretcher, then strapped the entire stretcher to the top of the Humvee, near Corporal Black's position. "If you have to fire, Corporal, just watch where you are aiming that fifty cal. We don't want to further injure our patient.

"Aye aye, Captain." Black responded with a grin. Torbin chuckled. That man sure enjoyed his work.

"All aboard. Let's head out." They were back in town within a minute.

"Thank you, Captain. I am forever in your debt. I couldn't stand to lose any more of my fellow warriors."

"As they say on the southwest border, Abigail, 'de nada'. I'm just doing what a decent human being should."

Abigail gazed at him with appreciation. Torbin had acted in a more humane and Christian way than many of her fellow Mormons had. She would always remember this day.

Torbin reached into his right fatigue shirt pocket, pulling out a hand calligraphed business card while he kept his eyes on the road. Aleks had made him a dozen or so of the handmade cards, each beautifully drawn and lettered. His future wife had many astounding skills, including the ability to produce detailed drawings and stylized printing. Torbin was lucky if he could draw recognizable stick figures, and he flunked handwriting in grade school. "Here, Abigail. On this card my betrothed made me are a couple of telephone numbers and a radio frequency you can use to contact me at Malmstrom Base. We have a cell phone system that is up and running through most of our States using microwave cell towers and connections with a couple of satellites the Tschaaa left up. Funny thing is, they don't try to block us. It's like we are gnats buzzing around that they ignore."

Abigail took the card. "Thank you. I will keep this safe. I can sense the love that went into its making. And I will tell my superiors of the help you provided."

"Please do. We would like to establish regular contact with your people. So far, it has been very much hit and miss."

Abigail sighed. "They closed the borders of Deseret, your Utah, in the first year. That enabled them to focus on organizing a rebuilding effort, even while we suffered the long winter. But our religion always had us prepare, with extra food, supplies in every Latter Day Saint's home. We lost almost no one to hunger, and few to sickness. Since then, they have been very hesitant to rejoin society, especially after some heathens tried to take by force what was not theirs, including women. That is when we Avenging Angels were created. No one is allowed to hurt one of our people and get away with it, no matter where they flee."

"How about Squids? Do you go after them?"

Abigail frowned. "I was told they tried to harvest our State in a couple of locations early on. Then they stopped. Our Living Prophet said it was our strong faith that made the Tschaaa leave us alone. I have no answer other than this."

Torbin did not tell her that his people had it on good authority that the Mormons had rounded up all the people of color they could find and sent them out along Interstate Highway 70 into Colorado. Some had made it to the bases and population centers being set up as the Unoccupied States by the end of the first year. Many died due to the long winter, others had been harvested by roving Falcons. No one would know for sure the numbers involved. What was known was the Tschaaa left Utah alone after a couple of months. They arrived back at the town, just as the two choppers called in and said they were a half hour out. Torbin checked with the Gunny, who reported they had set up a landing zone in a field on the outskirts of the town. The wounded and the surviving town residents were waiting, under the protection of a squad of troops. The one seriously wounded troop, plus one with a foot injury, were to be loaded with the badly wounded pastor and flown back ASAP, aboard a Blackhawk chopper set up as a Medevac Bird. A ubiquitous Huey would transport Heather and the children at a slower pace. Torbin and his men would transport their dead, along with the two prisoners.

"As usual, Gunny, you needed me about as much as a boar hog needs tits."

The Gunny smiled nervously. "Sir, you get the 'big bucks' to make all the decisions and get your ass chewed by the General. I just do what I'm told."

Torbin laughed. "That may be true to an extent, but NCOs like you still really run the military."

"By the way, Captain, there is a set of sealed orders onboard one of the choppers. They are from the General."

"Perfect. Looks he has something else he wants me to do. Carry on, Gunny."

"Aye aye, Sir."

Torbin walked back to his original Humvee. Out of his ditty bag, he grabbed a small twenty round box of .223 and a five shot box of double ought buck. He also grabbed three MREs. From the Humvee with the MG 240 attached in its gun position, he took two twenty round belts of 7.62 ammunition and slung them over his shoulder. He handed the guns over to Abigail. "Here, ma'am. This should help out. I wish I could talk you into coming with us instead."

Abigail smiled and shook her head. "I am sorry, but I have my orders. We will ask you to take the two Kraken scum with you as we have already... obtained information from them. We will stay here for a couple more days and kill as many Demons as we can find. Then, we will travel back the way we came, home."

Torbin knew all about orders, so he did not argue. He noticed the Kraken had signs of "questioning" displayed on their bodies, and they were very quiet.

He called to Corporal Tatupu. "Corporal, take a couple of men and check out that General Store. See if they have some canned goods or local produce for the Avengers here. Some water also."

"Yes Sir." The huge Corporal glommed onto two troops and headed out, weapons at a ready in case an Eater was hiding out.

Torbin turned to Mathew. "I see a cap and ball pistol in your shoulder holster. Need some black powder?" Mathew perked up. "Yes sir. I have spare caps and balls, but no powder."

Torbin reached into one of his pockets and produced a cylindrical object the same size as a toilet paper roll, because that was its basis. "Here. As one of my hobbies, I've made a couple of firecrackers as homemade flashbangs. Here's one. The center is black powder. Keep it away from flame, of course."

"Thank you. I can surely use this."

Torbin made small talk until he heard the sound of choppers. "Well, Abigail, I need to meet those whirlybirds. The Corporal will give you some food supplies when he gets back. I suggest you use that Church and its steeple to keep a eye out for the Eaters. Give me a call when you get a chance, please."

Abigail smiled again and stuck out her hand. Torbin took it, feeling her firm handshake. A connection only two warriors who have experienced combat, faced death together, passed between them. "Thank you, Captain. I will keep you in my prayers."

"I'd like that." He released her hand and stepped back. Abigail came to attention and snapped a salute that would have made an Honor Guard member proud. Torbin saluted back.

"Vaya con Dios, Angel."

"Thank you, Captain. May God go with you as well." She turned and strided toward the approaching Corporal with a wheelbarrow full of food and drink supplies.

Torbin returned to his Humvee, his driver, Private Martinez, starting it before Torbin said anything.

"Heading toward the choppers, Sir."

"That's what I like about you, Private. You can read my mind."

A few minutes later, the wounded and civilians were being loaded aboard. Torbin used his Ka-Bar to open the heavily sealed envelope. A quick glance over the terse message elicited a small curse from him. S-Day had to be moved up. The success of the recent space launches and all of the other material improvements the Director had overseen was resulting in more and more humans flocking to the Tschaaa controlled areas, like so many sheep. Time was running out. At a certain point, much like Occupied France and some Communist countries, the populace was more apt to accept the status quo as an extreme inertia set in. In those circumstances, the populace becomes almost as much of a problem as the occupiers.

"Gunny!" Torbin yelled. "Get everybody mounted up. We are going home."

As they watched Torbin and his unit depart, Ruth turned toward Abigail. "They are fine men, as fine as any man in Deseret. It is a shame they are non-believers."

Abigail sighed. "Yes, it is a shame. They would also put to shame some of our males who claim to be men of faith, warriors of virtue."

"Abigail, have you ever thought of leaving Deseret, and going to the U.S.A. so you could marry?"

Abigail paused. "Yes, truthfully. I've often thought of being able to marry. But right now, God, Jesus Christ and the Prophets have a different path for me. I know God will let me know when I have fulfilled my Mission as an Avenging Angel. Then, I will decide, with God and Jesus' council, what path I will take."

She turned to the others. "Come, let us take our food supplies to the Church. I agree with the Captain that the steeple is a perfect lookout post."

"And a perfect sniper perch." Mathew said with a smile.

Abigail smiled as well. "Yes, you will have ample opportunity to demonstrate your shooting skills, I am certain of it." The three young humans, mature beyond their years, began to move their supplies into the Church.

Once humans fall into a pit of depravity and degradation, even without alien help, it is often near impossible for them to crawl out unless helped by outside people and forces. What happened in Atlanta, Georgia, Cattle Country, is a horrible example of the concept.

> —Excerpts from the *Literary Works of Princess Akiko*, Free Japan Royal Family.

ATLANTA, GEORGIA, CATTLE COUNTRY

It was Fight Night again. Mayor Luther was happy, *very* happy, *extremely* happy because, due to the reported successes of the renewed space program, they were providing him with a whole boatload of extra food and drink as a way of saying, "Thanks for staying out of the way. Don't screw it up." With the addition of Joe's help and contacts, he had turned tonight into another extravaganza. The first fight had just ended, and a memorable one it was. Blue– he never did find out her real full name–had fought a young Filipina called "Orange" of the same size and weight. She had asked to fight again to gain more favors like the ones she had earned the first go around. Alas, her wish was not fulfilled. In a climax to the fight that would not soon be forgotten, Orange had wrapped her strong brown legs around Blue's waist from behind, squeezing with all her might. Then, she had wrapped her arms around her rival's body, using her sharp fingernails and strong fingers to claw and maul Blue's breasts. The piece de résistance was when Orange sank her teeth into her opponent's neck muscles, drawing blood.

Blue, shocked and beaten, had screamed for mercy, admitted defeat.

The Mayor had taken a chance of inciting interracial rioting by having one minority battle another. But he did not care now. The results had been fantastic, the crowds yelling for more.

"Hey, Joe, are they coming up?" the Mayor asked his right hand man.

"Yes, Boss. Just got the radio call; they are en route."

Mayor Martin Luther Johnson looked at Red. "Are you ready for this, Honey?"

She gave him a big smile. "Yes, Dearest, I am. I have waited for this for a while. Now, I will enjoy inflicting my payback."

The Mayor gave a big belly laugh. "Remind me never to piss you off."

Just then, the Mayor heard a shout cut short at the outer door to his office suite. Next there was a gunshot, followed immediately by the door being smashed in. Joe leapt to his defense, his signature Bowie in his hand. The Mayor started to reach for the Luger he kept loaded in his desk side drawer.

"Don't even think about it," a loud voice commanded. It was Malcolm, whatever his last name was.

He had a silenced .45 aimed at the Mayor, two other ski masked men at his side, with sawed offs in their hands.

"Sorry about the noise, Mayor. One of your guys got off a shot before I blew his brains out. Now, nice and slow, hands on the table. Joe, don't be stupid. Buckshot in the gut will do you no good. Now, please, put your knife away and raise your hands." Joe grudgingly complied. Another large man with a well-used but well- kept Winchester lever action came in. "Sir, our men are securing the other guards. A couple had to be knived. But we should have everything under control on the auditorium floor in just a minute. We have the communications booth already. In about ten minutes, you should be able to broadcast your message."

"Excellent, Tyrone. I am glad casualties have been kept to a minimum."

Malcolm continued to point the .45 at the Mayor as he spoke. "Consider this a recall election that you just lost. Sending those seven men to Talbot as sacrificial lambs was the straw that broke the proverbial camel's back. Especially when you picked ones you personally disliked. Sorry, but you will not be allowed to remain here."

He looked at Red. "You can stay or leave. I have nothing against the big house help. We are all in the same leaky boat. So, what do you wish?"

Red looked at Martin Luther, then at Malcolm. "I would like to stay, in one piece, if there is... something I can do... for you."

"*Red!*" the Mayor yelled, and lunging upwards and across the desk. Malcolm shot him through his right eye, the large round blowing the back of his head off. He toppled, slid and fell behind his former desk.

A second after the shot, Malcolm was covering Joe. "Same deal for you, Joe. I could use someone with your connections and abilities. I promise you, you will *not* be my pimp. However, do not think you can sit around and wait to take me out, because if you do, I have a few very loyal people who will draw and quarter you on general principles, and do it very slowly, whether I live or not. Get me?"

"Yes, Sir. I understand." Joe did not look at the former Mayor's body.

"Red. Is that your name? Well, let's just keep it that way for the time being. Do you have any office or management skills, other than screwing the boss that is?"

She looked at her feet. "I was attending business college and working part time at an import/export broker in Savannah when the Squids attacked."

"Good. Skills, brains, and knowledge of Savannah. Hey, look at me... I *said, look at me.*" Red quickly met his eyes. "No more of this looking down like you have something to be ashamed about. We've all had to do some nasty things to stay alive. But same deal as with Joe. If you think you can stab me in my sleep, forget it. You'll be sliced up by my people just like anyone else. Understand?"

"Yes... Mayor. I understand. But please understand also. Mayor Luther was nice to me. Treated me like he... cared. So please do not think I will degrade him to you. If that is what you want, you need to shoot me now."

"You have some fire in you. I like that. And you aren't willing to speak ill of the dead. Being as you chose to stay, you are pragmatic as well. Good. I can definitely use you. You can remain in this suite, as I know you have nowhere else to go. But, you are not my piece of ass. Okay?" She nodded.

"Now, how do you get a hold of the Squids to pick up bodies?"

Joe was the first to answer. "There is a large spotlight on top of this building. We shine it upwards, toward the clouds. A Falcon shows up, picks up the... meat."

Malcolm guffawed. "A bat signal. Some Squid has a sense of humor, and I bet I know who. His Lordship in Key West. Well, Joe, show Tyrone what needs to be done. I don't want to start off on the wrong foot."

A small radio that Malcolm held crackled to life. He held it to his ear as he had the volume turned down. A smile lit his very dark face. "Okay, I'm off to the control room. Joe, you need to get Mr. ex-Mayor's body out of here and have someone clean up the mess. Okay?"

"Yes, Mayor."

"Okay, I'm off."

Ten minutes later, he was broadcasting within the Arena and outside into Greater Atlanta. "Ladies and Gentlemen. As of today, there has been a change in management here in Atlanta. My name is Malcolm Carver. I am the new Mayor. Now, before everyone starts rioting, fussing and fuming... tonight, the show goes on. And, we will have future entertainment. *But*, and this is a big but–just like ones on some of those women you brothers like to look at– I will be asking everyone to start doing some things for me. Call it having a 'job'. That's right, a J... O... B. You want some fun and entertainment; you will have to do some *work*. I'll give you a while to think about that. Right now, enjoy the next fight." With that, Malcolm stopped broadcasting.

"Well, let's see how long before some brother starts breaking windows and acting the fool."

The rest of the fights went well. All the winners and losers went to the Mayor's suite as before. The one difference was that the losers were not simply exploited for the Mayor's pleasure. They were told they had to work it off some other way, to be determined. And were told to report back in two days.

Sure enough, the next day when things began to sink in, a bunch of mostly young people began to mill around in the streets. Soon, rocks were thrown. Then, a few molotov cocktails. Since so many buildings were vacant, it was hard to really see any damage. Malcolm sent out his trained personnel with some edged weapons gleaned from the local museums and one intact hardware store. A bunch of people were harvested, and a point was made. When one of his personnel was shot during a demonstration, he retaliated within the minute by having ten of the participants shot. Within another minute, a Falcon showed up overhead, and began lifting the bodies up with its well-known articulating tentacles. One dark-skinned Mexican-American young male was still alive, having been hit in the leg. He began to scream. Suspended some fifty feet in the air, a tentacle with a blade attachment eviscerated him, allowing his intestines and other internal organs to shower down on the streets and buildings below.

Malcolm was watching the scene via live video feed. He chuckled and turned to Red and Joe, who were with him in his office suite. "The Squids learned something that other oppressors knew. When someone resisted, terrorize everyone by brutalizing him publicly. Burn him, whip him, lynch him. Throw terrorist violence at them and you soon have a pliable populace. They may hide when possible but accept violence done to others, 'the Troublemakers'." Malcolm cracked his knuckles.

"Now, Joe. Use your contacts to get representatives from the various ethnic groups and organized neighborhoods here for a meeting the day after next. I am going to lay out what will be expected of them. They will be given the choice in helping me form a Resistance Movement, or they will be sent to Savannah for harvesting."

The new Mayor continued, "While on the subject of harvesting, we will not be filling our quota for slaughter. To achieve this, we must have sufficient hardened shelters, hidey-holes, as well as food and water supplies stashed for our city populace to survive. We also have to collect as well as build weapons to resist. Yes, we can develop weapons to take on Falcons and deltas."

Malcolm cracked his knuckles again. "Initially, Talbot and his white trash Krakens will be sent. We will wipe them out and take their weapons. Falcons and deltas will show up next, with some robocops on the ground. They will try to terrorize us by tearing open buildings and yanking people out, slaughtering them in public. We will not give in. The other population areas in Cattle Country will be given the chance to join us. If not, they may be expected by the Squids to make up the losses in harvesting. So, they either help us, or suffer the consequences."

Malcolm turned and looked out the window onto the bare street. "We will be like the Polish Jews in the Warsaw ghetto. We will fight with whatever we can. And, yes, most of us may die. But we are a populace of walking dead anyway, each of us eventually facing the butcher's block. However, since we are a necessary food supply, I think the Squids will have difficulty in trying to wipe us out completely. Killing off your breeding population is like killing the goose that laid the golden egg. No goose, no eggs."

Malcolm turned back. He knew that Joe and Red thought he was nuts. Too bad. He was in charge.

"I know you think that we have as much of a chance as there is in finding an ice cube in hell. Well, I think when harvesting us, fighting organized resistance, becomes too expensive in resources, the Squids will go back to hitting the white meat in the Occupied Areas as well as the Ferals, as they have been left alone for the last couple of years. Then, those pale bastards will be forced to fight again. Instead of selling us people of color as sacrificial lambs, they will either start resisting or they will be marched off to the slaughter like the rest of us." Malcolm realized he was becoming agitated. He took a deep breath and centered himself.

"Mayor, what about rocks?" Joe asked. "What's to stop the Squids from bombing us again?"

"They have too many young developing in our oceans, Joe. Creating another long winter, or some other climate change, not to mention the chance of an errant missile hitting one of their breeding areas, I believe will limit those types of attacks. Who knows, maybe we can find a way to attack those breeding areas. See how they like it when it's their babies that are dying, and being used as feed for other species. The more we hurt them, the more they will have to think, is it worth the cost?"

He stopped. He saw that Joe and Red understood what he was saying. They just did not have the confidence that he could succeed. Well, he had the confidence of a hundred Joes and Reds.

"That's enough ranting for now. Red, the losers from fight night will be here. You need to find tasks and jobs for all of them. We will house them here, so find some usable rooms in this former hotel. They will be fed and provided for a long as they work. Others who commit crimes in the streets will be given the same chance. Work it off, or wind up as a filet for a Squid whelp. Got it?"

"Yes, Sir. I will take care of what you wish."

Malcolm beamed. "Excellent. Now, excuse me while I go to the men's room. I've been drinking up our coffee supplies." He went to his private bathroom.

Joe glanced sideways at Red. In a low tone he asked, "What do you think?"

"I think I will do what I am told. I think I may have a chance of a better life with him. I will do anything to prevent me from having to give birth and having my child taken off to be slaughtered."

Joe nodded his head in agreement. "I guess you're right. I was always careful in my younger years in football not to get some girl pregnant. I am even gladder now that I did not. I would kill anybody who tried to take one of my kids away, to be used as fish food."

Red gave a tight-lipped smile. "This will not be an easy life, but it's a hell of a lot better than the death we are currently living."

CHAPTER 25

Kathy ran to the ladies room as fast as she could. The Major had been keeping her so busy preparing for the necessary follow up broadcasts to the Cape Canaveral missions, Eater threat and updates on rebuilding the infrastructure of the former U.S. A., that she barely had time to answer the call of nature. She dashed in, and grabbed the nearest stall. Weeks ago, she had tracked down janitorial support in the building weeks ago, slipped the young woman who cleaned some extra cash and asked her to spend as much time as possible keeping the women's toilets clean. Since that time, she had kept a steady flow of little "tips" to the woman and her sister. You could practically eat off the commodes now. Kathy thought it must have been a cosmic joke of God that men had the ability to stand up and urinate, no danger of infection, irritation, etc. and it was women who had the complicated plumbing that lent itself to these problems, yet had to sit down, close to potential sources of trouble.

She finished and stood up. As she started to open the stall door, another woman entered the bathroom in a hurry, and tried to enter her stall just as she was leaving. It was Mary Lou. They bumped, did the little dance of pedestrians, each trying to get around the other, but kept going to the same side.

"Kathy, if you don't move, I'm going to pee on you." Mary Lou snapped.

"Promises, promises." She quipped back, and then squeezed around Mary Lou.

Mary Lou quickly entered, slammed the door, and took a seat. Kathy waited, standing directly outside.

"What are you doing?" Mary Lou demanded.

"Listening. I just wanted to see if you are as human as the rest of us."

Mary Lou finished and flushed, glaring at Kathy as she exited the stall. "Oh, I'm definitely human. But what kind of *woman* lurks outside another woman's toilet?"

Kathy chuckled. "Of the two of us, I think I have more practice acting like a real woman than you. Are you even female? I didn't get to check if you pee standing up. Not that it would matter anyway. I prefer real men, like Adam." She knew she was being bitchy, but for some reason, could not help herself. She suddenly had a desire to really irritate Mary Lou. She succeeded.

"Are you trying to piss me off?" Mary Lou demanded.

"What's rude about stating my preference? Did you want me to make a pass at you? I just told you. I prefer large *male* members, like Adam's."

Mary Lou's face flushed with anger. "Look, I know you're screwing Adam. We both do. We have a truce about causing Adam problems. Now, you seem to want to piss me off. What's your problem?"

"Hey, lighten up, Mary Lou. I'm just joking."

"Yeah, right. You're just a comedian. You were on your back so much, I doubt you never developed a descent stand up routine."

Suddenly, Kathy was angry. She was tired having to defend her past as a porn star. Hell, she made a lot more money than Mary Lou had, and probably had more fun doing it.

"I said, I was just joking."

"Yeah, sure. You're just one big joke. Now, move so I can wash up."

"You're going to need more than a sink to wash that smell off you," a now angry Kathy hissed.

"Take that back!" Mary Lou yelled.

"Make me!" Kathy turned on her heel to exit. It was a mistake for her to turn her back on an enraged Mary Lou.

Two hands grabbed handfuls of her blonde hair and yanked back. Hard. She squealed in pain and surprise, then felt herself being pulled backwards and twisted back toward the stall.

"I'm making you now!" Mary Lou yelled in her ear.

The fight was on.

Mary Lou tried to force her down into the stall. Kathy grit her teeth to the pain in her scalp and reached back low with her right hand, finding Mary Lou's exposed thigh under her skirt. She dug her sharp fingernails into Mary Lou's soft flesh and tried to reach the brunette's panties. Shocked, Mary Lou let go of Kathy's hair with her right hand, grabbed at the woman's wrist to stop the attack, and went into a clutch. Kathy twisted around, jamming the nails of her left hand into Mary Lou's face. The participant in many a staged catfight, she fought instinctively, no fancy martial arts moves. She managed to push her way back out of the stall, as she felt some of her dark hair being pulled painfully from her scalp by Mary Lou's left hand. Both women began to curse and spit at each other, bumping into the bathroom wall as they wrestled. Shapely legs became intertwined, tripping each other. They slipped and fell to the bathroom floor.

"Ladies, *what* are you doing?"

It took a moment for them to recognize the voice. It was Major Jane Grant. They froze.

A strong hand grabbed an ear on each of their heads, twisting it painfully like a nun in a Catholic school. They both yowled in pain as Jane forced them to stand up, or have their respective ears seriously damaged. Neither woman even thought of striking the Major.

"What type of childish bullshit is this?" scolded Jane. "Two grown women fighting in the girl's room like a couple of spoiled cheerleaders? Do you think this helps anybody or accomplishes anything? Other than maybe working out spite and anger toward each other, I sure as hell can't!"

"Now look, Jane..." Mary Lou began.

"That's *Major* to you. You may be a glorified assistant to the Director, but that doesn't cut the mustard with anyone."

"And *you!*" Jane yelled at Kathy. "Do you think school aged kids who are sending you homemade cards and handwritten letters on scrap paper want to see you clawing and scratching another woman next to a toilet? Fighting over who gets to play with some guy's joystick?"

Kathy stood, stunned. She realized then that her old adult entertainment frame of mind about being sexy on camera did nothing for a whole new audience.

As if she could read her mind, Jane said, "That's right. There's a new generation who doesn't even know what a porn star was, but they sure as hell know what a hero is. In other words, Ms. Monroe, you've turned into a fucking role model."

Kathy almost cried. She was messing up a good thing and was too stupid to realize it.

"I'm not done with you, Mary Lou. You're supposed to be serving the Director, not just servicing him. Unless your goal in life was to be a concubine."

Mary Lou's rage got the better of her, and she tried to shove Jane away. She quickly found herself back on the bathroom floor, a painful wrist lock holding her right arm up, and Jane's shoe on the back of her neck.

"Want to try that again?" Jane hissed. "I don't catfight. I street fight." Jane released a subdued Mary Lou, then glared at both of them. "I expected that from you, Kathy, not her. I guess it goes to show that I'm as guilty of stereotypes as others." She let out an exasperated sigh. "I don't know why I put up with this shit. I could be a General in the Resistance, not having to catch two prima donna assholes pulling hair next to the commode. Especially after the death of a little girl."

There was silence for a few moments, save for the breathing of the three women. Then Major Grant added "This stays between the three of us. The Director needs another problem like this like he needs a bottle of viagra. But, if I hear of any more behavior like this, I am going to track you down, kick your asses and leave you hogtied naked in the Director's office. Are we *clear*?"

"Crystal," Kathy replied.

"Yes, Ma'am." Mary Lou said, rubbing her wrist.

"Good. Get back to work. Both of you."

The two women hastily did some damage control to clothes and makeup. Kathy wanted to say something, to try and apologize for her behavior but she saw Mary Lou was seething. They each left the ladies room separately.

CHAPTER 26

The workout with Heidi was kicking his ass. She had already helped Adam lose ten pounds of fat and tone up muscles that were getting soft. She didn't even begin the martial arts and weapons training, until after she had given him one hell of a warmup. He stood breathing hard, feeling his age. Heidi was sweating also, but had a big grin on her face. "Ready for another round, Director?"

He took a moment to catch his breath. "You're getting a sadistic glee out of kicking my ass, aren't you?"

Heidi laughed. "I just like to see a man sweat. But seriously, you need to train like you fight. Otherwise, you are just playing and wasting time."

Adam final began to slow his breathing. "I think I need to get some of my female staff in contact with you. Not only will they get in serious shape, but they will learn some fighting skills as well."

Heidi had a wry expression on her face. "I don't know if they need any more push in that direction. From what I've seen and heard recently, there are enough catfights in the ranks already."

Adam's brow furrowed. "What do you mean, Heidi?"

The Coasty hesitated. "I don't want to cause problems or be a rat, but, well, not only are many of the woman on base getting into nasty scraps with each other, but...two of your 'ladies' had another brawl recently."

Adam stood quietly. For a moment, Heidi was worried that she had just stepped in it. He continued, "Sorry to put you on the spot, Petty Officer, but I need to know exactly what happened."

"Well, Director, from several sources, it was like this..." After he had received the full story, Adam had Heidi run him through a series of doble daga and doble baston exercises, both against her and the large fighting dummy she had managed to have produced. For the first time, using live blades in doble daga, Adam had no nicks. In double baston, stick technique, he laid a couple of nasty hits on Heidi for which he apologized.

Heidi shrugged it off. "Hey. I'm the instructor. If I'm doing my job right, eventually you get good enough to smack me once in a while. So, I must be doing something right today."

Adam let a small grin show. "My anger is getting the best of me, Heidi. Don't feel like you did anything wrong by telling me. It has been building and I thought I had nipped it in the bud. Apparently not."

"Well, in their defense, it seems that women here are all suddenly throwing down on each other. It's like something is in the air or water, making them all eager to fight or, well, you know."

"Why not you, Heidi?"

"Honestly, I think it's because you and I have been working out, sparring a lot lately. It seems to help me expel my aggressive energy. And, of course, my martial arts-based spiritual training helps me keep my feelings centered, controlled."

Adam shook his head. "I'd like to accept your concept, but, since I already dealt with it, out in the open, they knew what was at stake. Now, I have to end this one way or another."

He took a deep, grounding breath before assuming a sparring position. "One more short round, okay? Then it's time to get back to work."

The next day, Kathy received a call on her radio phone. "Yes, Boss." "Kathy, could you come to my office? There's something I need to discuss."

"Sure, Boss." Kathy had been so busy she'd hardly seen Adam. She sighed. It was unfair, that bitch Mary Lou slept with him almost every night. Oh well, she couldn't complain. She walked up the stairs to Adam's office entrance door and met Mary Lou who was arriving at the same time.

"Kathy." Mary Lou's voice had a nasty edge to it.

"Mary Lou." Kathy gave Mary Lou a taste of her own medicine. The last attempt at a tussle with Mary Lou in the ladies room was just a short while ago. But no passage of time, no matter how long, would seemingly ever fix things between them.

She let Mary Lou knock and announce the both of them. Kathy frowned. Why both at once?

"Come in, Ladies."

"Director."

"Boss"

They both walked in and stood several feet apart in front of Adam's desk.

"Take off your clothes."

Mary Lou's mouth dropped. "Excuse me?"

"You heard me. Both of you. Now."

"Director..."

"Now!"

Kathy had no idea he had this level of red rage in him. She began to strip as if she was getting ready for another day in the adult film industry. Mary stood, frozen, until Adam rounded the desk and stood an inch from her face. In a harsh whisper, the Director instructed, "Now. Or I will do it for you." Mary Lou began undressing.

Within five minutes, both women were nude where they stood. Adam had them hand him their clothes, which he unceremoniously bundled together and threw behind his desk. "Do you really think you can hide things from me? How incompetent do you think I am, that I would be totally unaware of what is happening on my base, and behind my back? You two 'ladies' have embarrassed me for the last time. A catfight in the restroom?"

"Boss... "

"No. I don't care who started it. The Squids think our species is already too violent, too unpredictable, without two of my closest associates rolling around on a bathroom floor. I need my personal staff fighting like five year olds like I need a hole in the head. Today, we are going to adopt some Tschaaa concepts that seem a little more civilized."

"You two. Today. A personal duel. Here. No weapons but your own bodies. Rules? Squid duels are not to the death, so no eye gouging, no fists to the face, no karate kicks, throat strikes, rabbit punches.

"Instead, you two will use your god-given female talents only. Biting is fine, blood is fine, but no removal of flesh. Start doing that and you both lose. You wanted a fight so badly–now you've got one.

This timer goes off in three minutes. When the timer goes off, the fight begins. Submission only, unless someone is unconscious. The winner decides whether the loser stays or goes. I will be filming this for posterity. Start warming up."

As the two women began to stretch and loosen up, Adam noticed for the first time just how closely they resembled one another. Was that why he had chosen them both? He also knew that leaving here would be devastating for one them. He grit his teeth. They chose this path, not him.

The women finished their warm-ups just seconds before the timer went off. They had taken Adam's instructions to heart. Both exploded, lunging at their opponent with nails and teeth, slamming their bodies together. Adam had never seen two women tear at each other like this. Their pent up anger must have been enormous. They dug fingernails into each other's faces and bodies. They rolled on the floor, kicking and hitting each other's core. Adam thought Mary Lou was going to win as she went for a schoolyard pin but Kathy jammed a thumbnail up a nostril, drawing blood and forcing Mary Lou off her body. Kathy then bit Mary Lou's left shoulder, drawing blood. Mary Lou clawed Kathy's breasts, leaving red and bloody scratch marks. They attacked each other's extremities, trying like animals to inflict as much pain and damage as possible. Sharp nails left mute evidence of the attempts.

Both women randomly yanked at head hair, strands evident on the carpet. Kathy's right hand clamped down even harder, putting a vice grip on her opponent's blond hair. She began to try to pull and push Mary Lou around the floor. Her left hand clamped on her rival's throat.

Mary Lou tried to kick and scratch herself free. Kathy released her left hand and bit Mary Lou's throat. Mary Lou screamed louder. Before Adam realized it, Kathy was straddling Mary Lou, choking her with both hands. Mary Lou's lower body squirmed, helpless, while her hands still reached for her opponent. Kathy ignored Mary Lou's fingernails digging into her arms, and her wrists, now bloodied.

Saliva from Kathy's mouth drooled onto Mary Lou's face. Somehow, Mary Lou managed to croak out, "I give." Kathy immediately rolled off of Mary Lou. After struggling for breath, Mary Lou began to sob. Kathy sank to the ground, exhausted, bloody scratch marks adorning her body. She began to cry also.

"Chief," Adam radio phoned.

"Yes Boss."

"Could you have Dr. Fredericks, our senior surgeon, come to my office? I have a special project for her. Have her bring that Tschaaa medical and nanite technology we recently received."

"Will do."

Adam approached to Kathy. "You won. Decide."

Kathy sobbed. "She stays."

"Excuse me?"

"She stays! It's just as much yours as my fault it that it went this far."

Adam paused. She had a point. Adam had never dissuaded competition for his attention since he became Director. He had chosen his bed partners with little contemplation as to consequence. Now things had blown up.

"Fine. But you two live together, from this point forward."

"Work it out or leave. Kat, you and Mary Lou will move into the spare suite bedroom. Tonight."

"Jamey. Jeanie." They had been quietly watching the fight, unnoticed by Kathy and Mary Lou. Their faces both registered shock and concern.

"Take Kathy and May Lou to the spare suite. Clean them up. Help them move their stuff in. Medical attention will be there shortly." When they didn't react, he yelled, "Now!". They moved quickly, each taking a woman in tow.

Approximately two hours later, Dr. Fredericks called him.

"Director, may I speak with you?"

"Sure, Doctor. Come up to my office."

About twenty minutes later, an attractive middle-aged redheaded woman was standing in front of Adam. The doctor, Brigitte (Gitte) Fredericks was fifty-something years old with a slight German accent. When Adam had found out that the developer of new plastic surgery techniques was still alive three years ago, he had insisted that the Chief literally kidnap her from one of the few operating hospitals. Dr. Fredericks burst through the door, closed it behind her, and literally marched directly up to the front of Adam's large desk. "Mr. Director, I must be blunt. I do not know what you believed you were doing, but those two ladies are in extremely bad shape. A fight like that... I have only ever seen one that nasty before in a whore house in Zambia. *What* were you thinking? Are you having a breakdown? Is this a new sport? Because, let me tell you..."

"Halten sie, bitte." His use of his limited German cut her lecture short. "First, Herr Doktor, I did not start this fight, they did. I just finished it. And second, did the nanites and other things work?"

"Why yes, they did. Quite fantastic. The nanites are healing all the bites, scratches even old scars as we speak. They should be healthier than they were a week ago."

"Perfect. Third, and last, this was the perfect test case–nicht wahr, as you'd say?"

"Yes, Herr Director. It was."

He stood up, walked around the desk, and shook Dr. Frederick's hand. "Thank you. You're a miracle worker. I'd like you to return to your clinic and write an in-depth report. Now, if you excuse me, I have something else that has to be taken care of."

Dr. Fredericks left, convinced that Adam was having a breakdown. But now it was not her business.

About 8:00pm that evening Kathy woke in her double bed in the spare suite. She looked over and saw that Mary Lou was waking up as well. Kathy–now Kat, since Adam had called her by that name–sat up. The nanites made her feel like she had been infused with some magical potion. A quick check of her breast revealed that her old scar was gone, like it had never happened.

That was a wonderful notion. An idea came to Kat all at once. "Mary, it never happened."

Mary Lou lay silent, refusing to answer.

"Look at your body. It's like it never happened."

"But it did. You kicked my ass, humiliated me in front of Adam. How can I ignore that?"

"Because, dear Mary, you have to. We are in this together, now, thanks to our own selfishness."

Mary Lou answered, still lying with her back to Kathy, "We are both less in Adam's eyes than before. He needs your skills. I'm just the interchangeable pretty face at the front desk."

Kat sat up, and then stood up. Mary Lou turned and saw she was naked, and realized she was also. Mary stood up, and both women looked more closely at each other's bodies.

"Correct if I'm wrong, Mary," Kat began. "But… isn't everything just a little bit…. tighter? Less sagging. Fewer wrinkles. Hell, I'm a new woman. Like a virgin." Kat began to giggle. Finally, Mary Lou did also. The nanites and other Squid medical technology might have even helped their mental health.

"You keep calling me Mary, not Mary Lou, my full name."

"Adam called me Kat. New name for a new beginning. Likewise, Mary, instead of Mary Lou. We are different now."

Kat walked over and took Mary's hands in hers.

"Truth be told, Mary, I only beat you by a few dirty tricks and pure luck. Straight up fight in the gym, you'd probably have knocked me out. Now please. Truce. Honestly and truly --I need your help. If we don't make this work, we are *both* gone. Then he's left with the Barbies."

Mary began to laugh, hard, at that thought. Jamey and Jeanie taking over? Forget it.

Mary kissed Kat full on the lips. One thing led to another and they began loving each other in bed.

Later, Kat asked, "Mary, what brought that on? The nanites? Or, have you always wanted me? Is that how we make our truce official?"

Mary sighed. "I agree we seem to be new women. Maybe we can start over. We have to if we are going to stay here, and stay with Adam."

"Thank you," Kat replied, laying her head next to Mary's shoulder. "Since we are starting over, time for a history lesson. How did you and Adam meet?"

"He saved my ass, literally. Twice in one day."

"How so?"

"About three years ago, I was trying to stay alive in San Diego. Food was still scarce, various gangs were trying to run the city, and there was no government or police force. Groups of scavengers were grabbing attractive women, boys, and girls off the street and basically selling them for meat—either for sex or food. Yes, a certain segment of the population decided that if the conqueror could eat human flesh, why not the conquered. Some sick assholes even tattooed images of Tschaaa on their bodies and tried to emulate their own twisted vision of alien society."

Mary shivered. "I was grabbed and drugged. I woke up in some crap hole former hotel. Nude. Not only were there live nude humans there, there were the human equivalents of sides of beef hanging from hooks. All 'white meat', of course, so as not to unduly attract the attention of the local robocops. I was just about to discover my fate at the hand of my captors, when someone kicked in the door. It was Andrew–our cyborg–Adam, the Chief, and their security team. Adam and the Chief shot a few, the security team smashed a few, and the bodies were harvested–every one of those assholes.

They tried to take me to a security convoy. It seemed Adam had convinced the Lordship that this lack of local control in Tschaaa controlled areas was leading to disintegrating human populations. If our Lordship really wanted a productive client species, members can't be allowed to indiscriminately abuse each other. Bad for business. I tried to flee from Adam, and was almost captured by one of those ATV-looking robots attached to the harvesters. Adam whacked the robot before I was dragged to my death."

"Why did you run, Mary?"

Tears began to stream down Mary's cheeks. She sat up in bed. "I had a boy, a girl, and a husband waiting for me in a small compound we had secured with some friends. They were gone when I got there. Just blood, no other trace. Could have been harvested. A couple of our friends were mixed race, with darker skin. That's why I did a lot of the scrounging. That's what I was doing when I was grabbed."

Kat sat up on her knees; she took Mary's face in her hands. "Mary, I owe you an apology. I thought I had it rough. The only person I had to worry about after the first thirty days was me, myself and I. My experience in using sex to wrap people around my finger helped me obtain a lot of benefits the past few years others didn't. Like...Adam."

Mary took Kat's hands in her hers, and kissed them gently. "That's why I didn't want you here. I thought I was going to lose Adam. He saved me when I lost everything. He brought me back here, gave me a reason to live, to start over. He could have kicked me out of bed for the proverbial eating crackers, but he didn't."

"You actually ate crackers in bed?" Kat giggled.

Mary looked at Kat. "You have a way of relaxing tense situations. I wished I was able to do that. I'm afraid, I am Adam's 'Girl Friday', but that's it."

"You're more than that, Mary. Adam told me he was careful who he selected for important matters. I can tell by the way he looks at you. He wouldn't want to lose you."

"Then why did he put our fates in each other's hands? Do you honestly think I would have hesitated having you killed if I had won?"

"Yes, I do."

Both women paused, looking at each other. Finally, Mary said "I wanted you gone. But, not dead."

"And now?"

Mary sighed. "I realize that I don't own Adam. It is just that I have everything vested in him. *If* he failed horribly and was gone tomorrow, I'd go with him. I have no one else."

Kat put her arms around Mary, gently hugging her. "I think we have each other also. I think we need each other. To use an old hackneyed saying, er women have to stick together."

"Do you need, want Adam, Kat?"

"I want him as a man. I also know that if anyone can pull his weird balancing act off, between alien and human, it's him."

Kat continued, "Now I want and need you–not in a sexual way. I need your help to ensure Adam succeeds."

Mary gently pushed herself away from Kat, and stood up. "Kat, please stand up." Kat did, then stood so close to Mary that their naked bodies brushed each other. Mary shivered a bit. "Damnit, you know all the moves, know how to use sex to get everything. I don't want to be manipulated. If you really believe in Adam, then I need to trust you."

Kat met Mary's eyes "That depends. Can you share Adam?"

"With you, yes. As long as you share 'you' with me. I need to know what you are thinking."

Kat began to gently stroke Mary's hair. "You can have a personal part of me anytime you want. You and I need a formal relationship that includes Adam. The two of us together can make this work. As long as Adam does what he does so well... somehow keep us all from being just slabs of meat, give us a future beyond Earth. If we are stuck here with the Squids left behind when their ships move on, we are screwed. Eventually it will degenerate into a small group of humans watching the rest get eaten.

"Lord Neptune won't live forever; he could lose his position tomorrow. Having to depend on someone who may decide to cook you and eat you tomorrow is no future."

Mary put her arms around Kat, pulled her closer. Kat felt the strength in her arms. Mary leaned over, and whispered softly into her ear, "I hate Squids. They killed my family."

Kat whispered back, "I hate them too. They killed my fiancé, and my chances of a normal life."

"So, we both have a secret," Mary whispered. "Us versus them, which has gotten a lot of 'us' killed."

"Yes, that's true. How about a talk in the shower, as we may be wired for sound?"

"We might be. Good idea." She kissed Kat, took her hand and led her to the shower.

Kat pulled back a bit. "Mary, do you want Adam's children?"

Mary paused, started to stiffen, and then relaxed."Yes," She whispered. "And you?"

"As of today, yes," Kat whispered back. "Are you thinking what I think you are thinking? You and I are about to become what certain Mormons called 'sister wives'. That is, if you really want kids to survive. Adam must succeed, but we need a plan between the two of us for survival, also. In the tradition of many past ruling families, the wives are a power behind the throne. Adam's offspring may be allowed to carry on his survival plan if things take longer than he plans. Squids believe in generational family empires, so to speak."

"The... Crèches?"

"Yes, Mary. That's what they are. Super generational families. Children are everything."

"Let me get this straight. We once tried to kill each other, and now you want to be pregnant together?"

"Yes. If you will have me."

"And If Adam won't agree?"

"He will have no choice. He couldn't possibly resist both of us."

The Tschaaa surveillance program and sensors that were tracking Mary and Kat had shut down once there appeared to be sexual relations involved. The program was based on an artificial intelligence that did not understand human sexuality any more than a live Tschaaa did. As far as it was concerned, humans were a bunch of nasty primates that screwed whenever and whomever they could, gender be damned. Adam himself had suspicions that he was monitored sometimes, but had no real idea of the capabilities of Tschaaa technology. It probably wouldn't have done him much good regardless. He knew he lived at the sufferance of his Lord Neptune. He kept many thoughts to himself, but his honesty with the Tschaaa Lord had been a source of humor rather than fear or anger. A master can be very forgiving of a pet he adores, as long as his pet does not bite him badly.

It had been a week since The Fight. Everyone knew about it–although not the specific details–but no one broached the subject in front of the Director or his immediate staff. The work of the Base was completed on a timely basis. Mary and Kat showed up for work, now friendly, almost sisterly.

Kat made a special broadcast on Tschaaa interpersonal relations–including the concepts of limited physical conflict between individuals, limited dueling, no wars, everything for the survival of the species by complete protection of all the young. Could humans emulate it?

Adam shared a bed with Jamey and Jeanie, to feel the comfort of a warm human body, intimacy rather than sex. They seemed to sense this need, foregoing the games they might have otherwise tried to play to cuddle instead. Adam was somewhat surprised by their instinctive grasp of the situation. He had written them off as possible airheads, but he finally realized how wrong he was. Exactly one week to the day from The Fight, Kathy and Mary respectively requested his presence after work at the suite the women now shared. Adam completed his normal duties, took a shower, put on some casual slacks and shirt. He had two identical bouquets of flowers, as a peace offering.

He knocked on the door. Two voices as one beckoned him inside the dimly lit suite.

"Come to the bedroom, please, Director," instructed Mary. He walked into the bedroom, where two visions of sat on the end of the bed. Kat and Mary. Both in identical sheer silk robes, and nothing else. They let the silk robes fall, and Adam felt a rush of passion he had not experienced for quite some time. Maybe sex had become too mechanical to him, too much about stress relief. Tonight, it was all passion.

"I want you, Adam." Kat said.

"I want you Adam." Mary repeated.

Suddenly, the two women turned toward each other.

"I love you Kat."

"I love you Mary."

"Can you share Adam with me?"

"Yes. I love him as I love you."

"And I love him as I love you also."

They both turned to Adam. In unison, they said, "Come, Adam. We need you. We need you to make the love work."

Adam went to them, and both women grabbed his hand. "We want you, we want your seed. We need your complete love."

Both women stood up and kissed opposite sides of his neck and throat. In unison, they spoke, "It is time." Both women together pulled him to the bed.

Adam woke after a relatively short sleep between two of the most beautiful women in the world. He slowly, gently unwrapped their arms from him. He managed to climb out of bed, and stood up, though he felt almost lightheaded. He knew from experience certain muscles would be sore, but he did not care. He had never felt so good, so loved.

As he started to pull his pants on, Kat and Mary opened their eyes, smiled at him, and then slid close together, gently hugging. Adam had no idea of the plan behind the smiles. He made it back to his office suite and showered. The nice, long, warm shower, helped to soothe tired parts of his body. He exited, to find Jamey and Jeanie, laying out clean underwear and a clean pair of pants and shirt. In sheer nightgowns, they walked up, kissed him on each cheek, giggled, winked at him with knowing smiles, and then went back to the suite bedroom.

Now he was beginning to wonder. Just who really ran the show?

Adam was drinking a cup of coffee, when his phone rang. It was about 7:30am, so it was not that early. But with no Mary, he was his own receptionist. "Hello. Director here."

"Herr Director, Guten Morgan. I hope you had a good night's rest." It was Doctor Fredericks.

He laughed. "You don't know the half of it. What can I do for you

Doctor?"

"I was wondering, if I may be so bold to ask, could you meet me at the Sportsplatz, the sports field, please?"

"Couldn't you come here, Doctor?"

"I have something I need to show you here, please."

"Show me there? What…"

"Please, Herr Director. Here at the sports field." There was a sense of urgency, of concern he had not heard before in the Doctor's voice. Something was up.

"Okay, Doctor. I'll be right there."

Ten minutes later, he saw Doctor Fredericks circling on the running track wearing a wide brimmed hat. Adam walked quickly out to meet her.

"Please, Herr Director, please keep walking with me. I need the exercise. And please do not mind that I am looking down. The ground is very interesting." Adam knew she wanted to shield something she was holding from the eye in the sky, and was hoping this area was not wired for sound. "Here, please, look at this nanite in this small glass tube."

Adam took it, holding it low. "This is one of the newer ones that we just used to fix up the two women, correct?"

"Correct, Herr Director. Now, as I was reviewing the containers of nanites, I found some that had been infused, shall we say, contaminated with this." Adam looked at the second container. This small almost pill sized object looked more like a chemical pill or capsule than a nanite.

"That, Herr Director, is a highly sophisticated time release capsule with organic, literally living properties. There seems to be a form of virus also. The Tschaaa nanites are like our cruder nanites. Almost little robots designed to repair, to clean, and to make better, with little organic chemical compounds thrown in to speed and help the process. This capsule seems to contain living organisms that eventually wash out of our systems."

"What do they do?" Adam asked.

The Doctor walked a little faster. "As they say, the devil is in the details. We Germans had our devils, the most notorious was Mengele. He experimented with genetics and chemicals to influence the reproduction of the human race, to produce a superior race. He set back trust in German science at least twenty-five years. I think it took until the fall of the Berlin Wall before people began to trust German scientists again."

"And Doctor, the connection is...?"

Doctor Fredericks stopped short. "That and other capsules directly interferes with our reproductive system and its controlling DNA, genes and hormones. It produces ninety-nine percent fertility in all females, speeds up the development of the baby in the womb. Seven months will become the standard gestation period instead of nine. Maybe even quicker. Once born, I believe children will develop faster, age faster. A full grown adult at ten years of age, if a women and the child are given a large dose. A smaller dose, everyone gets pregnant, more normal development."

She shivered. "A large dose, massive growth in and out of the womb. Gigantism but without the crippling side effects. Seven feet tall supermen at twelve years of age."

Adam stared at her. "Brain development?"

"There, I am unsure." She chewed her lip. "Overstimulated brain development may cause psychological problems, psychosis. Humans need time to grow and process the worlds around them. Or, we may have geniuses all over the place. Right now, it is a crapshoot."

Adam stood in contemplation before he continued. "You have found this already in a human, haven't you?"

The Doctor paused, her brow furrowed with concern. "Six women are pregnant with signs of developing fetuses at a faster rate. After finding these capsules in with the nanites, I did a chemical and physical analysis. I used this as a basis to test the women. They have been infused with the materials in the capsule. Concentrations are hard to judge."

Adam stood stock still for so long the Doctor was beginning to worry that he had slipped into a fugue state. "Director Lloyd?" She finally said softly.

"Doctor, have you ever felt totally used, lied to?"

"Well, many of my relatives were used totally by the Nazis. By the time they realized that they were being used for the Final Solution, it was either too late or, they decided they did not really care. After all, they were not Jews, were they?"

"Can you keep this quiet, Doctor?"

"Of course. We are here, in the middle of a running track. Is not this secret enough?"

"Thank you." He started to walk away.

"Oh, Director, there is one important side effects in females I believe will show up."

"What is that?"

"They become very aggressive in seeking mates and mating, much more than normal. I believe the substances cause a rise in sexual desire as well as physical aggressiveness toward competitors. That is with even low doses, I believe. I also think in may cause a change in the natural scent of a woman, pheromones, that in men, when they get a whiff, seems to add to the normal randiness, nothing more. After all, women in civilized society limit their sexual availability. Now, their inhibitions have been reduced to a very, very low level."

Adam stopped. He was squeezing his hands in fists so tight his knuckles were white.

"Thank you, Doctor. You are a treasure to the human species." He strode off.

Doctor Fredericks sighed, and mumbled to herself. "My duty is done."

Adam strode back to his office a bit in a daze. He was still trying to process the ramifications of a modified human race along the lines the Doctor had told him. What if people were seven feet tall but so lacking in intelligence that they were easily controlled by the Tschaaa? Would they then be used to wipe out all but the Cattle? What if super intelligence evolved? Would the new oversized humans look on normal humans and even the Tschaaa as inferior beings to be disposed of? Did his Lordship and the other Lordships realize they may have created a Frankenstein monster that may turn on them?

He put his face in his hands. What a complete, horrible mess.

Who to tell? The Chief, of course. Then Kat and Mary. Hopefully they would help him figure this out before it became general knowledge. Adam hoped that anything Kat and Mary had in their bodies would not affect their ability to reason this out. He had no idea if nanites, the genetic and the organic material introduced into women's bodies had any mind control properties. But, he had to tell them, as he was sure, based the way they had been acting, they had some dosage of the, what he would call, the Sex Pill. He started by calling Kat and Mary.

Kat, Mary and the Chief stood together on the track at the athletic and parade field. All were in shock after he told them what the good Doctor had discovered. All four humans were wearing wide brimmed hats to help hide their faces from prying eyes form the sky. Adam waited for the information to sink in. Mary began to cry. Kat reached over and put her right arm around her and hugged her close. Kat's own eyes were beginning to tear up. The Chief had a look of stone cold anger.

"Well, friends, now what?" Adam asked.

"Someone owes us an explanation," the Chief finally said.

"Yes, I will be contacting his Lordship soonest. But, you have to remember that, down deep, we are like trained dogs to him. And we screwed with the genealogy of dogs for thousands of years. So, are we morally superior in any way?"

"But they are not sentient beings like us," Kat blurted out.

"From our standpoint, yes. But from the Tschaaa, not necessarily so. At least not at the same level of the Tscahaa. We can get as mad as we like. However, if we bite the hand, or in this case the tentacle, we could be put down."

Mary produced a tissue and dabbed her eyes. "Well, I am pretty sure I am now pregnant. Kat?"

"Ditto, Sister. Don't give me that look, Boss. Yes, we planned on a polygamist relationship with you. And do not tell me you hadn't given it a thought after last night. Sorry to bring this up in front of you, Chief."

"I'm just jealous that I don't have two beautiful wives to take care of me."

Adam harrumphed. "Well, if we are all finished with working over my mind and manipulating me, the question remains. What next?"

Kat answered first. "We get a complete checkup by Frau Doktor, and see if she can determine any side effects. If there is anything negative, I think I will be going Squid hunting."

Mary looked hard at Adam. "I will have to second that notion, Director."

"Chief? Any other suggestions?"

The Chief paused in thought. He sighed, and shook his head.

Adam addressed Kat and Mary, "Ladies, although I believe it is early for you to be certain you are pregnant, but go ahead and contact Frau Doktor in private. At the very least she can determine how much of a dose you both have received."

"In the meantime, I will have Andrew set up a secure video connection with our Lordship so I can talk to him without being there."

The Chief gave him a worried look. "You want to bring Andrew in on this? Now?"

"Yes, Chief. I am curious as to just how much of his humanity and ability for independent thought remains in him."

It took Adam a while to get back to his office. He pinged Andrew. Thirty seconds later, Andrew called back. "I seemed to remember, Director, a character in a television program that used to answer with, 'You rang?'"

Adam smiled. "Lurch, from *The Addams Family*. I think the actor who played him was taller than you are. He was one big man."

"So, how may I be of service, Director?"

"I need a secure video hookup with His Lordship, if you could, please."

"I will be in your office in ten minutes."

"Thank you, Andrew."

In exactly ten minutes, Andrew walked into his office. "I am here as you requested, Director." He removed the communicator from a hidden recess on his body and connected it with Adam's computer monitor to give an enhanced image. He made the connection, communicated silently thru his cyber connections, then handed the communicator to Adam. Lord Neptune appeared on the computer monitor.

"My Director. Andrew says you have some serious matters to discuss. I hope you are not distressed?"

Adam took a breath and exhaled. "Your Lordship, in the name of the continued truthfulness we have always shared, yes, I am distressed."

"How so, Adam?" The Tschaaa moved his tentacles in a gesture of concern.

"Lordship, just what modifications have you been making to our human females?" Adam held up the organic object Dr. Hendericks had found mixed in with the medical repair nanites.

The Tschaaa Lord paused. Then he answered. "My Director, I have been providing specially designed organic, genetic, and hormonal substances, including specialized nanites, to improve your species. They have been primarily aimed at your breeders, your women. These substances were introduced into your populace to help your species by making your offspring, your young, stronger, smarter, larger and more numerous. That is why these actions were taken. Not to harm you. To make your species better."

Adam tried to control his emotions. "Lordship, have you ever heard of the concept of unintended consequences?"

"Yes, of course."

"And, have you heard of the story of Frankenstein?"

His Lordship signed pleasure "Of course. The classic movie with Boris Karloff. His portrayal set the standard as to the image of the creature. And Lionel Atwell as Doctor Frankenstein."

"Did you read the book by Mary Shelley it was based on? "No, Adam. I must admit I prefer your cinema, your films. They are more enjoyable."

Adam drew a breath to calm himself. "Lordship, part of the original story emphasized the problem of trying to make human life, and specifically making a superior human. The unintended consequence was the monster."

His Lordship signed calmness. "My Director, trust me. That will not happen. I have studied your human species in depth for some sixty of your years. I was able to do this as an independent, outside observer, unclouded by being part of the grand experiment that is the human species. And yes, you are an experiment of what you call Mother Nature–your environment–and what you call evolution."

His Lordship shifted his body on screen. "We Tschaaa developed from much the same environmental pressures. Believe it or not, I do accept the possibility of a 'Higher Power' in the universe that may have an effect on us, what you call God. But, day to day, year to year, it is the environmental rules that you lump together as 'survival of the fittest' that govern our success as a species." The Tschaaa continued, "We Tschaaa have demonstrated our superior position in the food chain. We crossed trillions of your miles of outer space, the galaxy, and harvested you. Thus, we are the superior species. Therefore we have a superior ability to see what you humans need to succeed.

Adam, I am working to raise you up, to make you as close to equal of the Tschaaa as possible. How is that wrong?"

"Your Lordship, I appreciate all you have done for me, for the humans I have been able bring into your sphere of influence and control. But… why didn't you ask me, tell me, before you decided to try and modify us?"

His Lordship signed concern. "Adam, did you ask your canines, your dogs, before you began to change them through breeding?"

"Of course not. We did not know their language."

"My Director, if you had been able to communicate your desires, would you have told your subjects and asked permission?"

Adam answered carefully. "I would have liked to say yes, but that would not have applied to all humans. Hell, my previous government performed secret experiments on specific groups and populations without their knowledge. But, two wrongs do not make a right."

"My Director, how is improving your ability to evolve, to survive, wrong?"

Adam realized he had completely misread the Tschaaa Lord in so many ways. He had made the fundamental mistake that because this Tschaaa individual communicated in his language, a human language, that he processed ideas like a human being. The Tschaaa Lord did not. He had Tschaaa sensibilities, not human. Time for a different tact.

"May I ask Your Lordship, exactly what else you were trying to do to… improve human stock as a means to help us rise in our standing in the Universe?"

His Lordship gestured pleasure, the equivalent of a smile. "Of course, My Director. I, with consultation with the best minds in my Crèche and help from the human scientists on Platform One, was specifically modifying your females, and through them, your young.

"First, almost one hundred percent fertility among your females, and more twins. Next, shortened gestation. Your babies will now develop within seven months, freeing your mates to either reproduce more, or to free their bodies to perform the many other tasks that human females do, as opposed to Tschaaa breeders. Once born, your children will then live longer on average, at least one hundred of your years, possibly longer. Maybe eventually as long as we Tschaaa. That will make you more adaptable to interstellar travel."

Adam took a moment for the information to begin to sink in. Near one hundred percent fertility, and probably a great improvement in the miscarriage rate for all women. More multiple births and stronger offspring to help in species survival. "My Lordship, how do you know about the intellectual development? Physical stature is easy to modify and see results. But intellect? How would you determine that success?"

"My Director, nothing is perfect. But with our millennia of developing organic beings such as our grays, our robocops and other human-based beings, you must trust me that the possible problems are few and easily solved. Your human scientists are providing additional insights and suggestions that are greatly speeding up the developmental process."

Adam sighed. What a total cluster.

"Please, Director. Do not worry. In a month, we will revisit this subject. I guarantee that I will have solved any problems that may arise."

"Well, My Lordship, it appears we our fate is completely in your hands. But, may I ask one more question?"

"Of course, Adam."

"Did you try any such modifications on any males?"

Lord Neptune hesitated. "Just you, My Director. Before you worry, all we did was–shall we say–tweak your desirability."

Adam froze. Again, he clamped down his emotions. "And, sir, what does that really entail?"

"You are already sexually attractive by human standards. And power, I believe some of you humans say, is the ultimate aphrodisiac. All we did was a very slight change in the pheromones that you exude, your specific scent. The already receptive, almost always gravid females of your species, are thus given a slight push when they are around you. They become more receptive toward your ideas, and they are prodded a bit to find you sexually desirable more frequently. Not enough to eliminate their free will in the matter, but definitely a push to consider you more favorably."

"The side effect is that the females of my species are becoming more aggressive, more violent toward members of their own gender as they compete for sexual favors and gratification. How do you plan to deal with that?"

His Lordship gave the equivalent of a shrug. "Just a small, how you say, glitch in the development of the process. A slight modification in dosages, strengths of the substances used, slight tweaks to the genetic map, all will solve those side effects. To further allay your fears, we have performed previous tests in the so-called Cattle Country. Those helped us to develop the first baseline."

Adam could see that further conversation was a waste of time. The Tschaaa Lordship had decided long ago that he knew what was best for humankind. Unfortunately, as smart as Lord Neptune believed he was, he really did not and could not understand the possible consequences of genetic or hormonal modifications with as complicated a species as Homo sapiens.

"Well, Sir, we will make the best of it. But, as the information spreads, which it will, people in Tschaaa controlled areas will not be happy."

"My Director, I have complete confidence in your ability to convince your fellow humans that the course of action I choose for them will be, in the long run, beneficial. Now please excuse me, as I have some other pressing matters. Have a restful day."

Adam handed the communicator back to Andrew, who stowed it away within his torso once more. As Andrew disconnected the line to the monitor, Adam asked him a question. "Did you know of His Lordship's modification project?

Andrew replied directly. "It is in the voluminous data files to which I have access, but I never really actively review them. I have now, through my interfaces."

Adam knew Andrew had almost instantaneous contact with all databases, both human and Tschaaa in origin. "And now that you have reviewed them, what do you think?"

"I think, Director, that His Lordship's intentions were good. He truly believes he will improve the human race. But, as the expression goes, the devil is in the details. I think that because the human species is so complicated, and has evolved in a rather unique fashion on this planet, no one fully understands the ramifications of such strong modifications in such a short time. My human origins tell me that males and females developed the way they are over hundreds of thousands of years. Trying to change patterns of behavior as well as physical characteristics such as size and period of gestations over a year or two is very... problematical and troubling."

Adam regarded Andrew. He understand now, even more than previously, that there was a level of independent thought in him and other cyborg beings that was unrealized. "That is a very independent opinion, Andrew. Are you not afraid of angering your Tschaaa masters?"

Andrew paused. "I and my two hundred forty-nine 'brothers'–the part human, part machine, cyborgs created since the strike and invasion–have far more independent mental capabilities than those beings produced during the long voyage here. The next dozen or so produced over the coming weeks will be the same as I am. The Tschaaa seem to like us to retain this independence because we can operate with a level of autonomy, which means we do not bother the Tschaaa with day to day activities. As you have been told, the more senior Tschaaa have stagnated and become lazy. I function as part of a bureaucracy that keeps things running smoothly with little direction from above. The Tschaaa prefer it that way."

"If this... tweaking of Humankind produces literal Frankenstein monsters, what would you do?"

"I would do what was necessary to preserve life, especially young life, both Tschaaa and human, as it should be." Adam considered Andrew's use of the phrase, *"as it should be"*. He began to ponder the possibility that the Tschaaa had created a creature in Andrew which may be their undoing if he and his brethren decided that the Tschaaa were not acting in interest of the greater good. Like Gort, in the original 1950s movie, *The Day the Earth Stood Still*, these supposedly silent and stoic creatures were the hidden power behind the current system. If the system collapses, or seems to collapse, they may take charge... of everything.

"Thank you, Andrew. As always, your thoughtful analysis helps me greatly."

"I am at your command, Director. Within reason, of course." As Andrew left his office, Adam understood that this robocop was much more complicated than anyone realized. The original   versions brought for the invasion were noted for their cool efficiency in eliminating anything that disrupted the harvesting of the dark meat to feed the Tschaaa. Initially, they patrolled the population areas, taking out anyone who disrupted a quiet street, town, or city. Anything determined to be a drain on resources was destroyed. Those publicly intoxicated and the homeless were harvested on the spot. Start a fight when a robocop was near, and you were butchered for eating. Attack or resist a robocop, and you met the same fate. Large scale resistance resulted   in large scale destruction, with the blood from those slaughtered on the Falcons raining down on survivors below. After incidents like that, there was no more resistance, and there were no more disruptions in public. Everything became nice and orde rl y when the robocopy were watching.   The Tschaa used the robocops, with grey and lizard help, to set up the original electronic fence around what was now Cattle Country. With the assistance of the remaining flying squads, thousands of people of color not already in Mississippi, Alabama, and Georgia, were herded in like the beef cattle they soon resembled.   Adam had added a type of Guard Force and chain link fencing in the last couple of years to help keep the borders of Cattle Country secure. These actions backed up the thousands of miles of the original alien electronic fence. It all acted as an additional reminder that the Director was in charge.

But who was really in charge?

Adam fixed himself a double rusty nail. Too much was happening too fast. He decided he would sleep on it before he gave anybody else the full details of his conversation with His Lordship. The talk with Andrew he would probably only share with the Chief. He took a large swig of his drink and let it burn down to his stomach. Shit. Things were getting more complicated by the hour.

CHAPTER 27

Sometimes in the course of history, a confluence and convergence of independent events occur which somehow connect and form an overriding, forceful event. In the language of weather, this could be called a Perfect Storm. This confluence of forces creates an event of such magnitude that it changes or destroys everything in its path. In the area formerly known as the United States of America, such a storm of events began as Free Allied forces launched an assault on the seat of alien power in Key West, Florida.

> —Excerpts from the *Literary Works of Princess Akiko,* Free Japan Royal Family

THE PERFECT STORM

While Adam Lloyd was attempting to get a good night's sleep, Colonels Hunter and Bardun were on Platform One, their third trip to the large space station. After their return from the first trip, Director Lloyd welcomed Cliff Hunter back and offered him a position as a backup spaceplane pilot to Bettie Bardun. Within days of their return, the Tschaaa had grays and lizards replacing the original engines with early models of the pulse engines used in delta space interceptors. *The Hope* became a true spaceplane, using eject-able rockets to lift it off the runway, kicking in pulse engines at about one thousand feet altitude. They worked like a charm.

The two pilots were married in a simple ceremony, the Key West Base chaplain officiating. The Admiral provided a stocked honeymoon suite, called the Admiral Suite, at one of the refurbished shoreline hotels called, understandably, the Republic. Bettie and Cliff spent a glorious three days becoming reacquainted as man and wife. On the final evening they laid in each other's arms. "You sure know how to treat a girl right," Bettie playfully exclaimed.

"Hell, I thought I was out of practice. There weren't exactly a lot of available members of the female gender on the space station. I guess it's like riding a bicycle, you never really forget it once you're good at it."

Bettie giggled like a school girl, and gently poked him. "I didn't realize riding me was comparable to a bicycle."

Cliff kissed her forehead. "Ha. I wasn't referring to how we... fit together . I meant being able to love someone after six years house arrest in a small room in space. I'm glad I did not develop some type of psychosis."

"The strong survive, Cliff. I saw my share of humans who went insane while trying to survive the nuclear or long winter, whatever you want to call it. Even when things began to warm up after about sixteen months, there were still those who killed themselves, or committed suicide by attacking a robocop. The rest of us worked to survive, some even had children. The human species has a strong spirit of survival."

"Babe, did you ever think about heading North to the Unoccupied States?"

She sighed. "Yes. But I wanted to try and keep the Cape in one piece. I wanted something of my previous life to remain. I also saw a trip up north as just trading one prison for another one. At least living at the Cape gave me the feeling of some control over my fate, and a purpose for my life. If I had known about you, I might have chosen differently."

"But then you wouldn't have had the chance to man the spaceplane and find me. I don't see anyone else trying to go to space.

Things sometime happen for a greater purpose."

Bettie kissed Cliff. "I love you. The happiest moment of my life was when I saw you alive on Platform One. The second happiest was when you pulled this ring out of that beat up, bloody box. Now, we are permanently joined at the hip. Where you go, I go."

Cliff smirked. "I surmised we were joining a little south and to the right of your hip..."

Bettie kissed him again. "You can be such an asshole sometimes. Come here and show this old bicycle a few new tricks..."

Professor Fassbinder had spent his week on Platform One looking at the flying saucer in the photos the Director had shown him. He and the Olson twins had spent the first two days clambering around inside a large craft with absolutely no edges or corners. Everything was smooth, almost featureless. Attempts were made to examine its internal workings using x-rays, MRI-like machines, you name it. Everything was blurred. Finally, Joseph walked in the only thing they could get to work, the entrance hatch and stopped.

"Hm. Some craft used to have their hatches in the rear. I wonder…" He walked forward to what would be the "front" if the hatch was 180 degrees opposite of the bow of the ship. He suddenly sat down, cross-legged…

…and almost jumped out of his skin when the "floor" began to form a seat around his ass.

Somehow, he controlled himself. He was soon in a reclined "pilot's" seat. He felt the "armrests" and the area directly in front of him that might have been an instrument console. Parts of the ship formed around his fingertips and palms. When he moved his fingers, a heads up display appeared directly in front of his eyes. Or was it projected into his retina? He saw the wall of the large bay the saucer was in. Shit.

"Sandy. Sam. *Get in here.*"

A few hours later, the twins were able to get the saucer's interior to react to them as well. It seemed that the craft, ship, whatever you wanted to call it, took a while to "decide" it wanted to interface with each individual. The craft literally seemed to have a mind of its own.

The rest of the week Joseph spent with the Olson twins, trying to figure out its system. When he left with the two Colonels on the spaceplane, the saucer was slowly giving up its secrets to the three scientists. It was as if it was examining and testing them to see they were worthy enough to converse with, to share with. Joseph was glad he did not have to stick around. Not only because he really wanted to get back to his wife, but also he really disliked the Tschaaa Lord in charge of Platform One. Cliff called him the Wizard. Joseph called him Shithead. Whenever he was around him, Joseph felt the Tschaaa was sizing him as the main course of a meal. Joseph had visions of himself, on a big table, roasted, with an apple stuck in his mouth.

Joseph felt like kissing the ground when they landed at the Cape.

His wife, Sarah, actually brought her school class up to view the landing, getting a complete tour of the launch site. Joseph rode back with his wife in an old-fashioned yellow school bus. The experience brought back bittersweet memories. Back at the Key West Base, he kissed his wife. "Sarah, I need to check in with the Director."

She smiled at him. "Are you going to ask him about staying around because I may be pregnant?"

"Will do, darling. You'll be the first to know."

He went up to the Director's office, trying not to stare at Mary Lou. Damn, she still looked like Bettie Page. Joseph went into the office with his ducks in a row. When he found an opening, he started to explain about his new relationship with his wife, how they were going to start a family...

Adam stopped him short. "Let's cut to the chase, Professor. You think your wife may be pregnant. And you do not want to spend any more time away from her than you have to. You're afraid I wouldn't understand."

Joseph blushed. "Sir, I just..."

"You must think I am the most ignorant, uncaring asshole in the world. Professor, go home. Check in with your section here. You do not have to go back into space unless you really want to. The Olson twins, going by your reports, have things well in hand. Just keep an eye on this project of ours and use your talents with earthbound projects. Keep in touch. Talk to you later."

Joseph almost skipped home. He felt that his wife was pregnant. She was happy. Life was good. Little did he realize at that time a couple of catfights and major revelations on modifications of human biology threw everything in doubt.

Weeks later and the good Colonels were on their third trip, Professor Fassbinder staying home. Had he been along on the second and third trips, things may possibly have been different. They brought up needed scientific supplies, plus some creature comforts that were in short supply, making them the most popular temporary residents on Plattform One. Their expertise on aeronautical and space engineering made them welcome help on some of the projects with which the resident scientists were involved. Then Dr. Susan Smith and her husband, Robert, found out that Bettie had a minor in Biology, with a specialized study in extraterrestrial life.

"Colonel, please. Come to our lab. We have a special project we have been working on for His Lordship on artificial life. You must see what the Tschaaa growth vats can do, with a bit of tweaking by us humans."

Cliff cautioned Bettie before they set off to the laboratory that the Smiths were rather "intense". "I haven't been in their section in months. They have a tendency to corner you and go on and on and on. They also seem to think that the human species is just one big lab rat, ripe for experimentation. I know they were trying to develop new artificial food sources to replace Cattle for the Tschaaa. But they talk and act like they are just making a new kind of sausage." On the way to the section in which the Smiths' laboratory was located, Bettie and Cliff bumped into Sandy Olson. During the second, previous trip up on *The Hope*, Sandy had been very busy aboard the so-called saucer and had not had time to even say hello. She had even missed meals, spending every waking moment dealing with what the hell the saucer was and what it did.

This time, when Sandy saw Bettie and Cliff, she made a point of stopping to greet them. "Colonels. Congratulations on your marriage. How are the newlyweds?"

"Just great," Cliff answered.

Bettie felt a bit awkward, after the brief "affair" she had had with the other woman. She had not had a chance to talk with her, one on one, since Cliff showed up. She turned to her new husband. "Cliff, honey, can I have a moment for 'girl talk' with Sandy?"

Having had the situation previously explained to him, he smiled. "No problem. I think there is a latrine nearby and my bladder is calling. See you in a few." He headed toward a small side corridor nearby.

"Uh, Sandy..." Bettie began.

"Bettie, no need to explain anything. You found the love of your life, alive and well. You even told me about him, remember? It's perfectly understandable that our, shall we say, fling did not last."

"Sandy, it's just that... I was *not* trying to use you. I....we made a connection I didn't expect. I will always have feelings for you and would like you to remain a friend. Is that possible?"

Sandy kissed her on the cheek. "Of course we are friends. I am just glad that you're happy. I wished I could have been at the wedding, but I was stuck in space. One of these days, I'll give you a belated wedding present. Deal?"

Bettie hugged her. "Deal. I just hope someday you can find someone who will make you as happy as Cliff makes me."

Sandy sighed. "Yes, I wish I could find the 'one'. But to be honest, I'm having some... issues I guess you could say, with a level of sexual aggression that even my twin says is worrisome. From some reports I have received from groundside, a lot of women are having similar problems. I mentioned it to the Smiths, who are our primary biologists up here, and they said they would look into it. They mentioned about maybe a mutation or something brought here with the Tschaaa. After all, introducing non-native germs and other species can wreak havoc on an environment."

"Cliff and I are headed to their research wing right now. I'll mention it to them."

"Just one word of advice," Sandy cautioned. "They can get rather intense about what they do, and seem cold regarding the effect their research may have on individuals. They have been trying to grow some replacement meat products for the Tschaaa, in order to cut down on the harvesting of live subjects. But, I've stayed away from their work. Seeing a piece of human-looking flesh being tested for Tschaaa consumption gives me the creeps."

Bettie nodded. "Thanks for the warning. I have definitely seen my share of dead humans over the past six years, so I've probably built up thick enough skin to compensate. But I'll watch myself."

Sandy smiled at her. "Please do that. Now, I have to return to Sam. We have a gazillion things to do over the next few days. Our stay here has been extended for another month, but I suspect it may take a year or more to really figure the saucer out. Keep in touch."

"Will do, Sandy."

Cliff reappeared and the two Colonels continued their walk to the Smiths' research area.

"Get things worked out, babe?"

"Yes, Cliff. I just felt guilty, like I used Sandy. I still don't entirely understand what came over me that evening. I'm beginning to have some suspicions about what has been going on here in general... I feel like maybe my buttons are being pushed."

Cliff frowned. "Maybe our visit with the Smiths will shed some light on the whole subject. They are experts in human biology and physiology. However, I've heard rumors some of their work can be pretty gruesome; more like a morgue than a lab."

Bettie gave a small smile to her love. "As I told Sandy, after the last six years, it takes a lot to get to me. Unless it's a lover that is supposed to be dead showing up with a shit-eating grin and a ring." Cliff gave her waist a light squeeze.

"I'll never live that down, will I?"

"No, you won't. I love you to bits anyway."

They arrived at the entrance door to the Smith's lab area. When the doors did not slide open automatically, Cliff cleverly located a buzzer. A couple of minutes later, Dr. Susan Smith opened the access door. Susan was a short, fortyish zaftig woman with short, dishwater colored hair. She wore wire rimmed glasses, surprising, as those with access to Tschaaa medical technologies had used their nanites and procedures to fix most of the more mundane human physical deficiencies.

"Colonels Hunter and Bardun. Thank you for coming. I like to have new eyes look at our research once in a while. It helps us to get new ideas. Especially one with a biology background, Bettie."

A heavy set, white-haired and full-bearded man that looked like Santa Claus' twin, gut and all, approached them. This was Robert Smith, her husband and expert in all things concerning human biology. He stuck out his hand and gave both Colonels a robust handshake. "Welcome, my good people. Glad to have visitors of the human variety. I'll let my wife give you the cook's tour. I need to go to the supply area and look for a type of widget for an experiment I am performing. I'll be back in a few minutes, Susan." He kissed his wife on her cheek and strode off.

"If you will follow me, I'd like to start with something I'm especially proud of."

Dr. Smith took Cliff and Bettie into a large open area that had low illumination lights over at least two dozen large tubs or vats. There were also directional lamps over each of the vats, but only a few were turned on. Susan led them to a six foot long vat nearest the entrance.

"This, Meinen Herr and Frau, is my biggest accomplishment. Please take a look." Bettie and Cliff looked in under the lamp and saw an approximate five foot nude adult female form, with all secondary sex characteristics included. The head was enclosed in an opaque basketball shaped cover.

Susan grinned. "Say hello to the Other Me."

"What exactly do you mean?" Bettie asked.

Susan grinned more broadly. "I took my stem cells and, using Tschaaa vat technology, grew 'me'. A clone to be exact. I have that ball around the head as it is weird, even to me, to look at my face on a body sitting in a vat. But all of *my* organs are functioning."

"What about the brain?" Bettie asked, frowning.

"Just the automatic functions, if you notice the breathing tube. The lungs function at a very low respiration rate, as do the rates for blood flow and heart function. It is basically in a semi-comatose state, much like Tibetan monks claimed to achieve. The body and organs grew and developed quickly, much like the grays do. But, rather than awakening into a functioning being, like the grays, I keep it in this state."

"Why?" Bettie asked.

"Well, first, the project was to prove I could produce a full term human body, like the Tschaaa grow grays. I considered using a similar technique to introduce sentience at an automatic level, programmed to function in certain programmed fashions, like the grays do. However, as it is a human-based clone, not a gray, I might have to try and educate it to function at least at an idiot level. I really don't have the time nor the facilities to take the experiment to that level. Not to mention the disconcerting idea of an idiot level 'me' wandering around. So I keep it for spare parts and organs."

Bettie stopped in shock. Cliff's forehead was deeply furrowed.

"Spare parts, you say?"

"Yes, Cliff, if I may call you that...yes, thank you. Military rank seems so formal to me. Anyways, this is the medical wave of the future. Organ transplants from another 'you' to keep you alive and healthy for decades longer. All but the brain, of course. I still have no way to transmit your cognitive abilities to another body. Some brain cells for repair, yes. But right now, if the brain dies, that's it."

Something in the back of Bettie's mind screamed, 'Warning!'

"But, Susan, how do you decide if this has reached the level of being a ... person? "

"Easy. The same as at an abortion clinic, where I worked for several years. Until the fetus is 'born', it is not a person. Until we 'birth' a clone–in a sense, wake it up–it is just spare parts. This experiment was for us humans. The rest of these vats are for experiments and functions for Tschaaa needs. Specifically, meat sources that are indistinguishable from Cattle currently walking around on Earth. I have been able to achieve that for the fresher cuts of meat."

"Fresher?" Cliff queried.

"Yes. First, I took a few eggs and cells from the women up here at the station, Platform One. By the way, why do they call this a platform instead of a space station? It's confusing. Never mind, I'm getting off subject. Cells and eggs were brought up here, first by the Tschaaa, and then you two brought a small quantity up your last trip here."

"Wait a minute," Bettie interjected. "When you say eggs, you refer to human female ovum and gametes, maybe zygotes?"

"Yes. Let me show you what we can do with them."

A bit cautiously, Bettie and Cliff followed her to smaller vats a few feet away.

"Here. I can now grow them up to a stage of development where they resemble a fetus and thus provide a vat grown equivalent of veal or lamb for the Tschaaa."

Cliff and Bettie froze. In the smaller vats was each what appeared to be an unborn baby. The one difference was they lacked any part of the head past a rudimentary skull, possibly some jaw development.

"See, these are basically anencephalic fetuses, so called 'brainless' fetuses. We can easily produce them, without having the ethical complication of dealing with true brain development. Once again, the most basic automatic body functions are evident..."

All Bettie heard from that point on was a nonsensical drone from the doctor. She stared wildly around the lab, trying to focus on something, anything other than the horrors in front of her. She noticed some scalpels and a bone saw nearby.

Cliff, still shocked and staring at the contents of the vats, suddenly heard a soft keening coming from Bettie's direction. "Wha..." He had begun to turn toward Bettie when she flew by him, and drove a scalpel into the doctor's neck. Dr. Smith started to scream as Bettie, acting too fast for Cliff to react, slammed the second scalpel through her left glass lens and into her eye. Susan screamed, flailing her arms about. Bettie, with unnatural speed, slashed with the bone saw, opening up the scientist's jugular. Susan spun around, her blood spurting, and collapsed to the floor.

Cliff bearhugged Bettie, and almost had his nose broken as she tried to head butt him. She was acting on some primal defense level and did not even recognize who he was. He lifted Bettie off her feet and spun her around, his face pressed into the side of her neck. She tried to bite him, that keening noise from her mouth becoming a growl.

He yelled as loudly as he could into her left ear. "*Bettie!* It's me, Cliff! Goddamnit, stop it!" She struggled for a few more seconds, and then stopped. The animalistic sounds from her mouth also ceased.

 Cliff set her on her feet, still holding onto her arms. She started to retch. Cliff helped her bend over and she puked all over the feet and shoes of the dying Susan Smith. He tried to hold Bettie, to comfort her. She sputtered, "My...my...my sister gave birth to an anencephalic baby a week before... the first rock. It lived three days. They named it after *me*. Before they realized..." She retched again, and then began to dry heave.

"Deep breaths Bettie. Atta girl. In goes the good air, out goes the bad."

Bettie finally stood up, and spat at the still body near her feet. "I screwed this up. But she deserved it, evil bitch!" Cliff hugged her again, and stroked her hair.

His mind was racing a mile a minute. "Babe, we need to leave. Now. In the spaceplane. I don't think the Wizard will understand."

Bettie shook a bit, and stood up straight, pulling herself together.

Her military training and experience took over. "You're right, let's go."

Cliff did not see any cameras in the large laboratory, other than the one at the entrance door. He hit the open button, he and Bettie exited... and almost ran over Robert "Santa Claus" Smith, carrying a couple of boxes.

"Hey, what's up?" Cliff's right uppercut caught Robert Smith's jaw perfectly, and he went down like a sack of potatoes. "Those boxing lessons came in handy after all." Cliff stated. They began to run down the corridor toward the docking area where *The Hope* was berthed.

Platform One did have an internal surveillance system on the corridors and main areas. Over the years, the Tschaaa, grays and lizards had gotten used to such human activities as running, working out, sexual encounters, etc. The other species believed humankind was a bit "off" and got used to making allowances. The Tschaaa knew that eventually, they could be turned into meat, end of problem. Therefore, no one tried to stop them. Bettie and Cliff made it to the spacecraft in record time. There was no security on the spacecraft either. After all, why would anyone steal it, and where would they go? The Tschaaa knew they had control of all the good spots on Earth, and pretty much ignored the rest. The two Colonels dashed into the berthing area.

The berthing area was connected to the outer bay which would be sealed off by a large airlock when the craft was getting ready to launch. After being sealed in, the air was pumped back into the station, and then the outer door was opened. Small maneuver jets and rockets helped nudge and push the craft until it was far enough away to engage the main engines.

Cliff and Bettie snatched the pressure suits that were hanging up on their special racks, and with practiced ease, had them on in record time. Each checked the other over to insure everything was tight and secured. If they lost air and pressure in *The Hope*, these suits would keep them alive long enough to land somewhere on Earth. Helmets were last, more streamlined than those used during the old space shuttle program. Small intercom radios enabled them to talk to one another.

On board, Cliff grabbed the left seat pilot's chair. "I know you're senior, babe, but I have more experience in space combat maneuvering. Trust me, we may need it."

Bettie took the right seat without protest. "Dearest, I always have trusted you. I sure as hell got everything all FUBAR."

"Forget it. It was bound to happen. I'm surprised I didn't pull a berserker on the asshole Lordship that runs this place long ago. I think the chance of returning to Earth kept me at least partly in control." Bettie tried not to fog up her helmet as she started to cry. "Maybe if you left me…"

"Hey, dumbass. We're *married*. Remember? For better or worse, in front of God and country. Can't back out now, and wouldn't dream of trying. Okay, help me preflight this beast, just what we have to do to get it rolling."

"How do we get out the launch door?"

"Well, hopefully, no one has raised the alarm yet, so the automatic controls should work. If not, the main pulse engines may be able to knock the doors open. In theory, at least."

Cliff hit the release for the magnetic clamps that held *The Hope* in place. He heard the satisfying sound of the release. The landing gear on which the spaceplane was sitting had electrical motors attached with a drive mechanism, allowing a pilot to move the craft around a flat area at about two miles an hour, max. Engaging these motors and firing a couple of maneuver rockets to break the inertia, *The Hope* began to slowly move. "Remind me to figure out a way to increase the taxi speed on this thing." Cliff grunted in frustration.

Just then, Cliff noticed that his radio phone, attached to a small velcro pad on the control panel, was flashing. Cliff cursed, managed to untangle and unseal his helmet faceplate so he could hear it. Everyone on the Platform was given a small radio phone that worked in, on, and around the station.

"Hunter here."

"Cliff, it's Sandy. What's going on? I can't raise Bettie. The Tschaaa and their minions are rushing around at the Smith's laboratory. Was there an accident?"

"Yeah, you could say that. Sandy, I have no time, so listen carefully. Bettie and I are bugging out on *The Hope*. If you can get to the berth and launch area, I would appreciate it. I may need your help. But you may really piss off the Squids if you get caught helping us. Copy?"

"Tell Bettie I'll be there in five," Sandy replied. "Thanks." Cliff reattached his radio phone to the control panel.

Under Cliff's control, *The Hope* was now pointed at the airlock door. He hit the automatic door opener and was relieved to see the large airlock door begin to slide open. Slowly, on its motorized landing gear, *The Hope* crawled to the airlock. It seemed like an eternity, but finally they were in. Cliff hesitated for just a minute before he signaled the door to close. Now, they would be locked in if the Tschaaa realized what was going on.

"Cliff. It's Sandy. I'm at your launch berth. The doors locked and sealed so I guess you are cycling the airlock to leave."

"You got it. Anybody else there yet?"

"Not yet... wait. A soldier is approaching."

Bettie watched the closing airlock door. "We could try blowing the outside blast door. I know there is an emergency exit and launch protocol in case you had to get out of the bay with everything jammed up. I think we can do that without the airlock closed and cycling."

Cliff glanced at the small rear area view screen. "You had the original in-depth briefings on landing and taking off from this Platform. I just dealt with living on it. I'll leave it up to you. Work your magic."

Bettie quickly brought up the specifics on her monitor. A quick review and she had the correct emergency procedures in her head. She was poised, her hands over the controls. Turning her head toward Cliff, she asked, "Ready?"

"Yes. Blow the door."

Bettie's hands flew over the control panel keyboard, entering the correct codes in just the right pattern. A second's pause, and the outer blast door was blown open, just as the airlock door closed. The air rushed out, and Cliff hit the maneuver rockets, the combined forces easily lifting and propelling the spaceplane outward.

He quickly retracted the landing gear. "Boy, that's definitely going to piss off the Squids," he grinned. Ten seconds later, Cliff hit the Pulse engines. One moment they were slowly moving at maybe forty knots per hour, the next moment they felt a kick in the ass and were traveling at over six hundred knots. He angled the craft's nose downward, toward Earth. "Man, I will *never* get used to those sudden accelerations when I hit the pulse engines. Zero to six hundred is not exactly fun."He kept his eyes on the cockpit glass straight ahead.

"Bettie, keep an eye on the rear video feed. The Squids have at least one delta on board the Platform at all times." He activated the various search radars on board, trying to watch everything at once. *The Hope* was in the Earth's gravity well, and began to accelerate downward. Its skin and structure were designed to take the heat and stress of reentry at a high angle, using its wing and flap designs to help control the overall speed. It was easily stressed to take Mach 25, and could take probably a lot more in a pinch due to the "fudge factor".

"Cliff, we have company on our six." He glanced at the rear

monitor screen and tail radar. A delta had launched and was trying to acquire them on its sensor systems.

"Bettie, make sure you're strapped in tight and your G-suit's cells are inflated. This is going to be a wild ride." Cliff shifted the downward angle of *The Hope* to increase initial speed. He would have to then switch to a high angle of attack to induce drag to slow it down. Based on Space Ship One, it also had shape changeable airfoils that could help to control its descent.

"Let me tell you what I know about the delta fighters. They have rudimentary but fairly powerful search radar. This lack of radar capability is because those big eyes of the Squids provide them with outstanding vision, especially for moving objects at long range. The eye in the sky surveillance system they use is based primarily on lens-based optics, not electronic enhanced cameras and radars like our former satellites."

At that moment the spaceplane was passing quickly enough through sufficient atmosphere to cause a sonic boom. "I hope this bucket is as tough as they say it is. The delta behind us will pick up our direction of travel and hit their gravity pulse engines to start catching up. In the atmosphere, the ram jets will be used. They can pull more Gs than we can because of the delta's design and Squid physiology. We can't out turn them. I will dive as fast as I can and hope this beast doesn't overheat and come apart. I can jink and release landing flares. Eventually, I'll have to do some s-turns to try and slow us down. That's it. No offensive capabilities."

"You're not headed toward Key West or the Cape, are you? "No, Bettie. Luckily, our place in orbit gives us a pretty direct flight toward Montana, U.S.A.

Bettie patted his arm. "I love you. I my gut tells me we can do this."

"Babe, I love you to bits. I hope your confidence is not misplaced, or else we are going to make one hell of a fireworks display."

The initial delta's pilot was trying to catch up without overheating his craft. The delta had no specialized force field like protections that the Falcons had, just the tough organically-based structure. The delta was like a chunk of a super barrier reef, reinforced by metal.

The Tschaaa warrior radioed for assistance. Five more deltas were launched from one of the spokes of the wheel-shaped orbiting ship, the size of an aircraft carrier. They were soon plummeting downward in an attempted intercept solution. Bettie, monitoring everything on the rear-facing radar systems, picked up new hits on her monitor. "Cliff, we have new targets, coming in at a bearing of 160 degrees to our rear, about five o'clock high."

"Shit. Well, they won't catch us before the first one does."

It was a delicate balancing act, trying to maintain high speed in order to keep the delta from catching up, but having to flare out to control the descent to prevent the craft from becoming a flaming rock. Cliff knew the tough literally organic grown skin of the delta, like a super tough carapace of some superior crustacean, could take abuse and be able to disseminate heat in a superior manner to manmade materials. It had been built not as a true spacecraft, but rather a high atmosphere based attack craft; to swoop down from high perch, blow the hell out of its target, use its gravity pulse engines to boost itself back into orbit, then repeat. The ram jets gave it control and high speed in the atmosphere, up to about one hundred thousand feet. In a one-to- one comparison, the spaceplane's engines were nearly equal in power and mobility to the Tschaaa technology engines.

"Bettie, I have to start s-curves. The speed and heat are building up way too fast. Start looking for somewhere to hide, if possible." Bettie had a sinking feeling in her stomach. Hide? Where? It wasn't like there was a foxhole somewhere.

Suddenly, Bettie knew there must be a God. "Cliff. Two o'clock low. Thunderhead. A big one too."

In Cliff's attempt to closely monitor the spaceplane's gauges, he had missed the huge cloud formation over the Montana/North Dakota Area. It appeared that it might reach close to as high as seventy-five thousand feet. Inside were likely to be large electrical discharges. Lightning. Their craft, built for Earth weather and humans, was grounded and insulated for lightning strikes. Cliff had no idea to what degree the deltas were built to take electrical strikes, but now seemed like a pretty good time to try and find out. "Hang on! After this, rollercoaster rides will seem pretty boring." He pointed the spaceplane's nose down toward the weather formation. The speed picked up, and with it, heat and vibrations.

The forgotten Guard radio frequencies, standard still on all human aircraft, crackled to life. "Unidentified aircraft. We have you on our radar. Turn back or we will fire."

Bettie grabbed the emergency mike, and yelled, "*Mayday! Mayday!* Spaceplane *The Hope* with two on board. Request emergency asylum. Help us, goddamnit! The Squids are trying to eat us!"

Cliff focused on trying to keep the craft aimed toward the weather formation and in one piece. Something flew by the side windshield. "Aircraft, you are headed toward Malmstrom Air Base, U. S.A. You will be shot down." "Go ahead. And hoot the damned deltas following us while you're at it!"

The Hope hit the top of the huge thunderhead, as Cliff tried to flair the craft out more to slow it down. It began to shake and buck. "Bettie. Escape capsule ready status. Activate."

The spaceplane had been built so that the nose and cockpit area formed an escape capsule. No shuttle disaster for space trips in the future. The nose area separated from the body, being blown away from the spaceplane body and fuselage. Then, large parachutes hopefully executed a controlled descent to the ground. Hopefully.

The Hope took a large electrical strike. Monitors and gauges flickered; the powered flight controls cut in and out, and Cliff cursed and swore. "I thought this beast was grounded and shielded." He fought to keep the spaceplane under control, fighting the up and down drafts in the interior of the thunderhead. He changed the craft's angle of attack, nose up as best he could to slow it down, and began s-turns.

After a couple more minutes of an extreme rollercoaster ride, *The Hope* popped out of the other side of the thunderstorm. Cliff fought to steady the spaceplane. "Fuck! Come on, baby. Hold it together. At least until we get shot down." Somehow, he began to control the descent.

Something large zipped by the left side of cockpit. Cliff glanced over and saw a delta inverted in a power dive. "Shit. That Squid must have been hit by lightning also. Maybe the water in the cockpit they use as G-cushioning will fry him."

"Cliff... I think something is burning." Bettie unlocked and unlatched her faceplate so she could sniff the air. There was the smell of burning electrical wiring and ozone, as well as a little smoke. She could not locate the source. "Can you bring this thing under control? I can't figure out the source, but something got fried."

"Just don't turn on any oxygen sources. Seal your helmet back up, Bettie, so your suit oxygen won't help spread a fire." The suits had a small tank with less than pure oxygen because the cockpit was pressurized. If the cockpit failed and the air escaped, the small quantity in their suit system should last until they landed. They had been breathing it since they left Platform One, due to the threat of attack.

Cliff kept circling *The Hope* at a high angle of attack to slow their descent. He completely lost sight of the delta that dove by. "Bettie, can you get the rear search radar working? I need to know if those other deltas that were launched are headed this way."

Bettie attempted to get the monitor screens up. Nothing. "That burning smell must have been the circuits involved with the screens and monitors."

"Try the Guard Radio."

Fortunately, that still worked. Bettie repeated another version of her previous message. "*Mayday! Mayday!* Spaceplane *The Hope* requests emergency landing instructions. Two souls onboard. Request asylum."

Someone at Malmstrom Base Control must have figured out something more than a Squid incursion was occuring in their air space. A new voice answered.

"*Hope*, continue on your exact bearing. Two aircraft will be intercepting and will try to escort you in. Any sign of hostile intent will result in instant destruction. Acknowledge!"

"Colonels Hunter and Bardun acknowledge."

"I wonder what they are sending up to meet us."

"Well, good-looking, I hope it's something with some offensive capability. I think the other deltas may be catching up."

Cliff maintained the heading as ordered, keeping a high angle of attack to slow down the descent of *The Hope*. Years ago he had been at Malmstrom Air Base, after they had reopened the airfield primarily for rotor aircraft. He had a passing thought as to what it looked like now. Finally, he broke through a cloud cover and saw Great Falls, Montana, and located the Base. Everything seemed more sprawling with more recent construction. It looked like a lot of survivors had made their way there, away from the south and the coasts, and therefore less chance of being bothered by The Tschaaa. The Air Force Global Strike Command seemed to have survived the initial attacks. Cliff swung the spaceplane in a wide circle, trying to slow more as he lined up on Runway 47 Right. He noticed two F-15Es shadowing him as he started to drop below Mach One.

"Damn, Cliff. Those have Japanese Self Defense Forces markings," Bettie exclaimed. She called them on the Guard frequency. "To the fighter aircraft escorting us, do you read me?"

"Yes, Spaceplane *Hope*. We read you loud and clear. This is Colonel Yakashita. We will escort you until you touch down. Please do not make any rapid course changes. We have orders to launch missiles, fire if you violate instructions".

"Colonel Yakashita, do you have any other aircraft on your radar?"

"There are deltas some thirty miles out and closing. They are being engaged by ground to air defense... now."

Although neither Cliff nor Bettie could see anything being launched, it would not be worth the risks involved attempting a go around to check. Cliff tried to bring the spaceplane down as easy as possible, but landed a little hot. The landing gear had locked down, one of the few indicator lights that still worked on the instrument panel. They hit hard, and Cliff tried to brake with flaps, speed and wheel brakes. Security and fire rescue vehicles hauling ass down the runway after them, trying to keep up with the landing aircraft. Cliff used up the total airfield, and the overrun area, finally coming to rest with the nose gear in the dirt. Fortunately, *The Hope* had held together. Cliff patted the instrument panel. "Thanks, honey."

They went through the normal shutdown procedures, and finally popped their helmets. Cliff stood up with Bettie, giving her a quick hug and kiss. "We made it so far, Babe."

Bettie answered with a game smile. "Let's see what our reception is going to be. After all, we are in an enemy aircraft." They un-toggled the airlock, and not needing to pressurize, popped the outer door. Then they hit the automatic control to lower the stairs, and found at the bottom at least a dozen armed Security Police, weapons pointed at them.

Cliff quickly raised his arms, and Bettie followed suit."Don't shoot! We're unarmed."

"Get down on the ground, Squid loving bastards!" A dark skinned man with NCO stripes yelled at them.

Cliff and Bettie moved to comply. As they started to kneel, four uniformed personnel quickly closed on them. The two Colonels were slammed to the ground, arms painfully bent behind them as they were handcuffed. Cliff soon realized that the cuffs were put on so tight that his hands would soon go numb. "Hey guys, we're not going to try anything. How about loosening these cuffs?"

A foot suddenly forced his head to the ground, embedding rock and soil into the side of his face. "Shut up, Squidshit. If we want something from you, we'll squeeze it out of you," the black NCO spat at him.

Suddenly another soldier called out, "Ten *hut!* Good day, General."

A voice he had not heard in years asked. "Cliff Hunter, is that you?"

Cliff, the foot no longer on his face, spit some dirt out. "I think I hear John Reed. Yes, John, it's Cliff. And I'm in the shit again."

General Reed chuckled. "*That* is an understatement. Sergeant, let the Colonels up and take the cuffs off. If they were going to do something, they would have tried it by now."

"General, these Squidlovers killed my people." The NCO had the sound of hatred in his voice.

"Excuse me," General Reed began. "Did my stars fall off my uniform? Let me check... Nope still there. Let them *up! Now!* Take those cuffs off."

The security troops scrambled to comply. No one wanted a pissed off General, especially one that wasn't known to be shy about punishing those who didn't follow his direct orders.

Cliff quickly rose to his feet, and then helped Bettie to hers. "May I present Colonel Bettie Bardun, Astronaut Extraordinaire, and my wife."

"Now that *is* a surprise. It's bad enough everyone believed you dead. Now, someone actually married you? Good morning, Colonel Bardun, and congratulations on your nuptials."

Bettie attempted to salute. "General..." Suddenly, she went white, and her knees buckled. Cliff caught her before she hit the ground.

"EMT. Help the lady," General Reed commanded. The medics

seemed hesitant, and didn't move. In response, the General did something he didn't do often. He exploded. "*Goddammit! Move!* If no one likes the fact I'm in charge, then shoot me now. Otherwise, move!" Everyone was now scrambling. "Let's get something straight right now. They may have just come from the Tschaaa, but they are still human military officers. You will treat them according to Military Regulations, UCMJ and the Geneva Convention. Clear?"

"Crystal! Yes Sir! Yes General!" Suddenly everyone was trying to do everything at once.

General Reed impaled the senior NCO of the EMT personnel with his eyes. "*You.* Senior Sergeant. Take the Colonels to the hospital. Get them there in good order or you will wish you were never born. And tell the Doctors that I will be there and these officers had better be receiving the best care possible. Or else. Understood?" "Yes General."

General Reed wished that Torbin and Ichiro were here. They would go through these nimrods like butter, kicking ass and taking names. Then he realized. The sun was rising. The attack on Key West should be in full swing.

The General hotfooted it back to his staff car, where his driver already had it running and in gear. "Sergeant Pascal, hospital, lights and siren."

"Yes Sir." He took off like a shot. He was selected as the General's driver because he had some pre-strike experience with NASCAR. He beat everyone to the hospital by a wide margin. General Reed jumped out of the car, not giving the Sergeant the chance to open his door. "Once again, Sergeant Pascal, an excellent ride. Keep the motor running."

"Yes Sir, General."

Five minutes later, as Bettie was being wheeled into the ER, General Reed had almost the entire hospital staff on notice. "Screw this up, and you'd be up doing ear, nose and throat examines on the remaining Canadians in the Yukon."

"She's going into shock. Get an IV going. Colonel, can you hear me? Good. Hang in there. Focus on me. Atta girl."

Cliff stood by helplessly, watching his love being poked and prodded. He felt heartened when some color finally began to return to her cheeks.

"She'll be okay, Cliff." General Reed had snuck up on him. "Quick and dirty. What happened?"

"General, she saw something that shouldn't be done by fellow humans."

"What was that?" Cliff told him in a few sentences, no frills. He saw General Reed's jaw tighten to the point that Cliff thought his teeth would shatter.

"You were kept incognito on Platform One for six years, and had no indication what they were up to?"

Cliff took a deep breath. "General–John–to be honest, I think I was trying to be purposefully ignorant. Out of sight, out of mind. I was selfish, trying to survive. Then, we saw those… babies. The love of my life may never be the same again."

John Reed knew Cliff Hunter as one of the toughest, most competent fighter pilots he had ever known. He knew of Cliff's final kamikaze mission and, like everyone else, thought he was dead. Just like Captain Bender's brother, William. But while he survived, his soul was in hell.

General Reed then did a very un-General thing. He put his arm around his old friend.

"Cliff, it will get better. I promise you. She will live. She's tough. We know all about her history over her last six years. She survived just like you, doing what she had to do." He pulled back his arm. "We will work this out. There is a certain Madam President that will want to formally debrief both of you."

Cliff wiped his eyes. "I' m at your service, General. Just, if you need to shoot someone, shoot me. Bettie has suffered enough."

General Reed chuckled. "Colonel, people have done a lot worse than you and were not shot. Just be honest when you talk to Madame President. That old she bear gets pissed when somebody lies to her."

About an hour later, Bettie had markedly improved, even if she still felt like there was a huge weight on her shoulders. A light sedative had helped calm her down so that she has stopped alternating between nausea and hyperventilating. She had difficulty closing her eyes, however. Images from the lab kept replaying in her mind. She was in a private room, with two Security Policemen standing guard. From what she had overheard, this had more to do with General Reed demanding she be protected than to keep her from fleeing. She did not remember meeting John Reed while on active duty. But, since he was friends with Cliff, she knew he was a cut above other men.

There was a light knocking on the hospital room door. An attractive woman in Russian military fatigues entered, and saluted. "Colonel Bardun, Captain Aleksandra Smirnov of the Free Russian Military. Madam President asked me to check in on you before she met you. And, my apologies, but she also instructed me to ask you a few questions. Are you well enough?"

Bettie nodded yes. "Go ahead and ask away, Captain. But if I suddenly freeze up, I apologize ahead of time."

Aleksandra, with years of interrogation training and experience, could tell something horrific had shaken Bettie to the core. The Colonel had a feral look of fear and shock in her eyes, the type of expression Aleks had seen when someone had undergone torture. But, she had her orders to try and obtain answers.

"Colonel, what made you and Colonel Hunter flee?"

Bettie sat still for a moment. "Well, it was like this. I killed a vicious sick bitch... I mean, a human scientist working for the Tschaaa. She was doing some... things that made Mengele look like a boy scout." Tears began to stream down as she stared into space, her eyes focused on something horrific from another time and place. "I stabbed her in the eye, cut her throat, and then I puked on her."

"Colonel..."

"I killed her. And I wish I could do it, again, *and again, and again!*

Aleksandra recognized that Bettie was about to go into severe psychological shock. She slapped the Colonel's face. Not too hard, just hard enough to break the psychic loop she was about to enter, reliving something her mind did not want to relive. In a flash, Bettie's eyes refocused on Aleksandra. She began to wail. Not any type of wail that Aleks had ever heard before, but a wail from deep within the soul of a person who had just seen the face of evil itself.

Aleksandra stepped out of her role as interrogator and into her humanity as a woman. She went to the bed and hugged Bettie to her chest. She lapsed into Ukrainian, which had been her mother's language, forgotten when she had been forced by her Russian father to adopt his tongue instead. Before she realized it, she was cooing and whispering the same reassurances her mother had said to her as a little girl. When a Security Officer tried to enter the room to see who was wailing, her Russian military training came to the fore. "Get out. *Now!* I will call you if I need you." Her focus returned to Bettie. "It is over, dear lady. It is over. You are safe. You are with good men and women again. It is a bad dream, which will fade with time. Trust me. I know."

Finally, Bettie stopped wailing. Still holding on tight to Aleksandra, she quickly blurted out what she had witnessed.

For a few minutes after, the two women still clung to each other, finding comfort from the warmth of another human body. Bettie finally let go of Aleks. She tried to wipe her eyes with a corner of the bed sheet, but Aleks produced a very feminine lace handkerchief. "Here. My Yankee husband gave me a set of these before leaving. Pretty, isn't it?" Bettie wiped her eyes, blew her nose, and then realized she had made a mess of Aleks' present. "I'm so sorry, Captain."

"My name is Aleks, Colonel. May I call you Bettie?" Bettie nodded her consent. "Thank you. It is now yours. Keep it as a sign of a new beginning. Now, I must fetch Madam President. She wishes to have a few words with you. Are you up to it?" Bettie nodded again. "Good. Rest here. I will be back shortly." Aleks patted her leg, smiled, and left the room.

"Men, I will be back shortly with Madam President. Do *not* bother the Colonel unless she asks. And, as my husband Torbin would say, 'stay frosty'. Understood?"

"Yes, Ma'am," the two Security Policemen answered in perfect unison. Aleks turned and strode down the hallway.

"That's Captain Bender's wife?" one soldier asked the other.

"Yes, I guess she is. Man, I bet you he doesn't piss her off. She acts like she would cut your nut sack off in your sleep, and stick it in your mouth for grins."

The both chuckled, and then, remembering Captain Smirnov's admonition, returned to parade rest, stern looks on their faces.

Aleks rushed down the hospital corridor and rounded the corner. She made a beeline for a ladies restroom, entered, and stepped directly into a stall. When she was certain that alone for the moment, she bent over and vomited into the toilet bowl. She wiped her mouth with toilet paper, flushed, put the lid down, and sat. She began to sob quietly for about a minute or so, pulling out a handkerchief identical to the one she had just given away, and then dabbed at her eyes. She left the stall and went to the mirror for a quick light makeup repair.

The statement Bettie had given had shaken Aleks to her very core. Here she was, married all of two weeks, her husband on a very dangerous mission, and she was certain she was pregnant. Then to have in her mind image of babies, raised without brains, for *food*. It had hit her directly in the center of her body, where her own baby was developing.

Aleks pulled herself up straight and looked in the mirror. "You are a Free Russian officer," she reminded herself. "You have responsibilities." She inhaled, exhaled, gave herself a once over, and walked out of the restroom.

She found Madam President sitting with Mr. Williams in the cafeteria.

"Madam President, she is ready."

"Please wait here, George. I need to have some girl talk with the good Colonel."

"Yes Ma'am."

Aleks and Madam President walked toward the hospital room. In a few concise sentences, Aleks told the President what the two Colonels had seen, and why they had fled Platform One. The President stopped short, staring at Aleks. "She... said... *that?*"

"Yes, Ma'am. And I have interrogated many a... subject. Her reactions were completely truthful."

Madam President stood stock still. Then, she began to shake with rage.

"Those monsters! My God, we do things to our own species that the Tschaaa would not dream of doing to their own kind. Maybe they are right. We are a bunch of out of control monkeys who need someone to sit on them."

The President saw Aleks' reaction.

"Don't worry Captain. Just an old she bear growling a bit, to let off steam. I think we can figure out how to handle our own problems without some ten limbed monstrosities telling us what to do. Let's go see the Colonel."

A couple of minutes later, the two guards were snapping to attention. "At ease, gentlemen. Relax. I don't bite."

The President knocked lightly on the door to Bettie's room, and then she and Aleks entered. Bettie tried to sit up straight at the sight of the President. "Madam President. Sorry I cannot stand up, but I have these damned tubes…"

Sandra Paul walked straight up to Bettie's bed. "Forget damned protocol. Woman to woman, give me a hug." She sat on Bettie's bed and they hugged. Bettie began to cry again. "It'll be okay, dear. I can say that. I'm the damn President." She hugged and rubbed Bettie's back. President Sandra Paul noticed her own tears were beginning to flow. She untangled herself from Bettie, reached into the strapped large black purse she always carried and pulled out matching pink handkerchiefs. She handed one to the Colonel, and used the other to dab at her eyes.

Bettie wiped her eyes, and then spoke. "Madam President, I am asking for your mercy for me and for my husband, Colonel Cliff Hunter. I realize we have been working with the enemy, the Tschaaa. I ask that we be given a chance…"

"Now, stop that Bettie. I can call you Bettie, can't I? Good." The President continued. "You and your husband have not done anything that hundreds of thousands of others have done to survive this… infestation. Yes, I think that is a more accurate term than invasion or occupation. We have been infested by an alien species. They have been manipulating us ever since they landed. Besides, your escape has, by some great act of providence, helped us in our first great counter attack."

"How so, Ma'am?" Bettie inquired.

"You took the attention off our units approaching Key West, distracting one important Falcon and robocop stationed there. The eyes in the sky were distracted also."

"Distracted from what, Ma'am?"

"Well, it's no secret now. Over an hour ago, a tactical nuke hit the Squid Lord's stronghold off the tip of Key West. Initial reports are of heavy damage. We are hoping Lord Neptune is dead and is now irradiated fish food."

Aleks looked at Madam President. "Any word about… my husband?"

She regarded the Russian Officer, a serious look on her face. "Sadly, no. The last we heard from Captain Bender was the signal that the assault on the Director's quarters had begun. The nuke did what we hoped it would do… the majority of people at the Base headed toward hardened shelters. Their defense was disorganized. We have intercepted some transmissions from Director Lloyd's Security Control at a listening post we had set up. They are running around like chickens with their heads cut off."

Aleks still seemed concerned. "Now Captain, I ordered that crazy Marine you married to bring back my sainted husband's .44 Mag pistol. You know he wouldn't dare piss off this old she bear." The three women laughed nervously. They all knew the cards were stacked against eliminating the Director.

The President turned toward Bettie, and began speaking in a lower volume. "All right. Now, listen carefully. You and Cliff Hunter were part of a super-secret plan to help distract the Tschaaa and the Director from our assault. That is why you left when you did. The death of the human scientist was part of the plan. Your extreme reactions were part of this plan. Only Captains Bender and Smirnov, my assistant, George Williams, General Reed and I were privy to your plan. You are heroes, not villains."

"But, Ma'am, that would be a bald faced lie. We had to escape due to selfish actions on my part." Bettie's bottom lip began to quiver.

The President reached out and grabbed her hand. "Bettie, I believe everything happens for an eventual purpose. You, shall we say, 'saw the light', at just the right time. Who are you and I to defy divine providence? I know you want to punish yourself, to beat yourself up for surviving when others did not, for going back to space on a Tschaaa supported mission. But it helped you save Colonel Hunter. You brought the spaceplane here. You confirmed what we believed was going on with the 'scientists' on Platform One. Therefore, by the power vested in me as the President of the Unoccupied States, you and Cliff are pardoned for any past crimes, known or unknown. Penance is between you and God."

Bettie sat quietly for a few moments. "I don't deserve this. My Husband, Cliff, does. For his stake alone, I'll agree and not ask for a formal court martial for consorting with the enemy."

"You are extremely hard on yourself," the President commented, shaking her head. "But at least you agreed to my plan. A side benefit to your escape dash is that there are now four fewer Squid pilots and deltas. One was taken out by mother nature and her lightning. Three went down to six Hawk missiles, two of those because they collided by trying to dodge the Hawks. There were two more deltas damaged, hit by ground fire from a concealed fifty caliber quad meat grinder that a military collector donated to us in working order."

She chuckled. "Squids have a tendency to break off combat when their deltas are damaged, usually lacking the drive to risk pressing a kamikaze style attack. So, take my thanks and be done with it. Okay?"

Bettie swallowed the lump in her throat. "Yes, Madam President. Maybe someday I'll forgive myself." She laid back in her bed. "Sorry, but I'm exhausted. I am going to ring my nurse and see if she will give me anything to help me sleep... without dreaming."

Sandra Paul bent over and kissed her forehead. "Colonel, we are blessed that you and your husband are here. Please believe that. Now, get some rest. I will have Colonel Hunter come over soon to be with you." Madam President intercepted the assigned nurse, and had her ring up the head nurse and senior doctor on shift. Two minutes later, she was giving them their marching orders. She departed shortly afterward with her assistant George, and Aleks.

George walked ahead, but the President grasped Aleks' arm to stop her. "As soon as I have details about Captain Bender and crew, I will call you, Aleks."

"Thank you, Madam President."

The President grasped Aleks' other arm, and made full eye contact. "Thank *you*, my Free Russian friend. God willing, we women will save this planet. See you soon."

The Perfect Storm had many fronts...

The moment Bettie Bardun was stabbing Doctor Smith in the eye out, Adam Lloyd was sitting at his desk. He had not been able to sleep, aside from a few fitful minutes here and there. No one likes to admit they had been made to play the fool. Especially not one of the most, if not *the* most powerful human on Earth. He could not stop his mind from working on the situation at hand.

He now knew, definitively, that the genetic and hormonal manipulation of humans had probably started before the first rock strike. How else could up to one hundred thousand humans actually buy into helping an alien species into occupying the Earth without some major manipulation? It made no sense, no matter how racist people were toward each other. He himself had been turned into a guinea pig–the ultimate manipulation–as had Kat, Mary, and untold others about whom he cared. This rested on squarely his shoulders. He had helped to rebuild a system, a society controlled by an alien species, all in the name of survival, of life, of the Protocol of Selective Survival. But, as a human, was it "living" to exist at the sufferance of a species as genetically different from human primates as they were from a scorpion? All life in the universe may started out with the same basic building blocks, but there the connections stopped. Although cephalopods were native to Earth, the Tschaaa were *aliens*. Illegal and hostile aliens, to be exact.

He sensed another human presence. Actually, there were two. Kat and Mary, soon to be official sister wives, softly padded in. "Adam, are you okay?" asked Mary. "You aren't sleeping."

Kat walked around his desk, and started massaging his shoulders. "Boss, you are way too tight," Kat exclaimed. "Mary, I may need some help here."

Before he knew it, the two women had him lying on the floor on top of sofa cushions, as they worked, kneaded and massaged his entire body. Waves of relaxation washed over him, and his thoughts finally slowed. He began to lightly snore.

Mary whispered to Kat, so as not to wake him, "This is bad. I have never seen him so tense. Even after he executed that baby rapist."

"That talk he had with his Lordship must not have helped at all," answered Kat. "He won't tell us the details, but it looks like we are Tschaaa lab rats."

The odd tingling sensation that a Falcon produced when flying nearby woke him. He and his lovers felt, and then heard, the Falcon pass by. The Falcon rapidly accelerated, producing a sonic boom a few miles away. He bolted upright. "That must be Andrew leaving... fast. Something has happened."

Despite Kat and Mary's protests, he hit the hotline to Security Control. The phone conversation was short and to the point. The Director hung up the telephone. "There has been a murder on Platform One. Colonels Hunter and Bardun have fled in the spaceplane. Andrew flew to the Cape in case they try to land there. He has orders to take them into his custody if they show up."

The Perfect Storm began to form...

Because of the availability of deltas, with aggressive young Tschaaa pilots, levels of command lower than His Lordship had decided to launch them instead of the Falcons. The pilots needed combat experience. His Lordship was contacted immediately after, and was told it was just a matter of a few minutes before Bettie and Cliff were intercepted and shot down. His Lordship agreed to the action, and sent Andrew to the Cape, just in case. He knew the humans were building up their air defenses. As long as they had no noticeable offensive capabilities in the Unoccupied States, he did not care. He had no interest in the cold and dry Midwest.

The Perfect Storm continued to build...

A rebuilt B-25 World War Two Mitchell bomber, late of a private air museum, was droning its way down to Florida. Cutting across the Gulf of Mexico, in connection with the B-25, Ichiro Yamamoto leveled out his captured delta fighter, near the deck, at just under the speed of sound. With rough running injectable scramjets, the Japanese Captain alternated cursing the situation, with praying to any god who would listen. He needed to keep his speed up until he launched his payload– a one megaton hypervelocity missile.

The eye in the sky saw a delta, and ignored it. There was no Squid FAA, no flight plans filed. No real IFF. Tschaaa warriors followed the orders of the local Lordships, so it was their worry if one disappeared. Only a human craft traveling over three hundred knots an hour would have peaked their interest as a possible threat. The Tschaaa, never having fought an all-out air war on their home planet, had never developed a true sense of detection and defense. They had been the aggressors during the initial thirty days following the first rock, had achieved air superiority due to the subsequent strikes and attacks from space. Earth forces had made limited offensive responses, so the Tschaaa had seen no need to change their operations.

Now, the chickens were coming home to roost.

Captain Torbin Bender sat on the long jump bench that had been built into the modified B-25. There had been numerous discussions during planning for this attack mission on related subjects. For example, how big should the assault team be, and what aircraft should be used to transport it?

It was decided that a relatively small, hard-hitting assault force was all that was needed. Twelve troops were selected as the assault team, with two more staying with the B-25 as Rear Security. Torbin knew he made the thirteenth member of the assault team, but fortunately, he was not the superstitious type. The size of the team and its success was based almost entirely on surprise, and the concentration of force at a weakened spot. Torbin knew the chances of success were low.

The B-25 WWII-era aircraft was chosen for two reasons. First, it was not a current era military aircraft. A C-130 could have been obtained, or maybe two large military helicopters. But that might have raised questions as to who had access to most current military aircraft. The B-25 was similar to a lot of aircraft that had been found stashed in private collections or on private airfields the last couple of years. Aircraft built to fly low and slow were popular, because they drew little if any attention from the Tschaaa and their minions anywhere in continental America.

The second reason for the selection was that it was a tough, relatively simple military aircraft that had been easily modified for numerous missions. Pappy Gunn's ancestor had become famous in WWII for modifying the B-25 in a variety of ways, which it survived. The current B-25 was modified with jump benches, additional drop fuel tanks, and a larger access/jump door. The two Pratt and Whitney engines were completely rebuilt, unnecessary equipment stripped to make it lighter, with less drag. Crew was just pilot and co-pilot. It could hit an honest three hundred mph low down.

Now, the   B-25 droned along, headed to Key West, Florida. Refueling at an airfield in Kansas, with large drop tanks attached, the B-25 had the range to reach Key West. The Base at Marquesas Keys were some twenty-five miles away from the tip of Key West, so it would probably not take that long for the Key West Base to determine the level of danger.

The plan was to do a low-level airdrop of some two hundred fifty feet near the access causeway to the Base, now de facto capital of the Occupied States areas, just as the nuclear device delivered by Ichiro hit and detonated, likely resulting in some six thousand personnel fleeing for the blast shelters, with Security Forces assisting. The rebuilt Director's HQ was just over a mile from the main gate and ID building, located on the causeway off of Highway 1, the Overseas Highway. Therefore, they would make a low level chute drop near the causeway, then hot foot it down the causeway and through the main gate. It was hoped the gate would be minimally manned as everyone else hit the shelters. If not, they would hit fast, fight hard, and try to blast through. It was believed that the Director, having a "captain of the ship" mentality, would stay above ground in his office until the bitter end.

As a connected side note, the one megaton bomb was a penetrating "bunker buster". Rebuilt from some former Minuteman ICBM warheads, it would penetrate the coral and tough organic "concrete" that the Tschaaa used as its primary construction material, tunnel down several dozen feet, then detonate. Aimed at the center of the nearly four mile diameter enclosed complex that had turned the Marquesas Keys into a huge repair and manufacturing center, it was hoped the shock waves would cause the complex to collapse. The greater majority of the explosive force would be contained underground and underwater inside the circular Marquesas Keys. There would be a signature mushroom cloud, but the amount of crap thrown into the atmosphere would be reduced. The twenty-five mile distance from Key West would help reduce the negative physical effects on Key West itself.

Torbin had tried to suggest a second small tactical nuke–a "suitcase device"–to target the Director's Area specifically, but Madam President had refused. She did not want to risk killing women and children, not to mention the Conch Republicans. Her primary target was the Tschaaa, and the attempt at the Director would be performed in order to capture or kill the human head of the snake. Torbin was a Marine, a professional military man. If he was given a lawful order to "jump" he would reply, "Yes, Sir/Ma'am, how high?"

Torbin glanced at the fourteen people seated on the jump benches. The Senior NCO was Gunnery Sergeant Greg Smith. Thirty years old white male of generic heritage, he had been a Marine since age eighteen. Broad shouldered, he still had a lean look about him. He was one of the designated Riflemen with the ubiquitous M-4. He and the other four Riflemen had six thirty-round magazines of mixed armor piercing and ball .223/5.56 mm rounds. They also had two hand grenades, one blast, and one shrapnel, in addition to carrying a spare 40mm grenade for the three Grenadiers. Extra stripper clips of ammo were secreted in the spare areas of their combat fatigues for emergency resupply. Slung under his arm was a chopped down M-79 with two CS gas rounds in a small pouch. Corporal Manuel Martinez, former Private First Class and Torbin's driver, also filled a Rifleman's slot. He had one additional piece of equipment, which was a WWII-era silenced Hi Standard ten round .22 caliber pistol that had been "liberated" from some military museum. Light and proven, it was carried as an anti-sentry weapon. Martinez was a medium complexion and sized Mexican American who was quick and sure about anything he did. He had a Claymore mine in his small ditty bag.

Privates First Class Moore, Money, and Muller–"The Three M's"– rounded out the Riflemen. They all had similar builds, medium heights, brown hair, and light complexions. They were so similar in appearance that they said they were all brothers from another mother. But they were the best of the best, or they would not have made it to the assault team. In addition to the basic Rifleman load already mentioned, each had a ten round strip of linked ammo for the M-60 stashed in a fatigue pocket. In a flash, a thirty round belt could be put together for use. They also divided between them two LAWS and a Stinger anti-aircraft missile

Corporal Benjamin Black, the Gunner who loved his job, had turned the Ma Deuce in for a Barrett fifty with three ten round magazines and a heavy duty scope. In his small backpack he had a thirty round belt of fifty caliber for additional reloads. Due to the size and additional weight of the weapon and ammunition, he only carried a single hand grenade and a small smoke flare. Rolled up on his butt was a lightweight Ghillie Suit, in case he had to hide to shoot. He sat smiling; his large biceps and huge forearms gave him the nickname of Popeye. Black said his muscle development was due to him lugging around fifty caliber Ma Deuces the past years, often by himself with a unique bipod he had designed instead of the heavy standard tripod. He sat on the jump bench with his signature "boy, are we going to have fun" smile. When he jumped, he would have the Barrett broken down into two pieces, barrel and receiver.

Sergeant Joe Hagel, a typical dark-haired young of solid build and German descent, was equipped with a scoped M21, the semi automatic sniper version of a Match M-14 7.62 rifle. He had his five twenty-round magazines loaded with a dutch load of armor piercing (AP), match ball, and tungsten penetrator rounds. In addition to two hand grenades, in one of his fatigue tactical pockets he had a ten round linked strip of tracer for either his or the M-60's use. He had shot some five hundred practice rounds over the last two weeks, using the last twenty-five to sight in a new barrel. Everyone believed him when he said he could hit a gnat at fifty meters.

Sergeant George Washington, a very large black man, was the senior man after Gunny Smith. Sergeant Washington was one of the darkest skinned African-Americans surviving in the Unoccupied States. He carried a M-60E1 7.62 machine gun with a two hundred round combat pack of AP, ball, and tracer. In his tactical butt pack he had a rolled up one hundred round belt. He also carried two grenades and a red smoke flare.

The three grenadiers were Private First Classes Joe Trump, a nondescript medium-sized man of mixed European heritage; John Fein, a tall and skinny as a rail, dark-haired Irish/English mix; and Matthew Standing Bull, a very large Cheyenne Indian who needed to count some serious permanent scores to pay the Squids back for landing a harvester near reservation land in Wyoming. All three men had M16A3 Rifles with attached M320 40mm grenade launchers. Each man carried five 40mm grenades, three high explosive (HE), one newly developed high explosive anti-tank (HEAT) with enhanced anti-armor capability, and one white phosphorous smoke grenade that doubled as an incendiary device. They each also carried one hand grenade and five magazines of .223/5.56 ammo. Standing Bull, due to his size, carried a second Stinger anti-aircraft missile.

The final assault team member was Nick Nelson, a muscular five foot ten native Montanan who carried the M249 .223/5.56 Squad Automatic Weapon(SAW) with a two hundred round assault pack, seventy five round drum, and three thirty round rifle mags that would function in the SAW as well as an M-16. He had a light brown handlebar mustache that he refused to shave off until he had personally killed a Squid. Most of his family had been killed by a large rock in the early days of the invasion. He carried a smoke grenade as well as a blast grenade.

There were two Rear Security personnel: the Huge Corporal Tatupu and Private First Class Danny O'Brien. Jet black-haired "Danny Boy" came from a long line of Irish cops and carried a SAP that had been passed down generation to generation. It had busted many a head. He was the only team member dressed in a semblance of civilian attire, a Glock 26 9mm with a threaded barrel for a silencer concealed under his Hawaiian shirt. He was the front man, if someone needed to make contact with the civilian populace as they beat feet out of the Florida Keys at the end of the mission.

Tatupu would cover him with a Seal Version MP-5 submachine gun with the screw-on silencer that looked like a toy in his hands. He had also brought along a friend's .458 Magnum with three rounds of a special hand loaded armor piercing round for robocop protection, in addition to three commercial rounds. Tatupu had military camos on to help him stay in the shadows due to his rather dark skin. His specific emergency skill was as a Special Forces trained combat EMT/medic. He was to bring on board and patch up anyone who needed it as they hauled ass out. And, as added insurance, concealed under a tarp in the former Tail Gunner position, was a Ma Deuce with a one hundred round belt. The Rear Security team was to stay with the aircraft as it flew to land at the Marathon Airfield, some sixty miles or so from the Key West Base.

Because it looked like many a nondescript aircraft that had been put back into service as a "low and slow" transport, after the low altitude insertion during the confusion from the nuke strike, the B-25 would land at the Marathon Key Airport. Cover story was that they were operating as a "Gypsy" transport service, one of many that had sprung up over the last year to take items A to point B on consignment, then scrounge a load back. This old style type of transport and capitalism was helping to re-develop an American form of commerce. The Squids couldn't care less, as long as their meat source was not interfered with. Rumors were that some pilots also hauled dark meat for a price when asked. The two B-25 Pilots, Captains French and Vandenberg, were wearing non-descript flight jackets and utility slacks. Stashed in the Cockpit, should their cover be blown, were two M-4s.

Torbin carried an M-4 with optics, four magazines of ammo, one smoke grenade, one blast grenade, and a Markarov 9mm pistol with threaded barrel and silencer. He had a Claymore mine in a small butt pack. He also had a special weapon in a shoulder holster with a unique story.

He still remembered the meeting they had in the hangar at

Malmstrom some forty-eight hours prior. Madam President Sandra Paul had joined General Reed, George Williams and Pappy Gunn for a quick goodbye. As usual, she walked in the room and took charge of everyone.

"Alright, gentlemen, let's form a circle please." The sixteen troops, including Ichiro and two pilots, quickly complied. Before he knew it, Torbin had his right hand grabbed by her left.

"Gentlemen, everyone please grab the hand nearest you. We are about to have an old-fashioned prayer circle." When everyone was clasping hands, the President bowed her head a bit, and proclaimed with her clear, resounding voice, "Lord, we may not be all the same religion here–we may even have an atheist or agnostic or two. No matter. We are all humans! Humans of different beliefs and backgrounds about to make a perilous mission to attack an evil that has come to your Earth, home of the first humans. We ask you for your divine help, and blessing on this endeavor. If one of these fine men should fall, please accept them into your Kingdom. For, no matter what flaws they may have, what sins they may have committed, this day they go to fight and maybe die for all humankind. Please accept my prayers. And all God's children say *Amen*."

At that moment, Torbin believed the likelihood of the old saying that there are no atheists in foxholes was probably true.

As everyone made last minute equipment checks, Madam President approached Torbin.

"Captain, I have one small, unusual request for you." "Of course, Madam President."

Sandra Paul pulled a fairly large object from her signature large purse. "Here. This Smith and Wesson .44 Magnum four inch revolver was my husband's backup bear gun. I believe you can get this shoulder holster attached to your gear. You have five rounds of a special armor piercing load for any robos and one of my husband's 'bear loads' for a Squid. I have engraved *Property of the President of the U.S.A.* on the back strap so you won't forget where you got it."

She looked him straight in the eye. "I lost my son, only to gain a hell of a lot more sons, including you and Ichiro. I hate sending you all out. But, I must. Please. Do what you can to come back. I'd love to be godmother to your child."

Tough, nasty Torbin Bender had a huge lump in his throat. He swallowed, came to attention, and snapped off a salute. "Yes, Madam President."

She chuckled despite the tears in her eyes. "You can take the Marine out of the Corps, but you can't take the Corps out of the Marine. May God speed you on your journey, Captain Bender."

As she walked away with George Williams, she reached out and grabbed his arm for support. George worriedly looked at her. "You okay, Sal?"

"Not really, George. This old broad suddenly became very, very, weary. Help me back to the General's office, and maybe I can borrow something from his liquor cabinet. Then, I think I need a long sleep."

Torbin snapped his attention back to the present. Sometime in the next ten minutes, Ichiro, piloting the captured delta, would reach Key West. He would launch the hyper velocity cruise missile with the one megaton bunker buster bomb. As it sped toward the His Lordship's complex, the pilots would get ground control on the horn, tell the story that they were a bit lost and would need to follow the overseas highway up to Marathon to find the airfield. In his day of limited air travel support, most pilots followed known highways to the desired destination. Ichiro would also try and take out the three ex-shipboard Phalanx air defense gun systems arrayed in a triangle around the Base. All this activity should distract anyone from noticing the parachute drop.

From some two hundred fifty feet, using Russian D6 drogue stabilized chutes, Torbin and twelve team members would hit the silk and land a few hundred yards from the causeway entrance that led to the main gate of the base. The main gate was about halfway down the almost two hundred meter long causeway that bisected the channel near the entrance of the Former Key West Naval Base. Hopefully, although some twenty-five miles away, there would be some effects from the nuke that would draw the attention of everyone in the area. Since the attack and air drop were scheduled at dawn, there would be a substantial flash and as well as wind, though dissipated by the distance involved. Metrological research pointed to the fact that the prevailing winds would be away from Key West in the impact area, so radiation exposure from any fallout would be reduced.

Torbin scanned his troops one more time. If the job could be done, they were the ones who could do it. He knew there would be casualties, probably death. That came with the territory.

Aleks was pregnant. He knew she was worried sick. Russian officer or not, she was still a mother to be. Torbin wanted to be there when she finally gave birth. But first, duty and humankind called. They had married two weeks ago, a simple ceremony with the base chaplin to give his first child a legitimate name. No bastards for him. If he did not return, he knew Aleksandra would raise their child, with help from his military mates at Malmstrom. He shook his head. No more woolgathering. It was time to be focused. Just then, he heard the pilot's radio crackle. It was time.

As the B-25 and delta both approached their destinations, Ichiro cursed and swore in every language he knew. The delta's injector scramjets were losing power, and when he tried the pulse engine... nothing. He had gained substantial momentum while gliding down from a couple of thousand feet as well as the distance where the scramjets had worked at full power. So, he would get near the launch point. Past that, all bets were off. Ichiro had decided that, if the already armed hypervelocity missile failed to launch, and he could not reach the Tschaaa complex, he would nosedive into the Key West Base. He knew there would be huge civilian casualties, but he had to at least kill the Director. The assault team would die with him. That was unavoidable.

Somehow, Ichiro nursed the delta along. He knew that the Key West Base personnel would not attempt to contact the delta, as Squid pilots did not carry translators. Ichiro was hoping no robocop tried an informational interface, as that would prove be disastrous. Such an attempt would quickly reveal something was wrong, and a Falcon would intercept him. What Ichiro could not know was that two former USAF Colonels had done something on Platform One that had everyone out of position for any intercept.

The scramjets sputtered once more. Whether he liked it or not, it was time. Ichiro said a short prayer and then launched the missile. At the same time, he tapped out quick a morse code broadcast of the letter "S" twice. A quick three dot reply from the B-25 acknowledged the reception. The missile launched straight and true, accelerating to some thirty-six hundred miles an hour in seconds, turning and headed toward Marquesas Keys.

Yelling, "Banzai!", Ichiro fired the plasma energy weapon in the nose of the delta, taking out the Phalanx System. He skid and jinked the delta and tried to snap off some reduced power shots at the other two Phalanx sites. He did not see a satisfying explosion as he had from the first shot. However, he was pretty sure he had at least fried some of their electronics, limiting their ability to shoot at the missile as it zipped by Key West.

Just then, the scramjets quit completely. He was horked. Ichiro made a quick decision. Using the remaining momentum, he turned the delta and tried to aim it at the Headquarters Building. By this time, all hell had broken loose on the various radio freqs, with one Phalanx blown up and the other two unable to function, Security Control quickly became aware that something was wrong.

Ichiro was rewarded with fifty caliber strikes and a Stinger AA missile blowing his right jet pod apart, taking some aircraft control with it. The Key West Base Security Forces were pretty well trained to respond this fast. Dammit. A three inch former shipboard gun firing air burst rounds also got a big piece of him. The delta began to veer to the left, heading toward the entrance causeway. Ichiro tried to bring it back toward the Headquarters Building. No Joy. Knowing he was going down, he managed to regain some control of the delta. He flared it out, dumped air brake and flaps, and popped the canopy of the modified to human cockpit, anything he could think of to slow it and bring it down into the channel water west of the causeway. If he struck the causeway road and bridge, he would damage the route Torbin and his assault team needed to take to quickly get to the Director's office. That must not happen. The delta flared on the edge of a stall then pancaked into the channel water. It slid on top of the water, then began to dig in. It finally stopped and began to sink, its nose some four yards from the causeway's rocky edge. When the B-25's pilot, Captain French, received the morse code from Ichiro, he realized he was about thirty seconds early. He had just been contacted by Key West Security Control, which was telling them that they were a bit off course and trying to locate the Overseas Highway to follow to Marathon Airport. Just as the Controller on the radio was telling him to turn to a heading toward Marathon, he suddenly yelled, "Number one Phalanx just blew up! B-25 aircraft. Leave the area immediately!"

"Fuck!" Captain French exclaimed. He hit the jump light to flashing amber. "Captain. Gotta move now. Hang on!"

The assault team, seeing the amber light, had already stood up. They had been automatically checking their chutes and gear as they neared the destination, so everything was Go. They all grabbed the solid bars suspended from the top of the fuselage interior, and were lucky they did. The pilot banked to the right. Then, he rolled the WWII Bomber into a tight left hand turn, trying to line the aircraft up so as to fly straight up Highway 1. The modern stall warning horn began blaring, and the large airship began to shudder a bit.

"Come on, baby. You can do it. Did I ever tell you my great-granddad, Joe, flew B-25s in WWII?" Captain French commented to his co-pilot, Captain Vandenberg.

Torbin said a quick prayer, "Lord, send an angel and give us more lift." He called aloud to his team. "Visors down!" They had visors attached to their goggles that would automatically darken if there was a bright flash, like a nuke. He knew that the missile Ichiro had launched would take about thirty seconds to reach the target. It would spend a second or two boring down into the Tschaaa complex, and then detonate. Regardless, there would still be a flash and mushroom cloud. The twenty-five miles or so the blast would cross would take a little time, and the distance would hopefully reduce the physical effects. The original plan had been to hit the ground in their chutes just before the wind hit so as not to screw up their tight landing pattern. Now, it was going to be catch as catch can.

Miraculously, the B-25 did not stall. Captain French was leveling out when Captain Vandenberg hit the green light and yelled, "Jump!" At that exact moment, unnoticed by either pilot, Ichiro's delta hit the channel water. The B-25's wings were just level when Gunny Smith went through the door, with Corporal Black on his ass. The plan was for the Gunny and Black to get to the ground first and provide cover of the landing zone area, Highway One, just northeast of the causeway entrance. Like clockwork, everyone was out, tight on the ass of the man in front. The drogues they threw out quickly deployed the chutes, and everyone landed just yards apart. Torbin who was the last out, yelled, "Geronimo!" just because he could. Because they had to jump early, their landing zone was actually closer to the where the causeway connected to Highway One. Gunny Smith and Black hit almost at the signal light that controlled the traffic between the highway and the causeway. Despite their darkened clothing and dark chutes, the small street light illuminating the traffic signal area made Gunny extremely nervous. The main gate guard shack was about two hundred feet down the causeway. Fortunately, the timing of the assault offered cover to the team due to compromised visibility. Early dawn causes problems with human eyesight, as the eyes are trying to switch from rods to cones. Therefore, for a short while, things are a little indistinct, sometimes blurry.

Just after Gunny and Black hit the silk, there had been a large flash from the southwest direction of the Base. Ichiro's weapon detonated.

After a couple quick twists and turns, the missile had pointed directly at its intended target. However, a glancing hit from a small plasma weapon had knocked the missile off course. It veered down to the left, and then went straight into the outer southeast quadrant of the circular Marquesas Keys. No longer striking the center of the complex, the nuke hit the outer structures. It had burrowed only some thirty feet down before it detonated. Taking the path of least resistance, a large portion of the blast was directed in a southwesterly direction into the surrounding sea and reefs.

Moments prior, Adam had hung up the telephone with security control after an update on the spaceplane. Suddenly, his office windows shook. His radio began to broadcast the yells from the security controllers that a Phalanx had just blown up.

He yelled at Mary and Kat. "Shelter. *Move!*"

"Adam."

"Don't argue, Mary. Move!" Jamey and Jeanie came from the sleeping quarters, robes on. "Shelter. *Move!*" Adam repeated a third time. The two made a beeline to the escape elevator. Air raid sirens began to undulate.

A little over two years ago, Adam had started the construction of a complex of underground shelters capable of holding the population of the Base. It had not been easy, as the Florida Keys sat primarily on coral reef materials–some soil the mangroves grew in and some rock. Using Tschaaa energy weapons, and some assistance from the other alien species, he had shelters constructed about two stories down. Soon, local Conch labor came to help, as did some of the new recruits for the New Capital that came from the rest of North America. The shelters were constructed using a form of Tschaaa organic "cement" to build buried waterproof block houses (waterproof due to the shallow water table) for defense against a nuclear or biological attack. What Adam did not tell the Tschaaa was that the shelters were built as much for defense against a Tschaaa attack as from any rogue humans.

The elevator dropped three stories from the second floor, where his office and the living area suites were situated. It automatically hit the patented Otis elevator emergency braking system that let it slide to a stop on the bottom floor. It opened to a blast door, which allowed entrance to the large two rooms and a small shower/bathroom room. With substantial emergency supplies, and an escape tunnel modeled after the Minuteman missile launch control facility tunnel, survivors could last for weeks.

As the women descended to the shelter, Adam activated a hotline he had installed a few weeks ago directly to His Lordship. He buzzed the connection. A few moments later, His Lordship picked up.

"Director. It is early and I was still resting. What is happening?"

"Lordship, we are under attack. Get to shelter!"

His Lordship signed off immediately. Adam stood up to retrieve his body armor and weapons when there was a flash of light across the lawn near the Headquarters Building. Not overly bright, but bright enough to know that a nuke detonated in the distance. Adam heard a distant rumbling, followed by substantial winds blowing across the base. Based on the direction, Adam could tell that a nuke had detonated on top of the Tschaaa complex at the Marquesas Keys. He punched a direct line buzzer to Security Control that signaled evacauation. Security Control, if they hadn't already figured out what was happening, would immediate begin the planned and practiced shelter evacuation plan. A special klaxon went off. Every single Security Soldier, all five hundred or so of them, were mobilized to get the populace to the shelters. They rushed to put MOPP gear on, as most were to remain above ground to secure the base from further attack. If there were a tactical nuke strike follow-up, this would be a death sentence. Adam was expecting another nuke in the first minute after the first strike at the Tschaaa Complex. When this did not occur, he knew that they had been spared, for whatever reason. But, depending on prevailing winds, fallout could be the death of them yet.

Chief Hamilton picked that moment to enter his office. "Well, Adam, I think the balloon just went up."

"I think you are right, old friend. The ladies are in the shelter. You need to take the ladder down to join them."

The Chief snorted, "Yeah, right. You can order me all you want, but I'm staying next to you, watching your back. Just like old times."

Adam smiled at his friend. "Willie, no matter what happens, it's been a pleasure."

He reached his hand out. Willie took it. "Hell, Director. We're not dead yet. Let's have some fun."

On Highway 1, the wind had hit just as the assault team landed. Only their extensive training enabled them to hit their quick release clasps before the wind began to blow them around. As it was, Torbin was pulled onto his butt before could release his open chute. Luckily, this early in the morning in a limited populated area, there was no one nearby. However, they had landed so close to the entrance to the causeway that Torbin was certain someone would see them and sound the alarm. The Gunny, thinking the same thing, had already told Corporal Black to get his Barrett 50 caliber operating and cover the guard shack. A hundred yard or so shot would be easy for Black. So far, no signs of reaction as the assault team formed-up.

What no one knew was that the Sergeant and Security Patrolman who manned the entry point were already scrambling to throw on their MOPP Gear. The explosion of the Phalanx had drawn their attention first, then the air raid Sirens. As soon as the warning sounded after the distant flash, even before the accelerated wind hit, they put the MOPP head pieces on, and scrambled to zip up their coveralls. There was no thought of anyone attacking their position on foot. After all, anyone doing so would be hit by radiation. The idea that the detonation was too far away to really irradiate much had not sunk in. They heard a large object strike the channel and send water shock waves up into the causeway. They had also heard the approaching delta, but had seen many before this. The idea that a delta could be behind the attack was not credible to them.

"Hey, hurry up with your gear and see what hit the water," the Sergeant ordered.

Grumbling about possible radiation exposure, the Security Troop finished with his MOPP gear, not bothering to put his weapon and ammo harness back on. He grabbed his M-16 and went outside to look.

Ichiro had survived the impact thanks to tight cockpit straps, though he knew there would be some bruising. He hit the quick release clasps and was out of his unused ejection seat. He had designed and had made a special quick release G-suit. A few velcro straps and a long zipper and he was out of it. Underneath, he wore a black Ninja suit, traditional headgear and all. Only his eyes showed, though he had a pair of smoked pilot's glasses on to protect him from any residue light from the flash of detonation. He took those off and tossed them into the delta cockpit.

The Security Troop was hampered by several things when he went to see what had hit the channel. First, the MOPP Gear head piece was not conducive to good sight, it being built primarily for protection with an integral gas mask. Second, his eyes adjusting to sunrise, then the weird flash, had made his normal good vision a bit indistinct. Next, the tendency of the human mind to see what it expects to see. When he saw Ichiro clamber into the water and head to the rocks that surrounded the Entry Control Point on the causeway, he surmised it was a gray or maybe one of those new soldier class of artificial being that had been recently introduced. He knew grays flew Tschaaa craft sometimes, so why not the new soldiers. Humans did not.

"You, there! If you can understand me, grab my rifle barrel and I will help you up. The safety's on." The figure grabbed his rifle barrel. Instead of pulling itself up, the figure yanked and jerked the Troop forward and down toward the water. Off balance from standing on the large rocks, he quickly fell into the channel, the rifle twisted from his grip. His cries were muffled inside the MOPP gear, and he soon struggled to stay afloat in the restrictive suit. The Sergeant had heard another large splash and went out to investigate.

"Hey, did you fall in or..." He was face to face with a figure all dressed in black. The Sergeant had a .308 G-3 late from the German army that he tried to bring into play. A katana parried the barrel up as he fired a single round off into the early morning light.

Ichiro, actions born of a thousand practice sessions, brought his sword down in a half circle and then stabbed upward, into the Sergeant's lower body to avoid body armor. The Japanese warrior's sharp blade penetrated the lower abdomen, nicking the right lung and then bumping the spine. Ichiro twisted the blade sideways, hitting the spine with the cutting edge, and then pulled it back out. The move was over in less time than it took to read this passage. The Sergeant collapsed to his knees, his spine partially cut, then fell forward onto his face as he grabbed his abdomen. Ichiro struck the base of his neck with the hard blunt end of his blades grip, and the Sergeant lay still. This was only the second man he had ever killed. His mission in life was to kill Squids. But sometimes circumstances dictated actions. He wiped his katana on the dead Sergeant's MOPP uniform, and then ran low down the causeway onto the base, trying to keep to the shadows. As he exited the area, he smashed an overhead light attached to the building with his sword.

When the .308 went off, Cpl. Black was just getting into position with his Barrett. He saw the rifle flash, tried to use his scope to see what was going on. The sun was working its way up over the horizon, to replace the short flash of light from the nuke. He saw a dark figure move, then disappear past the guard house as a bright light on the front of the building went out.

"Whaddya see?" Gunny Smith asked, crouching down by him.

"I saw the muzzle flash, then a figure running off into the dark, down the causeway. Wait. There is another figure getting out of the channel, and there's something partially submerged in the water. Maybe an aircraft. Should I take that figure out?" "No, too much noise, even with the air raid sirens going off. This 50 has a distinctive bark."

At that moment, in low crouch, the assault team showed up on the entrance to the causeway, Torbin in the lead.

"Cover us, Black." Gunny said. Black just smiled. He loved his work.

Gunny joined the rest of the team across the four lane causeway road, and told Torbin what had just happened.

"Damnit, I bet that was Ichiro, and that is his delta, sure as shit. Come on, let's get there before that troop getting out of the water blabs we're here."

They ran crouched down the along the causeway, thankful that the Base personnel had been stingy in putting up lights. The one Ichiro had taken out had been a bright flood light, aimed into the eyes of oncoming traffic to slow down approaching vehicles and people. However, the sun was working its way up over the horizon. They had to move fast.

The waterlogged Security Troop had made it up out of the channel and onto the causeway, sans his rifle. He finally deigned to remove his MOPP headpiece as he couldn't see out of his soaked gasmask eyepieces.

"Soldier, what is going on here?" A stern voice commanded. He gazed upward and saw a Captain he did not recognize, sans MOPP gear, standing in front of him. He heard running figures.

"I don't know Captain. Some gray threw me in the water, and–*ohmygod*–the Sergeant's down!" As he turned to look at the Sergeant, Torbin hit him at the base of his skull with the butt of his M

4. The man collapsed. Torbin checked his pulse. Still alive. No need to kill people unnecessarily. He retrieved the Sergeant's rifle. Good, a .308, hopefully with some distinctive tracer rounds in it. Nothing like perceived friendly fire to confuse the issue. He slung his M-4 and held the G-3 at low ready and ran after his troops. As soon as he saw Torbin take out the remaining sentry, Black jumped up, grabbed his Barrett and began running to catch up on the causeway. He saw Hagel waited for him by the guard building. As he closed, he saw the sniper had a handheld radio in his hand, apparently obtained from the building.

"Come on, Black. I don't want to miss the party." He stepped back into the guard shack and ripped the direct land line to Security Control from the wall. Torbin was still behind the team. He glanced back and in the brightening morning, saw Hagel and Black hot-footing to catch up. The front part of the team exited the causeway onto the Base proper. Off to the right was the Headquarters Building. Gunny Smith used hand signals to spread the team out into a line assault formation. They were approaching the HQ Building from the northwest side, some half mile away. Torbin was catching up when he heard vehicle engines. From his left came three security vehicles, a Humvee with a 50 caliber mounted on top and two Jeeps. Each had two MOPPed out soldiers in them, so the drivers were trying their hardest not to hit something due to their limited vision.

He turned and began waving at them like he had something to tell them. As the drivers began to slow down, keyed on him, Torbin went into the CQB Groucho Marx walk, raised the .308 rifle and fired full auto. He fired at the Humvee driver first, the heavy mixed bag of armor piercing, tracer and ball rounds punched through the front semi armored windshield and hit the driver. The Humvee skewed off to its right and hit a palm tree lining the HQ entrance road, the Gunner on top almost thrown off. The middle jeep's driver was hit by the next burst, which caused him to cut the wheel so sharply that the jeep flipped on its side, and rolled, the passenger being thrown free. Torbin hit the third jeep with the final rounds in his magazine. The driver slammed on the brakes and try to back up. The radiator was trashed and a round clipped the steering wheel. The driver and his passenger bailed out.

Sergeant Hagel arrived on the scene, having heard on his purloined radio screams of, "Cease fire. Blue on blue. Cease fire!" Someone thought Captain Bender was a friendly who had opened up by mistake on the vehicles. The Gunner on the Humvee began to fire his 50 caliber as Torbin dropped his now empty .308.

Luckily, the first rounds went high, and Torbin flattened himself to the ground, trying to make himself as small a target as possible. The Humvee gunner started to adjust his fire when his weapons receiver exploded. Sgt. Hagel had hit the Ma Deuce with a .308/7.62 AP and a tungsten penetrator round, detonating the round in the chamber and destroying the receiver. The gunner fell into the interior of the Humvee. Torbin jumped to his feet and signaled to Black, running up behind Hagel, to take a cover position underneath some bushes in a small depression. This spot would give the Barrett operator the ability to cover the main entrance of the HQ Building as the assault team members entered.

The two Security Soldiers from the third jeep fired from some bushes near their disabled vehicle. Once again, the restricted vision from the MOPP head gear was not conducive to accurate fire and the first rounds went high. Torbin rolled behind an old U.S. Post Office mailbox that someone had left in place. He leaned around the right side of the box and fired his M-4 on full auto. Sgt. Hagel fired his M-14 into the bushes as well, sending three rounds down range. The firing from the bushes stopped.

A burst of fire from the HQ Building parking lot set rounds ricocheting around the assault Troops. Before there were any casualties, Sgt. Nelson let loose with his Mini 249. The Security Soldier hidden behind a vehicle was hit and went down. The gunplay stopped. Torbin saw the gunny, about twenty five yards in front, looking at him. Torbin signaled to continue the assault to the HQ Building. Torbin started to stand up and leave the cover of the mailbox. Then, all hell broke loose.

30 caliber auto fire came from the roof of the HQ Building. Chief Willie Hamilton had gotten into the fray with his beloved BAR. Of course, Torbin did not know who it was. The 30.06 AP rounds began striking around the assault team members, as they scrambled for cover behind the few vehicles and light poles in the lot. An AP round went through both of Sgt. Nelson's thighs, taking him to the ground. Rounds hit the mailbox Torbin was hiding behind. He tried to crouch even lower. From behind a palm tree lining the parking lot entrance, Sergeant Hagel responded with his scoped rifle. Just as Chief Hamilton shifted the BAR to reload with a fresh magazine, Hagel fired. The AP rounds smashed into the BAR rather than the Chief's head. He sprawled backwards. Torbin could tell things were heating up, so he yelled at the gunny, "Take them into the building!"

As he started to leave the cover of the mailbox, more rounds of a different caliber began to hit it. He ducked back again. "This is getting damned ridiculous," he mumbled to himself. Director Lloyd was firing from his second floor office window with a 10mm Ex FBI MP-5. The heavy rounds hit the mailbox like a drum. Torbin snapped a burst out in the general direction before he ducked back behind it. Just as Adam ducked back into his office, Sgt. Hagel blasted the window area with his M-14. Adam was splattered by pieces of wood molding and he dropped to the floor. Torbin, seeing Hegel's action, leapt up and ran toward the rest of the assault team. Hagel, seeing no motion from the second floor window, began to head forward also.

Torbin yelled at him, "Did you hit anyone?" "Can't tell, Captain." Although Torbin was supposed to try and capture the Director alive, that option was rapidly disappearing. He considered blowing the shit out of the office with HE rounds. But then, he would not be able to tell for sure if he got him or not. Damn. He had to try at least one assault, as per orders.

As soon as Major Jane Grant had realized that an assault team was on Base, she started to form a fire team sans MOPP gear. She knew that no logical commander would waste a highly trained team if he was planning on nuking or hitting the Base with a bacto-bomb. She also knew they were after the Director with the least amount of collateral damage. Security Control was only some six blocks from the HQ Building and she began to throw a team together.

Adam was on the office floor, when a voice crackled over a small radio receiver he had on his desk. "Director, I will be there in ten seconds." It was Andrew. After getting word of the nuke strike, and verifying here was no chance of the Cape being the destination of the spaceplane, Andrew had elevated his Falcon off the tarmac, rotated toward the direction of Key West, then took off like a bat out of hell. Now, he was almost there. Once again, the people on the ground felt the odd vibrating electricity that preceded the arrival of a Falcon. Then it was over the parking lot.

Torbin swore. "I need the Grenadiers, Stingers and LAWs up front. Fire at will!"

Andrew sat the Falcon down between the assault team and the front entrance. He had considered just blasting away, but did not want to cause any more collateral damage that he had to. For once in his existence, Andrew had underestimated the capabilities of his former fellow humans and overestimated his Falcon.

Andrew set the Falcon down, and started to scan the area with his sensors. Then the Falcon shuddered with the hits from two HE 40mm and one HEAT round. This was quickly followed by a LAW rocket. A Falcon had a force field or "shield" system. However, it was made to operate in near vacuum conditions, as atmosphere degraded its capabilities. Therefore, the system was rarely operated close to the ground. Only the tough organic barnacle like skin was there for protection. The LAW Rocket, capable of penetrating eight inches of hardened steel, blew a satisfactory hole in the hull, damaging some of its control systems in the process. The 40mm grenade shells did lesser damage, but some damage nonetheless. Andrew quickly dropped to the parking lot pavement through an escape hatch. As he dropped, the Falcon began to power up and rise in the air. As it rose, the Stinger missile, with an enhanced warhead, struck the underside of the Falcon, blowing a satisfactory hole. The craft wobbled a bit, and then dashed toward the ocean. Andrew sprinted to the entrance door of the HQ Building at an Olympic games speed.

Andrew's interface system told him that the Falcon had taken substantial damage, more than he had considered possible. He sent it to a safe distance, saving it from further harm. He might need it to bug out with the Director. Andrew realized he had made a significant error in not taking the chance of collateral damage and should have targeted the parking lot, blasting anything that moved. He had become so used to people acting in abject fear to the Falcons and the capabilities they reflected, that the concept of a substantial attack had become foreign.

The assault team let out various whoops of joy and satisfaction at the sight of fleeing robocop and Falcon. Torbin ordered, "Forget the Falcon! Hit the building!"

There was a loud report from the roof of the building. A .338 Lapua round smashed through Sergeant Hagel's body armor and he collapsed. Chief Hamilton, a bit banged up, was still in the fray with a sniper rifle he had as backup. Torbin was close enough to the Gunny that he dashed over and grabbed the loaded Shorty M-79. He spun around and lobbed the CS shell onto the top of the HQ Building just as the .338 rifle spoke again. The heavy round hit Rifleman Moore's M-4, smashing and jamming the receiver. He yelped and dropped the weapon. Before Willie Hamilton could fire again, the CS shell hit the roof, began spinning and shooting CS gas about. With no gas mask, the Chief was soon spitting, sputtering, and then retched. He stumbled to the exit hatch in the roof to escape the gas.

Handing the M-79 back to Gunny, Torbin ran over to Hagel. He was dead, the heavy round overpowering his body armor and hitting his heart. Torbin grabbed his dog tags, the M-14 rifle, and a spare magazine. He would grieve later. Three large figures came striding from the far side of the parking lot. Torbin immediately recognized them as the new Soldier class being the Tschaaa had developed. A smaller, poor man's robocop, they were still well over six feet tall and tough. Torbin slung his M-4 and began shooting the M-14 at the figures. He was joined by the Riflemen and Sgt. Washington with his M-60-E1. High velocity bolts of energized metal needle-shaped rounds came from the odd-looking, large weapons they were carrying. PFC Mooney took a round full in the chest. The round from the bolt gun, of the type demonstrated to Adam Lloyd some time ago, blasted through his body armor and through his body. Mooney toppled over, dying. A similar round hit Cpl. Martinez in the chest, and he fell backwards.

Sgt. Washington screamed out a curse and began slamming 7.62 machine gun rounds into one, then another of the Soldiers. Torbin concentrated on one as he shouted, "Grenades!" Sgt. Washington concentrated his fire on the head of the nearest Soldier, and was rewarded with the head toppling off the being's shoulders. The legs locked and it fell like a tree. Torbin smashed several rounds into the face and neck of one of the remaining Soldiers. Blinded, it started to fire in all directions, a bolt catching Gunny, knocking him over. There was a loud report. Black's 50 caliber slammed into the being's chest, knocking it over. It lay still.

A 40mm grenade caught the third Soldier full in the chest, blowing it apart. Torbin dashed to Gunny, just as he began cursing and trying to get up. The bolt had hit his body armor at an angle, singeing and bruising his ribs before exiting.

"Going to make it, Gunny?"

"Fuck yeah, Skipper. This is just a scratch," he grimaced.

Cpl. Martinez stood up, yanking and pulling at his body armor. There was smoke rising from the front of his fatigue top. He threw off his armor, and then pulled a smoldering object from underneath his t-shirt. It looked like a book.

"Santa Maria—my mom's bible saved me!" Cpl. Martinez exclaimed. The bolt had penetrated his rifle's receiver, his front armor plate, coming to rest in the back of a small bible he was carrying inside his fatigue top. His chest was singed by the fire started in the bible and his chest was bruised, but that was it.

Torbin gave him his M-4. "Here, use this. Your rifle's trashed."

Torbin heard the Gunny curse loudly. "Skipper, something hit my rifle. The bolt is fused."

"Go grab Nelson's SAW M249. He can't move with his thighs shot to hell."

Moore checked on Mooney. The bolt round had penetrated his body armor and into his chest. He was dead. Moore grabbed his dog tags and his rifle. "See you later, Buddy."

A 30 caliber tracer zipped by. Everyone grabbed cover behind the few vehicles, light poles, and palm trees in and around the parking area. Some three hundred yards away a line of some non-MOPPED troops were approaching, about seven in number. Torbin yelled for smoke, and two Grenadiers each fired a 40mm smoke round in front of the assault line. The WP round set up a thick barrier of white smoke between the attacking Security Forces and Torbin's group.

Gunny Smith crouched next to Torbin behind a staff car that was parked on the edge of the parking area. Torbin said, "Excuse me." He grabbed the Shorty M-79 from the Gunny again, loading the last CS round. He fired it and the CS round hit near the barrier of smoke.

A couple of Security Troops dashed through the smoke, firing, and then proned out on the ground to provide fire for the others trying to attack through the smoke. They began to cough, choked, then retched as the CS gas, hidden in the smoke, hit them. With no gas masks, they had no protection. Two more armed human soldiers came through the smoke, and ran into the CS concealed gas. They tried to keep firing, but soon choked, coughed, retched, and their eyes blurred with tears. Two other Security Troops swung wide of the smoke barrier, coming around the north end of the smoke, missing the CS gas. One fired a grenade, and then was blown apart by Black's Barrett 50 Caliber. His comrade tried to flee and was hit and downed by rifle fire. The rifle grenade exploded at the feet of Joe Fein, slamming him backwards. It nearly amputated his right leg, and he lay with his life's blood spurting out from a cut femoral artery. Cpl. Martinez tried to stem the flow of blood, but was unsuccessful as there was more than one puncture. Fein was dead within a minute.

Torbin had to make a quick decision. His small force was being whittled away; the blocking Falcon has delayed the assault just long enough to allow other forces to arrive.

"Gunny. Base of fire with that SAW. Sgt. Washington. You, Trump, Moore, Muller. Hit the building. Everyone else, on me, covering fire."

Technically, the twelve man squad was divided into two fire teams, under Sgts. Smith and Washington. Or, it could be reconfigured into three four-man teams. All twelve men were trained to operate with any others as part of any sized force. No matter who was left, they slid into whatever slot was necessary. With the squad automatic weapon as the base of fire, Torbin, Standing Bull, and Martinez spread out and began suppressive fire across the parking lot. Sgt. Washington, Trump, Moore and Muller began the mad dash to the entrance door. Nelson lay cursing next to Black's concealed position, his shot up legs preventing him from doing much of anything. Someone had thrown him Fein's rifle with grenade launcher before they all got busy. He checked it over and it seemed to be still operational. He turned, slid around and faced backwards, cursing from pain. He had refused to take the morphine in his first aid kit, not wanting to dope himself up to the point of ineffectiveness. At least he could be rear security.

The four CS gassed soldiers tried to fire at the figures running at the door, but were too gassed to be effective. Finally, they began to crawl and roll back through the smoke barrier. One was hit and stopped moving. Torbin had the rest hold fire until another threat appeared. The lone gunman, who had fled when his grenadier buddy had been hit by Black's 50, tried to engage Washington and his men from behind a light pole, as Major Jane Grant tried to help the three gassed survivors to safety behind a nearby small utility building. She received a good dose of residue CS for her trouble. The Major called for backup over her radio. The lone gunman, for his bravery, was sieved by the assault team. Then they were through the front door of the Headquarters Building.

The original passenger from the Humvee Torbin had taken out finally made another appearance, MOPP gear and all. He had recovered a rifle and tried to hit the assault team in the rear. Sgt. Nelson shot him through his forehead with one round, killing him instantly.

"Get something, Sarge?" Black asked, still providing long cover with his Barrett.

"Yea, some dumbass still in full MOPP gear trying to sneak up on us. You'd have thought he would realize that a full-fledged nuke or germ attack would have taken place by now. Now, he can't realize anything."

"Yeah, Sarge. War is hell. But it sure can be fun." Black smiled again, this time unnoticed under his Ghillie camouflaged poncho.

Through the two sets of double doors in the front of the HQ Building was the foyer, with a large, winding staircase that led to the left up to the second floor. Here were the offices and the living suites. Andrew had already sped up the stairs, went into the Director's office.

Adam heard something and spun to face it, gun in hand. "Please do not shoot, Director. I just had a new finish put on my body."

Adam smiled. "I still have not figured out how you, being so large and heavy, can move so quietly."

"Superior technique and technology, Director. In that order. And now, I must get you out of here."

"Can't do that, Andrew. I'm the Captain of the Ship. Can't leave with crewmen still aboard."

"Director. Adam. The subject is not up for discussion." Andrew seemed to glide over and picked Adam up effortlessly, holding him under his left arm like a small dog.

"Goddamnit. Put me down!"

"Sorry, Director. Higher orders." He walked through Mary's office toward the exit to the stairs. He stopped, then set Adam down. "The enemy is too close to the front door, and too well armed to risk running with you. I will have to dispose of the threat first, and then move you."

"What about the Falcon?"

"Sadly, due to my misjudgment, I underestimated their capabilities to do damage. The Falcon is sitting well offshore. Now, I must engage the attackers and beat them back. Please stay away from the windows, Director, and in the center of the office. I shall return."

Andrew slowly walked toward the winding staircase. He was interfacing with the various cameras, radios, and surveillance equipment in the area to obtain a true picture of the attacking force. He saw the Tschaaa Soldiers had been taken out rather quickly. Then, the Security Forces beaten back. And the attackers were coming straight to the Headquarters Building.

Just then, Chief Hamilton came sputtering, choking down the hallway from the ladder that went to the roof.

"Chief, are you well?"

"As well as one can be, after being gassed and hit with shrapnel."

"Please, join the Director in the office. I must deal with these attackers directly." The Chief did not have to be told twice. He went in.

Andrew decided he would wait at the top of the stairs, giving him space and distance to use his targeting systems. He had the capability to target any incoming object, including a bullet if given a good distance for response, and hit it with the MP-5K compact weapon he carried on his hip. He had found, as many of his brothers, that their integral interfaced targeting system worked just fantastic with conventional human weapons that threw bullets downrange. One bullet, one hit, at the most vulnerable spot on the target. Using his computer interfaces, he dimmed the lights in the foyer and the upper stairs landing. He stepped back into the shadows and waited. He did not have to wait long.

Washington burst into the building first, and immediately noticed it was darkened. The sun had begun to rise, so there was some ambient light coming in through the small sun dome that the Director had built above the staircase and foyer. However, all the interior lights were off. He slipped on his night goggles.

"Let me take a look with my night goggles first," he told the other three, as he motioned for them to stay put at the entrance. He moved slowly into the foyer. Andrew spotted the night goggles and hit them with a pencil beam of light. The goggles' safety feature to prevent blindness shut them down, but Sgt. Washington still saw stars and dark dots. He swung his M-60EI up and began firing. The other three assault troops hit the doorway and came boiling in.

The small light had told the humans the threat was on the second floor, so they began firing in that general direction. Andrew began to take a few rounds on his armor, so he moved swiftly to the right toward the top of the winding staircase and opened up one-handed with his MP-5K. Four targets, four hits on the torsos to start. The small rounds were stopped by the body armor and had been more of a last minute warning to flee than anything. As he fired, PFC Trump fired his 40mm grenade at Andrew. The cyborg's fifth shot hit the round halfway to its target, detonating it. Surely the blast would make the troops realize who and what they were dealing with! But Andrew, having dealt with a fairly passive population the last couple of years, dulled by his interface with so many emotionless databases, had again underestimated the enemy's capabilities. And anger.

Sgt. Washington charged up the stairs, through the back part of the blast, firing his M-60 as he moved two steps at a time. In his hands, the M-60 seemed to be as light as a BB gun. The AP and Ball rounds smashed into the robocop, denting the front armor plate. Surprised with the ferocity of the attack, Andrew sped along the top of the stairs back to the shadows where he had been. Sgt. Washington kept firing, some of the rounds hitting Andrew. The cyborg fired a round into the large man's head, hitting the helmet because the human happened to duck his head just as he had fired. Washington fired at the muzzle blast, smashing the MP-5 barrel, causing it to jam.

"I got you now, *bitch!*" Sgt. Washington screamed as he reached the top of the staircase. The MP-5, propelled with great force, smashed high into the man's chest, knocking him on his ass. Somehow, the NCO remained cognizant enough to reach for his hand grenade attached on his left shoulder. He saw a figure approach from his left as he started to pull the loosed pin with the thumb on his right throwing hand. It was the Director, approaching with his sub gun.

In a microsecond, Andrew processed the scene. The Director had not stayed back, and was now in danger. He launched himself with inhuman speed, smashing into Sgt. Washington. He ripped the hand grenade from the human's grasp and tossed it into the foyer. He ripped the M-60 from the assault strap. Andrew held it with his left hand as he turned and threw the African-American human by his throat, down at his fellow soldiers near the bottom of the stairs.

Trump was hit with the flying body just as he tried to bring his 40mm to bear again. His left arm sustained a compound fracture as the heavy human body in body armor smashed the M-16 to his body. The grenade discharged from the launcher, impacting and detonating above the top of the staircase. Andrew was peppered with shrapnel, but did not seem to notice as he threw the M-60 like a spear. The barrel penetrated the skull of Muller between his eyes, completely destroying his face and head. He died in an instant, never knowing what hit him. Moore emptied the rest of his magazine at the robocop, then ducked out of the foyer back into the entranceway, just as the spoon popped completely free of the hand grenade that bounced around. Five seconds later it exploded.

With the explosion of the hand grenade, Andrew stopped his descent down the winding staircase. He was on autopilot, en route to turn any surviving attackers into mush. The explosion ended that line of thought; his quick assessment was there were no humans in the foyer. The cyborg turned and hotfooted back to the Director's office. Moore, outside when the grenade went off, was safe from the shrapnel. He popped a new magazine in and tried to sneak back into the foyer as smoke boiled around. Trump started to scream in pain, which drew his attention. Moore heaved the dead Washington off the wounded man, and helped Trump up. He half carried him out from the foyer to near the entrance. Once under more light, Moore saw the bone sticking out Trump's left arm. He used a large bandage to secure the arm across Trump's chest. He then helped him out into the sunlight.

Torbin and company had heard the shooting and explosions, then nothing. They stayed in position, waiting to see what happened next. Finally, two figures appeared, one supporting the other. "Friendlies. Cover them."

About three minutes later, Moore helped Trump lay down behind the staff car Torbin and Gunny used as cover.

"Did you see him? Did you see the Director?" Torbin asked.

"I don't know, Captain. We blew some shit up, but that damned robocop was in the way. We blew the shit out of him and he kept coming."

"Fuck." Tobin had a quick decision to make. He could try with his remaining personnel now, or try a tactical withdrawal. The decision was made for him. He saw at least a couple of dozen Security Personnel approaching from the northwest. He yelled at his remaining grenadier, Standing Bull.

"Lob a grenade at that office window, then lob another! Start firing at those troops! Moore, get Trump back to Black's position. Get Nelson ready to bug out!"

"Everyone with 40mm. Hand it to Standing Bull and me."

Torbin grabbed the Shorty M-79 from Gunny Smith and loaded it with a HE round.

Andrew went into the office. "Director, Chief, you must go to your shelter. Go, or I will carry you. I do not know if I can stop another attack. "

Adam hesistated. "Okay. I guess you are right..."

Andrew heard and sensed the 40mm rounds approaching. He grabbed the Chief and Adam like small children under his arms and dashed from the office. The grenades exploded on the window sill, filling the office with shrapnel. He carried them over to the escape ladder that ran parallel to the escape elevator. "Go now!" Andrew ordered. After the last explosions, Adam did not argue.

"Be careful, Andrew."

"Of course, Director. Caution is my middle name. As of right now."
Andrew's droll humor became more noticeable every day.

The Security Forces began to fire at Torbin's remaining team. They fought back, hitting many of the soldiers who were crossing the open field. But more were coming, trying to encircle them.

"Captain, you need to go."

"Gunny, you stay, I stay."

Gunny Smith stopped firing the SAW long enough to yell at him. "Bullshit! You have a wife and soon a child waiting on you. I lost everything years ago. It's my time to stay. Please, go."

Torbin hesitated. Smith continued. "Besides, you need to report to Madam President what happened. Go."

Torbin looked at him. Time to go. "Semper Fi, Gunny. I go with the wounded. Surrender if you get a chance. I was told the Director still has some honor."

Gunny Smith laughed. "See you on the Sands of Iwo Jima." A mortar round landed close. Torbin turned and sprinted back to Black and the wounded. Gunny kept firing. Standing Bull began to sing and chant a possible Death Song. He let loose with another grenade at the advancing forces.

Martinez and Moore were doing a fireman's chair carry for a protesting Sgt. Nelson.

"Goddamnit. I can walk."

"Like hell you can, Sergeant." Cpl. Martinez scolded him. "That AP round must have tumbled sideways when it was in your right thigh. You're missing a hunk of primary thigh muscles from the exit wound."

Torbin arrived at their position, and heard the nearby Barrett start to fire one round after another. Each round was a kill, and would hopefully help to break the resolve of the attacking force, as they watched their people getting torn apart from long range. A Humvee had made the mistake of exposing itself and now had a ruptured gas tank and a hole in its engine from a SLAP (Sabot Light Armor Piercing) round. However, firing so many rounds would eventually lead to it being located for mortar strikes.

"Corporal Black. Time to leave."

"Alright Sir." Torbin knew he was smiling although he could not see him. That man enjoyed his work. Nelson had a rifle in his hands, being the shooter from the seated carry position for the three troops.

Trump, holding his arm in pain, had no weapon. Torbin stepped up, hit him with a morphine shot, and then handed him his Makorav. "Eight rounds, Private. Don't waste them."

Torbin looked back and saw the Gunny had popped his smoke flare, trying to generate some more confusion. He tried to move faster.

Ichiro Yamamoto had actually crossed the causeway first. He saw the armed guard in the parking lot of the Headquarters Building and heard the vehicles driving around. He decided that rather than draw possible attention to himself by a frontal assault, he would try and sneak around and find a back way into the HQ Building. The sun had just started to peak its rays over the horizon when he snuck down the fence line along the causeway, then began to swing wide, stayed in the shadows. He snuck to and from bushes, along small ditches.

He was on the southwest area from the HQ Building when the Humvee and two jeeps drove by. Ichiro flattened, willed that they could not see him, and had his katana ready for action. They did not see him. A couple minutes later, all hell broke loose toward the front of the headquarters. Torbin had arrived. Ichiro jumped up, and ran toward the back of the building.

Just as he reached a back window, a few human soldiers jogged around the corner. They must have emerged from a concealed room or basement somewhere. They almost bumped into him before they saw him.

"Hey!" one yelled in surprise. Then Ichiro was on top of them.

Five seconds later, they were laid out. He had managed to knock them unconscious, not kill them. After all, they were just ignorant peons, trying to survive. However, judging by the firing, everyone had been alerted to the assault. Ichiro swore. Just five minutes later, and he would have been inside the building. Five minutes more, and the Director would have been captured or dead with a slit throat. He was not ignorant; he was the leader, a good target for a ninja.

He sighed. Well, sometimes fate was just fate. He started to work his way back to the causeway.

It looked like the survivors would make it onto the causeway before they were blocked. Gunny and Standing Bull were still drawing all the attention, with the Security Forces swinging around close to the HQ Building to encircle them. Torbin and his wounded had made it outside the encircling force. They were about fifty yards from where the causeway intersected with the Base proper. Trump was out front, still holding his badly injured arm close to his body. In a sudden move, what looked like a changing colored mass literally engulfed him. He was gone.

"Martinez. Get them to safety." He ran in the direction where Trump had been and took a hard left. It was official sunrise, things were lightening up. The extra light helped him see that the mass was a Tschaaa. Torbin had not been this close to one, ever. He'd shot at one from a distance during the invasion, that was it. He saw the characteristic the Tschaaa shared with Earthly octopi; the ability to change color and camouflage.

He raised his rifle before he realized how close he really was. The long social tentacles wrapped around his ankles and upended him. As the rifle went off, he heard an odd hissing noise, and the rifle was ripped from his hands by the same tentacles that had upended him.

Torbin rolled to his feet. He grabbed for the .44 Magnum in the shoulder holster. Nothing was there. Somehow, it had been knocked loose from its holster. Out came his Ka-Bar. A calm came over him. This is like what Ichiro did. Facing a large alien beast with a blade.

"Come on, you ugly calamari! Let's dance."

Dropping the rifle, the adult Squid lunged at him, its limited cartilage skeleton structure giving it better mobility on land than its earthly cousins. The Marine couldn't tell if the rifle shot had winged it or not. It didn't matter. He went in under the long grasping social tentacles, slashing and stabbing. The next he knew, the shorter arms where throwing him up and over. He hit hard, some soft grass helping mute the impact. As he got to his feet, the Squid was hissing, clicking, and making deep belching noises. One of the tentacles was cut almost all the way through, hanging limp. It clambered toward him. He leapt up, then threw himself onto the main torso and head area. He sunk the Ka-Bar in as deep as he could, and the blue-hued blood began spurting from around the knife wound. He sailed through the air again, this time sans knife. He performed a judo breakfall and managed to get to his feet. The Squid was trying to pull the knife out of its body. Torbin frantically searched for another weapon, any weapon. Stuck in a nearby flower bed was a five foot aluminum pole with a small photocell powered light. Torbin lunged and yanked it out of the soft dirt, just as the Squid charged him with his own knife.

The rest was a little blurry. He remembered colliding full on with the three hundred pound alien, using the pole as a crude lance. Then, he was on his back, looking up into the sky. Combat training and instincts took hold, and he managed to scramble to his feet, almost falling over from vertigo. Then, his sight cleared and he saw the Squid, with its arms wrapped around the pole, which was jammed deep into its mouth. It shuddered, and all of its arms twitched. Then it lay still. As his head cleared, he noticed the body of Trump. His neck had been broken. He saw his Ka-Bar lying in the flower bed, and he retrieved it. He looked at the M-14 and saw the scope had been ripped off and the magazine was nowhere in sight. He started to look for the .44 Magnum pistol. There it was, half buried in the flower bed.

"Where the fuck do you think you're going?" He heard the slightly throaty female voice from behind him and he turned around. A very strong-looking female in a set of combat fatigues was glaring at him with red, somewhat puffy eyes.

Torbin thought, she looked like she had a dose of the CS gas. And was now royally pissed off. He had never heard of Heidi Faust before, nor she him, but fate from the perfect storm dictated their paths would cross.

"Lady, I just killed this Squid. All I want to do is leave the area. I don't see a gun on you, so I don't think you can stop me. I don't make it a habit to smack women around, military or otherwise, but I don't have time to screw round. Don't get in my way."

In a flash a rather good sized butterfly balisong knife appeared in her right hand. She had a throaty, sultry laugh. "I'm in your way. I suggest you surrender so you don't get hurt."

"Shit. Why can't things be easy?" Torbin mumbled.

He tried to feint and get around her. She exploded at him. Her knife was a blur as she performed a type of figure eight Eskrima attack. Somehow, partly due to his body armor taking a couple of nasty strikes and partly due to his ability to move backwards, he managed to keep damage down to a couple minor cuts. He tried to score with his Ka-Bar in return, but was not even close.

Heidi paused in her attack. "Give? Or do I have to kill you?"

Torbin sighed. "Sorry, not in the mood to surrender." He saw the .44 in the flower bed dirt and decided he would make a go for it.

A familiar voice came from his left, Heidi's right.

"Torbin-san. Leave it to you to find an attractive woman in the middle of a battle."

It was Ichiro. Heidi quickly shifted to her left, so that she could see both men at once.

"Please, gentle lady. No more fighting. There has been enough death today." Ichiro slowly approached with both palms up, hands empty. Torbin thought he saw his katana handle protruding a bit over his left shoulder. He had removed his ninja headgear so that Heidi could see his face.

"You want a piece of me too? Come on, *bitch!*" Heidi yelled at Ichiro.

Once he appeared in range, Heidi attacked. Heidi was excellent; fast, sure, experienced. But Ichiro was at a whole other level. In a blur, he was inside her attack, knife hand trapped under his left armpit. Before she could react, Ichiro hit her left temple with the heel of his right hand. Her eyes fluttered, and her knees buckled. Ichiro gently lowered her to the ground, removing the knife from her hand as he did.

"She is the fastest woman I have ever met, Torbin-san. You're lucky to be alive."

Torbin quickly strode over and recovered his .44 Magnum. "I sure am glad you have a habit of showing up at just the right time, Ichi." He pulled a plastic tie he carried and secured her wrists behind her back. He checked her dog tags. "Heidi Faust. I think I'll remember that name."

"Let's go, Ichiro."

"One moment, Torbin-san. I have something for you." Ichiro sprinted a few feet and pulled a long arm from a slight depression in the ground. He went and handed it to Torbin.

"Damn. A BAR and a spare magazine. Where did you get this?"

"Let us say, the person I took it from has no current use for it. Come, let us move quickly. There is a weak spot in the fence bottom over there that we can bend over and slip through. But we must hurry. We are being encircled."

Torbin followed Ichiro to the spot in the fence. It was a spot where an animal had dug under, probably a dog or raccoon. Torbin pulled a set of wire cutters he carried and clipped the fence wire until he and Ichiro easily bent a section up. Now, they had more than enough room to slide through the fence. Within a minute, they were on the other side, near the water.

He and Ichiro began to head toward the causeway along the channel bank. They moved quick and sure. Some fifty feet from the causeway, Ichiro stopped so suddenly, Torbin almost ran into him.

"What..." Ichiro drew and slashed with his katana in one smooth action at something suddenly rising from the water. It was a camouflaged Tschaaa. Two more slashes, then a thrust thru the eye, all in a blur of motion.

"Give me room, Torbin-san." Torbin jumped back and Ichiro became a whirling dervish, slashing and cutting at figures trying to exit the water. Torbin raised the BAR, a former Navy version re-chambered and re-barreled in .308/7.62 with two taped together magazines. He fired at something in the water that did not look right and was rewarded by a splashing Squid losing its color blending camouflage. Here he was, after six years without being close to a Tschaaa, and in the last few minutes, had quickly been inundated with them. What was going on?

Ichiro scrambled toward the causeway proper. Torbin followed. From under the causeway as it crossed the channel, figures seemed to be boiling out of the water, some armed with cutting weapons, some not. Torbin swore and began picking his targets.

Corporal Martinez had managed to head his small four man unit onto the causeway, carrying Sgt. Nelson in a two man fireman's chair carry. Corporal Black was watching the rear. They still heard some shots coming from the Gunny's last position, which seemed to have distracted the Security Forces from noticing people were fleeing from the Base across the causeway. They scrambled down the four lane road on the causeway, nearing the guard shack at the entry control point. On the way out, Sgt. Nelson had been given

a .308 rifle that a defender had no further use for. He carried it as his fellows supported him, scanning in front. He swore and fired up the causeway. "Squids!" Everyone looked up and saw Tschaaa crawling up the sides of the causeway road, over the guard rails. Some looked much the worse for wear, many appeared as if they had been injured. Some were armed, some not. However, rage was driving all of them. Most were not even trying to use their natural camouflage ability. It was if they wanted to be seen, to strike fear in their opponents.

Andrew, after he ensured that the Director and Chief were climbing down to the blast shelter, strode quickly toward the causeway. He knew that a couple of the attackers were pinned down in the HQ Building parking lot. He also knew the others were fleeing across the causeway. Confusion reigned, despite Major Grant's attempt to regain control. Security Forces, having now secured everyone else in blast shelters, were flowing to the sound of gunfire. Andrew knew he must go to the causeway and organize what personnel he could as a blocking force. He saw a squad of Riflemen come jogging down from a side street toward the causeway. He began a high speed dash to them when multiple Tschaaa came scrambling out of the channel water. The Riflemen slowed as their supposed allies approached. Without warning, a harpoon skewered one of the Riflemen in his abdomen. Then a Squid literally threw itself on a human, trying to rip the man apart with its arms and tentacles.

Just at that moment, a stream of data updated his information systems. There had been massive casualties in the breeding Crèche's from a watery blast wave emanating from the nuclear strike. Because the blast had not been contained in the center of the Marquesas Keys Complex, which would have been the result if the bunker buster had burrowed itself in the center of the complex, the blast had sent a heated and radioactive tsunami crashing across the ocean. Right into the reef breeding areas. It was believed over one thousand young and adolescents had been killed, were dying or injured. Dozens of adults were killed or dying, including twelve breeders. Many others were injured. Still more were insane with rage. They were attacking any humans they found.

Major Jane Grant appeared and emptied her M-9 pistol into the Squid on top of the Security Troop. The creature shivered, then lay still.

"Don't just stand there! Get it off him!" Major Grant yelled at the surprised and frozen men. Two ran to help their comrade; the rest stared at Major Grant. As this happened, Andrew was broadcasting a cease and desist order in the Tschaaa language and frequencies. Some dozen individuals were approaching the Rifleman while he broadcast. Half stopped, but the other half, enraged, ignored his instructions. Seeing the Tschaaa approaching with murderous intent, Major Grant gave the only order she could. "Fire at the ones approaching."

The Riflemen opened up, semi-auto. Most were armed with 30 caliber weapons, so one or two well place rifle rounds seemed to either kill or cause the Tschaaa to flee, wounded. The half dozen attackers were neutralized. Then, one Rifleman began to fire full auto on the Tschaaa that had stopped. High velocity rounds ripped into the stationary Squids, ripping alien flesh.

"Fucking *Squids*. Kill them all, like we should've done before!"

The security man screamed in a rage to match the Tschaaa's. Andrew was then beside him, grabbed the rifle and yanked it from his grasp. Andrew's right hand clamped on the human's throat, and he lifted him up to look him in the eye.

"I have stopped those Tschaaa you are shooting. You are wasting bullets, and exasperating the situation. You will stop. Yes?" The man's eyes were bugged out, his breath cut off. Andrew held him for a moment, and then let him fall to the ground. The man laid gasping for air, held his throat.

Andrew looked at Jane. "Major Grant. If you would be so kind as to follow me with these armed soldiers. There are some attackers trying to flee down the causeway.

"Yes, Andrew. Alright. You heard him. On me." The remaining effectives formed an assault line on Jane, and they began to follow Andrew, who had already begun striding ahead. Other Tschaaa crawled, lunged, slithered, and scrambled from the channel. Andrew tried to stop them with repeated warnings in the Tschaaa language. One refused to stop advancing and, in a blur of motion, Andrew picked up a rock and threw it with blinding speed. It imbedded between the Squid's eyes, stopping it dead. The others began to part away from the approaching Andrew, like the Red Sea to Moses. They hissed, clicked and grunted as the humans passed. Only Andrews' presence stopped them from mobbing the security personnel.

Major Grant called to Andrew. "What the hell is going on? Why are they attacking us? I thought they said we were their allies."

"They have just experienced a horrible loss in their young, due to that nuclear strike. A loss in such numbers, all at once, is unknown since the Plague hit on their home world. They are in a murderous rage, a vicious mob similar to others in human history. But almost unknown in Tschaaa history."

Major Grant felt a cold hand grip her spine. If they were not controlled, the base could be wiped out. Andrew heard shots further on ahead, on the causeway. He began to stride faster.

Ichiro and Torbin dashed up unto the causeway. Ichiro slashed a rapidly approaching Squid, at least his seventh, taking off two arms and a social tentacle before thrusting home into its brain. Two Warriors came clambering over the causeway railing, edged weapons at the ready. Torbin gave out a war cry and fired the BAR full auto. A half a dozen rounds smashed into the nearest one, a couple penetrating on into the torso of the second Squid. The second Tschaaa slid and twisted, trying to reach Ichiro. The Nippon warrior parried the long halberd weapon, sliced off the end of the arm holding it, then reversed his katana and thrust its blade through the right eye and into the alien brain. The creature shuddered and died.

"Quite impressive, Torbin-san." Ichiro said as he flicked Squid blood from his katana's blade.

"And, let me congratulate you on killing that Tschaaa with your Ka-Bar. Most excellent."

Torbin snorted at him. "I'm going to hurt for days. Let's get moving. My men are ahead, up on the causeway."

Just then, Ichiro looked backwards. "Torbin-san, a robocop approaches from our rear."

Torbin spun around. "Damnit! Ichi, head down the causeway and catch up with my men. Get them to the pickup point. I'll delay that robo."

"I cannot leave you, my brother. We will meet it together."

"Captain Yamamoto, that is not a request, that is an order. Move!"

Ichiro paused for a second, and then saluted with his katana. "Hai. I go. I will sing your praises to my ancestors. I serve you with honor, my brother."

"Just go, and keep my men safe. I'll catch up when I can."

As Ichiro began to run up the causeway, he yelled back at Torbin. "I killed the excrement Russian Colonel."

"I already figured that out long ago. Now, goddammit move!"

Torbin turned and sighted the BAR on the approaching robocop.

The weapon seemed to have a dutch load of AP, ball, and tracer. He had at least a few rounds left, so hopefully he could do some damage. He fired at Andrew's face at fifty yards. Andrew deflected the round with his arm at blinding speed. Torbin fired a round at the robocop's chest that ricocheted off. Then Andrew threw a rock with a windmill overhand pitch. It smacked hard into Torbin's helmet, knocking him on his ass and leaving a divot in his helmet. Torbin sat stunned for a few seconds. As he tried to focus his eyes, a large hand grabbed the BAR from his hands. Then, another hand was grabbing his left leg and he was lifted unceremoniously upside down into the air. Andrew dropped the BAR, and yanked Torbin's dog tags from his neck.

"Hmmm. Captain Bender, Torbin R. Captain, you have caused us many problems and the Tschaaa much pain. I salute the abilities of you and your men, but now I must take you to the Director." Torbin tried to reach the .44 Magnum pistol, and Andrew yanked it from his grasp.

"The inscription says… *Property of the President, U.S.A.* That is your Madam President, yes?"

Torbin glared at him upside down. "Yes. Now can you put me down, you big trash can!"

With that, Andrew dropped him on his head. A moment later, Torbin was hoisted up by the nap of his fatigue top, and suspended in the air again. Andrew began to stride toward the HQ Building with his catch.

Sgt. Nelson soon found out that a 30 caliber bullet between the eyes of a Squid usually put it down. He fired at a fifth Squid, an adolescent, trying to climb over the guardrail of the causeway. The round hit the guardrail top, just below the many-armed creature, and it fled back into the channel water. The bolt stayed open on an empty magazine. "Out of .308. Set me down so I can get the '16 off my back."

Martinez and Moore set him down gingerly, Moore giving him a shoulder to lean on and help him stand with his injured legs. The morphine helped with the pain, but the damage to his thigh muscles made movement difficult. He unslung the M-16 with grenade launcher off his back and adjusted the tactical sling for forward carry.

Cpl. Black, watching the rear with his Barrett 50, called out.

"We've got company. A robocop and some armed soldiers are

approaching the causeway. Shit. They just engaged some Squids. Something is definitely weird, the Squids attacking their lap dogs."

Moore looked back, and then turned to Sgt. Nelson. "Okay, you go across my back in a shoulder carry. You can watch my rear. Corporal Martinez, can you take point?

"Gladly. Black, let's get moving."

"Roger." They started to move again, Sgt. Nelson held the M-16 by the pistol grip as he was carried across Moore's shoulder. Wounded extraction had been practiced many times, so all the team members were used to carrying or being carried. Corporal Black turned around and looked through his scope again.

"Well I'll be... the Captain's on the causeway, shootin' at the robo. And Captain Yamamoto is high tailing it to us."

"Keep moving. He can catch up," Martinez said. Black turned forward again for a few steps, then looked back. An adult Squid had managed to climb up one of the support pillars and was clambering over the guardrail some ten yards back. Black paused long enough to fire a single 50 caliber at it. One second the Squid was there, the next minute it was cut almost in two, and tumbled back into the channel.

"Goddamn, you're loud!" Sgt. Nelson exclaimed.

"Maybe so, but when I shoot you, you stay shot."

Ichiro had almost caught up to the fleeing men. He had momentarily thought about disobeying Torbin's direct order, but that would have been a dishonor to his friend. He could only hope that Torbin could extricate himself from the enemy. He knew that if anyone could, it would be his blood brother. As he neared the four survivors, he called out, "I am approaching your rear."

"We saw you, Captain Yamamoto," Cpl. Martinez called back. "Glad you could join us. Now what, Sir?"

Ichiro reached them and matched his speed to theirs. "Captain Bender is delaying the pursuit and ordered that I was to ensure you escaped to the pickup location at the airport, where the plane is waiting."

"How do we achieve that, Sir?"

"We find transportation for the wounded Sergeant, some type of vehicle or boat. I think a vehicle might be best as the Takos–Squids– seem to be all over the water. The faster we move on land, the harder it will be to get to us. The bomb blast made them extremely angry, so they are attacking all humans. As a result, the Security Forces may not be able to chase us effectively."

"Lead on, Sir. We'll follow."

Ichiro surged ahead. Then, as they neared where the causeway connected to Highway One, several Tschaaa rapidly clambered onto the roadway from the nearby channel. Before the men could raise their weapons, Ichiro called out, "Hold back! I will clear them. It is much quieter than gunshots."

Cpl. Martinez, PFCs Moore and Black, and Sgt. Nelson were then presented an exhibition of sword play they would never forget. Ichiro strode up to the armed Tschaaa, who seemed to be caught off guard by the fact lone human was approaching a group of very angry Squids. In the blink of an eye, the Samurai was among the leading two. A blur of sword slashes and strikes, and the two adults were down, eviscerated. He next took on the two warriors. Parrying and slashing, he sliced off the tentacles of both, and then slashed the forward arms almost in half. He left them writhing on the pavement as the last two adults tried to encircle him. Cpl. Martinez pulled his silenced .22 caliber pistol and fired two rounds at the one Tschaaa trying to attack Ichiro's from behind. It turned toward the source of the pain and started slithering toward the four men, rising up on its eight arms. By this time, Ichiro had performed his patented three slashes and a stab through the eye to the others. He glimpsed the last Squid trying to get to the men, dashed behind it, and slashed the rear two arms nearly in half. The Squid plopped to the pavement. He lunged to the left side and stabbed the Squid through its left eye, then leapt back. Writhing in pain, it tried to reach him with its grasping social tentacles. Ichiro danced out of range and signaled the four surviving assault team members to pass to the rear of the Squid. They did not have to be told twice.

Ichiro danced around as the wounded Tschaaa bled out from its wounds. Dodging the badly wounded and still-writhing warriors, he sprinted to follow his unit. They were now moving northeastward up Highway 1 toward Marathon Airport. Sgt. Nelson, who still laid across PFC Moore's shoulders, whistled. "Man, I'll never watch old kung fu movies the same way again."

Ichiro snorted. "Japanese swordplay is superior to Chinese."

The four enlisted troops chuckled at his comment. Then Ichiro added, "But hear and remember this. Captain Bender killed a Squid with his fighting knife. I saw the end, so take it as true."

Sgt. Nelson, the Montanan, whistled again. "Just like Daniel Boone or Davy Crockett. We worked with a living legend." "Yes, Nelson-San. Tell the story, pass on the tale. No matter what happens, his honor must never be forgotten."

KEY WEST, FLORIDA TWENTY FOUR HOURS LATER

Torbin Bender had been dozing on and off for most of the time he had been in the cell. His sore body needed to recover from the beating he had taken fighting the Tschaaa, and frankly, there was not a hell of a lot else to do. There was a faucet that provided water in the cell, so he had had plenty to drink. He had refused the food they had brought, for fear that it was drugged. They had not tried to torture him for information, which was a bit surprising, given the circumstances. Knowing the Tschaaa, he would not put it past them to introduce some mind control substance instead.

He also had time to reflect on the sequence of events after Andrew, the cyborg, had grabbed him up…

Andrew carried him through a gauntlet of Tschaaa at the end of the causeway that had grown to at least a couple of dozen. Some appeared as if they had been singed, others battered and bruised. All were almost black with rage. They knew he was involved in the nuke strike.

He felt some vibrations emanating from Andrew which suggested that the cyborg was trying to communicate with the Squids using frequencies out of human hearing. Whatever he had said before or was saying now, the effect was wearing off. The Tschaaa began to crowd ever closer, Torbin feeling their murderous intent.

"Major, be prepared to open fire again. They have ceased listening to me." Andrew reached into a hidden compartment in his battered torso and removed what looked like a flexible length of car antenna. Torbin recognized it as a sheath for a monofilament wire blade, which was capable of slicing almost anything. Major Grant grouped her ten armed men around Andrew and his prisoner. Her pistol was out and at the ready. Bayonets appeared on the many of the rifles. Without warning, a long grasping social tentacle, five fingers and all, grabbed at Torbin. A blur of motion from Andrew and the Tschaaa's "hand" was neatly sliced off. "Shoot, Major."

"Fire at will."

Torbin had been involved in mad minutes–short periods of intense fire–before, but never starting this close, not even the eater ambush. Hot, expended casings were everywhere, some bouncing off of him. A couple of the Major's men were dragged from the formation, and torn apart. Another died from a harpoon bolt through his throat. The humans began to slip on the Tschaaa blue blood as the close range carnage continued. Torbin saw Andrew slice three arms off of one Tschaaa, leaving it floundering on the roadway. Then, it was over. Major Grant tried to recover the dead, but the surviving Tschaaa had scattered, taking the human remains with them.

Jane Grant, shaking with anger and fear, glared at Torbin. "I hope you are satisfied. You just signed our death warrant."

The cell Torbin now occupied was largely empty except for a table and two chairs–bolted to the floor–a commode, and a metal sink and faucet. His clothes had been removed, and a large chain with a huge clasp had been fitted around his left ankle. The chain and clasp looked like they had last been used in some movie about the French Bastille. Torbin could reach the commode and the sink and shuffle around a bit. Mercifully, the floor was warm, as was the air. Last night, a mattress, pillow and blanket had been brought in for his use. Small comforts.

His jailer pointed out a camera in the room, letting him know that if he tried to tear anything up or to harm himself, he would be quickly hogtied. The sleep items had just been removed. He sat cross-legged and leaned against the wall. He heard the key in the lock again, and stood up, almost hoping it was some good-looking woman that he could show his muscled body off to, just for shits and grins. The door opened, and in stepped Director Adam Lloyd.

The Director had a small serving cart with a huge bowl of freshly popped buttered popcorn on the top, and Torbin's clothes and boots on the second shelf. Two unopened cans of Miller Light beer completed the scene. Without a word, Director Lloyd unloaded the contents of the cart onto the table, then pushed it behind him. A very large man wheeled it out and shut the door. Torbin heard the key turn in the lock.

Adam tossed the clothes and boots to Torbin. "Here. Make yourself more presentable, Captain. But a warning, if you try to bean me with your boots, you will be put down like a rabid animal."

Torbin began to dress, and Adam sat down. He set the bowl of popcorn in the center of the table, and pushed one of the cans of beer to Torbin's side. The leg chain kept Torbin from reaching the other side of the table.

"The popcorn is fresh, see, I am eating it. Mm, I am addicted to this stuff. The can of beer is unopened, from a private stash in someone's deep wine cellar. It shouldn't be too skunky. So, please, join me." He popped his beer can top and sipped it.

Torbin finished putting his clothes on, leaving his boots off as he did not want to screw with the chain on his ankle. He also had no interest in committing suicide by attempting an Iraqi shoe attack. He set the boots on the floor next to the table, sat down across from Adam, and opened his beer, taking a long, slow sip. "Not bad. Tastes a little like can, but not bad." He tried the popcorn. "Now, *that* is good. Good old-fashioned theater popcorn. Kills you with cholesterol, but hell, no one gets out of here alive anyways."

Torbin looked directly at Adam. "So, no torture, no drugs? Not even feeding me to the Squids? I have to admit, you have me astounded. Not even a good beating, other than Andrew the robocop dropping me on my head."

Adam chuckled. "He and the other recent converts to cyborg kept their human sense of humor. They are basically enhanced humans rather than machines built on a human frame."

"Well, Lloyd, that still begs the question. What now?' Torbin asked.

Adam sighed. "Well, Captain, to say you and the Unoccupied States have started a shitstorm would be a monumental understatement. To tell you the truth, if I am alive twenty-four hours from now, I'd be surprised."

Torbin measured his response. "I take it from the reactions of the Squids–attacking everything that moved on two feet–that there was a lot of collateral damage."

Adam snorted. "Your nuke was hit and sent off course. Instead of impacting in the center of the complex–which, as you know, was his Lordship's location–it struck the northeast edge. It had burrowed only part way into the structure when it exploded. Thus, a shockwave of heated water and debris was shaped outward. The wave and everything in it slammed into the reefs and shallows in the area, which were being used to raise their young. Over one thousand young and adolescents have died so far. Many are also injured. Twelve breeders are dead, some with child. Dozens of attending adults were killed or seriously wounded. And now we have a large area of radiation contamination. All breeding activities in the area are being moved up to Key Largo and north."

Torbin knew now that Adam Lloyd was in deep shit; both his loyalty and his effectiveness as the Director was in serious question.

"So, Director, is his High Lordship alive, or is he fish food?"

"He is alive, though badly injured. I spoke to his second in command, one of his offspring we call El Segundo."

Adam flashed back to the conversation he had over voice com. The Tschaaa El Segundo had picked a human voice that sounded like a broadcaster from a Midwestern radio station, no accent. "He is alive, Director, and has asked about your well-being. He should heal, but it may be a while. I will remain in charge until then." El Segundo paused. "He wants me to assure you of your continued position, but in all honestly, I cannot. Unnecessary deaths of young are a psychic blow to all Tschaaa. Some say the young were targeted. After the attack, there are many Tschaaa who wish that all humans be wiped off of the Earth. Their rage is far from over. Since you served my Sire loyally, I suggest you get your affairs in order and be prepared to leave if you wish to survive."

Adam's attention snapped back to the present conversation.

"Let me guess. El Segundo was less than positive about us humans." Torbin commented.

Adam gave a wry smile. "That would be an accurate appraisal. The attack shows us to be nasty little monkeys, to be locked up until we are eaten."

Torbin shrugged. "With all due respect, Director, by cooperating with the Squids, you perpetuated a system–the Protocol of Selective Survival–that would always keep us as potential prey for an entire species. I and my cohorts were doing what comes naturally to humans; resisting a threat to our survival."

Adam replied. "I know you will not believe this, but I have helped save millions by sacrificing one segment of the human genome, the people of color. I did this to buy us time. Eventually, I hoped to find a way to replace live meat with types grown in vats, of a type that the Tschaaa could not tell the difference between it and actually human."

"Would there be any... people of color left by the time this happened?" Torbin responded. "Why should we not question the morality of feeding someone our young, our babies. Living under the heel of such an oppressor is not living; it is existing at the expense of some innocent stranger sent to slaughter."

Adam sighed. "Life, and the universe, are not fair. I did what I could to rebuild the infrastructure to pre-strike levels. We have the internet, food and medical distribution, cross-country transportation, operating hospitals. I have not heard of a single case of starvation within the last year. The new space program was just an attempt to demonstrate our excellent capabilities and intellect as a species. We would soon be working alongside the Tschaaa as near equals, as are the ones we call lizards. We would be traveling amongst the stars within a generation."

There was an almost religious fervor in his eyes. Adam believed that eventually, his way would lead to a better life for most humans. The problem was the word "most". Those not part of the "most" would be the "least", which in this instance would mean being food for someone else.

"I have a question, Director. Did the Squids ever eat lizards?"

Adam stopped. Then frowned. "Not that I know of."

"Then, we are in a little different situation. We would, no matter what we did, always be a hunk of mobile meat on the hoof."

They drank their beer in silence for a couple of minutes. Torbin could tell that Adam Lloyd really wanted to help humanity, to be a real good guy. He just did not want to admit that, no matter how nicely his Lordship treated him now, Adam would still be on the menu when the chips were down.

Adam finally spoke. "You will be transported to the former State of Utah, now Deseret. I cannot, in good conscience, hand you over to the enraged Squids to be ripped apart and eaten. You are an honorable soldier who acted according to human rules of warfare. For your information, you and your people cost us two dozen dead personnel, and an equal number wounded and injured. Not to mention the vehicles you shot up. Plus, a small group escaped to Marathon, and left by plane before we could get organized. The sudden violence perpetrated by the Tschaaa caught us completely by surprise."

Torbin, upon hearing that his wounded men had escaped with Ichiro, found it difficult to contain his joy. Yes!

"If I may ask, how many people did you lose to the Squids?" Torbin asked.

"They killed at least a half a dozen, as well as an equal number of Conch Republicans. There would have been more but for your people's ability to engage and dispatch the Squids, which drew many Tschaaa toward you. Whoever that man is with the Samurai sword, he is quickly becoming a legend. He seemed to intentionally go out of his way to incapacitate rather than kill. He apparently only killed one sentry, at the main gate."

Calmly, Torbin spoke. "That is Captain Ichiro Yamamoto, of the Free Japan Defense Force. He's a skilled warrior, as well as my blood brother in arms."

"Well, he must have taken out close to a dozen Tschaaa with his sword technique. I must confess, taking on a Tschaaa hand to hand is not something I would want to do."

Then Adam laughed. "A certain Coast Guardsman by the name of Heidi Faust said you took on one with a knife. How did that go?"

Torbin snorted. "I am beginning to feel the aches and pain from that. I was lucky, and I have no interest in ever doing that again."

"It seems you have a legend developing around you as well.

Especially after the murderous attacks on us by our so-called 'friendlies', anyone killing a Squid is beginning to be looked on very favorably. I am working hard not to have an all-out war here."

Adam leaned in closer to Torbin. "I am about to tell you something I want you to pass on to Madam President. I am not trying to ask for help or mercy for myself, to justify some of my actions. I realize I've made some serious mistakes. But I made my proverbial bed, and now I must lie in it. I will ask that, should my people come under your control at a later date, please show them some mercy. If there is a war criminal, it is me. They were just trying to survive per my instructions. After I tell you what I know, maybe you will understand."Adam pulled a vial out of his pocket containing small, pill-shaped objects. He then began to tell Torbin a story about manipulation and control.

Sometime later, Captain Torbin Bender sat rigid at the table. A rage was building in him that he was having difficulty controlling. He concentrated, and began some of the breathing and mental exercises that Ichiro had taught him as part of some additional martial arts training.

"When things are untenable, when your rage begins to grow to an uncontrollable level, you must breath, control your anger, and become centered. Uncontrolled rage controls you, and makes you do stupid things. Control the rage, focus it, and use it, Torbin-san. It gives you additional strength with which to battle your enemies. It can help you survive when all seems loss," Ichiro had instructed.

Finally, Torbin had obtained an appropriate level of self-control. He could speak without exploding. "Those evil motherfuckers. To manipulate and endanger our unborn. How dare they?"

"We did something similar to our dogs to create all of our various breeds," Adam cautiously responded. "His Lordship has said he was just trying to improve our 'breed'."

"We love our dogs. Most of us do, anyways. And they love us. I have known canines to give their lives for their handlers. I know of handlers who risked all for their dogs. This mutual love between us, two different species, is strong. I know the Squids do *not* love us, and we sure as hell don't love them. I doubt we ever will."

There was a knock on the door. Adam rose and waited for it to be unlocked. Chief Hamilton came part of the way in, speaking in a low tone. Adam thanked him and shut the door. Torbin heard it being locked again.

"Pardon me, but did the Chief there have some bandages on his face?"

"Yes, Captain. You snagged a piece of him when he was on the roof. And, as you can tell, I have a few dings myself that are not from shaving. It was close. If not for Andrew returning, we would not be speaking."

Torbin nodded. Adam continued. "And, whoever was working the

Barrett set a new standard for sniping. Six men and a Tschaaa soldier were felled by him, and a Humvee was destroyed. Not to mention he scared the shit out of a bunch of people. He needs a promotion."

Torbin gave a small smile. "Corporal Black. What can I say? The man enjoys his work." He paused. "I had a Gunny and a PFC who were holding you up, letting the others escape. What happened to them?"

"Gunny Smith and PFC Standing Bull, by their recovered dog tags. We had to blast them out with several mortar rounds. Standing Bull was bleeding out when the final assault was made. Someone said he was singing and chanting. I guess he had his own Death Song. They died as soldiers. To many, they would be called heroes. Any remains or bodies I recover will be sent to your commanders with the appropriate honors and decorum."

Torbin was quiet, with a lump in his throat. The Gunny had sacrificed himself for him. So had Standing Bull. He would make sure they were remembered.

Adam cleared his throat. "And now, Captain Bender, it is time for you to leave for Deseret. By the way, the contact person we used knew your name. I guess you get around."

Abigail must have passed on their meeting to the powers that be. It would be good to see her. Maybe, they would use her as a go between. That would be nice.

"I see a small smile on your face. I guess, Captain, you have a friend with the Mormons."

"Yes, I have a friend. Now Director, I guess I need to put my boots on. Can someone come in and unlock my ankle?"

"Of course." Adam stood up to leave, taking the popcorn bowl with him. He stopped. "Captain, in other circumstances, it would have nice to have served with you."

Torbin snapped to attention and saluted the Director. "I will pass on the information and the vial. I am certain that the President will try and contact you. May God speed you in your journey."

"Thank you, Captain. Now, if you will excuse me, I have some things to rebuild."

Two very large men came in and removed his chain, watching him closely as he put his boots on. Then he heard a familiar voice.

"Well, Captain, you will now get a ride in my Falcon." It was Andrew. "A bit banged up, but we managed to patch it up enough so it is operational. Not pretty, just functional. I have else something I will give you when we arrive in Deseret." He held up a large plastic bag containing the .44 Magnum and the six rounds. "Please return this to Madam President, with my compliments."

"Thank you, Andrew. I guess I owe you my life. But I don't understand. Why didn't you hand me over to the Squids? Don't they give you orders?"

"Captain, I am assigned to the Director. My orders from his Lordship were to follow Director Lloyd's orders, as long as they were not suicidal or subversive. I have not received any new orders from his Lordship, so they stand. I was told to collect you, and so I did."

"What about the Squid you killed with a rock? And the one you cut protecting me? What about those actions?"

Andrew paused for a microsecond, and then answered. "I have been given the ability to decide who lives, who dies. I decided you live. So, the others must die. It is simple, really."

Torbin wondered, as had many others, how much humanity did these Earth-based cyborgs retain? He would have to watch Andrew during the flight, and see if he could figure it out. As exited the cell, Andrew informed both very large men that they would not need to escort Torbin to the Falcon. "I do not think Captain Bender will attempt to flee."

Torbin snorted. "What, and get drilled in the back of the head with a one hundred mile an hour plus fast ball? I don't think so."

Torbin thought he saw a ghost of a smile on the exposed mouth of Andrew. The protective visor with a heads up display covered the robo's eyes, so he could not see a twinkle. But he could swear there was one.

They walked down the hallway to an exit door when he suddenly saw a familiar face. He called out, "Kathy. Kathy Monroe!"

She stopped at the sound of his voice. Kathy looked as if she was torn, trying to make the decision whether to disappear down the hall or greet him.

"You wish to speak to Miss Monroe?" Andrew asked.

"Yes, please."

Andrew put a powerful hand on Torbin's right shoulder and walked with him toward Kathy. She tried to beam her signature smile, but seemed to have difficulties doing so. "Hi Torbin."

"Hi, Kathy. Long time no see, at least in person. You look great."

Kat tried to reply, but she was blinking back tears.

"Hey, no need to turn on the water works. I'm just happy to see you're alright."

Then she was hugging him. She buried her face in his shoulder and began to cry. Torbin immediately stroked her hair and rubbed her back. "Hey, sweetie, it's Torbin. Remember, Mister Smartass? No need to cry. Everything is working out. Andrew is helping me get home, in a roundabout way, but home nonetheless."

Finally, she stopped crying, and looked him in the face. "Sorry, you just brought back... memories of a much better time. I've kind of been on an opposite side for a while."

Torbin kissed her forehead. He reached into his pocket and produced the vial the Director had shown him. "I just had an illuminating talk with the Director. I don't think any of us has been working with a full deck."

She looked at the vial. She hugged Torbin again, and then kissed him. "I missed you, and I still miss William. I always will. No matter what happens, just remember I loved him with all my heart. He was the best thing in my life."

"I miss him, too." A tear tumbled down Torbin's cheek. He quickly wiped it away, hoping no one saw it. It would ruin his reputation of a hard ass Marine.

"Hey, before I go, I'm married, and my wife has a bun in the oven." He looked in an interior pocket of his fatigues and found one of the business cards Aleks had hand drawn for him, a little crumpled but still readable. "Take this. Get a hold of me when you can. I will find a place for you if you show up. Okay?"

Kathy beamed. "Okay. Congrats. Tell your wife to treat you right or she'll have a lot of angry people on her doorstep." She hugged him again and kissed him. Then she turned and walked quickly down the hall.

Torbin drew a deep breath.

"Shall we go now, Captain Torbin?"

"Yes, Andrew. Thank you for letting me speak with her. She was like family once."

Andrew stood still for a few moments. "Yes, we all had family, once. For some, like you, family will happen again. The human family is what makes humanity good, no matter its flaws. Now, come. We must leave. We have some distance to cover."

He and Torbin walked toward the Falcon.

CHAPTER 29

As Torbin was saying hello and goodbye to Kathy Monroe, Aleksandra was giving an orientation briefing to a twelve man team of Free Russian spetsnaz at Malmstrom Operations, now Armed Forces Base. They had just arrived, having been held at an outpost in Alaska until the word came down that the nuke strike had occurred.

Three days prior, the Russian President had died of a stroke. The second in command–the Prime Minister–was a former female General. Madam President had called her upon hearing of the death. The former Russian President seemed very hesitant to commit much of anything to the Free Alliance, as it was now being called.

A short conversation with new President Alina Federov, Free Russia, and all that changed. She had said, "Madam President, I have lost children, you have lost children. If we are to lose any more, let us lose them together, fighting these filthy aliens."

Finally, the offensive arm of the Free Alliance was coming together. As Aleksandra was explaining the layout of the base, where their quarters were, where to report in the morning, they suddenly all came to attention and saluted. "Good morning, General," the Senior Lieutenant called out in excellent English.

Aleksandra spun around and came to attention, caught off guard by the unexpected presence of General Reed. "At ease, please. I just need to borrow the good Captain for a minute. Aleksandra, please walk with me."

As they turned and walked away, General Reed shared his

information. "I have just received word about our wayward Captain." Aleks held her breath.

"I do not know how that sneaky Marine did it, but he is being taken to Deseret, formally the state of Utah. We just got a long distance phone call at Security Control that the Squids and specifically the Director, had made arrangements to let him return home.

"Apparently, the Mormons have heard some positive things about Torbin, and are more than happy to help him on his way. They will provide land transport in the next day or so, and we will meet them on the road. They asked that a young officer be allowed to come to Malmstrom to act as an unofficial liaison. Looks like The Latter Day Saints are having giving some thought to how they'd like the future to look."

Aleksandra had not really been paying much attention to what the General was saying past the fact that Torbin was alive and coming home. Tears began to trickle down her cheeks. General Reed handed her a clean handkerchief. "Here. Can't let the *spetznaz* see you blubbering. Blow your nose, and dab your tears. The father of my godchild is coming home. Now, carry on."

Aleks slowly began to recover her composure. They had heard yesterday that Ichiro and a few others had made it to the Tamiami Trail in the Everglades on the B-25, and were making the rest of their trip by foot, unless the General could arrange some clandestine air travel. But, at least they were alive, and had a chance of sneaking back if they stayed away from the coasts.

Last she knew, Torbin was being grabbed by a robocop. Now, he was *alive*. And soon to be free. The rest of the day Aleks felt like she was floating on a cloud. Her love was coming home.

CHAPTER 30

In Atlanta, word quickly spread that a nuclear weapon had been detonated over the Squid stronghold. Malcolm Carver ordered all further meat shipments to Savannah immediately stopped.

"Well, what do you know? That trash attacked without us pushing them." Malcolm pulled a couple of cigars out of his desk and threw one to Joe. He knew Red did not smoke, so he did not offer her one. But he flashed a big smile at her, which she returned. He had to remind himself that she was not his bitch, but a needed member of his staff.

"Now, the fun begins. Joe, Red, help our Captains find as much shelter from attack as possible. We are not going to have time for any more construction. We'll make do with what we have." He lit his cigar and blew a smoke ring. "Ol' Nat Turner, I wished you could see what's about to happen."

CHAPTER 31

The Olson twins had been working for over twenty-four hours straight. The Tschaaa minor Lord the humans called the Wizard had flown into a rage over the death of Dr. Smith, the damage to his station, and the theft of the spaceplane. Dark with wrath, he almost had Dr. Smith's husband throttled when the doctor began to blubber about his wife. "Shut up, you worthless monkey!" he had screamed over the translator. "Get back to work and give me results… *now!* I will not be embarrassed again!"

The nuclear strike at His Lordship's complex had outraged the Tschaaa. As they stormed through the corridors, humans on the station largely went into hiding, other than a couple of individuals who went catatonic. When the aliens' tantrum subsided, the humans were dragged out of their quarters and told, again, to get to work.

Samuel glanced over at his tired twin Sandy. "Well, here goes, might as well see if we can get this thing to turn on. I don't know how much more time we have." A soldier was posted outside the work area. They clambered into the "saucer", and Samuel took a seat in what passed for the pilot's position. Another one of the form-fitting reclined seat positions enclosed Sandy's body. Every hour, the craft had become more and more attached to them personally. Samuel crossed his fingers, and then manipulated his fingers in the joystick that formed around his hand. He thought what he wanted to happen, moved his digits…

Suddenly, they were no longer inside the station known as

Platform One. In fact, they were nowhere near it. "Damn, Sandy. We're in another system." He thought of the hangar they just left and they were back. He turned to his twin and grinned.

The perfect storm had ended. Another kind of storm was brewing.

www.ingramcontent.com/pod-product-compliance
Lightning Source LLC
Chambersburg PA
CBHW060306100726
47907CB00002B/307